Evil Intent

Evil Intent

Kate Charles

Poisoned Pen Press

First Edition 2005

10 9 8 7 6 5 4 3 2 1

Library of Congress Catalog Card Number: 2005925481

ISBN: 1-59058-200-4   Hardcover

Poisoned Pen Press
6962 E. First Ave., Ste. 103
Scottsdale, AZ 85251
www.poisonedpenpress.com
info@poisonedpenpress.com

Printed in the United States of America

*For three wise and wonderful women
Jacquie Birdseye, Joan Crossley, and Christina Rees*

Chapter One

On the afternoon of her first official Sunday as Curate of All Saints', Paddington, murder was the last thing on Callie Anson's mind.

Instead, her head ached with trying to process and remember all of the people she had met: their names, their faces, their attitudes. By and large, she had been given a warm welcome. Those who were opposed to having a woman curate—and she knew that there were a handful in the congregation—had presumably stayed away. And there had been a few barbed comments which could be taken more than one way, along the lines of 'I never thought I'd live to see the day when we had a woman in the Sanctuary.'

But most people had been lovely. Old women had greeted her with tears in their eyes, wishing her all the best. Young men had gripped her hand, declaring that it was about time.

And the Vicar, the Reverend Brian Stanford…

Brian, as he had insisted she must call him, had been kindness itself. 'You must come to supper tonight,' he'd said. 'Relax and take it easy this afternoon, and come to us in the evening. It's time we all get to know each other. Isn't that right, Jane?' At that point he had turned to his wife for confirmation.

She had nodded; she had even smiled, but her eyes had narrowed fractionally. Callie, a woman who noticed things like that, told herself that it was only to be expected. After all, it was generally known that wives did not always appreciate having guests sprung on them at the last minute by well-meaning husbands, and this must be as true of clergy wives as of anyone else.

'If it's not convenient...' Callie had said, addressing Jane Stanford.

But Brian had answered for the both of them. 'Oh, of course it's convenient. After Evensong, just come across to the Vicarage. Jane will rustle something up.'

In the end, of course, Callie had accepted the offer of hospitality. It wasn't as if she had anything better to do, she told herself. No one to cook for. Nothing in the diary. There wasn't even anything particularly appealing on the telly that night.

Though she *should* get on with her unpacking. Callie sat on her sofa and looked at the tea chests which ranged along the wall. She'd had a week to unpack, in between her ordination and her first day on the job. And what had she done? She'd gone to Venice for three days, leaving the tea chests behind in the otherwise empty flat. On her return she'd managed to get the kitchen in order, as well as the bedroom and bathroom, so she could eat, sleep, and keep herself clean. But the book shelves gaped at her emptily in silent reproach at her laziness, and the tea chests reinforced her guilt. She was by nature an orderly person; living in any sort of chaos depressed her. Sighing, Callie roused herself from the sofa and opened the nearest tea chest.

Novels. She would put them here in the sitting room, on the built-in book shelves, and the theology books would go into the tiny second bedroom which would serve as her study.

Her new flat was not large, but Callie felt that it would suit her very well, once it was sorted out to her satisfaction. It was, almost literally, living above the shop: the flat was on the first floor, above the church hall. The proportions were pleasing, with high-ceilinged rooms, and the sitting room boasted an original Victorian fireplace flanked with book cases. The kitchen was rather old-fashioned and overdue for a refit, but Callie thought she could live with that.

She emptied three tea chests and arranged the books in alphabetical order. Then, feeling that it was time for a break, she went through to the kitchen and switched the kettle on.

The doorbell buzzed.

Callie wasn't expecting anyone. She went to the door and opened it a crack. Her younger brother stood on the landing outside of her door, half obscured behind a large sheaf of flowers.

'Peter!' She opened the door more widely, smiling in delight.

'Aren't you going to invite me in?'

'Come in! I've just put the kettle on.'

'Music to my ears. You must have known that I was coming, then.' He presented the flowers to her with a graceful flourish. 'Here, Sis. For your housewarming.'

'Peter, how sweet.' She hesitated for a moment as she accepted them. 'Let's see if I can remember where I've put the vase.'

He followed her into the flat, neck craning unashamedly in curiosity. 'So this is where they've put you, then. Not bad, is it?'

'Sorry. I'm still not quite unpacked.' Callie indicated the tea chests as they passed through the sitting room toward the kitchen.

Peter Anson laughed. 'I moved three years ago, and I'm *still* not quite unpacked. To say the least.'

'I've noticed.' In Callie's opinion, her brother had made disorganisation into an art form. His packing crates had become part of the decor of his flat, almost replacing the need for furniture.

'The kitchen's a bit small,' Peter observed. 'And surely those units have been there since about 1950?'

Callie opened the cupboard under the sink and found a large vase, which she filled from the tap. 'True. But wait till you see the bathroom. They've left the Victorian claw-foot bath, but they've put in a brand new power shower. Perfect for a curate on the go.'

Peter, who had started rummaging in the nearest cupboard in search of the biscuit tin, turned to stare at her. 'I still can't believe it,' he said. 'My sis—a curate.'

'Well, it's true.'

'What do they call you, then?' he asked. 'They surely don't call you "Father", do they? Or "Mother"?'

Callie laughed as she took a scissors from a drawer and began snipping off the bottoms of the flower stems. 'Good question. To tell you the truth, I don't think they quite know *what* to call me. They've never had a woman curate here before. So I've been telling them just to call me "Callie". Some of them don't seem very comfortable with that. Any bright ideas?'

'I'll give it some thought.'

While Callie arranged the flowers, Peter made himself useful by preparing the tea and carrying the tray through to the sitting room. He placed it on a convenient tea chest; Callie followed him and put the vase of flowers on the hearth in front of the fireplace.

'Thanks so much for the flowers,' she said. 'They really lift the place, don't they?'

Peter surveyed her handiwork and nodded. 'I like the fire-place. Does it work?'

Callie shrugged. 'I think so. I haven't had a chance to try it yet.'

'That will be nice and cosy come winter. Given the right person to curl up next to—'

She cut him off, aware that her voice was sharper than she'd intended. 'Peter, don't.'

'Sorry, Sis.' He looked repentant. 'I thought maybe what's-his-name had come to his senses by now.'

'You know perfectly well that his name is Adam. And no, he hasn't changed his mind. I haven't seen to him since… well, since the ordination.' Her tone, controlled and chilly, warned him to drop the subject.

'Sorry,' Peter repeated, and took the hint as she sat down on the sofa and began to pour the tea. He reached over and accepted his cup, reaching for a biscuit with his other hand. 'Have you seen Mum?'

Callie grimaced. 'Yes, I dropped by a couple of days ago. To give her something I bought for her in Venice.'

'Let me guess. She didn't like it.'

Her laugh was rueful. 'Well, I should have known. I got a little cat for her collection—a glass one, from Murano. And she said that I ought to have remembered that she collects *china* cats, not *glass* ones.'

'Well, that's Mum for you.' Peter lifted his eyebrows and sighed.

Callie felt a tightness across her shoulders. She consciously relaxed, laughing again. She shouldn't let her mother get to her; she knew that. And at least Peter understood—the one person in the world who did.

'You had a good time in Venice, then?' Peter asked. They'd talked on the phone, briefly, since her return, but they were both in a hurry on that occasion and this was the first opportunity she'd had to tell him about her trip.

When it came down to it, though, she found it impossible to put her experiences into words. 'It was… wonderful,' she said. 'Having a good time doesn't begin to describe it. I've never seen anything as beautiful in my life as that city.'

'Did you take lots of photos?'

Callie shook her head. 'No. That wouldn't have done it justice. Venice is so much more than the sum of its parts. I just… well, I just absorbed it. I walked for hours and hours, and just soaked it in.' She sipped her tea absently, remembering. She recalled the play of light on the stone of San Marco, the way the gold mosaics of its domes lit up the interior like millions of tiny lamps…

Peter put his cup down with a clatter, cutting into her thoughts. 'What did you bring me?' he demanded, reverting to the little boy he'd been years ago. 'You said you'd brought me something.'

His eagerness made her smile. 'Just a minute. Let me finish my tea.'

He helped himself to another biscuit. 'I hope it's not a glass cat. Or a china one either, for that matter.'

'I'll have to find it. I think I've put it in the bedroom. I wasn't expecting you today, after all.'

It was impossible to be cross with Peter, she thought as she searched for where she'd put his gift.

⌾◍ ⌾◍ ⌾◍

Peter had made himself comfortable in her absence; he was sitting crosswise on the chair, his head tucked into the angle of the wing and his long legs dangling over the arm. Callie's heart lifted, as it always did at the sight of him: he was so graceful, so elegant, grown up yet boyish still.

'Here,' she said. 'A gondolier's hat.' Callie proffered it—a straw boater, festooned with dangling ribbons.

Peter took the hat, settling it at a rakish angle on his head.

'Thanks, Sis.' He grinned mischievously. 'At the risk of sounding like Mum, I would have rather had the gondolier.'

Callie chose to misunderstand him. 'I don't think Mum would have fancied the gondolier.'

'Very funny.'

'Anyway,' she went on in the same bantering tone, 'what would Jason have said about that?'

The grin faded from his face, and suddenly he seemed very young indeed, far younger than his twenty-six years. 'Actually,' Peter said, gulping, 'Jason's left me. Last week. Went off with a nineteen-year-old chorus boy.'

Callie's heart welled with sympathy. 'Oh, Peter. I'm so sorry.' And she was: Peter seemed to go through boyfriends the way most people went through paper tissues, but Jason had been around for several months, and the two of them had appeared almost settled together. Peter had confided to her that he had hopes for a long-term relationship with Jason; evidently Jason had not shared those sentiments.

He made an effort to smile, but he looked like nothing so much as a miserable schoolboy whose pocket money had been stolen, and his voice quavered. 'So you see, Sis, it looks as if the two of us are in the same boat, doesn't it? We've both been ditched.'

Callie went to him, her arms outstretched.

⌒⟶⟶⟶ ⌒⟶⟶⟶ ⌒⟶⟶⟶

In a way, Callie wished that she didn't have to go to Evensong. She and Peter had hugged, had shared their misery and even shed a few tears together. It was therapeutic for both of them; she hated to have to cut it short. But on the other hand, as she was going to the Stanfords' for supper, it was useful to have Evensong in between to collect herself and regain her equilibrium. Peter had dredged up emotions in her which she had kidded herself had been successfully squelched. Now she admitted to herself that it was far from the case.

As she knelt for the prayers, Callie took deep breaths. She had to get on with her life. She had a new job, a new flat, and the prospect of many new relationships as she got to know the people in the parish. She should be thankful that it was so, thankful that her life was full of promise and possibility. But she couldn't stop thinking that somewhere less than a mile away, Adam was probably also at Evensong. And someone else might be at his side.

⌒⟶⟶⟶ ⌒⟶⟶⟶ ⌒⟶⟶⟶

Jane Stanford hadn't gone to Evensong. No, she'd been left behind to prepare supper. Offering hospitality was one of the accepted duties of a vicar's wife, and she had never resented that. Throughout Brian's ministry Jane had always been conscious of her privileged position at his side, embracing the obligations that position brought with it: she had, in her day, taught Sunday School, run the Mothers' Union, headed up the flower rota, made countless cups of tea and produced endless traybakes and scones. She had edited the parish magazine, typed it herself and duplicated it on an old hand-cranked Gestetner machine in the days before high-speed photocopiers. She had typed Brian's sermons, often improving them subtly, hoping that he wouldn't notice. Many times through the years she had even been a surrogate vicar, listening to the whispered confessions and guilty tears of people who were too afraid or in awe of the vicar to speak to him; everyone knew that something told to the vicar's wife would reach his ears, and no one else's.

It was a high calling, that of a vicar's wife. There were moments, of course, of being fed up with it all, of wishing that one's home were one's own and not an extension of the parish hall. There were times when the burden of making the meagre vicar's stipend stretch to the end of the month, to put food on the table for her family every night and still eke out enough money for everything else, seemed impossible—for unlike many clergy wives, it was a point of honour with Jane that she had never worked outside of the home. But when Jane had met Brian all those years ago, when he was an ordinand and she embarked on secretarial training, she had determined from the start that it was what she wanted: to be married to Brian, and to have all that came with being the wife of a clergyman in the Church of England. She had never, for more than a passing moment, regretted that choice.

Tonight, though, Jane was feeling a bit low. She told herself that it wasn't really surprising. She had worked flat out over the past few weeks as the boys prepared to go off to university, making sure that they had everything they would need to take with them and that it was all packed properly and in a fit state. Buying all those last-minute things for them had stretched the budget, as well. It had always been one of the difficulties of having twins, she recognised: the demands on the budget had inevitably come in twos. When Charlie needed new trainers, Simon always needed them as well, and the same was true now of tuition fees and books. For the first time in her married life, Jane had thought seriously about getting a job to fund the expensive proposition of having two boys going up to Oxford.

But when she'd broached the subject to Brian, he'd been horrified. 'You can't do that *now*,' he'd said. 'Not after all these years. I mean, who would look after *me*?' Then he'd given her a hug. 'We'll manage somehow, Janey. *You'll* manage. You always do.'

So that had been that. And she *had* managed.

Jane had always prided herself on being able to produce a reasonable meal for visitors at short notice; it was something she was called upon to do with some regularity. Usually this wasn't a problem, with judicious use of things from the freezer and a stock of tins in the larder. At the moment, though, the larder and the freezer were both a bit depleted. It wasn't very sensitive of Brian to have invited the new curate to supper tonight, of all nights. She couldn't very well give the woman beans on toast.

There was a packet of spaghetti in the larder. But what to put on it? Jane got down on her knees and pulled things out of the freezer. At the back she made a serendipitous discovery: a container labelled 'Bolognese sauce'. It was a legacy from a parish supper, some months ago now, when they had ambitiously over-catered; the left-overs had been prodigious in quantity. 'You take it, Jane,' the other women on the catering team had urged. 'You have those boys to feed, and Father Brian.' So Jane had filled a shelf of the freezer with little containers, and they'd eaten Bolognese until the boys were sick of it. This one little remnant of that bounty had escaped undetected, and now was welcomed by Jane as a positive Godsend. Never mind that it might not be at its best. There was a nub of cheese in the fridge, and if she grated that over the top, perhaps it wouldn't be noticed.

❦ ❦ ❦

'Do you fancy a pint, mate?' Neville Stewart paused by the desk of his colleague Mark Lombardi.

'Great, Nev.' Mark looked up at him, distracted from his paperwork for just an instant. 'I've nearly finished.'

They were among a dwindling number of policemen left at the station, early on Sunday evening. Neither of them was scheduled to be there, but both had come in for their own reasons, and now it seemed the right time for them to call a halt to their activities and leave together for some liquid refreshment.

Neville Stewart was an Irishman by birth. His name, with its roots so strongly on the eastern rather than the western side of the Irish Sea, was a source of mild amusement, sometimes hilarity, amongst the English. But in Dublin, where he'd grown up, it was little short of an incitement to riot. 'I can't tell you how many times I've had the crap beat out of me because of my name,' he'd once told Mark. 'Very early on, I knew there were only two things I could do about it: change my name, or leave Ireland.' London had proved a safe haven for him, and in spite of the soft Irish lilt in his voice which he'd retained, and his predeliction for drinking Guinness, he had assimilated very well. Now in his late thirties, he had risen through the ranks of the CID to become a Detective Inspector, and a very good one, with responsibility for major crimes.

Mark Lombardi was a few years younger—just over thirty—and a Detective Sergeant whose speciality in the CID was as a Family Liaison Officer. He was London born and bred, though both of his parents had come from Italy, and he was proud of his Italian roots.

There was a natural affinity between the two, not least because of their non-English backgrounds, and they often had a drink together when their schedules permitted it. These drinking sessions sometimes went on for rather longer than intended, but unlike most of their colleagues, neither of them had anyone at home waiting for them—no wife, no girl friend—so it didn't matter, as long as they turned up fit for duty.

The pub to which they regularly repaired was an anonymous sort of place without a great deal of character, but it possessed the virtue of being close to the station, and the beer was a few pence cheaper than in the more upmarket pubs. Besides, they offered Guinness on draught.

'My turn to buy, I think,' Neville announced. Mark found a table, and Neville joined him a few minutes later, balancing a pint of Guinness in one hand and a Peroni in the other, trying hard not to lose a precious drop of either.

'So,' said Neville, after they'd quaffed the first few refreshing mouthfuls, 'I haven't seen you since you got back from Italy. Had a good time, did you?'

'Fine. I always enjoy Venice.'

'And your granny was in good health?'

'Remarkable,' said Mark. 'She's in her eighties, but she's very fit. She still does her own shopping every day.'

'She's still on at you to find yourself a wife?'

Mark shrugged and nodded. 'She won't give up until I do. And of course she keeps trying to help me out—every time I'm there, she dredges up some young women and makes sure I meet them. It's my duty, she says. My duty to *la famiglia*.'

'Sounds just like my granny,' Neville commiserated. 'Though in Ireland, no one expects a bloke to get married before he's forty. It's well known that the sap doesn't start to rise till then.'

Mark, in the process of sipping his beer, sputtered and choked. When he'd recovered, he pointed out to his friend, 'You don't have much time left, then. You'll be forty in a couple of years. Then no more excuses.'

'Don't remind me,' Neville groaned.

Neville wasn't averse to women: far from it. On the contrary, he was well known amongst his colleagues for his success with the ladies. Blessed with more than his fair share of charm, and above-average looks to boot, he could have had his pick of any number of women. But he preferred to sample their goods— freely offered—rather than buy into anything permanent. 'I'm just not ready to settle down,' was his mantra. So far he'd managed to get away with it.

'Let's change the subject,' said Neville, knocking back half his glass in one swallow. 'What were you doing at your desk this afternoon? I thought you were off until tomorrow.'

'As a matter of fact, it had something to do with my trip to Italy.' Mark followed suit and took a long drink, aware that the next round was his and that Neville would soon be ready for a second Guinness. 'Tying up some paperwork. Turns out there was some bloke on the plane who had bumped off his wife in Venice, and thought he'd get away with it.'

'Oh, I heard something about that.' Neville assumed a look of professional interest.

'The usual story, it seems. Clearing the way for another woman. His Italian girlfriend came back with him on his wife's passport.'

'Doesn't sound like Immigration were doing their job,' grumbled Neville.

'I'm sure they'll catch hell for it, if that's any consolation.'

'So how did he get caught? If they made it through Immigration?'

Mark drained his glass. 'That's a long story, best left for the next pint. I'll get you one, shall I?'

Evensong was over; in the vestry, vicar and curate took off their surplices and cassocks. 'Shall I go home and change?' Callie asked.

'Mufti? Oh, no need for that,' Brian Stanford assured her. 'Just come along with me. Jane will be waiting.'

It was only a short distance, but the wind was blowing cold, and Callie didn't have the benefit of a clerical cloak like the one Brian wore; she was glad to reach the vicarage, with its promise of warmth.

The warmth, though, was merely relative, as the heating had only just come on. Brian apologised, adding, 'If it were up to Jane, we wouldn't put the heating on at all until the end of October, no matter what the weather. She tells me that I have no idea how expensive heating oil is.' He shook his head. 'And I'm afraid she's right—I don't worry about things like that. I leave it all to her.'

Jane appeared at that moment, proffering a small bowl of crisps. 'Would you like a drink, Miss Anson?' she asked. 'Wine? Sherry? Fruit juice?'

Brian intervened before Callie could reply. 'I'll open a bottle of wine, shall I?'

'Yes, all right.' Jane sat on the sofa, and indicated that Callie should take one of the arm chairs.

'It's so kind of you to have me,' Callie said impulsively. 'I do hope it hasn't caused you any trouble.'

'It's our pleasure, Miss Anson,' said Jane, without warmth.

'Oh, please—do call me Callie. Everyone does.'

Jane seemed to be inspecting her. 'An unusual name.'

She was used to explaining it. 'My given name is Caroline,' she said. 'But when we were small, my younger brother couldn't say his "r"s. So I've been called Callie ever since.'

Brian came through from the kitchen with a bottle of red wine and three glasses. 'Here we are,' he announced, beaming jovially. 'This will warm us up.'

'Miss Anson—Callie—was just telling me about the origins of her interesting name,' Jane addressed him, then turned back to Callie. 'So do you have other family? Other brothers and sisters?'

'No, just the one brother. There are four years between us, but we've always been quite close. He lives just across the river, in Southwark.'

'And your parents?'

Callie felt as if she were being given the third degree. 'My father died a few years ago. He was a Civil Servant, in Whitehall. My mother still lives in London.' She made an effort to deflect further questions. 'I understand that you have two sons.'

Jane softened visibly. 'Yes. Twins. Very clever boys, both of them. They've just gone up to Oxford for their first term. Charlie is reading Theology at Oriel, and Simon is reading Law at Christ Church.'

'You must be very proud,' said Callie. That, at least, was a safe thing to say.

'Oh, yes,' Brian agreed, handing Callie a glass and sitting down beside his wife on the sofa. 'Cheers, Callie.' He raised his glass. 'Here's to a successful partnership at All Saints'.'

'Cheers.'

Jane didn't look overjoyed at the toast; she raised her eyebrows at Brian and took a sip of the wine. 'I've always looked on our marriage as a partnership,' she said to Callie, almost belligerently.

'And so it is,' Brian assured her, draping an arm across her shoulders and giving her a casual squeeze. 'You know I couldn't possibly manage without you, my dear.'

Callie observed them, middle-aged and content with each other: Brian, with his sandy, receding hair and prominent nose, and Jane, the almost quintessential vicar's wife, chunky in her ancient Laura Ashley skirt, round-faced, bespectacled and with her dark hair skinned back from her face into a lank pony tail. A team, dependent on each other. What sort of partnership would she and Adam have had in another fifteen or twenty years? She didn't want to think about that…

But Jane was on to the next question. 'What did you do before you were ordained? Brian went to Theological College straight from university, of course—everyone did in those days. But I believe that nowadays they like their ordinands to have another career first.'

Callie gratefully turned her thoughts from Adam. 'To tell you the truth, when I was at university, ordination was something that never crossed my mind. I wasn't much of a church-goer, in fact. I wasn't even very much aware of the battles over the ordination of women.'

Brian seemed interested. 'What happened?'

'Well, I followed my father into the Civil Service. It was a good career. I enjoyed it. Then… well, then my father got sick. Cancer.' Now she was back on painful ground; she told the rest as quickly and non-emotively as she could: how during his illness, she had come to know and respect the hospital chaplain, Frances Cherry; how the respect had grown into a deep friendship; how after her father's death, Frances had helped her to discover her vocation to the priesthood and put her on the path leading to ordination.

'So that's it,' she said. 'Before I met Frances, I didn't even know that women could be priests. Afterward, I knew that I had to be one.'

And then, with the second glass of wine, came the question that she should have been expecting, but wasn't.

'Have you set a date yet?' asked Jane.

'A date?' Callie echoed, not yet comprehending.

'Your wedding. Brian told me that you're engaged to a fellow ordinand. He's the new curate at Christ Church, I believe?'

The question struck Callie like a physical blow, and for a moment she was breathless with the pain of it. Of course Jane would have known about Adam, she realised. She'd told Brian all about him at their initial interview, had explained that it was one reason why she was so interested in serving her curacy at All Saints', in the adjoining parish to Adam's. In a year or so, she'd told him, when they were both settled into their parishes, they would get married.

Oh God, oh God, oh God, her head hammered. If only… If only Adam hadn't gone on that particular parish placement…

The silence stretched out painfully, as Callie searched both for her voice and for something to say. The voice, when she spoke, was less wobbly than she'd feared it might be. 'I'm afraid that's not going to happen,' she said. 'It's been called off. We… changed our minds.'

'Oh,' said Jane, narrowing her eyes. 'Oh, I'm sorry.'

⌀⍟⍟⌀ ⌀⍟⍟⌀ ⌀⍟⍟⌀

Somehow Callie got through the evening. She was going to rub along just fine with Brian, she decided—he was quite sweet, if a bit wet. And Jane?

Fortunately, she thought, she wasn't going to have to work with Jane, at least not directly. Jane had been perfectly civil to her, but there was something there that she just couldn't quite put her finger on…

Letting herself back into her flat, Callie was unexpectedly assailed by a feeling of desolation at its emptiness. It was silly— she had lived alone before, and that had never bothered her. Now, though, she longed for some living creature—a dog, or even a bird or a goldfish—to welcome her back. Fighting back a lump in her throat, she went to her phone and checked for messages. There were three, according to her call minder.

Not Adam, she told herself, while hoping against hope that one of them might be. Even if he weren't ringing to say he'd changed his mind and seen the error of his ways, even if he just wanted to say hello and see how she was doing…

The first message was from Frances Cherry. 'I just wanted to know how your first Sunday went,' her friend said. 'And I need to have a word with you about the Deanery Chapter meeting. Give me a ring in the morning, if you have a chance. I'll be at home until late morning.'

The second was from Peter. 'Good to see you this afternoon, Sis,' he said. Odd, thought Callie—not for the first time—that the person who had been responsible for her nickname never called her anything but Sis. 'Hope I wasn't too much of a wet blanket. Give me a ring whenever. And by the way, you're better off without what's-his-name, in my humble opinion. I never did think he was good enough for you.'

Callie supposed that was meant to make her feel better. Holding her breath, she pressed the button to listen to the final message. She exhaled slowly as she realised that the male voice wasn't Adam's. 'This is Mark,' it said, then paused. 'You know—Mark, Marco, from the Venice flight. You gave me the tip about Mr Hawkins and his wife, and I thought you'd like to know what's been happening. Here's my number.'

Callie wrote it down, with an unexpected flutter in her chest.

Chapter Two

Unlike Callie, whose vocation had come to her late, Frances Cherry had always wanted to be a priest. Her father was a priest; she had grown up steeped in church life, a child of the vicarage. From earliest days, her favourite games involved not dolls and tea parties but playing at celebrating Mass. Carefully she would lay out her 'altar' on a little table, meticulously placing the elements. As an only child, she rarely had a live 'congregation', making do with a variety of dolls, but that didn't seem to matter. With great solemnity she would say the words of consecration, lifting her plastic chalice of Ribena in reverent elevation.

To his credit, her father never told her that she couldn't be a priest, that the Church had not yet caught up with her sense of vocation. It was years before she discovered the horrible truth: women could not be priests.

'But it's not fair!' she raged.

'You can serve God in many other ways,' her mother tried to soothe her. 'You can marry a priest, like I did. Or you could be a Deaconess.'

In the end, Frances did both.

She was accepted for training as a Deaconess, and went to theological college. It seemed to compound the injustice that she was educated alongside men who would one day be priests, receiving exactly the same training as they did. Those were difficult years for her.

But it was there that she met the man who would be her husband: Graham Cherry. Unlike some of the other ordinands, he never dismissed her strong sense of vocation. 'The Church will see the light one day, Fran,' he would say to her. 'Just hang in there.' That didn't make it any easier to bear on the day, a few weeks before their wedding, when a bishop laid hands on Graham Cherry and made him a deacon. And a year later, when he was priested, it was even worse for Frances. She was happy for him, of course, and shared in his joy, but she felt as though she would forever be locked out of the only club she had ever wanted to join.

Frances, by then, was working as a hospital chaplain. It was one of the few fields of ministry which was available to her as a woman, since she could administer communion to hospital patients using elements which had been consecrated by a man. She enjoyed the job, and discovered that she had a real gift for working with the sick, the dying, and their families.

Within a year of their marriage, though, Frances discovered that she had achieved perhaps the one thing her husband was incapable of: she was carrying a child. The baby hadn't been planned, but when it happened, they were both delighted. Frances continued working until virtually the last moment, and went back to her job a few months after Heather's birth.

She told herself that she should be the most content of all women: she was a wife and mother, she had a rewarding job at which she excelled. Yet still, deep in her soul, she knew that something was missing. She felt it most strongly each Sunday morning as Graham elevated the chalice and said the words of consecration, but the ache was with her always, gnawing at her contentment.

Needless to say, when the Movement for the Ordination of Women arrived, Frances was ready to be enlisted for the battle.

That was where she had first met Leo Jackson, now the Area Dean of Bayswater. He was one of the handful of brave men whose sense of justice and equality had put him in the forefront of the fight. Then he'd been a young vicar, working in a deprived area of London. He'd felt so strongly about the cause that he had campaigned for a seat on General Synod, and won. His vote had counted, that day in November of 1992.

ᲛᲘᲛᲘᲛᲘ

Frances recognised Leo's voice as soon as she picked up the phone. Leo didn't just talk, he boomed. And his West Indian lilt seemed to get stronger through the years, rather than diminishing.

'Frannie, my love!' he shouted down the phone. 'How are you, my pet?'

She held the receiver a foot away from her ear, smiling. 'Doing very well, Leo. And you?'

'Couldn't be better!' He paused, lowering his voice a notch. 'Listen, Frannie. I want to ask you to do me a favour.'

'Ask away,' Frances invited; there was little she wouldn't do for Leo Jackson.

'This Clergy Chapter meeting tomorrow. I know it's short notice, pet, and I know that you don't usually come to Clergy Chapter, but I'd like for you to deacon for me at the Mass before the meeting.'

'Well,' said Frances. 'You know why I don't usually come.'

'Oh, THEM,' he exploded. 'They're not worth worrying about.'

They might not be worth worrying about, Frances reflected, but they could certainly make life quite unpleasant for her.

'They'll be very upset if I deacon the Eucharist. They might walk out.'

'Let them walk. It's at *my* church, and I can have any deacon I want!' He added, 'They wouldn't come at all if we weren't having a speaker they're interested in.'

'Something about silver?' Frances remembered.

'Yes. Just up their street. Silver, vestments, all that sort of poncy stuff that they love. Tat. They wouldn't miss it for anything.'

'Well…' said Frances again. 'I was planning to come, actually. As moral support for Callie Anson.'

'Brian Stanford's new curate.'

'That's right. She's a good friend of mine, and I don't think it's fair to let her walk into that lion's den on her own.'

'Good for you, pet.'

Frances hesitated a moment before going on. 'And there's another reason why she needs moral support, Leo. A more personal reason. She was planning to marry Adam Masters.'

'Richard Grant's new curate at Christ Church,' Leo said at once. 'Yes, I knew that.'

'But he dumped her, just a few weeks ago. Right before their ordination. Apparently he met some girl on his parish placement, and that was the end of his engagement to Callie.'

'Oh, God.' Leo's reaction was heart-felt. 'Poor kid. And he'll be at the meeting.'

'I expect he will. So I thought I'd go along with her and hold her hand, so to speak.'

'Good woman.' Leo paused. 'And you'll deacon for me, then?'

'All right,' she capitulated. 'As you say, if they don't like it, they can walk.'

⚬⚬⚬ ⚬⚬⚬ ⚬⚬⚬

Callie made a bit of time in the morning to return her phone messages. She wanted to hear what Mark—or Marco, as she thought of him—had to tell her, but she was strangely nervous about talking to him. Buying time, she rang Frances first; the number was engaged. Even though her brother's message hadn't indicated an urgent need to speak to her, she tried him next. He answered after a number of rings, grumbling at her for ringing so early in the morning. Apart from that, he seemed to have regained his equilibrium and was his usual bouncy, optimistic self. So much, she thought, for his broken heart over the perfidious Jason.

On her next try, she reached Frances.

'You must have felt the vibes,' Frances said. 'I was just talking about you.'

'Who to?'

'The Area Dean. Leo. I was telling him that I was planning to break a long-standing habit of avoiding Clergy Chapter to give you a bit of moral support.'

Adam, Callie thought. Frances must know how she was dreading the prospect of seeing him. 'I really appreciate that.'

'I thought I ought to prepare you for what is likely to be a fairly unpleasant experience,' Frances added.

'Well, I did figure out that Adam would probably be there.'

Frances gave a mirthless laugh. 'It's not just Adam I'm talking about. There may very well be some people there who think you're an abomination, and won't hesitate to tell you so.'

'An abomination?' Callie was shocked at the word, and at the depth of feeling in Frances' voice. 'But they don't even know me!'

'Nothing personal, mind you,' Frances assured her. 'But you're one of those hateful creatures who have destroyed their Church. Someone who thinks she can be a priest, even though they know better.'

'I don't understand.' Callie had never encountered any overt hostility to her new vocation; at theological college she had been affirmed in it, and though she knew there were people out there who weren't so positive, she was unprepared for anything like what Frances was talking about. 'I thought that all the people who were against the ordination of women had left the Church of England. Had gone off to be Roman Catholics or Orthodox or something.'

'Oh, would that it were so. The Church is still ordaining young men who don't believe that women can be priests. Insane, or what?' Again Frances laughed. 'At any rate, I didn't mean to alarm you, just warn you. And they might not be there anyway.'

'But who *are* they?' Callie asked. 'What do they look like, so I'll know to steer clear of them?'

'By their shirts ye shall know them,' intoned Frances solemnly. 'Avoid the men in black.'

Callie echoed her words, thinking of the film. 'Men in Black?'

'The blacker their shirts, the higher their Churchmanship.'

'Of course.' Callie realised what Frances was talking about: the coded messages given out by clerical shirts. By and large, she knew, Anglo-Catholic clergy almost always wore black, mimicking the Roman Catholics, whilst those of a more Evangelical bent might wear pastels, bright colours or even stripes, and middle-of-the-roaders often favoured grey or pale blue. And then there were the clerical collars, from the narrow Roman bands worn by the High to the broad expanses of white at the necks of Evangelicals. 'By their shirts ye shall know them' was indeed an apt observation. 'I'll watch out for the black shirts,' Callie promised.

Frances added, 'I have to say, though, that the Evangelicals probably won't like you much, either. '

Callie sighed. 'Because of the Headship thing, you mean.'

'That's right,' affirmed Frances. 'Women having authority over men is a big no-no for them. They have real problems with women priests for that reason. But they'll be much nicer to your face than the other lot will,' she added. 'They'll be all smiley and nice, and you'll never know what they really think of you.'

'I'm not even a priest yet,' Callie protested. 'I'm just a lowly deacon. I don't have authority over *anyone.*'

'True. And for that reason, the Evangelicals might just about let you get away with it.'

Again Callie sighed, wondering what she'd let herself in for. 'I can see why you avoid Clergy Chapter,' she said. 'That sounds like the safest thing to do.'

And that, she thought, was even without the question of Adam.

⁂

It was mid-morning before Callie rang Marco Lombardi. She had a clear picture of him in her mind as she picked up the phone: the curly black hair, the warm brown eyes, the smile. On their one meeting, when he'd sat next to her on the plane from Venice, she'd found him attractive in personality as well as in appearance. He had drawn her out, encouraged her to talk, made her feel like an interesting person. There was something about him, about the way he'd smiled at her…

But she was being silly, she told herself firmly. He had been displaying good manners, no more than that. He would have been the same with anyone. He hadn't singled her out; he had found himself with her as a seat-mate, and had made the best of the situation.

And besides, it was way too soon to be thinking about anything like that.

With renewed determination she punched in the number he'd given her.

'Marco?' she said when a male voice answered.

His response was immediate. 'Callie. Thanks for ringing.'

'How did you know it was me?'

He laughed: the warm, deep laugh she remembered. 'No one but my parents ever calls me Marco. And you certainly aren't my mother.'

'Oh,' she said, gulping. 'Shall I call you Mark, then?'

'Not at all. I like it,' he assured her. 'It reminds me of Venice.'

Venice. For an instant Callie was there, walking along the Grand Canal…

'Speaking of Venice,' he went on, 'I thought you'd want to know what's happened with your Mr Hawkins.'

'Hardly *my* Mr Hawkins,' she laughed. 'But of course I want to know.'

'The body. It was his wife, all right—it's been positively identified. And the paperwork is underway for him to be extradited back to Italy.'

'So he *did* kill her,' Callie said, satisfaction in her voice.

'At this point, I don't think there's anything more than circumstantial evidence that he did, but I'm sure that my Italian colleagues will put that to rights.'

Callie wasn't sure whether that was meant to be ironic or not; she didn't know Marco Lombardi well enough to tell. 'What about the woman?' she asked. 'Gabriella? Will she be extradited as well?'

'No need for that,' he assured her. 'She's already back in Italy. Deported. Don't forget, she entered the country illegally, on someone else's passport. HM Immigration don't fool around with that sort of thing—as soon as they nabbed her, she was on the next plane back.'

'Well. That's that, then.'

'I wanted to thank you for your part in it,' Marco said. 'Without your keen eye, they might very well have got away with it.'

Callie felt satisfied, yet oddly deflated. 'Well, thanks for letting me know.'

'Not at all.'

There was a pause as Callie tried to think what to say next. She considered 'see you around', but realised it was unlikely that their paths ever would cross again.

Marco finally spoke into the silence. 'Callie,' he said, tentatively. 'I was wondering whether you might like to go out some time. For a meal, or something.'

Her heart thudded. 'You mean… like a date?'

'Not if you don't want to think of it like that,' he said. 'It can be just on a friendly basis, if you'd prefer.'

'Yes, I'd like that,' she assured him. 'I don't mind what we call it, but I'd like to see you.'

'How about Saturday evening? I'm off duty.'

Callie laughed. 'Well, I'm *on* duty on Sunday morning, but as long as it's not too late…'

'How about an early pizza? Say, seven o'clock?'

'That would be perfect.'

They made arrangements to meet. This time, when Callie put the phone down, she was smiling.

⌒⠑⠑⠊ ⌒⠑⠑⠊ ⌒⠑⠑⠊

Later on Monday morning, Frances Cherry was at the hospital, making her rounds. Walking down a corridor between wards, she was so lost in her own thoughts that she didn't see Leo Jackson until he boomed her name.

'Frannie, my love!'

Her head jerked up and she found herself engulfed in a bear hug, acknowledging his greeting against a massive chest. 'Hello, Leo,' she said, muffled.

He released her, grinning in delight. 'Just imagine. I talked to you earlier, and now I have the pleasure of seeing you in the flesh. That's amazing!'

'Leo, I work here,' she reminded him, returning his grin.

'And so, sometimes, do I. One of my parishioners is in for a little op, and needed a bit of hand-holding. In spite of your wonderful ministrations,' he added.

Frances took a step back and looked at him, altogether larger than life. He was, as usual, wearing a clerical collar and black stock under a wildly coloured African tribal dashiki, looking like an exotic tropical bird—albeit a gigantic one—amongst the hospital greens and drab hues of the rest of the people in the corridor. Leo was like some primal force, pulsating with energy. Seeing him always made her smile; being with him invariably made her feel better about life in general.

'Are you busy, pet? Come for a cup of coffee,' he urged.

'I was on my way to the caff for a bite of lunch,' Frances said.

Leo took her arm. 'Better yet. I'll come with you. If you don't mind being seen with me, that is,' he added with a twinkle. 'People might talk.'

'Let them talk,' Frances laughed, falling into step beside him.

They must be quite a sight, she thought: the enormous black man, and the petite, slender woman with red hair and the very fair skin that so often goes with hair of that colour. Both in clerical collars, and neither fitting in any way the traditional stereotype of the British clergy. This, though—like it or not—was the Church of England in the twenty-first century.

❦ ❦ ❦

Together they went through the queue and then, in the midst of the busy lunch hour, found a table which had just been vacated. Frances sensed, as they settled down with their food, that Leo had something he wanted to tell her. She also knew that he would do it in his own time; it would be counter-productive to rush him.

So for the first part of the meal, they talked about the Deanery.

'You probably don't realise what an uproar there's been about the curates,' Leo said, sighing.

'What do you mean?'

'Well, in the first place, there's your friend Callie Anson.'

Frances frowned. 'How is Callie a problem?'

'That should be obvious,' Leo said wryly. 'She's a woman. You of all people ought to know that this Deanery hasn't been very woman-friendly.'

'So why is she here?'

Leo paused as he conveyed a forkful of an unidentifiable curry mixture to his mouth. 'Because the Bishop and I wanted her here. Brian Stanford kicked up a bit of a fuss about it—he's not been known as a strong supporter of women priests.'

'Then why did he agree to have her?'

The Area Dean wiggled his eyebrows at her and grinned wickedly. 'Because we told him it was Callie Anson or no one. Take her or leave her. And at the end of the day, Brian Stanford wanted a curate more than he didn't want a woman, if you know what I mean.' He added, 'I'm not saying that he's bone idle, but our Brian doesn't like to do any more work than necessary. He's been coasting for years.'

'Callie will be all right,' Frances said stoutly. 'She's a hard worker. And she's more strong-minded than she seems.'

'She'll need to be, with that other lot baying for her blood.'

Frances scowled. '*Father* Vincent, you mean.' Her emphasis on 'Father' was deliberate and ironic.

'And Father Jonah. Our local chapter of Forward in Faith.'

'Backward in Bigotry, more like,' Frances muttered. 'I don't know how they have the nerve to use the word "forward" when all they want to do is hang on to the past for dear life, and pretend that women priests don't even exist.'

'In their books,' Leo reminded her, 'they *don't* exist. You remember that famous—or infamous—remark by one of their lot: that it was no more possible to ordain a woman than to ordain a pork pie. A woman may *believe* she's ordained, and other people may believe it, but that doesn't mean she's a priest. Not as far as they're concerned.'

Frances stabbed her fork at a lettuce leaf. 'It makes my blood boil.'

'You can almost understand where someone like Vincent Underwood is coming from,' Leo said thoughtfully. 'He's a dinosaur. An old-fashioned Anglo-Catholic, who's been surrounded by "Father knows best" all his life, and doesn't know any different. He just can't accept that today's Church isn't the Church he's always known. There are times when I almost feel sorry for him.'

'Not for very long, I hope,' said Frances with another savage stab.

'The one I don't feel sorry for is Father Jonah,' Leo grimaced. 'He's young enough to know better.'

'I haven't had much dealing with Father Jonah,' admitted Frances.

'Best to keep it that way. Jonah loathes everything that you stand for—I don't suppose he would throw you a life preserver if you were drowning. And he doesn't have much use for me, either,' he added.

'Because you're…' Frances caught herself in time, and left the sentence dangling.

'Because I'm West Indian,' Leo stated. '"Son of a slave", he calls me in his more charming moments.'

Frances lowered her fork and stared at him. 'But he's…'

'Nigerian. And thus pure-blooded and vastly superior. Which he never lets me forget.'

For a few minutes Leo was silent, applying himself to his curry, and Frances didn't know quite what to say. She picked at her salad, then ventured, 'You said there had been an uproar over the curates. Plural. I can understand why the fuss about Callie, but…?'

'Adam Masters,' Leo said. 'With him, it was a question of money.'

'Money?'

'You know how desperate our finances are in the Diocese. Everywhere in the C of E, in fact. And the Deanery's resources couldn't stretch to two new curates in one year.'

'Then how…?'

Leo gave a rumbling laugh. 'The only ones in the C of E who have any money are the Evangelicals. Apparently, with Richard Grant's guidance, the people of Christ Church prayed about it, and God told them that they were meant to have a curate, so the congregation put their hands in their pockets and are paying for him themselves.'

'But doesn't that go against everything?' Frances frowned. 'Against the structures and the discipline of the parish system?'

'Of course it does. But they don't care.' A note of bitterness had crept into his voice. 'It's God's will, they say. You can't argue against that. Even if that sort of thing ultimately brings the Church down.' He shook his head. 'Who'd ever want to be Area Dean, I ask? It's a thankless job.'

'It must be difficult for you, holding everything together,' Frances sympathised. 'No end to the problems. Not to mention dealing with the great range of Churchmanship.'

'I don't know which are worse,' grumbled Leo. 'The bloody Evangelicals, or the bloody-minded Anglo-Catholics.'

'And you in the middle.'

'No one knows what to make of me.' He had regained his equilibrium, and gave her a sly grin across the table. 'Liturgically High Church. Theologically liberal. In favour of everything that both sides hate: inclusive worship, women priests.'

'You're a real trouble-maker,' Frances said with great affection.

'I suppose,' he chuckled, 'that's why they made me Area Dean. Just to get up everyone's nose.'

'That, and the fact that you're brilliant at it.'

Leo threw his head back and laughed his booming, full-throated laugh. 'Tell *that* to Vincent Underwood, pet. Or Richard Grant.'

༄༅༄ ༄༅༄ ༄༅༄

It wasn't until they had finished their meal and gone back through the queue for coffee that Leo got round to what he'd really wanted to tell Frances. The lunch-time crowd had thinned out a bit by then, and they were able to find a table with no immediate neighbours.

Leo tore open a sachet of sugar and sprinkled it over his coffee. 'One of these days I'll give it up,' he said, almost to himself. 'I know it isn't doing me any good.'

Frances waited, sensing that he was working himself up to it.

He stirred his coffee, took a sip, then leaned forward and announced, 'Frannie, I'm in love!'

'Oh,' said Frances carefully.

It was an open secret, at least amongst those he counted as his friends, that Leo Jackson was gay. Indeed, he had never particularly tried to hide his orientation. On the occasion of Frances' first meeting with him, many years earlier, he had told her that he had felt impelled to join the fight for women's ordination because of his own circumstances: as a gay black man, he had said, who knew everything there was to know about marginalisation, he had no choice but to stand beside his sisters at the barricades.

But as far as Frances knew, at least in the years they had been friends, Leo had never had a partner. She had always assumed that he was celibate, or if not that, at least extremely discreet.

That was what had protected him, as far as the Church was concerned: though official Church policy was clear in its condemnation of homosexual acts, especially amongst the clergy, it was more understanding on the matter of orientation. People couldn't help what they *were*, the Church seemed to say, but they could help what they did about it. In practice, of course, things were quite different, and the unofficial policy of 'turn a blind eye' was prevalent throughout many quarters of the Church of England, not least in the Diocese of London. Still, Leo would almost certainly not have found preferment, would not have been made Area Dean, if he'd been living openly with a partner.

'Aren't you happy for me, then?' Leo said, beaming at her.

She took a deep breath. 'Yes, of course I am.'

Then it all came out in a rush. His name was Oliver Pickett. Leo had met him some weeks earlier, when Oliver had turned up at church. 'A seeker after truth,' Leo said. 'He was looking for something, looking for answers.'

Apparently he had found them.

He had asked Leo if he might come round to see him at the rectory, to discuss some questions about the Christian faith. It had gone on from there.

'We fell in love,' said Leo simply, his face shining with a touching wonder. 'I'm not sure how it happened. But it did. I love him. And he loves me. That's the most amazing part of it, Frannie. He loves *me*.'

Her heart ached for him, anticipating the problems that he, blinded by love, couldn't foresee. 'Leo, you *are* being careful, aren't you?' she had to say.

'Careful?' he countered defensively. 'If you mean safe sex, then of course we're being careful. I'm not stupid, you know.'

'That's not what I meant. I meant… careful. Discreet.'

The smile returned to his face. 'Oh, that. Yes, we're being careful. He hasn't moved in or anything. We don't go out in public together. And I haven't told anyone. Not a soul, till now. But I just had to tell someone. And I knew I could trust you, Frannie my pet.'

'You can trust me,' she assured him. 'I just want what's best for you.'

Leo leaned across the table and took her slender white hand in his large black one. 'Oliver is what's best for me,' he stated with a radiant confidence that almost convinced her. 'He makes me happy. Happier than I ever thought I could be. He's made me realise that, after so many years of self-denial, I really can have it all. I don't have to give up the Church for love, or deny myself the love of another human being for the sake of the Church. I can have both.'

Frances swallowed and squeezed his hand. 'Then I'm very happy for you, Leo.'

'I want you to meet him,' Leo said impulsively. 'I want you to see how wonderful he is.'

Frances realised that he was asking her to compromise herself, but for the sake of their long friendship, she didn't hesitate. 'Yes, I'd like that,' she said, forcing a smile. 'I'd like to meet this paragon.'

Leo responded to her smile with a dazzling one of his own. 'Come to tea tomorrow. Before the Clergy Chapter meeting. You can meet him then.'

Chapter Three

Callie hadn't had much opportunity, in her scant few days in the parish, to familiarise herself with much more than the location of the shops, so she welcomed Brian Stanford's suggestion that she should accompany him on his weekly Monday afternoon round of home communion visits. She would meet a few more of Brian's flock—now hers as well, and it would give her a chance to learn a bit more about her new territory. And besides, it was a beautiful early October day, sunny and warm.

The parish of All Saints', Paddington, was a diverse one, encompassing a quantity of very grand Georgian terraces, some of them still single-family dwellings while others had been broken up into flats or bed-sits or converted into upmarket nursing homes; in addition there was a council estate, albeit a well-maintained one.

The parishioners who merited a weekly visit from the vicar were in various stages of decrepitude which prevented them from coming to church; some lived alone, while others were in nursing homes or care facilities. Brian and Callie went round the parish on foot, and in between each visit he filled her in on the circumstances of the person they were about to call on.

The first few visits were to people of some means and social standing, people who had once been forces to be reckoned with in the church, and still exerted influence through their steward-ship cheques.

Elsie Harrington, though, Brian explained as they walked toward the council estate, was quite a different matter. She and her husband Dennis had been members of the church for years, but their contributions toward its life were largely in the form of labour—time and talents—rather than money. Elsie had cleaned the brasses weekly, polished the eagle lectern till it gleamed, washed and ironed the altar linen, even scrubbed the stone flags of the floor. Dennis' stewardship had been exercised outside of the building: he had kept the tiny bit of grass in the churchyard mown, and had planted and tended the flower beds with loving care. He'd made sure the railings and steps were in good repair, and the gutters and drains clear of leaves. Dennis continued to provide those services; Elsie was no longer able to do her part, nor was she able to get to church at all. While not totally bed-ridden, she was incapable of negotiating the stairs to and from their second-floor council flat, and the council had not yet managed to re-house them on the ground floor. Therefore every Monday afternoon Brian took her the sacrament and stayed for a chat. He tried to make it the last visit of the day, he explained; the Harringtons could always be counted on for a good cup of tea and a slice of cake.

Callie was fairly winded by the time they'd climbed the two flights of stairs to the flat. While Brian rang the bell, she admired the profusion of pot plants on the narrow exterior landing.

'Dennis has real green fingers,' Brian said. 'There's nothing he can't grow, if he sets his mind to it.'

'What a shame he doesn't have a garden.'

'All the better for *us*,' grinned Brian. 'He's made the church-yard his garden.'

The door swung open; Callie took in a compact, wiry elderly man with scant hair plastered to his skull, very prominent ears, and wearing a well-darned cardigan of pale green. He smiled at Brian, then his face fell. 'Hello, Father,' he said with something less than enthusiasm, narrowing his eyes in Callie's direction.

'Afternoon, Dennis. I've brought the new curate with me. Callie, this is Dennis.'

She smiled and put out her hand; he ignored it. 'Not meaning to be rude, Father,' he addressed Brian, 'but I didn't shake her hand yesterday, and I'll not shake it today.'

Stung, she withdrew her hand, though she made an effort to keep the smile in place.

Dennis Harrington stepped aside to let them into the flat. 'You may as well come in,' he said grudgingly to Callie. 'But I'll not have you bothering my Elsie.' To Brian he said, 'It's one of her bad days, I'm afraid. She's in bed. She'll be glad to see you, Father.'

Callie followed Brian into the flat. 'You go straight through to see her, Father,' directed Dennis. 'I'll bring some tea through directly.' Then he turned to Callie. 'You can come in here.' He led her into a tiny lounge, neat as the proverbial pin. The windows gleamed, the net curtains were scrupulously clean. With its magnolia walls and neutral carpet, the room might have seemed quite sterile, were it not for the colourful array of lush African violets and pelargoniums on a shelf in front of the window, and the rather gaudy pattern of the upholstery on the three-piece suite which dominated the room, taking up most of the available floor space.

Dennis gestured to the chair. 'Have a seat,' he said. 'I'll make some tea.'

Callie sat, still a bit bemused by her reception. In his absence, she looked round the lounge. Its furnishings comprised the three-piece suite, a set of stacking occasional tables, a television set on a stand, and an electric fire. A shelf above the fire displayed several framed photographs, and surmounting that, on the wall, was a large reproduction of Constable's Haywain.

There were no books in evidence. It was almost the first thing Callie noticed, and it unsettled her nearly as much as Dennis Harrington's hostility. She was used to making a quick assessment of people based on the books they chose to display in their public reception rooms; here the absence of books was in itself the only clue.

She rose and looked more closely at the photographs. One, in sepia tones, was a formal wedding portrait of some years past, the groom—with Dennis Harrington's unmistakable ears but a good deal more hair—in uniform, the bride in an elaborate confection of creamy satin and a veil of fine lace. Another photo showed a willowy young man wearing an Edwardian frock-coat, his hair in a Beatle cut. This, also, was a studio portrait; there were no informal snap-shots, and none of the generic school photos of grandchildren which she had dutifully admired in the sitting rooms of others.

Callie returned to her chair almost guiltily when she heard the approaching rattle of tea paraphernalia, as though she were about to be caught out doing something naughty. She needn't have worried; Dennis delivered tea to the bedroom before coming through into the lounge, so she had plenty of time to compose and prepare herself. In spite of her efforts to relax, she felt tense, unsure how to deal with a man who clearly did not want her there.

Dennis arranged the occasional tables, then busied himself pouring the tea. The pot was a workmanlike brown stoneware, but the cups and saucers were made of fragile bone china, garlanded with garish red and yellow roses. 'Sugar?'

'No, thank you.'

'Would you like a bit of cake?' he offered. 'My Elsie's best fruit cake.'

Callie didn't really want any cake, but felt it would be churlish to refuse. 'That would be lovely,' she said. 'Just a small slice, though. I need to watch my figure.'

That, at last, elicited a ghost of a smile from Dennis Harrington. 'Your figure looks just fine to me, girl,' he said, handing her a plate.

Callie relaxed slightly; perhaps it was going to be all right, after all. She broke off a corner of the cake and nibbled at it. 'It's delicious.'

Dennis nodded complacently. 'My Elsie is known for her cakes.'

'I've never been very good at baking,' Callie admitted.

'Maybe because you don't spend enough time doing it.' Dennis put his cake plate down and fixed her with a baleful squint. 'Maybe if you spent more time in the kitchen, where you rightly belong, instead of trying to do a man's job...'

Callie shrank back into her chair. 'I take it you don't approve of women clergy,' she said with all the bravado she could muster.

'It's not right,' Dennis stated. 'Not proper. Not at all.'

In spite of herself, she was curious about what was behind his opposition. 'But why?' she asked.

'Jesus was a man, wasn't he?' He glared at her triumphantly, as if he'd just delivered the ultimate, unarguable answer.

'Well, yes.' She waited for him to elucidate, and after a moment he did.

'Father John, as was here before Father Brian, he didn't hold with women priests at all. He said that women couldn't be priests, because Jesus was a man, and the priest represents Jesus.'

Callie searched for the right words. 'Jesus was a human being,' she said. 'He came to earth in human flesh. He had to be one thing or the other—either a man, or a woman. There weren't any other choices, if he was going to be here as one of us. But the significant thing was that he was *human*, not that he was male. It's Jesus' *humanity* that the priest represents, not his gender.'

Dennis considered that for a moment, taking a thoughtful sip of his tea. Then he renewed his attack. 'It's the Bible, too, isn't it? In the Bible, Jesus goes out and gets himself some disciples. The twelve apostles. And they were all men. All twelve of them.'

It was an argument that Callie had heard before. 'You have to consider the culture,' she said, trying to sound conciliatory rather than embattled. 'It just wasn't the sort of thing that women did in those days. It was a pretty rough life the disciples led, after all.'

'My point exactly,' the old man stated. 'There are some things women just aren't suited for. There's men's work, and there's women's work. Our Lord knew that.'

Callie was beginning to accept that she was on to a loser: she would never change Dennis Harrington's mind. Instead she changed the subject. 'This cake is wonderful,' she said, extending her plate. 'Do you think I could have a tiny bit more?'

'Of course,' he said, then added with a sly smile, 'And if you like, I'm sure that my Elsie would write out the recipe for you.'

She laughed, and the atmosphere eased.

'I'll just go and offer Father Brian another slice,' Dennis said. 'Father Brian has always been very partial to Elsie's fruitcake.'

During his brief absence, Callie finished her tea, stashed the rest of her second helping of cake—which she didn't really want to eat—in a tissue in her handbag, and rose once again to look at the photographs.

This time, when he returned, she was emboldened to ask about the photos. 'This is your wedding?'

'That's right. We married in the war.' He moved to her side and gazed at the photo with a fond smile. 'Doesn't my Elsie look beautiful?'

'She looks amazing,' Callie said. 'What a fantastic dress. I thought that it was difficult to buy dresses like that during the war, with rationing and everything.'

'Difficult? It was impossible!' snorted Dennis. 'You think my Elsie could buy a dress like that, girl?' Shaking his head, he looked at her with something approaching pity for her naivety.

'Then how…'

'She borrowed it, didn't she? From Gainsborough movie studios. They had all those beautiful costumes from their pictures, and they'd loan them out to girls for their weddings. As long as they were in uniform, that was—women in the forces, and nurses. My Elsie was in the ATS. That's how she qualified. And she looked a dream in that dress, if I say it myself.' He sighed reminiscently. 'Had to give it back the next day, of course, but we have the photo to remember it by.'

'And this?' Callie indicated the photo of the young man in the trendy garb of the Sixties. 'Is this your son?'

Dennis nodded. 'That's our Stu. Our one and only.' His voice was warm with pride as he took the frame in his hands. 'He's done well for himself, has our Stu. Back in them days, he was mad for music—all that rock and roll rubbish, as I used to call it. The Beatles, the Rolling Stones. Hundreds of bands, it seemed like, and London was the place to be.'

Callie, who had not yet been born when the Beatles broke up, knew about London in the 'Swinging Sixties' only as an abstract concept. 'So what did he do?'

'Oh, he followed them bands around till one of 'em gave him a job. A "roadie", they called it. Not much of a job, if you ask me, but it was what he wanted. It was hard work—don't get me wrong. Hard graft. And after that he worked his way up. All the way to the top!'

'The top?'

'Now he's a big record producer. In California, USA. Los Angeles. Hollywood, no less.' Dennis' chest expanded. 'Our Stu, in Hollywood!'

'Do you get out to visit him very often?'

Dennis deflated a bit, but he continued to smile as he shook his head. 'No. We went out there once, years ago. He sent us plane tickets and everything. Treated us like visiting royalty, Stu did. Nothing too good for his mum and me—posh hotel, fancy food. But all them palm trees and cars—it just wasn't for us, like. I don't mind telling you, girl, that we couldn't wait to get back home to our nice little flat, where we could put our feet up and have a decent cup of tea!'

Callie couldn't help smiling at the mental picture. 'Well, I suppose he must enjoy coming here to visit instead, if only for his mother's cakes.'

'Not very often.' As soon as he'd said it, Dennis looked as if he wished he hadn't. 'Not that I'm complaining,' he added quickly. 'He's very busy, is Stu. Well, somebody as important as that would be, wouldn't he? He can't just go off and leave it to some assistant. It's a hands-on business, he says.'

She judged it a good time to change the subject. 'Do you have grandchildren?'

Dennis sighed. 'No, we haven't been blessed. Stu... well, he just never found the right girl. Makes for a lonely life for him,

I always think, and his mother does worry about him, being on his own like that. But he says he's happy.'

'And I suppose it still isn't too late,' Callie said. 'Lots of men marry when they're a bit older.'

'That's right.' Dennis gave her an approving look. 'Maybe he'll find the right girl yet. One of them Hollywood starlets. They could do a lot worse than our Stu, believe me.'

'He's very handsome,' Callie said, thinking that at least he he had been, all those years ago. By now he was probably bald and paunchy.

'He gets that from his mum,' Dennis grinned. 'Not from me, you can be sure of that.'

He was still holding the photo when Brian came through from the other room. 'Well, Elsie and I have set the world to rights,' Brian said. 'I hope I haven't tired her too much.'

'She always enjoys seeing you, Father,' Dennis assured him. 'Tomorrow, God willing, she'll probably be up and about again.'

'Well, I'll be back next week,' promised Brian. 'I'll hope to see her up.' He glanced toward Callie. 'I hope you two have been getting on all right?'

'Fine,' said Callie, looking in Dennis' direction. 'Haven't we, Mr Harrington?'

The corners of his mouth turned up. 'We have, girl.' He cleared his throat. 'Perhaps I was a bit hasty, earlier on.'

He put out his hand toward Callie, and she shook it.

'Then I can come back?' she asked.

Dennis Harrington nodded reluctantly. 'Yes, girl. Yes, I suppose you can.'

⁂

On Tuesdays, as on most days, Marigold Underwood met one or another of her friends for lunch. They had a certain number of perennially favourite luncheon spots—Fortnum's, Harrods, Peter Jones—but today she and Beatrice were going to try something different, a new restaurant which had just been opened by a celebrity television chef. So popular was it that it had taken them several weeks to obtain a booking, and they were looking forward to the experience. So Marigold prepared herself with perhaps even just a bit more than her customary care. She spent over an hour of the morning in the bathroom, soaking in a steaming tub with a skin-firming paste hardening on her face.

Marigold Underwood had never been a typical clergy wife, in any sense. It was a point of pride with her. For a start, she didn't bake: never had, never would. She didn't even cook, at least not any more than she had to. That's what places like Harrods were for, she reckoned—to supply beautifully prepared things which didn't need much additional attention from her. And Marks and Spencers were brilliant, with their ever-expanding range of ready meals.

She never went to church—apart from Christmas and Easter and rites of passage—and despised the sort of women who did, those dim parish spinsters who had nothing better to do. It followed that her friends were not people connected with the church in any way; they were the friends of her youth, who had all come out together as girls and grown together into middle age.

Yes, she had always led her own life, and Vincent had understood that and accepted it, right from the start.

Her friends had thought her mad when she married him.

Marigold had been a deb, back in the late Sixties, and had been the toast of her Season. She could have had any eligible man in London, or beyond. Beautiful and rich, she had lost count of the proposals of marriage which she'd turned down, the spurned suitors and the broken hearts left in her wake.

As her friends married, one by one, they whispered amongst themselves that Marigold was too picky—after all, she had rejected the eldest son of more than one duke, and a handful of lesser nobility. Their speculation gave rise to a rumour that she was hoping for an even more exalted suitor, that she was in fact holding out for the soon-to-be invested Prince of Wales himself.

But she had confounded them all.

It was at Beatrice's wedding, in fact, that she had first spotted Vincent Underwood. The wedding had been the grandest of the

Season, held in considerable splendour at a church favoured by high society. Marigold had been a bridesmaid, and not for the first time—by then her wardrobe was stuffed with confections of satin and chiffon in all shades of the rainbow which she'd worn in the weddings of various friends.

Vincent was the curate. His role in the wedding had been minimal, standing off to the side wearing a black cassock, lacy cotta, and a biretta. She'd had plenty of time to observe him during the lengthy nuptial ceremony, and Marigold liked what she saw. He was dark and rather mysterious-looking, self-contained, somehow aloof from what was going on. He seemed to her like a man with secrets, with unplumbed depths.

He had been at the reception, and she had contrived to speak to him. Her impression of aloofness was borne out, and it made her all the more determined to get to know him.

It was only later that she discovered she was not alone in her fascination with the smoulderingly handsome curate: Vincent Underwood was sought after and pursued by any number of women in his parish. They wooed him with cakes and casseroles, with demonstrations of domestic skills, with signs of suitability for a future as his wife.

But Marigold had triumphed.

The marriage had evolved on its own terms, not like the marriages of any of her friends. While she was not the dim clergy wife of the type she so despised, nor was she the sort of complacent, worldly wife who viewed her husband's affairs with detached amusement, as so many of them did. It was the one thing she felt she couldn't have borne: for Vincent to be unfaithful to her, to favour another woman over her. To prove that her friends had been right to question her choice of husband.

Not that Vincent gave her worries on that score. In spite of the women who continued to throw themselves at him even after their marriage, she was certain that he wasn't even tempted.

Of course there had been that silly business all those years ago, but that hadn't really counted. And no one had ever known about it. Not the people who mattered, anyway. As far as Marigold was concerned, it was ancient history.

There were no children of the marriage. They hadn't planned it that way; it just hadn't happened. Marigold didn't think she minded. She'd never known her own mother, and didn't consider herself a particularly maternal person.

And as for the physical side...

If she'd been expecting grand passion from her husband, Marigold would have been disappointed. It had been years since they'd shared a bed. As far as Marigold could recall, Vincent was the one who had suggested separate rooms, and she had not objected. In her circle of friends, that sort of thing was commonplace.

So, too, were affairs. Her friends had all had them, with men of varying suitability. It was always discreet. Sometimes their husbands didn't know; often they did. But the husbands were all engaged in affairs of their own and weren't generally bothered. Now her friends were at the stage of life where they all seemed to be involved with younger men. Beatrice, for instance, was having a wild fling with a young man who was some sort of minor functionary at Number Ten, and this connection provided Beatrice with enviable titbits of gossip as well as the thrill of illicit passion.

Marigold, though, was not the sort of woman to have affairs. It wasn't that she'd never had the chance; indeed, she'd had ample opportunity, not least with the husbands of most of her friends. They let her know in ways sometimes subtle and often forthright that they wanted her. She was flattered, especially now that she'd reached her mid-50s, but she just wasn't interested. She'd never even been tempted; she was too fastidious to find the idea of sharing her body with men she scarcely knew—or knew all too well—to be the least bit appealing.

Marigold rinsed the mask from her face, climbed out of the tub, towelled herself dry with a fluffy bath sheet, and regarded herself dispassionately in the steamy full-length mirror.

For her age, she wasn't bad at all. She took care of herself, and it showed. Even in the glare of the bathroom light, the little lines on her face were not too noticeable. Her body was good: slender still, with taut muscles and a bottom free of droop. Her breasts had never been large, and at this point she was glad of it; they didn't sag as so many of her friends' now did, unless they resorted to surgery.

And there was her hair, which had always been her crowning glory. It was, in fact, the source of her name: when she was but a few hours old, her mother had held her and remarked that the aureole of gilt hair with which she'd been born made her look just like a tiny marigold. A few days later her mother was dead of septicaemia, and her light-hearted remark was forever enshrined in her daughter's name.

That hair had been truly golden, and thick as well—the envy of her friends. She had worn it long for years, sometimes loose over her shoulders and sometimes swept up in an elegant chignon. In time, though, its brightness had faded. Marigold's hairdresser, who was very good at his job, had convinced her that rather than trying to retain the colour through artificial means, she should accept the inevitable and go progressively lighter. The process had been gradual if no less artificial, and Marigold's hair was now a light ash blond, cut flatteringly and stylishly short, and as becoming to her at her stage of life as the luxuriant mane had been in her youth.

Marigold went through to her bedroom, dressed in a new outfit, and carefully applied her make-up. She checked her watch: she'd lingered over-long in the bath, and Beatrice would be waiting when she arrived at the restaurant.

At the bottom of the stairs, though, her progress was blocked by her husband, who was just showing his curate to the door.

'The speaker should be very good,' Vincent was saying. 'I think it will be worth going.' Vincent's voice, which Marigold had once thought beautifully sonorous, now possessed an unattractive hooty quality, though he continued to regard it as a fine instrument.

'Very well, then,' said Father Jonah. 'I will meet you there.'

As Marigold descended toward them, Father Jonah turned and looked at her, his eyes deep black pools. He inclined his head respectfully. 'Good morning, Mrs Underwood,' he said with grave courtesy.

She had to brush past them in the narrow hallway to get to the door. 'Good morning, Father.' Her tone was as cool as his.

But she was suddenly hot—burning as if with one of the hot flushes she'd experienced a few years ago. She slipped out of the door, closed it and stood with her back against it for a moment while she tried to remember to breathe. Unconsciously her hand cupped the arm where his sleeve had brushed against hers.

In all of her married life, no man had ever had this sort of effect on her.

Her friends talked about this kind of thing casually. 'Oh, he just melts me,' they would say about a new lover.

She'd never known what they meant until now. Now she knew. At the sight of her husband's curate, her insides liquified.

And she didn't know why. It wasn't as if he had ever given her any encouragement, or telegraphed availability or interest.

Quite the opposite, in fact. He was untouchable, reserved, austere. It was, she realised, the same sort of remoteness which had originally drawn her to Vincent—the detachment of one whose character had led him to choose a life of celibacy.

Whenever they met, he was coolly polite. Nothing more.

Why, then, did she dream of him at night? Why did she think of him a hundred times during each day?

When she'd first known Vincent he had been handsome, though his good looks had hardened into a perpetual expression of self-regarding pomposity.

But Jonah was beautiful. Beautiful, with the lithe grace of a panther or some other exotic jungle cat. When he moved, he didn't walk as ordinary men did: he glided, almost as though he were on wheels.

Marigold loved to picture his face, sculpted and lean, with impossibly high cheekbones and those deep, deep eyes. She wished she were an artist so she could draw that face, paint it, fashion it in clay or marble or wood. Sometimes she thought she was obsessed with his face.

There was more, though, and it was even more shameful.

In the sleepless hours of the night, in her solitary bed, she thought about him, and it was not his face which obsessed her then.

Beneath his cassock he was not just a priest, but a man of flesh and blood. If someone—if *she*, God help her—were to unbutton those 39 buttons and free the man beneath, what would happen? She imagined that it would be like unstopping a flood, unleashing a torrent of passion all the more uncontrollable for having been kept so tightly in check.

Marigold Underwood knew that life had been good to her in every material way. She had been born into a life of privilege, and she had never been denied anything she really wanted. With that in mind, if a genie had magically appeared before her and offered to fulfil one wish, she would not have been greedy. She wouldn't have asked for the secret of eternal youth, or true love that would last a lifetime.

No, she wouldn't have been greedy. She would have asked for just one night. One night—free from guilt, free from inhibitions and free from consequences—with Jonah Adimola.

⌘∽⌘∽⌘∽

By Tuesday afternoon, in spite of Leo's encouragement and her own bravado, Frances still had serious misgivings about her promise to act as deacon for him at the Eucharist before the Clergy Chapter meeting. She was used to facing hostility from a certain type of male clergy; at times she had even courted it. But she did not underestimate the capacity for venom from the likes of Vincent Underwood and Jonah Adimola, especially when they had not been warned. And she was feeling a bit fragile as the result of something else entirely: a telephone conversation with her daughter Heather.

Frances had always known that Heather was a restless sort of girl, who would take more time than most to find her place in the world. Heather had never had a clear idea of what she wanted, except in the short term; she followed her enthusiasms and whims without heed to their consequences. To her parents' disappointment, she had refused to go to university, although she was a very bright girl who could have had a place at any university she'd fancied. Instead she had thrown herself into a series of dead-end jobs and no-hope relationships.

She was almost twenty-five years of age, yet she showed no signs of settling down, either with a permanent job or a permanent man. By the time she was Heather's age, Frances reflected, she had a husband, a baby, and a job which was a vocation. Heather hadn't even decided what she wanted to be when she grew up.

For over a year Heather had been travelling round the world, stopping for a while whenever she needed money for the next leg of her journey and working at whatever menial job she could find—waiting tables, cleaning hotel rooms, operating the till at a supermarket. She'd been to Australia, New Zealand, and India; at the moment she was in America. She had, she'd just told her mother, taken a job as a fund-raiser with an animal rights charity in which she believed passionately. She was on a three-month contract, which she hoped might be extended—especially as she had fallen in love with one of her co-workers. As a result, she would not be home for Christmas. She was sure, she said, that her parents would understand. There was always next year.

Frances *did* understand. But that didn't mean she wasn't bitterly disappointed. She hadn't seen Heather in more than a year, and she'd been anticipating her return in time for Christmas and her twenty-fifth birthday, which would follow just after. Heather rang infrequently and e-mailed intermittently from far-flung Internet cafes; Frances longed to see her, to reassure herself that Heather was well and happy. Now that did not seem likely to happen any time soon. She tried to console herself that at least Heather's characteristic lack of success in love meant that she would be back at some point: the new romance was as unlikely as those which had preceded it to display any sort of longevity and keep her on the other side of the Atlantic for more than a few months.

So when Frances went to pack up her gear for the service—a cassock alb and stole—her mood was more reflective than defiant.

She always preferred cotton albs, crisply ironed and snowy white, but they did not transport well, so for travel she kept a polyester cassock-alb which would come out of her case as wrinkle-free as it went in. Her stole should be seasonal green; she discovered, though, that she had left her green one at the hospital. She picked up her ordination stole, which had been specially made for her in a spirit of jubilation and triumph after the vote to ordain women: it was fashioned of rough white silk, on which were painted in blue the names of all the women mentioned in the Bible. It was a beautiful thing, but it was also a statement, bound to ruffle feathers amongst the misogynists at Clergy Chapter. Frances hesitated for a moment, then thought of Leo's cheerful disregard for their sensibilities, and put it in her case.

☙☙☙

As she walked along toward the rectory of St John's, Lancaster Gate, Frances tried to switch her thoughts away from Heather and to prepare herself for meeting Leo's new lover, Oliver Pickett. She didn't have any ironclad preconceptions about him. Her mental picture of him was vague at best: a professional man, perhaps, around Leo's age. Perhaps black, perhaps not.

What she was not expecting, though, was the young man—scarcely more than a boy—who opened the door to her at the rectory. Slim and tall, with a flop of straight golden hair which almost obscured one very blue eye, he wore an immaculate white tee shirt and a pair of artfully faded jeans. His feet were bare: slender, long and pale.

'I'm Oliver,' he said in a soft, unaccented voice. 'You must be Frances.'

Trying to mask her astonishment, she took the hand he extended. 'Nice to meet you,' Frances said; all the while she was thinking 'Leo must be mad.' Mad to fall in love with a child like this, mad to send him to the door when the person who rang the bell might have been anyone—a casual caller, a parishioner, even the Archdeacon or the Bishop.

Leo was waiting for them in the upstairs sitting room, where he had just finished laying out an elaborate tea. He gave Frances his customary bear-hug, then draped an arm round Oliver's shoulders. 'This is Oliver,' he announced, glowing. 'Isn't he gorgeous, then?'

There didn't seem to be any proper response to that, so Frances made do with a smile.

Somehow she found enough things to say to Leo as they had their tea. Afterward she couldn't have told anyone what those things might have been. Oliver Pickett, for his part, was almost entirely silent. He sat on the polished wood floor at Leo's feet, smiling enigmatically.

Leo did most of the talking; he was almost manic in his excitement. Most of the time he rested his hand on Oliver's head, his fingers twining in the golden hair. Once in a while Frances saw him stroke the youth's downy cheek with a hand she would not have thought capable of such delicate, tender movement. She had known Leo for years, and never had she seen him remotely like this: the man was clearly besotted to the point of madness.

Whatever she managed to say to Leo, carrying on an ostensibly normal conversation, her real consciousness was of an interior dialogue.

'I thought you said you were being careful,' she wanted to say to him. 'Don't you know what might happen if people found out?'

But who was she to cast a cloud over Leo's happiness? Oliver didn't seem to mind Leo's caresses, so what business was it of hers? And Leo was unquestionably happy.

She cared about Leo, that was the trouble. He had always been there for her, had been enormously supportive and a good friend. She was helpless in the face of the passion which now gripped him, seemingly rendering him incapable of rational thought. If she had felt uneasy yesterday, when Leo told her about Oliver, now she was positively terrified for him. What could—what should—she, as a friend, do?

Nothing. She could do nothing. He hadn't listened to her when she had tried to warn him yesterday, and he wouldn't listen to her now. He was like a runaway freight train, careering toward self-destruction. All she could do was watch, and pray: pray that her worst fears would end up being unfounded, that Leo would come to his senses, that he would somehow get over it—or get away with it.

ᕙᕗᕙᕗ ᕙᕗ

Callie took special care as she prepared herself for the Clergy Chapter meeting. Usually a brush through her hair and a swipe of lipstick would have been sufficient. But tonight she would be meeting people for the first time, making an important first impression on them.

And Adam.

She would be seeing Adam.

Callie knew that she should no longer care what Adam thought of her. It wasn't important. He probably wouldn't even notice what she looked like.

Once he had thought her beautiful, Callie remembered, looking in the mirror. He had told her so, though no one else ever had. He was the first and the last. The Alpha and the Omega, she thought wryly.

It was for Adam that she had grown her hair. When she'd met him, and for years before that, she'd worn it quite short—easy to care for, if not stylish. But Adam had said that he liked longer hair, so for two laborious years she had grown out all of the layers. Now it was a chin-length bob, shiny and smooth even if the colour was an undistinguished brown. She had to admit that it suited her, framing her face.

On that terrible day when Adam had told her about Pippa, one of her first impulses was to cut her hair, to hack it off herself with a nail scissors if necessary. Fortunately she had resisted that self-destructive urge, realising even in the extremity of her pain that it was Adam she wanted to hurt, and cutting her hair would hurt only herself. Now she was glad she hadn't done it.

She applied her makeup with care, choosing a bolder shade of lipstick than she usually wore; perhaps, she thought, it would boost her confidence in the pulpit.

Not beautiful, she told herself when she'd finished, standing back from the mirror to get the full picture. No, not beautiful—but she looked attractive and respectable. Curate-like, even. That would have to do.

She looked at the clock. If she didn't hurry, she would be late.

In just a few minutes, ready or not, she would see Adam.

Chapter Four

Jane Stanford's Tuesday had started out well. She, like her mother before her, adhered to the old routine: laundry on Monday, ironing on Tuesday. And though she found washing a chore, she had never minded ironing. One of her chief joys, in fact, was to be found in transforming Brian's clean white surplices and albs, wrinkled and stiff as boards, into crisp garments fit for him to wear at the altar or the pulpit. It was, she felt, part of her high calling.

So she was humming to herself at the ironing board when the post came through the letterbox. With practised ease she whipped a snowy surplice off the board and onto a hanger, then, as Brian was out, she went to collect the post.

Most of the letters were addressed not to her but to Brian; she appropriated the bills for herself, and put his letters on the desk in his study. One of the letters, though, was intriguing enough for her to take it along with her as she went back to the kitchen. The envelope revealed that it had been sent from St Cuthbert-in-the-City.

St Cuthbert-in-the-City was one of the glorious Wren churches in the heart of the City of London. Each year before Christmas they hosted a gala charity concert, followed by a reception at one of the livery companies; tickets were very expensive and much sought-after. Jane had never even contemplated the possibility of attending until the year before, when the newly-appointed incumbent, a good friend of Brian's from theological college days, had sent them a pair of complimentary tickets.

It had been the highlight of Jane's year. In her best Laura Ashley frock, she had reveled as much in the company of the great and the good as in the music, and the reception had been outstanding, with delicious food and freely-flowing champagne.

Now, she hoped, the envelope would contain the promise of a repetition of that splendid evening. And her hopes were not disappointed: two tickets nestled in the envelope. With a smile, she propped them on the mantelpiece and returned to her ironing.

When it was all done, she went out to do a bit of shopping. She felt that a celebration was in order, and wanted to prepare a special meal for Brian—perhaps the housekeeping money could stretch to a steak and kidney pie.

But on the way to the butcher shop, she passed a charity shop and stopped to look at the display in the window, her attention caught by a dress on a headless dummy.

It was a deep royal blue velvet, with long sleeves and a nice neckline—not too high nor too low. Instinctively she knew that it would suit her, bringing out the colour of her eyes.

For several minutes Jane stood and looked at the dress. Her Laura Ashley would do, she told herself. She'd always felt good in it. But a little voice at the back of her mind countered that she owed this to herself. No one wore Laura Ashley any longer. Last year the women had been dressed in frocks such as this, frocks which made her Laura Ashley seem dowdy and outdated.

It wouldn't hurt to see how much it cost. That didn't commit her to anything. So she pushed the door open and went into the charity shop. The woman at the till was happy to check the price: a mere twenty pounds. 'That's a real bargain,' she confided. 'I'd buy it myself if it fit me.' She looked Jane up and down. 'Would you like to try it? I think it should be your size. I can whip it off the mannequin in a jiff.'

'Oh, I don't think so,' Jane demurred. 'I don't want to put you to the trouble.'

'No trouble at all. That's what I'm here for.' Deftly the woman took the dress off of the dummy and carried it to the tiny changing room.

Jane undressed in the confined space, then slipped the dress over her head and contemplated herself in the mirror.

It looked as though it had been made for her. A perfect fit, and just the right colour.

'Oh, it suits you!' the woman said when Jane came out to show her.

That was all the confirmation she needed. 'Yes, I'll have it,' she said impulsively. 'It *is* a bargain, isn't it?'

While the woman wrapped the dress, Jane glanced at a rack of assorted clothing next to the till. At the front was a negligee—pink chiffon and white lace. It was, thought Jane with a rush of nostalgia, almost identical to the one she'd so carefully purchased for her honeymoon. For their wedding night, in fact. Brian had loved it.

That negligee was long gone; Jane had been a size eight in those days—a mere slip of a girl—and now she was a size fourteen.

She checked the one which hung before her. It was a size fourteen. And it was priced at only two pounds. 'I'll take this as well,' she said, and put it on the counter.

In fact, Jane realised as she left the shop with her prizes, she was feeling a bit frisky. She began to make plans for the evening. First she would cook a special dinner for Brian—it couldn't be steak and kidney now, but another one of his favourites would do; he liked chicken casserole and dumplings nearly as well, and the money left in her purse would stretch to a nice bit of chicken. There was a good film on the telly tonight, so they could watch that, and afterward she would slip into the negligee and surprise him.

⚬⚬⚬

The chicken was already in the pot when Brian arrived home. 'I'm exhausted,' he declared, sniffing the air appreciatively. 'I've been on the go all day.'

'We'll have a nice, quiet evening,' promised Jane, smiling to herself.

Brian shook his head. 'Not a chance, I'm afraid. I did tell you that I had Clergy Chapter tonight.'

'But you usually don't go to that,' Jane reminded him. He *had* mentioned it, and she had discounted it. Brian always said that after a hard day of work in the parish, the last thing he needed was to sit around with a bunch of clergy moaning about their problems.

'I thought I would this time,' he said. 'For Callie's sake. She doesn't know anyone in the deanery, except for that new curate of Richard Grant's, so I really need to go and make sure she meets everyone.'

Jane bit her lip; she could see that he had made up his mind, and she wasn't going to talk him out of it.

'She's nearly run me ragged,' he said. 'Callie, that is. We've been all round the parish today. We did a baptism visit and a bereavement visit. She's a very quick study, Janey. She's going to be a great help to me here in the parish. You'll see.'

'How nice for you,' she said stiffly.

'What has *your* day been like?' he asked a bit later, as she spooned dumplings onto his plate.

'Oh, the usual. Ironing, shopping.' Jane paused. 'But I do have some news. Something that arrived in the post this morning.' She fetched the tickets and laid them on the table beside his plate.

'Ah, the concert!' Brian picked up the tickets with a smile. 'I'd hoped he'd send these again this year,' he said. 'I thought I'd take Callie. There will be so many people from the diocese there—useful people for her to know. It never hurts to treat the curate to a nice evening out, eh?'

Jane turned her head away so he wouldn't see the tears.

⟩∭⟨ ⟩∭⟨ ⟩∭⟨

It seemed to Callie, tucked in what she hoped was an inconspicuous way into the far end of the middle row of the chapel at Leo's church, that the most dramatic events of the evening must surely have occurred at the very beginning.

The meeting of the Deanery clergy was to begin with an act of worship, a short Eucharistic service. Callie had arrived early, and chosen her seat without a word to anyone. She'd tried not to look at the other clergy as they arrived, composing herself for the evening by kneeling in prayer. With her eyes closed, she'd had a sense that the chapel was filling up, that someone was in the row with her.

At the sound of the bell she stood, and her attention was on the altar party as they arrived: Frances, wearing her ordination stole, and a massive black man in a chasuble. They turned to face the congregation, and the black man raised his hands. 'The Lord be with you.'

It was then that the drama began.

'Infidels!' boomed a resonant voice.

A second voice, softer and accented, said, 'Church-killers!'

Two men seated near the front pushed their way past the man next to them, toward the centre aisle. Callie had just a fleeting impression of them as they stormed past her: one was florid-faced and white-haired, the other as black as ebony. Both were wearing black cassocks.

⌘⌘⌘

After the service the clergy trickled toward the church hall, where the urn steamed away comfortingly and one of the women of the parish spooned coffee granules into styrofoam cups.

Callie hung back, wishing that Frances would appear. She'd had rather a shock during the service, when the time came to exchange the Peace: she'd turned round to find that Adam was behind her. He'd clasped her hand warmly, looked into her eyes, and said, 'Peace be with you, Cal.'

For the rest of the service she'd been shamefully distracted; her hand still burned from his touch, and she was sure she could feel his eyes on the back of her head.

She knelt at the end of the Eucharist, trying to pray, hoping that he would be put off from trying to speak to her.

It seemed to work; when she eventually rose from her knees, he had gone, and she was alone in the chapel.

But she realised that she couldn't stay there indefinitely, and perhaps Frances had gone into the church hall already.

When she got into the hall, though, Frances wasn't there. Callie hovered in the doorway and assessed the situation.

Adam was in one corner, talking to a tall, wiry man in an open-necked shirt. Brian Stanford was nearby with an elderly man in a black shirt. Everyone, styrofoam cups in hand, seemed to be engaged in conversation. And she, it appeared, was the only woman in the room, apart from the one who presided over the urn.

If this had been a Barbara Pym novel, Callie reflected, the woman at the urn would have been elderly or middle-aged, wearing a hat and capably pouring out cups of tea from a large, battered metal pot. But this one didn't fit that mould at all: she was quite young, with spiky red hair and a gold ring through one nostril. And the beverage on offer was instant coffee.

Callie headed for the table. She didn't really want coffee, but she felt that holding a cup in her hand would be some sort of defence.

'Sorry about the brew,' said the young woman cheerfully. 'It's pretty nasty stuff, even if it is fair-traded.' She proffered a plastic bowl of sugar. 'This might help.'

'I'll take it as it comes,' Callie said.

She turned from the table and noticed that there was one person on his own, standing slightly to the side and nursing his coffee with a bemused expression. Callie thought that he looked a rather nice man, with an expressive mouth and attractive eyes; in spite of the fact that he was wearing a black clerical shirt, which she had vowed to avoid, she decided to risk talking to him.

'Are you new here, too?' she ventured. 'This is my first time. I don't know anyone.' Anyone but Adam, she said to herself. Adam, and Brian Stanford.

'Actually,' said the man, smiling at her, 'I'm the speaker. And I don't know a soul. Except by reputation, of course.'

They chatted for a few minutes; she discovered that he was a recently-ordained priest who had come to it even later in life than she had, after a career as a solicitor, and that he had a wife who was an artist. 'It was touch and go,' he told her. 'She'd always said that she would never want to be married to a priest, as her father was one, and she knew what it entailed to be a vicar's wife. That was before we were married, before it ever occurred to me to be ordained.'

'You must have managed to change her mind,' Callie observed.

'Well, it got to be crunch time. We'd been together for a few years, and everything was fine, but when I was accepted to train for ordination, we knew that we either had to make it legal, or go our separate ways. Maintaining the status quo, continuing to live together, wasn't an option as far as the Church was concerned. So something changed her mind. I'm not sure it was me.' His mouth twisted in a self-deprecating smile. 'Perhaps it was divine intervention. But it's very reassuring, in a way. I know that she must really love me, to have married me in spite of the way she feels about the Church.'

'She hasn't come round, then? Joined the Mothers' Union? Taken up baking?'

'No, she still hates it.' He shook his head. 'That's what *I* had to accept—that Lucy would never be a traditional vicar's wife. And I wouldn't want her to be,' he added earnestly. 'She's a very talented artist. That's her vocation, just as the Church is mine.'

'Callie,' called a voice off to the side.

She turned to see Brian Stanford, who had another man in tow.

'I wanted to introduce you to Benedict Burton,' he said. 'A retired priest in the Deanery who helps us all out by taking the odd service or covering for our holidays. I've been trying to convince him that he'll like you.'

That, Callie thought, was not a very promising start. 'Hello,' she said warily.

The man nodded. He appeared to be quite advanced in years, his shiny head covered with liver spots rather than hair. 'It's nothing personal,' he said with a smile. 'I'm sure you're a very nice person.'

'Benedict isn't very keen on women priests,' explained Brian in a hearty voice.

The other man shook his head. 'It makes me sad, that's all. That the Church of England should take a decision like that all on its own. And why change things that have worked for centuries?' There were tears in his rheumy blue eyes. 'It's no longer the Church I grew up in, the Church I've served for so many years.'

Callie found herself feeling unexpectedly sorry for him: things *had* changed, and as she knew in her own life, change was usually painful. 'Why have you stayed?' she asked him. 'You didn't have to stay.' There was, she knew, money on offer for those who were unable to accept the new order, and many had taken it.

He bowed his head. 'Because it's my Church,' he said with touching simplicity. 'I may not agree with the direction it's taken, but it's still my Church. And unlike others, who don't believe that women's ordination is valid, I only go as far as to say that it's valid but irregular. Irregular,' he repeated. 'To say it wasn't valid would be to cast doubt on my *own* ordination.'

All at once there was evidence of movement, as people began drifting toward the semi-circle of chairs which had been set up at the other end of the room. It was as if some inaudible bell had rung, but as Callie followed Brian, she saw that Leo Jackson had taken the chair in the centre, and his arrival was a signal to the rest that the formal meeting was about to get underway.

There was still no sign of Frances. Callie chose a seat beside Brian, leaving an empty chair on her other side for Frances. Adam, already seated, was at an oblique angle to her, so at least she wouldn't have to look directly across at him during the meeting.

The man who had identified himself to her as the speaker sat next to Leo, and at the last minute, Frances slipped into the empty chair to Callie's right, giving her arm a discreet squeeze of greeting. 'Sorry to have left you on your own,' she whispered. 'You seem to have survived.'

'It's not been too bad.'

'You've managed to avoid *them*, then?' Frances nodded her head across the semi-circle in the direction of the two men who had walked out of the service.

'Yes. Who are they, anyway?'

Frances whispered close to Callie's ear. 'Father Vincent is the white one, the one who looks like a slug. And the black one is Father Jonah.'

A slug. Callie studied him while Leo made a few introductory remarks. The description seemed apt, though she wasn't quite sure why. There was, perhaps, a sluglike inertia about him in his posture, his hands folded complacently over his substantial belly. The expression on his very round, very pink face was smug, self-satisfied. He had a thatch of abundant white hair, styled in a way which suggested that he was proud of it, considering it a virtue to have retained such a quantity of it at his age when so many around him had lost theirs.

She was snapped out of her reverie at the sound of her own name. Leo was mentioning her, welcoming her to the Deanery, waving his hand in her direction. She composed her face into what she hoped was an appropriate expression and nodded in acknowledgement.

'And we also welcome Adam Masters, who is serving his title at Christ Church with Richard Grant.'

Adam did her one better: he stood up. Callie's eyes went to him without volition.

Till now, she'd managed to avoid looking at Adam; even when she'd shared the Peace with him, when she'd seen him in the corner, her eyes had slid over him without really looking. Now, though, she saw him.

He had changed.

He seemed taller somehow, his back straighter. And he had cut his hair.

Adam's hair was auburn and wavy. In the years she'd known him, he'd always worn it on the long side, curling luxuriantly round his collar.

Now it had all been cut off, shaped into short back and sides. Very establishment, very traditional.

To Callie's eyes, the hair cut seemed to have removed part of his charm—part of what had made him Adam, and loveable. Like Samson, he had been shorn of some of his power over her.

And she was glad. This was not the Adam she had known and loved, this well-groomed young man in the neat blue clerical shirt and wide white collar.

His voice, though, was the same. 'Thank you,' he said. 'It's good to be here.'

Across from Callie, Father Jonah leaned toward Father Vincent and said something *sotto voce* behind his hand.

'Before I introduce our speaker,' Leo went on, 'are there any other announcements or notices?'

The man next to Adam put up his hand.

'Yes, Richard?' acknowledged Leo.

Richard Grant stood. 'I just wanted to let everyone know that we have a new Alpha Course beginning next week. All are welcome to attend, of course.'

This time Father Jonah's voice, though intended only for his companion, carried across the room. 'Oh, joy.'

But Richard Grant was not fazed. 'Yes, it *is* a joy,' he said firmly. 'A joy and a privilege to have the opportunity to bring people to Jesus.'

Callie observed that he was not wearing clericals; rather he had on a striped shirt with the sleeves rolled up to the elbows, revealing sinewy forearms covered with dark hair. 'Muscular Christianity' was the phrase which popped into Callie's head, and it seemed particularly apt. His face was lean and sculptured, with high cheekbones and deep vertical grooves, and his black hair was cut in a style similar to Adam's, the short sides revealing sprinklings of grey. He was not, Callie thought, a man to be trifled with.

'Thank you, Richard,' said Leo in a voice which precluded further discussion. 'I'm sure we'll all be happy to steer interested parties your way.'

Richard Grant nodded, apparently satisfied, and sat down.

'Now I'd like to introduce our speaker—' Leo began, but Richard Grant bobbed back up and Leo stopped, raising a quizzical eyebrow. 'Yes, Richard?'

'Aren't we going to begin with prayer?'

'Very well. Since you're up, why don't you lead us in prayer?' From Leo's straight face, Callie couldn't tell whether he was amused or annoyed, serious or ironic.

There was a moment of shifting about, heads being bowed and suitable attitudes of prayer being assumed, as the two black-clad men opposite muttered to each other in an inaudible hiss.

'We just want to thank you Lord,' said Richard Grant, 'for bringing us together here tonight...'

Several minutes later he had finished, and sat down once again.

'Now,' said Leo, and this time there was no mistaking the irony in that one word, 'I'd like to introduce our speaker, David Middleton-Brown. He is a priest in this diocese, in the Kensington area. And he is a recognised, though very modest, expert in the area of church furnishings and silver. Tonight he is going to talk to us about the treasures in our churches—how to recognise them, and how to take care of them.'

The talk was interesting, but after a few minutes Callie found her attention wandering. Surreptitiously she looked round the semi-circle at the people she could see without swivelling her head too obviously. Directly across from her, Father Vincent and Father Jonah were raptly attentive, their heads turned toward the speaker. Benedict Burton seemed quite interested, nodding now and again. Richard Grant looked bored. Beside him, Adam looked... well, like Adam. She knew him so well; she'd always prided herself on being able to read his face, to know what he was thinking. Now he was wearing the expression of polite interest which he had so often assumed during lectures at theological college, and she knew that his mind was far away. On *her*, then? Pippa, the paragon? The perfect, the pulchritudinous.

Unwilling to go there, Callie tuned back in to the talk. The proper way to hang vestments was something which she was sure she ought to know about, but the people here, in all of their variety, were far more interesting.

Hands, then.

Not Adam's hands, though. She couldn't bear to look at those well-loved hands, capable of such tenderness. Instead she slid her eyes past him to Richard Grant. His hands were as sinewy as his arms, tanned, the veins standing out on them, the fingers blunt. They were the sort of hands that Jesus might have had, she reflected: the hands of a working man. Idly she wondered what Richard Grant had done before coming to the priesthood.

Benedict Burton's hands were as mottled as his scalp, the bones showing through and the flesh flaccid. Beside him, Father Vincent's hands remained folded over his ample black-clad girth. Though his face was pink, his hands were white—soft and plump as undercooked dumplings. She couldn't imagine those hands doing anything more energetic than lifting a cup of tea.

Father Jonah was a complete contrast, though he was equally still, his hands resting on his knees. They seemed to be carved out of some beautiful, tight-grained black wood, shiny and hard, every vein and muscle defined, strong yet delicate.

There was nothing delicate about Leo Jackson's hands. A more coffee-coloured brown than Father Jonah's black, they were as massive as the man himself. And they were far from still. Restlessly they moved—tapping out a beat on his knees, clasping and unclasping, scratching his scalp or rubbing his nose.

And then the leathery palms were coming together, leading the round of applause, as Leo thanked the speaker for his fascinating and informative talk.

⚬⚬⚬⚬

There was no rush to leave after the speaker finished, as Callie might have expected. Leo produced, as if by magic, a couple of bottles of wine, and plastic cups were found somewhere.

Callie picked up a cup of wine and took a sip. Out of the corner of her eye, she could see that Adam was headed in her direction. Quickly she turned toward the nearest person; unfortunately, that happened to be Father Jonah.

It was too late to turn away, so she gave him a nervous smile. Up close, she realised he was younger than she'd thought—

tainly not much older than she. 'I don't believe we've met,' she said brightly. 'I'm Callie Anson.'

'I know very well who you are.' His voice was clipped, accented—and very cold. 'You are one of the people who have destroyed our Church.'

'But…' she sputtered, her eyes widening.

'You have no excuse,' he went on stonily. 'There *is* no excuse.'

'Leave her alone,' said Frances as she materialised at her side, slipping her arm through Callie's.

'It's like that, is it?' the man sneered, his nostrils flaring. 'I should have known. Abomination on abomination.'

Frances tensed, narrowing her eyes. 'What, exactly, do you mean by that?'

'I should think it's fairly obvious.' He looked pointedly at their linked arms. 'You're not content with taking away from us a church which has existed for centuries, divinely instituted by Our Lord. You have to flout God's will as well, committing unspeakable acts together. "God gave them up unto vile affections: for even their women did change the natural use into that which is against nature."'

It was so ridiculous that Callie wanted to laugh, but Frances wasn't laughing. 'How dare you,' she hissed, not bothering to deny it. 'How dare you pass moral judgements on us?'

He pressed his lips together. 'The words are not mine. They are St Paul's words. And Our Lord himself judges you, not me. He knows what grievous sins you have committed, against His Church and against natural law and common decency.'

'You… sanctimonious hypocrite!' Frances exploded.

Heads swivelled in their direction, and Leo crossed the room in a few strides to Frances' side; his protective arm was long enough to encompass the shoulders of both women. 'Steady on,' he said warningly, then glared at Jonah Adimola. 'Are you upsetting my sisters?'

Again the man's nostrils flared. 'I should have known that you would come to their defence, Son-of-a-Slave. After all, you allowed your altar to be desecrated, to be defiled and tainted, to be polluted by this woman, this spawn of Satan.'

Frances' arm shot out, and a full glass of wine went into Father Jonah's face, dripping down onto his cassock.

For a few seconds there was total silence; everyone seemed frozen in place. Then the spell was broken as Father Vincent, who had been watching the scene with bemused approval, moved to the side of his colleague. 'Father Leo,' he boomed in a carrying voice. 'May I take Father Jonah to your vestry to clean up?'

Leo nodded, but his attention was on Frances, who had begun to tremble with shock.

Callie took a step back. 'Frances, are you all right?'

Frances' voice shook, but her words were firm. 'I'm not sorry,' she said defiantly. 'He deserved it. He deserved worse than that. If I'd had a blunt instrument, I would have killed him.'

Leo put his arms around her, enveloping her in a hug against his chest. 'Frannie, my pet,' he crooned in a gentle voice. 'He did deserve it. But you don't mean that.'

'I do.'

'Come on, my love. Let's get some fresh air.' His arms still around her, he steered her toward the door.

Callie, along with everyone else in the room, watched them go. The silence was complete. What now? thought Callie. Should she wait for Frances, or should she make her own way home?

Indecisively, she turned. Turned, and found herself face to face with Adam.

He was smiling down at her, that lazy smile she'd always loved.

'Hi, Cal,' he said easily. As if none of it had ever happened, as if they were still together. He was the only one who called her that—Cal, a diminutive of a nickname.

'Hi.'

'What was that all about?' Adam raised a quizzical eyebrow. 'All I heard was the last bit.'

'Don't ask.'

'All right, I won't.'

She waited, looking down at the floor, reminding herself to breathe.

'Actually,' Adam said, 'I've been meaning to catch you all evening. There was something I wanted to ask you.'

Involuntarily she raised her head and looked into his brown eyes, her heart constricting. 'Yes?'

'I wondered if you were free on Saturday night.'

'Free?' she echoed in a tight voice she didn't recognise as her own. 'Saturday?'

'I wondered if you might come to my place for a meal. You could see my new flat. And you could meet Pippa,' he added enthusiastically. 'She's coming up for the weekend. I'd really like the two of you to be friends, Cal. I know you'd love her.'

'I'm sure,' said the voice that wasn't really Callie.

Adam was beaming. 'The thing is, Cal, she doesn't know anyone in London but me. When we get married in a few months' time, when she moves here, it would be great for her to have a friend.'

All for Pippa's benefit, then. Not an attempt at reconciliation, or trying to salvage something—a vestige of friendship—from a relationship that had meant so much to both of them. It was all about Pippa. Callie swallowed a lump in her throat.

'Say you'll come on Saturday, Cal,' he wheeled, with a pleading look on his face which had never failed to get him his own way where she was concerned. When the silence had stretched out for a few seconds, he added, 'Pippa makes a great curry.'

Callie lifted her chin and looked him straight in the eye. 'I'm sorry, Adam,' she said firmly. 'I won't be able to join you and Pippa on Saturday.' She paused and took a deep breath. 'I have a date.'

Chapter Five

When DI Neville Stewart reported for duty on Wednesday morning, it was with the sincere hope that it would be a routine day, with nothing more challenging than a few minor infringements of the law to occupy his time. If at all possible, he planned to spend the day at his desk—he had a heap of paperwork with which he needed to catch up. At least that was the excuse he gave to the duty sergeant on his way to his office.

The truth of the matter was, Neville Stewart was rather the worse for wear.

Although he didn't usually indulge in late nights when he was on duty the following morning, the night before had been an exception. He'd met a girl at the weekend who had expressed an interest in traditional Irish music, and he'd arranged to meet her at a pub in Kilburn which was renowned in equal measure for its live music and its perfectly-pulled Guinness.

The girl had stood him up, but Neville had remained, finding the pub's reputation to be well founded. The music was as good as he'd ever heard in Dublin, and as for the Guinness…

The long and the short of it was that he had stayed till closing time, singing along with the music with increasing confidence, volume and merriment. And though his capacity for Guinness was prodigious—even legendary—he had sunk at least one pint too many. Maybe more. He couldn't quite remember.

On his way to his desk, he collected what was sure to be the first in a series of mugs of strong black coffee. Perhaps that would help, though the bitterness of the coffee was decidedly unpleasant on his furred tongue.

As he put the mug down, coffee slopped over the edge onto the surface of his desk. Neville gave it an ineffectual wipe, but wasn't too bothered, as the desk was already marred by discoloured rings and various scratches. For a moment he contemplated the mound of paper in the in-tray, wishing he knew where to begin. Wishing he had a cigarette.

Neville was a reformed smoker, and usually a zealously self-righteous one—the first to point out to a smoking colleague the dangers of the evil weed. Though once he had made up his mind to quit, he had never so much as sneaked a clandestine puff, secretly he was envious of those who continued to blacken their lungs without regard for the consequences, and nothing made him happier than to be in a room full of smokers, breathing in second-hand smoke.

The pub last night had been a winner on that score, as well: at times it was difficult to see the musicians for the fuggy haze which enveloped the place.

Neville sniffed the sleeve of his tweed jacket reminiscently. Yes, it still had that lovely redolence of stale tobacco. Maybe that would help to get him through the day.

He had just begun to thumb through his paperwork when Mark Lombardi stuck his head round the door. 'Morning, Nev,' he said.

'Morning.' He grimaced. 'At least I think it is.'

Mark wrinkled his nose in distaste. He had never smoked, and felt this gave him the moral edge when it came to disapproval of the habit. 'Whew—you smell like you've been sleeping in an ashtray.'

'Pub,' Neville mumbled. 'Irish pub.'

'Ah.' Mark grinned, altogether too knowingly for Neville's liking. 'That explains a great deal.'

'I'll have you know I'm perfectly sober,' Neville said with all the dignity he could muster.

'That's as may be. But let's hope you don't have to get behind the wheel of a car any time soon.'

It was at that moment that Neville's phone rang. He jumped slightly, then picked it up. 'DI Stewart.'

'Sorry, Guv,' said the duty sergeant. 'Your paperwork is going to have to wait for another day. Or two.'

'What's up, then?'

'A body,' said the sergeant succinctly. 'Murdered. DCS Evans wants you there right away.'

'You're sure about that?' Neville gulped down the rest of his coffee, now cold as well as bitter. 'Sure it's murder?'

'Sure as sure. I don't think the poor bastard strangled himself.' There was a pause on the other end of the phone. 'I haven't told you the best part, Guv. It's in a church—St John's, Lancaster Gate. And the dead bloke's a priest.'

⌘﹏⌘ ⌘﹏⌘ ⌘﹏⌘

'You did what?' Graham Cherry stared at his wife with undisguised astonishment over their Wednesday morning cornflakes.

'I threw a glass of wine over Father Jonah What's-his-name,' Frances repeated patiently. 'Red wine.'

'What on earth did you do a thing like that for?'

Frances sighed. 'I was provoked. He was incredibly rude.'

'He's always been rude to you,' Graham pointed out. 'What did you expect?'

'It wasn't so much on my own behalf.' She poured herself a second cup of tea and a ghost of a smile twitched at the corners of her mouth. 'Though he did call me a spawn of Satan. But he was picking on Callie, and then he brought Leo into it. I just... lost it. The wine was in my hand, and the next thing I knew, it... wasn't.'

Graham shook his head, as much in wonderment as in reproach. 'I suppose in your place I might have done the same. But it just doesn't seem like you, Fran. After all you've put up with through the years...'

How nice it was to have a supportive husband, Frances reflected. They'd always been able to talk things through, even if they didn't always agree on everything. 'It was more or less the last straw,' she admitted. 'I was already upset about... various things. He caught me at a bad moment.'

He leaned forward, frowning in concern. 'What other things were you upset about?'

'Heather, for one.' There was a slight tremble in her voice, even now. 'I haven't had a chance to tell you. She rang yesterday afternoon. She won't be home for Christmas.'

'Oh.' Graham's eyes widened, the pupils dilated. 'That's bad news.' His relationship with their only child was a far less complicated one than Frances': he had always adored Heather unreservedly, and that was reciprocated, even if Heather's behaviour didn't always accord with her love for her father.

'She said to tell you she's sorry.'

'So am I.' He looked down into his cornflakes, overwhelmed with disappointment.

Frances was glad she'd been able to distract him from asking any more questions: she didn't want to tell him about Leo and his young lover, and her unease over that situation. It was Leo's secret rather than hers; the fact that he had trusted her with it made it all the more important that she not pass it on, not even to Graham.

⚭⚭⚭

DI Neville Stewart allowed his young sergeant, DS Cowley, to drive him to the crime scene, though from the moment he received the phone call, he was stone cold sober; he couldn't afford to be anything else.

They arrived at the church a few minutes after the SOCOs and the doctor; Detective Chief Superintendent Evans had already come and gone. Neville always thought it was important for him to view a crime scene as soon as possible, and before anything was disturbed by the SOCOs, but this time he was too late. Having had the go-ahead from DCS Evans, the white-suited officers were already about their business, efficiently and without a lot of superfluous chat. The room at the focus of all the activity was a small one, located at the back end of the church. Deciding that it was the better part of valour to wait a few minutes until he could get into the room without being in the way of the SOCOs' necessary ministrations, Neville left his sergeant in the narrow corridor and went through into the nave of the church.

The interior of St John's, Lancaster Gate, looked not at all as Neville had imagined it. In his Irish Catholic childhood, he had always been told—in tones of derision—that the Anglican Church was Protestant, and in his mind that conjured up pictures of whitewashed walls, pitch-pine pews and no decoration save the Ten Commandments on a wooden board behind a simple wooden communion table.

This church was nothing like that. Indeed, it was far more richly decorated than the church of his childhood, with jewel-like stained glass windows, carved stone pillars, and painted statues on pedestals. A flickering red candle suspended near the stone altar indicated that the Blessed Sacrament was reserved. Neville hadn't been inside a church—any church—for years, but he realised with a jolt of surprise that he had just crossed himself as he walked in front of the altar.

Maybe this wasn't an Anglican church after all, he told himself.

There was a middle-aged woman near the pulpit, fiddling with a large flower arrangement, picking off a few wilting heads and titivating the rest to hide the gaps. Perhaps he could ask her.

'Excuse me,' he said tentatively. 'Is this church the Church of England?'

She stopped and peered at him over the tops of her glasses. 'It most certainly is,' she said in an accent of cut-glass purity.

'I just thought maybe it was Catholic.'

'It's that, as well,' the woman stated. 'The two things aren't mutually exclusive, you know.'

Now he was confused, and he felt as though the woman were subjecting him to a rather detailed inspection which he was sure to fail. It must be obvious to her that he was not a sightseer or a religious seeker, and in a moment she would probably tell him to be on his way. She belonged here; he didn't. Defensively he said, 'I'm investigating a murder.'

'Oh, yes.' It didn't faze her at all. 'Then I suppose you're looking for the young woman who found Father. She's in the chapel, I believe.'

It was the first he'd heard of that, but it gave him a legitimate excuse to take his leave of her. 'Thank you,' he said. It was only as he walked away that he realised the woman shouldn't have been there at all—the church was now sealed off as a crime scene; he himself had had to duck under the tape to get in. She must have been in here when the body was discovered, and no one had been able to shift her. He could understand that: he certainly wasn't going to try. Maybe Sergeant Cowley, with his lack of sentiment and total obliviousness to nuance, would have better luck.

The small side chapel was in semi-darkness, and it was a moment before he saw the young woman in question, kneeling in one of the back pews. Neville felt awkward about disturbing her, so he slid into the pew next to her and waited. Her hands were clasped tightly together, their knuckles white with tension, and her head was bowed over them. As his eyes adjusted to the dimness, he noted that she was a rather pretty girl, in spite of her efforts to disguise the fact, her short carrot-coloured hair moussed into rather aggressive-looking spikes. She had a ring through her nostril, and wore distressed blue jeans, a shocking pink fleece and thick-soled DM boots. Her fingernails were painted the iridescent green of an exotic beetle.

Sensing his presence, she looked up at him. Her eyes were large, either naturally or because of shock, and the heavy kohl make-up had smeared a bit, giving her the appearance of a surprised panda.

'I'm sorry to bother you,' Neville said quietly.

She shrugged. 'That's all right. You're the police, aren't you?'

Neville nodded. 'Detective Inspector Stewart.'

'I was waiting here because I figured you'd want to talk to me.'

Automatically Neville reached for the notebook in his pocket. 'That was good of you, Miss… err…'

'Tree,' she said.

'Christian name?'

She twisted her fingers together. 'Promise you won't laugh?'

'I promise.' He was, Neville thought wryly, the last person to laugh at anyone else's name.

'Willow. Willow Tree.'

In spite of himself he smiled. 'That's… unusual.'

'My parents were hippies,' she explained bitterly. 'Eco-warriors, really. They thought it was clever. *They* don't have to live with it. And I get tired of people taking the mickey about it.'

Neville bent his head over his notebook and wrote her name at the top of the page. 'Yes, I can see that.' He wanted to tell her about his name and the problems it had caused him over the years, but this was not the time or place for that. 'I guess it's better than Christmas.'

It took her a few seconds to get his meaning, then she relaxed and smiled. 'Yes. I suppose it could always be worse.'

Neville gave her a moment, then asked, 'Do you feel able to answer a few questions now, Miss Tree? I promise I'll try not to keep you too long.'

'I'm all right,' she said bravely. 'Just a bit shaken, that's all. And please—call me Willow.'

He noted down the details of her address and telephone number. 'You can always get me on my mobile,' she said.

'If you could just begin, Miss… err… Willow, by telling me what brought you to the church this morning? How did you happen to be here?'

Willow looked at the altar in the chapel as she told him, concisely and without fuss. She was, she explained, the sacristan at the church. That meant she had responsibility for setting up for services: getting the communion vessels out of the safe in the sacristy and putting them on the altar, and also laying out the vestments in the vestry. Although today's Mass wasn't until noon, she had come in early, on her way to work, as was her custom.

'But today's not Sunday,' Neville pointed out.

She turned her head and looked at him. 'We have a service here every day. At least one.'

He was more confused than ever about the practices of the Church of England, but this was not the occasion to go into that.

'And that's when you found...' he said delicately.

'Yes.' She nodded, bowing her head. 'In the vestry. It was... horrible. He was lying on the floor, with a stole wrapped round his neck.'

'You could tell he was dead?'

'There wasn't much doubt about that.' Willow swallowed hard.

'And you recognised him?'

'Oh, yes.'

Neville could feel her distress, so he deliberately shifted his questions away from that painful subject. Willow Tree intrigued him; it seemed strange to him that a young woman—and one who didn't even live in the parish, according to the address she'd supplied—should be so involved with the church. 'What brings you here?' he asked, as much as anything to satisfy his own curiosity.

'I told you. I'm the sacristan, and...'

'That's not what I meant.' he tried to formulate the question so it didn't sound too insulting. 'Most young people these days don't go to church. Let alone get involved in doing a job like that, when it means you have to be here every day. Is it your parents? Do they make you come?'

For the first time, she laughed, a single musical peal of amusement. 'My parents stopped trying to tell me what to do a very long time ago.'

'Then why...'

She gave him a searching look. 'Do you really want to know? Is it relevant?'

Neville realised that he did really want to know. 'Yes, I do,' he said. 'And no, I don't suppose it's relevant. But humour me.'

Willow seemed to ponder for a moment, choosing her words. 'I suppose it was Leo,' she stated. 'The vicar. Don't get me wrong. I love everything about this place—the beauty of the building, and the drama of the worship. It all speaks to me in a very powerful way. But I don't suppose I would have come—and stayed—if it wasn't for Leo.'

'Tell me about Leo.'

Again she paused. 'Leo... well, from the first time I met him, I could tell that he was special. A man of great faith... and so much more. I mean, he's not just interested in the Church, like so many clergy. Don't get me wrong—he takes the Church very seriously. But it's in the context of the world we live in. And our responsibility to our world.'

Poor kid, thought Neville. She was talking about him in the present tense, as though he were still alive, and not lying in that little room surrounded by police. Even though she'd seen it herself, she hadn't quite taken it on board yet. 'What do you mean?' he asked.

'Social issues. Justice. Equality for all men and women, regardless of colour or nationality or religion or sexual preference.' Her voice was passionate. 'The environment. The homeless. Asylum seekers. The Third World. There are so many things he's interested in. And he does something about it, as well. He doesn't just sit on his backside and talk about it, like lots of people do. He campaigns. He writes letters. He uses his influence in the Church—on General Synod—to speak out publicly. Lots of people resent him for that, of course,' she added.

At that, Neville's brain suddenly revved up into first gear: if people resented him, that meant he had enemies. Enemies meant motives for murder. 'What sort of people?' he asked.

Willow shrugged. 'Oh, the sort of people you'd expect. The old guard here at St John's. It's a very wealthy parish, you know. Conservative. Establishment. People who don't like rocking the boat.'

Neville thought about the woman with the flowers, and could imagine that she'd not been a great fan of the dynamic, social activist Leo. But he couldn't quite picture her committing murder over it. Though Willow Tree had said that he'd been strangled with a stole…

'But there are lots of people like me here, as well,' Willow went on. 'Younger people who care about the things that matter. Leo's brought us all on board. We come from all over London, not just from this parish. And it's because of Leo.'

He sounded like the sort of man who aroused strong feeling. 'He must have meant a great deal to you. I can see why it was so upsetting for you to find him like that,' Neville said sympathetically. 'I'm sure he'll be greatly missed.'

Willow turned and stared at him, her eyes wide. 'What on earth do you mean?'

'Well, now that he's dead—'

'But Leo's not dead!'

Neville felt as if the ground had shifted beneath him, as if he had been pitched into a surreal world where the rules did not apply. Perhaps, he thought, she was comforting herself with some theological malarky about the dead being alive in Jesus. That's what old Father Flynn had said at his granddad's funeral. 'In the vestry. You said you could tell he was dead,' he said patiently.

Her face cracked into a smile. 'Oh, you thought that was Leo in there!' Willow laughed with relief. 'That's not Leo, Inspector Stewart. It's Father Jonah.'

⁂

Callie was to preach her first sermon at All Saints' on Sunday, so on Wednesday morning she settled down at her desk to try to put a few ideas together. She was determined that her first sermon would be a good one; it would set the tone for her curacy. The congregation would judge her on it, and more importantly, so would Brian. It was important to her that she impress Brian, right from the start.

At theological college she had discovered that she was rather good at preaching. Her years in the Civil Service had accustomed her to organising her thoughts into logical points and synthesising material from different sources into a cohesive whole, and that had stood her in good stead when it came to preaching. She liked to write sermons the old-fashioned way, sketching out ideas on a legal pad; when she had a good sense of what she wanted to say, she would commit the words to her computer and get them into final shape on the screen.

But this morning she was finding it very hard going. Unsurprisingly, she hadn't slept very well, and now her thoughts kept wandering to the events of the previous night. Two images continued to rise to the surface of her mind: the astonished and angry face of Father Jonah, dripping with wine, and the astonished and disbelieving face of Adam.

Callie kept an open mind on the subject of love at first sight: though she had never experienced it herself, she knew people who insisted it had happened to them. Nonetheless she was certain that it was impossible to fall out of love in an instant. Love was a habit, a mind-set, a pattern of thinking that would surely take time to change. But last night, at the moment when Adam stared at her, she felt she had taken the first step away from loving him. For an instant, looking into those startled brown eyes, she had seen him in a very different light—not the Adam she had loved for over two years, but a stranger, and not a very attractive one at that. Self-assured, self-absorbed. Selfish, even. Blinkered, seeing the world as he wanted it to be rather than how it really was. Lacking in imagination, humour, empathy. Perhaps, she thought with a sense of shock, not even terribly bright.

The memory was disturbing yet exciting in its implications, and she intermittently probed it in the way a tongue continues to return to a sore tooth. There was hope: in a month, in six months, in a year—who knew how long?—a time would come when she no longer loved Adam. Not even a little bit.

When the phone rang, it was with a feeling of guilty relief that she abandoned her sermon to answer it.

'Listen, Callie,' said Frances. 'I want to apologise for last night.'

'Apologise? To me? Whatever for?'

'For abandoning you,' her friend said. 'I was supposed to be there as moral support, right? But I ran out on you, and left you to... whatever. Adam. Those neanderthal men in black. All the things I was supposed to be protecting you from.'

'But you were standing up for me!' Callie protested. 'When Father Jonah said those horrible things.'

'He just made me so furious,' Frances said with asperity. 'On your behalf, and... well, for all of us women. I can't remember ever feeling so angry—honestly, Callie, I could have killed the smug bastard.'

'You got home okay?' Callie asked. 'I was a bit concerned.'

'Leo was an absolute star. He took me outside and gave me time to calm down and blow off steam. Then he walked me all the way home. Fortunately,' Frances added, 'Graham was out at a meeting. So I poured myself a stiff drink and went straight to bed.'

'Are you feeling better now?'

'In the cold light of day, I know I shouldn't have done it,' she admitted. 'But given the same circumstances, I'd probably do it again.'

⊙❦❧

'Who,' asked Neville Stewart, baffled, 'is Father Jonah? Or should I say, *was* Father Jonah?'

Willow Tree glanced toward the altar of the chapel. 'A priest at another church. I think it was St Mary the Virgin, Marble Arch.'

'And do you have any idea what he might have been doing here?'

'There was a meeting here last night, in the church hall. Deanery Clergy Chapter, it's called,' she explained. 'For all the clergy in this area. It was mostly a social sort of thing, with a speaker and refreshments.'

'And it's likely that this Father Jonah was at the meeting?'

She turned to face him and spoke with the sort of directness Neville was beginning to admire her for: if only, he thought, all witnesses could be so co-operative and precise. 'I know for a fact he was. I was here myself, for at least part of the evening. Leo had asked me if I'd serve the coffee. When the speaker started, I tidied up the kitchen and went home.'

'So you definitely saw this Father Jonah last night,' he stated, then added, as another thought struck him, 'and you could give me a list of the other people who were here, as well?'

'I can't really be much help to you there, I'm afraid. They were from all different churches. A few of them I recognised, but I didn't know them all.'

'You did know Father Jonah?' he pressed her.

She shrugged. 'Not really—I couldn't even tell you his sur-name. He was hard to miss, though. African. Leo's black, but Father Jonah was... well, he was *really* black, if you know what I mean. The darkest skin I've ever seen.'

A racially-motivated crime, then? Neville reflected. Not impossible, even in a church.

'Leo's the one who could give you a list,' Willow volunteered. 'He's the Area Dean. He knows everybody.'

Leo. He'd assumed that Leo was the murder victim; now, having been proved wrong about that, Neville demanded, 'Where *is* Leo? Why isn't he here?'

She had a ready answer, at least for the second question. 'On Wednesday morning he always has a meeting with the Arch-deacon. That's why the Mass isn't until noon on a Wednesday.' Willow consulted her watch. 'It's twenty to twelve. He should be arriving at any minute.'

As if on cue, Leo erupted into the stillness of the chapel. Leo was, Neville discerned instantly, the sort of man who not only dominated a room—he filled it with his presence.

'Willow!' roared Leo, manifestly agitated. 'There you are. Thank God. What the hell is going on here? There's tape around the church. I can't get into the vestry. There are people every-where—police, and people in white space suits. No one will tell me anything. What in God's name is going on?'

'Did you manage to avoid Adam?' Frances wanted to know.

Callie sighed. 'Actually, no. He caught up with me after you left. Said he wanted to invite me to supper on Saturday night.'

'He's having second thoughts, then? He wants to patch things up?'

'In a manner of speaking.' Callie made an attempt at mimicking Adam's voice. '"Pippa makes a great curry."'

'Oh, no,' Frances groaned. 'Not that "I hope the two of you will be great friends" crap.'

'That's exactly what it was.'

'I hope you told him where to go. In no uncertain terms.'

'I told him,' Callie said, 'that I had a date on Saturday night.' Once again she remembered the look on his face when she'd said it.

'Oooh, good one, Callie. Brilliant. If you'd like to make your confession, I'll give you absolution for that little porky. It was entirely justified in the circumstances.'

'But it wasn't a porky. It was true,' Callie stated, feeling a flush move up from her neck toward her face. She was glad that Frances couldn't see her at that moment, blushing like a schoolgirl.

Once Leo was apprised of the situation, and had calmed down sufficiently to be coherent, Neville told Willow Tree that she could go. 'I know where to reach you if I have any further questions,' he said to her, and when she'd gone he turned to Leo. 'If I could have a few words with you, then, Mr... err... Reverend... err... Father...' Or should it be Vicar? he wondered. The titles of the Anglican clergy were a mystery to him. The girl had said he was Area Dean. Did that mean he had some special honorific title, like 'Your Deanship'? With the RCs you knew where you stood: it was 'Father', and that was the end of it. Why did the Anglicans have to make things so complicated?

'Leo. Just Leo's fine.'

'Guv—there you are.' A London-accented voice announced the arrival in the chapel of his sergeant, Sid Cowley. 'I've been looking for you. The pathologist wants a word.'

'Good.' Neville moved toward the chapel entrance, out of Leo's earshot, to where the pathologist waited for him. He went straight to the point. 'What can you tell me?'

The pathologist heaved the sigh of a man who had heard that question many times before. 'I guessed you'd want to know. Cause of death: strangulation, without a doubt.' He sighed again and rolled his eyes. 'And I suppose you want some idea of time of death as well.'

'It would be helpful.' Neville tried to keep any hint of sarcasm from his voice; his experience with this man told him that it wouldn't get him anywhere.

'As you well know, I won't be able to give a precise time till I have him in the lab—if then. But I'd say last night. Before midnight.'

'Thank you.'

The pathologist nodded in acknowledgement. 'Oh, and he died where we found him. He wasn't moved after death.' He turned and moved away, adding over his shoulder, 'He's all yours. For the moment. But the sooner you let me have him, the sooner I'll be able to tell you more.'

It was Neville's turn to sigh. 'I suppose it's time for me to go and make the acquaintance of Father Jonah,' he said as much to himself as to DS Cowley. 'Just what I've been looking forward to.'

Then he remembered Leo, behind him in the chapel.

Leo was standing in front of the altar, facing the chapel entrance; he was still, not moving a muscle, but it was the stillness of a coiled spring. 'I have a Mass here in a few minutes,' he said. 'People will be expecting it.'

This threw Neville: was the man seriously proposing to hold a service while a man lay dead in his vestry?

'I'm afraid,' he said firmly, 'that won't be possible. This church is a crime scene. No one will be allowed in past the tapes.' A thought struck him. 'For that matter, how did *you* get in?'

'It's my church,' stated Leo with unassailable authority. 'I have a right to be here.'

Neville could well imagine that no one would have dared stop him. 'Well, I'm afraid that a service is out of the question. No one else is coming in here for the moment.'

Leo inclined his head in silent acknowledgement.

'And I *will* need to talk to you. In a few minutes.' As soon as he'd done the necessary in the vestry. 'Do you have an office somewhere? Or a room where we can talk in private?'

Neville told himself that he might have been imagining it, but he thought he detected, for just a fraction of a second, a tiny flicker of hesitation.

'At the rectory,' said Leo. 'I'll wait for you there.'

Chapter Six

The Reverend Vincent Underwood—Father Vincent to his flock—was up early on Wednesday. This was not unusual; he was up early every day, and in church by eight. It was his duty as a priest to say Morning Prayer daily, and while he could have done that at home, in the sanctum of his study, he preferred to do it in church, especially as Morning Prayer was always followed by Mass. Some days he took the service, and on other days it was Father Jonah. Father Vincent liked to be there even when it was Father Jonah's turn; it was a joy to him to be at the altar—the essence of what priesthood was all about, as far as he was concerned.

Father Vincent lived at some distance from St Mary the Virgin, Marble Arch. The church was north of Marble Arch—though it still boasted a respectable W1 address—while Father Vincent lived south of Oxford Street, indisputably in Mayfair, in a gracious Georgian townhouse facing onto a tiny green square.

It wasn't that St Mary's didn't possess a clergy house. Indeed, there was one, and Father Jonah lived there. But Father Vincent was in the fortunate position of having a wife with private means. Marigold Underwood's father had been an Honourable, and had died at a relatively young age, leaving her—an only child—the family house with all its goods and chattels. The early years of their marriage, living in tied clergy housing, were long forgotten; since inheriting the Mayfair house they had resided there. Father Vincent had served his entire career in the London diocese, and had been Rector of St Mary the Virgin for more than twenty years. It was longer than priests usually stayed at a church. Father Vincent knew that, yet he felt that he had found his niche, the place where he belonged, and it would be foolish to move on just for the sake of moving.

He would not, however, have been averse to preferment. If nothing else, it was the Church's mark of esteem, of recognition, for a priest of outstanding gifts. After all, when he was a mere ordinand at theological college, he had always been the one tipped to be a bishop one day. But the mitre had not come, nor had a canonry at the cathedral, or even an honorific like a prebendal stall. Several times he had been passed over for the office of Area Dean, and plum livings in the diocese had been bestowed on those far less worthy and experienced than he.

It was well known, though, he consoled himself, that the Church had an overt if not official policy of discrimination against priests like him: priests, that is, who vocally and actively opposed the abomination of women's ordination. The Act of Synod had decreed 'two integrities' and promised that no distinction would be made when it came to appointments and preferments. On paper it sounded fine; in practice it had not worked out that way. Anyone who held membership in Forward in Faith, who led their congregations to pass the resolutions which made their churches no-go areas for women clergy, was sure to be overlooked when the good jobs were being dished out.

Father Vincent tried not to be resentful about it. But it seemed bitterly unfair that he should be punished for adhering to the true faith.

Still, if he had to be stuck in a job, it was preferable that it should be in W1 rather than somewhere in the East End.

On that morning, as usual, Father Vincent had ridden his bicycle through the streets of Mayfair and across Oxford Street to the church. He'd said Morning Prayer and celebrated the Mass. There was a congregation of six that day. Father Jonah was not among them, which was unusual but not unprecedented. No one had remarked on his absence.

The rest of the morning had seen Father Vincent at his desk, working on his sermon. His study was at the front of the house on the ground floor, overlooking the leafy square. He always enjoyed watching the people passing by, as well as observing the changing of the seasons as reflected in the little patch of green and its trees. October was now underway, and although it would be a while before the leaves fell, they had begun to change hue.

Father Vincent prided himself on being a fine preacher, with his mellifluous voice and his incisive grasp of theology. Today, though, he was aware that his mind was not really on his sermon. The words flowed effortlessly from pen to paper with the fluidity of long practice, but his thoughts were elsewhere.

He was aware of noises in the house: the tick of the carriage clock on the mantelpiece in the study, the distant sound of the daily hoovering the stairs, the even more distant rumble of the washing machine somewhere beneath him. And then there was that wretched cat, meowing for her lunch. Already.

Father Vincent threw down his pen with a bad-tempered grunt.

When Marigold was out at lunchtimes, which was almost every day, the daily was supposed to feed the cat. It didn't always work out that way: she would get involved in whatever she was doing, and if she were running the hoover, she didn't always hear the insistent meows.

He made his way downstairs to the kitchen, resisting the impulse to kick the cat as she twined round his legs. Usually she had no time for him, but she knew that he had it in his power to feed her.

Father Vincent didn't like cats in general, and he most certainly didn't like Jezebel, a sleek Siamese. In the first place, he thought her name highly unsuitable. And he hated her air of smug superiority, regarding the world—and him—with disdain. She was Marigold's cat, not his, though she wasn't noticeably more friendly toward her mistress than she was to him. Except at feeding time. This didn't seem to faze Marigold, who lavished an inordinate amount of affection on the beast.

He tore open the pouch of expensive cat food and dumped it in her bowl. In spite of her frenzy of hunger immediately before, she inspected the food with a fastidious sniff, nibbled it tentatively, then walked away, her tail in the air.

'Blasted cat,' said Father Vincent under his breath.

He looked at the clock: almost mid-day. There would be a news broadcast on the television at noon.

The only television set in the house lived down here, in the kitchen. Marigold considered it an abomination to have a television above stairs, so if they ever wanted to watch anything, they had to descend to the kitchen. That didn't happen very often; it was mostly used by the daily, who kept it on as a background to her work in the kitchen, or settled down in front of it with a periodic cup of tea.

He switched the set on and sat down in the lone arm chair, long since discarded from upstairs.

The broadcast began with the usual: wars and rumours of wars. Then there was the latest government scandal, a funding crisis in the NHS, and the Queen's state visit to some far-flung country where they wore funny hats. At the end they got round to a few minutes of local London news.

Father Vincent leaned forward and stared at the screen. It showed St John's Church, Lancaster Gate, and there was blue-and-white crime scene tape stretched across the door. The voice-over named the church, then reported that the body of a man had been found inside. Although official identification was unavailable, pending notification of next-of-kin, sources indicated that the man was a priest. The circumstances were suspicious, and police were at the scene.

It lasted for just a few seconds, no more. And then the relentlessly chirpy weather girl was there, standing in front of a map and talking about isobars.

Father Vincent allowed her to witter on for a minute. Then he switched off the television and went back upstairs to his study. This time there was no question of working on his sermon. He was waiting for the police.

Neville Stewart, trailed by DS Cowley, who was smoking a quick cigarette, walked the short distance to St John's Rectory, his head filled with the image of the dead man in the vestry. The first glimpse of the body had been a shock from which he was still recovering. It was at moments like that one that his Catholic childhood reared its head unexpectedly. 'Holy Mother of God,' he'd breathed at the sight of the murdered priest.

His witness, Willow Tree, had said that Father Jonah had been strangled with a stole, and what Neville had expected to see, had pictured in his mind, was the sort of stole which women wore round their shoulders—perhaps a pashmina. But the stole which had permanently stopped the breath of the dead priest was nothing like that: it was a ceremonial vestment of a type worn only by clergy.

Strangled with his own stole, he'd thought, then he'd taken a closer look. The stole was white, with blue writing on it. The writing turned out to be names: Ruth, Rebecca, Naomi, Rachel, Mary, Eve, and a host of others. All women's names, he observed. A very odd thing to have on that sort of garment.

Some echo of his childhood resonated in his head, and Neville realised that the names belonged to women in the Bible.

Perhaps Leo Jackson would be able to enlighten him.

The rectory door swung open almost before Neville had rung the bell, and Leo Jackson loomed above him.

Neville was not easily intimidated, but Leo Jackson had that sort of effect on him. It wasn't just Leo's size, though he was massive; there was something about his very presence which radiated authority and power, in a spiritual rather than a physical sense. Leo Jackson was not someone to be trifled with.

His face, so distorted with emotion when they'd first met, had by now been composed into a mask of sombre courtesy. 'Come in,' he invited, and led the way into his study. He offered them coffee, which Neville was happy to accept; it seemed like a very long time since he'd downed that cup of coffee at his desk.

'I'll just be a minute, then,' Leo said, and disappeared.

In a habit born of long practice, Neville looked round the room for clues to the man he was about to interview. It was clearly a room with a function, and that function was work. The walls were ranged with filled bookcases, there were two filing cabinets in a corner, and the large desk was covered with untidy stacks of paperwork. Not at all unlike his own desk, thought Neville ruefully. One corner of the desk held a stylish-looking iMac computer—switched on, but nothing could be seen on the screen except the shimmering waves of a screen saver.

Neville scanned the room for photos or other revealing personal mementoes. There was, as far as he could spot, only one photo, hanging on the wall in a space between the bookcases and the door. He stepped up to it for a closer look.

Leo was at the centre of the photo, a huge smile splitting his face. In the background was the façade of St Paul's Cathedral. On either side of Leo, his long arms spanning their shoulders, stood two women, also smiling.

Something about the picture caught Neville's attention. The woman closest to Leo on the left side was a pretty redhead, fair-skinned, so tiny that her head barely reached Leo's shoulder. She was wearing some sort of a loose white garment and a dog collar. And round her neck was a white stole with blue writing on it: the names of women in the Bible.

⟆⟆⟆ ⟆⟆⟆ ⟆⟆⟆

Leo was glad that the police had asked for coffee. It gave him a few precious extra minutes while the kettle boiled to complete what he'd started to do before they arrived. He'd already checked the sitting room and kitchen for anything which might betray Oliver's presence, removing a few golden hairs from the sofa cushions and a magazine from the coffee table. Just in case. Now he picked up the cordless phone and carried it through to the kitchen. He dialled Frances Cherry's mobile phone number and listened in frustration as an impersonal voice told him that the number could not be reached and he should leave a message. She was at work, then—the hospital required that mobile phones be switched off.

Speaking as softly as he could, almost whispering, he left a message. 'Frannie, love. It's Leo. I have some bad news, pet. Jonah Adimola's dead—he's been murdered. The police are here. I'm going to have to tell them about last night—about the row. If I don't, someone else will. I'm sure they'll want to talk to you. I just wanted to warn you, pet.'

⚬⟁⟁⚬ ⚬⟁⟁⚬ ⚬⟁⟁⚬

Neville heard Leo coming, and moved quickly away from the photo to take a seat.

'Sorry to have taken so long,' said Leo, pushing the door open with his foot and setting down the coffee tray on a small table. One corner of the study was arranged as a seating area, with three comfortable arm chairs; it was where he would sit with people who came to see him for counselling or marriage preparation. He handed both policemen mugs of black coffee, and kept one for himself. 'I suppose you have some questions you want to ask me,' he said in a neutral tone.

Neville sipped gratefully at the scalding brew. It was strong enough to strip the varnish from the table—God, it tasted good. That gave him a moment to collect his thoughts, to decide what to ask first and how to ask it. There would be nothing to be gained by being high-handed or demanding with this man, he realised. He would treat him with deference and courtesy.

'First of all,' he said, 'I suppose I'd like to know what the man—Father Jonah—was doing in your church. He wasn't officially associated with it, I understand.'

'Good Lord, no.' Leo's mobile face betrayed with a grimace what he thought about that scenario. 'He was there for a meeting last night. Willow must have told you about it—she was there serving coffee.'

'Yes, but… why would he have been in that part of the church? That wasn't where the meeting was held.'

'The meeting was in the church hall,' Leo affirmed. 'After a service in the chapel.'

'Did this Father Jonah have a reason to be in the—what's it called?—vestry?'

Leo spoke with deliberation, weighing his words. 'I sent him there, after the meeting. There was... an incident. He needed to clean himself up. The vestry seemed the best place for that.'

'What sort of an incident?' Neville could scarcely imagine anything happening at a church meeting that would merit a description like that.

'I need to explain a few things.' Leo took a gulp of coffee, then leaned forward. 'Jonah wasn't an easy man to get on with. He was opinionated, to say the very least. One of the things he hated—and I say one of the things, because there were many—was women priests. He couldn't accept them, not at all. And last night I had asked a woman to assist me with the service. He and another priest, his boss, walked out—they didn't stay for the service at all.'

'Why did you ask a woman to assist you if you knew he would hate it?' Neville asked, believing he already knew the answer; Leo's dislike of the other priest came through loud and clear.

A smile twitched at the corner of Leo's mouth. 'Partly to get up his nose, if I'm being honest. But also because it was *right*. I don't think you should stop doing what's right, just because it might upset people.'

'Fair enough.'

'Anyway, at the end of the meeting I opened a few bottles of wine. Jonah picked a fight with the woman. Frances Cherry, she's called—she's a hospital chaplain. He was unspeakably rude to her. Deliberately rude. So she... well, Frannie threw a glass of wine over him.'

'Ah.' Neville had scarcely begun to come to terms with the idea that priests might dislike each other, and now he was being told that things could go even beyond that. Suddenly this case was looking very interesting indeed.

'I don't blame her,' Leo added. 'She was provoked.'

'What happened then?'

'I sent Jonah off to the vestry to clean up. And I took Frannie outside for some fresh air, to calm her down.'

'Did you go back to the meeting after that?'

Leo shook his head. 'No. It took a good while to calm Frannie down. We walked a long way. I ended up walking her home. By the time I got back to the church… well, everyone had gone, or at least I assumed so. The lights were all off, the place was deserted. I locked up and came home.'

'Did you lock the vestry?'

'No.' Again he shook his head. 'I didn't even go near it. It wasn't usually kept locked. All of the valuables—the silver and so on—are in the sacristy. And that's always locked. But nothing is stored in the vestry except for vestments.'

'So anyone could gain access to it.'

'Theoretically, yes. As long as the church was open.'

The church *had* been open, which meant that anyone at the meeting, or anyone off the streets for that matter, could have got into the room where the priest was murdered. 'What time, exactly, did you get back? What time did you lock up?' Neville didn't yet know—possibly might never know—at what time the murder occurred, but this could be important.

'I think it was gone eleven,' said Leo. 'Ten past, quarter past. Something like that.'

'And after that?'

'I came home, as I said. Went to bed.'

Neville dreaded asking his next question; it was always a difficult one, implying as it did that the person was under suspicion. 'You understand that I have to ask you this,' he began. 'Apart from this Frances Cherry, is there anyone who can vouch for your actions, your whereabouts?'

'An alibi, you mean,' said Leo flatly.

'I have to ask,' Neville repeated.

Was there a flicker of hesitation, a heartbeat in which the man across from him decided what to say?

'I am a bachelor,' stated Leo. 'I live alone.'

Neville sensed that he would not progress any further by pressurising Leo, by putting him on the defensive, so he moved on to a more neutral question. 'This Father Jonah,' he said. 'Can you tell me anything about his personal life? Where he lived, anything about his family?'

Leo put down his coffee mug, leaned back in his chair and tented his fingers. 'About his family, no. I don't think he had one, at least not in London. He lived in the clergy house at St Mary the Virgin, Marble Arch. The person to ask about his personal life would be Vincent Underwood, his vicar.'

'You'll give me his address?'

'Of course.'

'And the other people who were there last night for the meeting?'

Leo went to his desk and pulled a directory from under a stack of papers. He sat behind the desk and wrote out a list, consulting the directory for addresses and telephone numbers. Neville waited in silence, glancing at his sergeant, who hadn't said a word but who was taking assiduous notes. 'Here you are,' said Leo, handing over the list. 'That's everyone. I've put Vincent Underwood at the top.'

Neville glanced at the list and passed it on to DS Cowley. 'Thank you very much. You've been very helpful.' He rose to go, then did something which he'd deliberately borrowed from the old American television detective Columbo. 'Just one more thing.'

'Yes?'

'Have you ever seen a white stole with blue names painted on it? Names of women in the Bible?'

This time there was no hesitation. 'Of course,' Leo affirmed. 'It belongs to Frannie. Frances Cherry. She wore it for the Mass last night.'

'Does anyone else you know have a stole like that?'

Leo shook his head. 'No. It's a complete one-off. It was an ordination gift, made specially for her.'

'Did she have it with her when you walked her home last night?'

'No. I told you, we went off in a hurry. I suppose she must have left it in the vestry.' It was at that point that Neville reckoned the penny dropped. He had never seen a black man go pale before, but Leo Jackson suddenly went ashen grey, as though the blood had drained from his face. 'You're not saying...'

The stole was an important clue, Neville realised, and now that its ownership had been confirmed, he was no longer prepared to give away his advantage. 'I'm not saying anything. It might be relevant to our enquiries, that's all.'

⚬⚬⚬ ⚬⚬⚬ ⚬⚬⚬

So the redhead in the photo was Frances Cherry. Neville considered the implications of that fact. She and Leo Jackson were friends; he had been at her ordination; he had been responsible for her involvement at the service last night; he was the one who had looked after her following the debacle with Father Jonah, and had walked her home.

Or had he?

Neville spoke reflectively to DS Cowley as they got in the car. 'Do you suppose he's been shagging her, then?'

'Who?'

'Him. Leo. Shagging that woman Frances Cherry.'

Cowley, in the process of lighting a cigarette, turned a shocked face to him. 'But they're both vicars!'

Neville smiled humourlessly. 'Don't you read the tabloids, sunshine? Vicars are the worst.'

'But...'

He ticked the points off on his fingers. 'First, he's known her for years. He said so. And they were in that photo together, looking pretty chummy. Second, he calls her "Frannie". Like a term of endearment.'

'That doesn't mean anything.'

Neville ignored the interruption. 'Third, he's hiding something.'

'Is he?'

'Didn't you see the way he hesitated, when I asked him about where he was later last night? I'll bet you a pint of Guinness that Leo Jackson wasn't alone in his bed.' He nodded his head thoughtfully. 'And who more logical to have shared it with him than Frances Cherry? We only have his word for it that he walked her home.'

'Maybe he knows that she killed that Father Jonah, and is covering for her,' said Cowley, his imagination finally engaged. 'Or maybe they did it together—maybe they went back and killed him.'

Neville was still nodding. 'Maybe they did.'

⌘ ⌘ ⌘

Inevitably, their first call was the address supplied to them for Frances Cherry. It was rather farther than Neville expected, in Notting Hill, to the west of Lancaster Gate beyond the point where the Bayswater Road becomes Notting Hill Gate.

The person who answered the door was not Frances Cherry: it was a bespectacled middle-aged man in a grey clerical shirt and dog collar, who looked startled when they proffered their identification.

'We'd like to speak to Frances Cherry,' Neville said.

'I'm afraid she's not at home. She's at work.' He hesitated. 'Is there anything I can help you with? I'm Graham Cherry. Her husband.'

Somehow Neville hadn't anticipated that she would have a husband. 'You're a vicar, as well?'

Graham Cherry nodded in the affirmative. 'Yes. This is my parish.'

'But you weren't at the meeting last night with your wife?'

'No. It was a deanery meeting, and I'm in a different deanery.' Graham hesitated, his brow furrowed, then blurted, 'Look, I know Frances lost her temper. But surely it isn't a criminal matter? Surely he's not pressing charges?'

So he knew about the wine incident. That, thought Neville, was interesting. How much did he know about Leo Jackson, and his wife's relationship with him?

He glanced at his watch. They needed to be getting on with other urgent matters, and those were questions which could wait.

'It's just not like her to lose her temper like that,' Graham insisted. 'I'm sure it won't happen again.'

'We'll need to speak to her nonetheless. What time do you expect her home?'

DS Cowley spoke for the first time. 'Or do you have a number where we can reach her?'

'She's usually home by half six. I'm afraid it's difficult to reach her when she's at the hospital, as she has to switch off her mobile.'

'We'll be back,' Neville promised, adding, 'and I'd appreciate it, sir, if you didn't tell her about our visit.'

⚬⚬⚬ ⚬⚬⚬ ⚬⚬⚬

The reaction of Vincent Underwood, when he was told by DI Stewart that his curate was dead, was suitably dramatic: he staggered backward, clutched at his heart, and burst into tears.

A few minutes later he had recovered sufficiently to speak, and led them into his study, dabbing at his eyes with an immaculate linen handkerchief. 'Excuse me, Inspector,' he said. 'I just can't believe that Jonah is dead. But how? When? Was it a traffic accident of some kind?'

'No, sir,' said Neville impassively. 'He was murdered.'

'But… but that's not possible!'

'I'm afraid it's true.'

Father Vincent sat down heavily on the nearest chair and pressed his fingers to his temples. 'When? How?'

'We're still waiting for details from the postmortem,' Neville hedged. 'He was found in the vestry of St John's, Lancaster Gate this morning.'

'Then she did it,' Father Vincent said at once in a ringing voice, raising his head to stare at the policemen. 'That woman. She killed him.'

'And which woman would that be?'

'That dreadful woman, that hospital chaplain. Frances Cherry. It must have been her.'

Neville waited for more, and it came. Father Vincent imparted his version of the row. According to him, Jonah had been minding his own business, drinking his wine, and Frances Cherry had accosted him, spoiling for a fight. She had attacked him verbally, then she had thrown her wine over him. 'I was shocked. Shocked! I'd never seen such disgraceful behaviour in someone who calls herself a priest.'

'Surely she *is* a priest,' Neville pointed out.

Father Vincent shook his head, briefly distracted into a lecture. 'Oh, no. Not at all. She just *thinks* she is. Like all of those women. They're deluded. They think that because they went through an ordination ceremony, it makes them a priest. But God knows better. It's just not possible for women to be priests, whatever they may think. And this,' he added pompously, 'shows us exactly why. They're not stable, are they? Women, that is. Their hormones make it impossible for them to act rationally. Menopausal, I wouldn't doubt. Not that it's any excuse for her appalling behaviour.'

Neville tried to digest this, and finding it impossible, encouraged him back onto track. 'So what happened after she threw the wine over him?'

'Leo Jackson—he's the vicar of the church—suggested that I should take him to the vestry. There's a wash hand basin there, so we were able to repair the worst of the damage. Most of the wine had gone onto Jonah's face, though some had dripped onto his cassock. I helped him to clean up.'

'And how long were you in the vestry together?'

The priest considered the question for a moment. 'Oh, I suppose it was ten minutes, quarter of an hour—something like that.'

'Then what happened?'

'We left,' Father Vincent said promptly. 'We went out together. Jonah had walked to the meeting, and I'd come in my motor. I offered him a lift home, but as he was getting in the car, he remembered something and said he needed to go back into the church. He said not to wait for him. And that,' he added, his voice trembling, 'was the last time I saw him.'

'And you, Father? What did you do then?' Neville slipped the necessary question in.

'I came home,' the priest stated. 'I was still quite upset by what had happened. I had a drink, then decided to have an early night.'

'So you didn't see anyone, or talk to anyone.'

'My wife was out last night. At the opera, I believe.'

This was the first that Neville had heard of a wife, and the reference to her surprised him. He knew, of course, that Anglican clergy were free to marry, and many of them did, but he somehow expected that one who called himself 'Father' would not have done so. It seemed to him rather like having one's cake and eating it.

This led him onto another train of thought, and another line of questions. 'Did Father Jonah have a wife?'

'Oh, no,' the priest said. 'He was a true celibate. He lived on his own, in the clergy house.'

'No girlfriends, then?' Neville probed.

'No.'

'Or boyfriends?'

Father Vincent bristled. 'I take that as an insult to his memory, Inspector. There may be some in the Church who think that sort of thing is acceptable, but I can assure you that Father Jonah did not. He was adamantly opposed to it. As I am myself, of course,' he added. 'Sodomy is a sin, abhorrent and repugnant, incompatible with true Christian faith. Jonah and I agreed about that. We are... were... as one on most things.'

Neville meekly accepted the rebuke, then went on to his next question. 'Did he have any family at all, then?'

'Quite a large family, back in Nigeria,' Father Vincent said. 'By family, I mean parents, brothers, and sisters. That sort of thing. Aunts and uncles, cousins, nieces and nephews. None of them ever visited him here.'

'Friends?'

'Jonah was a very... private person. He kept himself to himself. Don't misunderstand me—he was a wonderful priest. He always had time for his parishioners. *Our* parishioners. But there were strong boundaries. He didn't socialise with them, ever. He never would have considered them friends. And he didn't have time for friends outside of the parish. Didn't seem to need them. He was… aloof.' Father Vincent leaned forward and added in a confidential voice, 'I admired him for that. Envied him, even. To live happily without the need for human companionship—well, that seems to me to be a very special gift from God.'

It sounded dead boring, thought Neville. Unnatural. And it didn't help them at all. A man without family, without friends.

But not without enemies.

Frances Cherry had been an enemy. They needed to talk to her as soon as possible, Neville realised. He made a move to get up, trying to catch DS Cowley's eye.

The front door opened and closed, and a blonde woman looked into the study. 'Vincent?' She took in the presence of the policemen and frowned. 'Whatever—'

'These men are the police,' Father Vincent announced, rather too loudly. 'They've brought me some very bad news, I'm afraid. It's Father Jonah. He's been murdered.'

Chapter Seven

It was well past lunchtime when Callie first heard about the murder. She'd gone into the church to help with early preparations for Sunday's Harvest Festival—something which even in the countryside seemed of dubious relevance in the twenty-first century, and in the middle of London was a ludicrous anachronism. But it had been celebrated at All Saints' for many years, having been introduced by a long-ago vicar, and was a much beloved institution. Periodic suggestions to drop Harvest Festival were always firmly quashed by the traditionalists, as well as the flower ladies, who relished the opportunity to exercise their skills on something different once a year.

The actual flowers wouldn't be done until Friday and Saturday. On the Wednesday, though, the custom was for the women of the church—those who had nothing better to do, at any rate—to gather and make corn dollies. This comparatively modern addition to the ritual had been introduced to All Saints' by Jane Stanford, who had learned the technique when she and Brian had done a stint in a country parish some years earlier.

By now they all knew how to do it, and Jane's tuition was no longer necessary. Still, by tradition, Jane was in charge of the activity, so there was some uncertainty when she had not arrived by the appointed two o'clock starting time. A quarter of an hour later, Callie suggested that they might begin without her.

'Or maybe we should ring,' someone countered nervously. 'Perhaps Jane has forgotten.'

'She's had a great deal on her mind, with the boys going off,' added someone else.

Callie produced her mobile phone, into which she had already programmed Brian's home number. The number was engaged.

The women looked at each other helplessly. 'Well, if you think we should begin…' one of them said.

A few minutes after they had started, Jane Stanford burst into the room, bright spots of colour on her cheeks and gasping for breath. 'Oh, you'll never believe it!' she cried. 'Brian's just heard! It's Father Jonah! He's dead—murdered!'

⌒⌒⌒ ⌒⌒⌒ ⌒⌒⌒

Frances had been sitting for several hours at the bedside of an elderly man who was dying. He knew that he was dying, and that fact did not trouble him, but he was fretting about whether his family would arrive in time: he did not want to die alone.

'I'm here,' Frances murmured continually, stroking the back of his emaciated hand. 'I'm sure they'll be here soon, but I'm here, and I'm not going to leave you.' Now and again she stole a peek at her watch. Surely they *would* arrive soon? They didn't have that far to come. Perhaps they'd been delayed by traffic. She didn't mind for herself; after all, this was her job, and there was nowhere more important for her to be at this moment. She minded on behalf of the old man in the bed, longing for the comfort of his loved ones around him when he breathed his last.

So when the two men appeared in the doorway, Frances looked up at them expectantly, then realised with a stab of disappointment that they weren't the awaited family.

'Frances Cherry?' said the older of the two men, stepping into the room.

'That's right.'

He flashed a warrant card in her direction. 'DI Stewart. This is DS Cowley. We'd like a word with you, please.'

Her mind raced in a spiral of panic. It was Graham: he'd had an accident. His church had burnt down. The vicarage had burnt down. Heather had been killed by a crazed gunman in the lawless streets of America.

In spite of her thoughts, she kept her face tranquil and her voice calm, aware of the man in the bed beside her. 'I'm afraid you'll have to wait,' she said quietly. 'I can't leave just now.'

'It's important,' stated the policeman.

'So is this.' Deliberately she turned away from them, bending over the bed and resuming her soothing noises. 'Don't fret. I'm sure they'll be here any minute now. I'm here. I'm not going anywhere.'

Surely not, she told herself, even as she continued to speak words of comfort. Surely nothing had happened to Graham or Heather. Then why were they here? What could be so important that the police would seek her out at work? She hadn't done anything—

Yes, she had, she realised, and it was like a blow to the solar plexus, making her both breathless and dizzy.

She had assaulted Jonah Adimola. At least that would be his story. And he had decided to press charges against her. Yes—that must be it. That was the only explanation that made any sense.

She would be arrested, charged. She would have to stand trial.

She shouldn't have done it—she shouldn't have let her temper get the better of her. Leo would vouch for her, and so would Callie, that she'd been provoked. She'd been defending them, not herself. Surely the courts would let her off lightly. A fine, perhaps, or community service. Perhaps just an apology to Jonah. They couldn't send her to prison for throwing a glass of wine, could they?

But no matter how the legal process turned out, it would get her on the front page of the tabloids: Woman Vicar Assaults Colleague. The fact that he was black would make it even worse; she'd probably be forever dubbed 'Racist Woman Vicar'.

Conscious of the minutes ticking by, imagining the increasing level of anger in the police she was forcing to wait for her, she glanced again at her watch.

At that moment they arrived: a stocky man, a woman who looked as though she'd been weeping, two teenagers. 'Dad!'

said the woman, going straight to the bed without a glance at
Frances.

'I'll just go, then,' Frances said, but they were too intent upon
the figure in the bed to notice when she slipped from the room.

The two policemen were standing in the corridor, leaning
against the wall. The younger one was fiddling with a packet of
cigarettes, glaring through narrowed eyes at the 'No Smoking'
notice, while the other one sipped at a cup of vending machine
coffee.

They both looked at her as she approached them, and they
weren't happy.

'I'm sorry,' she said, in the same calm voice she'd adopted
earlier. She wouldn't get hysterical; that would do her cause
no good. 'Sorry to keep you waiting. But he's dying, you see. I
couldn't leave him until his family got here.'

The older policeman made a disapproving noise. 'Is there
somewhere we can talk?' he asked.

Frances weighed up the possibilities. She could do with a cup
of coffee, she thought longingly, but the caff was at the other
end of the building. There was a small day room nearby, mostly
used by patients' visitors while dressings were being changed or
bedpans used. And it had a vending machine—presumably the
one the policeman had already found.

She led the way into the room—unoccupied apart from a
tearful young man at the window—and went straight to the
vending machine. She didn't carry a handbag when she was
working; while she fumbled in a pocket for change, the policeman came up beside her. 'Allow me,' he said in a sardonic voice.
'Milk? Sugar?'

'Black.'

He fed in some money and handed her a plastic cup of steaming black liquid, then got another for himself. 'Sid?' he asked.

The younger policeman shook his head. 'No, thanks. I'd
rather have a smoke.'

'Not in here,' said Frances, pointing out the ubiquitous
notice. 'Sorry.'

They sat on wood-framed chairs with seats and backs uphol-
stered in coarsely-woven royal blue hessian, Frances facing the
policemen across a low table littered with a variety of out-of-date
magazines. The pictures on the wall were anodyne: watercolour
prints of Mediterranean harbours with impossibly blue water,
masses of flowers spilling over wrought-iron balconies. The
view from the window, of urban Paddington, was something
else entirely.

Frances had been thinking about what to say to the policemen, and was determined to get in there first, before they had
a chance to put her on the defensive. She took a bracing sip of
the coffee and said, in what she hoped was a conciliatory tone,
'Listen. I think I know what you're here for. It's about Father
Jonah, isn't it?'

The two policemen exchanged a look. 'Yes,' said the elder—
the Inspector—cautiously.

'He's decided to press charges, then, has he?' Without waiting
for an answer, she continued with what she'd planned to say. 'I
know what I did was wrong. It was unprofessional of me, not
to mention un-Christian. And I'm very sorry. Do you think he
would be prepared to accept an apology, instead of making a
legal issue of it? After all, he didn't suffer any permanent damage.
It was just a little wine.'

'Jonah Adimola is dead.' The Inspector's words cut through
the room like a knife.

Frances gasped, as the blood drained from her face and the
fingers holding the cup of coffee went slack. The cup fell to
the floor, spattering her legs, the old magazines, and even the
policemen's trousers with hot coffee.

'You seem to make rather a habit of throwing your drinks
over people,' said the Inspector ironically. 'I'd watch that, if I
were you.'

'It wasn't... it wasn't an accident?' she faltered. 'Jonah?'

'He was murdered.'

'Oh, God.' Frances' brain, which seemed to have ground to
a momentary halt, now kicked into overdrive. Jonah murdered.

They would think she had done it. 'Listen,' she said urgently. 'I didn't know. I didn't see him again. Not after... the wine incident. You have to believe me.'

The younger policeman—the Sergeant—was writing in a small notebook. The Inspector looked across at her, seeming to take in every detail of her appearance, before he responded. 'You went straight home, did you?'

'Well, sort of.' She remembered the jumble of emotions—anger, indignation, shame, guilt—which had overwhelmed her in the aftermath of her impulsive action. She remembered Leo's soothing voice, his comforting arm round her shoulder. She had no idea how long they had walked and talked. 'I walked around for a while,' she said. 'With Leo Jackson—the Area Dean. He took me home.'

'Your home, or his?' The Inspector's expression was unreadable.

'Mine, of course.'

'And then?'

'Then... nothing.' She tried to remember what, exactly, she'd done. 'He left, when he was sure I was going to be all right. My husband was out at a meeting. He wasn't back yet. So I went straight to bed.'

'Leo Jackson,' the Inspector went on. 'What is your relationship with him?'

'I told you. He's the Area Dean.' She paused, then added, 'I've known him for years. We're friends.'

'Close friends?' the Inspector asked neutrally.

'Quite close, yes.'

It didn't escape her notice that the Sergeant looked up from his notebook and caught the Inspector's eye. The Inspector gave a minute shake of his head and the Sergeant frowned.

The Inspector let the silence stretch out for a long moment as Frances wondered what could possibly come next. Would they arrest her now, drag her off to gaol? Or did they believe her, that she'd had nothing to do with it?

'Well, thank you, Reverend Cherry,' said the Inspector in a formal voice. 'You've been very... helpful. We know where to reach you if we have any further questions.'

Frances couldn't believe that was the end of it; she sighed with relief as the two policemen stood.

'One more question, though,' said the Inspector. 'Did Jonah Adimola have any enemies that you know of?'

'Every ordained woman was his enemy,' Frances stated bitterly. 'Or I suppose it would be more accurate to say that he was ours. He always made it very clear what he thought of us. And other... minorities... as well. He was opinionated, outspoken. Rude.'

'You didn't like him,' said the Inspector; it was a statement rather than a question.

'No. I didn't like him.' She paused. 'I didn't like him. But I didn't kill him.'

The Inspector raised his eyebrows and gave her a long, speculative look. 'Then answer me just one question, Reverend Cherry.'

'Yes?'

'You have a white stole with blue writing on it. Names. Women's names.'

'Yes,' Frances confirmed breathlessly, beginning to go cold. Her mouth filled with saliva, tinged with the bitter after-taste of coffee.

'Then maybe you can tell me how your stole happened to get round Jonah Adimola's neck?'

⌘⌘⌘

DS Cowley lit up as soon as they were through the hospital doors. 'God, that's better,' he murmured, drawing deeply on the cigarette. 'Bloody hospital.'

'I'm glad your nicotine craving doesn't rule your life,' Neville said acidly.

Sid Cowley, though a fairly uncomplicated soul, was able to recognise sarcasm when it stared him in the face. He also knew better than to cheek an inspector, so he contented himself with a muttered, 'Bloody ex-smoker.'

Neville gave him a sharp look. 'What did you say, Sergeant?'

'I said,' he enunciated clearly, 'that I wish I could quit smoking.'

'You wouldn't regret it,' Neville stated. 'Best thing I ever did, giving up the fags. Apart from leaving Ireland, of course.'

They got into the car, Neville behind the wheel. But before he turned the key in the ignition, he sat for a minute, collecting his thoughts. 'I'm glad we decided to track her down,' he said. 'Before anyone had a chance to warn her.'

'She seemed pretty surprised,' Cowley recalled. 'Did you believe her, Guv?'

Neville took a deep breath, trying not to be too obvious as he leaned toward the curl of smoke from Cowley's cigarette. 'She was pretty convincing,' he admitted. 'But what you have to remember, Sid, is that priests are sort of like actors. They're used to performing in public, to playing out roles. That's one thing I learned in Ireland, and I don't suppose the Church of England is any different. Quite honestly, I don't think we can take any of them at face value. Not Frances Cherry, nor Leo Jackson. Or even the husband, or that Father Vincent.'

'So you still think they're having it off? Cherry and Jackson?'

'I don't know,' he said frankly. 'It would explain a lot if they were.' It would explain, thought Neville, why they were so protective of each other. And it would discredit their alibis, which at the moment consisted only of the fact that they'd each said the same thing: that they'd walked about while she calmed down, and then he'd walked her home. That could so easily have been cooked up in advance, Neville reasoned. They might have committed the murder together, or she might have done it and enlisted him to cover for her. Maybe even the other way round, if Jackson had killed the other priest to avenge the honour of his lady love. One thing he felt for certain, in his gut: the two of them, as neatly as their stories coincided, were not telling him the whole truth. They were hiding something, and a love affair between them would be a logical thing for them to want to hide. A story like that—prominent black churchman bonks married woman priest—would provide juicy fodder for the tabloids, and possibly put an end to two careers, not to mention a marriage.

They had a long way to go before they had reached the bottom of this case, he realised. It was early days yet, but they had a very long way to go. For one thing, they were dealing with the Church, with too many people who had a vested interest in keeping the lid on unpleasant truths.

He switched on his mobile phone, listened to a couple of messages, and checked in briefly with the station. The body had been formally identified; the postmortem would be held shortly, and they were of course expected to be there. He imparted the information to the sergeant, who nodded.

'Where now, Guv?' asked Cowley, adding hopefully, 'Could we grab a bite to eat somewhere?'

Neville looked at his watch: it was getting on for tea-time, and they hadn't had any lunch. In fact, all that stood between him and the meal he'd had at the pub the night before was a packet of crisps which he'd got from a machine in the hospital. As if reminded, his stomach gave a rumble.

From his pocket he took the list which Leo Jackson had written for him, and studied it. There were nearly a dozen names on the list, all of whom had to be interviewed. All of whom, he noted gloomily, were Reverends. It was going to be a long night.

'I don't think we'll have time for anything like that,' he stated. 'Not if we want to be on time for the postmortem, plus do all these interviews.'

'But, Guv...'

'All right, then,' he relented as Cowley's stomach echoed his own. 'Let's see if we can find a chippie that's open.'

'There's a sushi bar in Paddington Station,' Cowley suggested. 'That would be quick.'

'Sushi bar?' He turned and stared at the sergeant in amazement.

'It's quite tasty,' Cowley said defensively, flushing to the roots of his close-cropped blond hair.

Sid Cowley, a fan of sushi? Raw fish, and poncy bits of rice? Wonders, Neville told himself, would never cease.

⌒⣿⣿⣉⣿⣉⣿⣿⣉

Callie tried to ring Frances, but found Frances' mobile wasn't switched on. She left a brief message to ring her at home.

She didn't know what to think about Father Jonah's death. Jane Stanford had imparted the bare facts: he'd been found dead in the vestry of Leo's church, and it was definitely murder. On her return home, her answer phone held a brief message from Leo, with the same information. He was, evidently, ringing round to all the clergy in the Deanery, or at least those who had been present at the meeting the night before.

She tried to apply herself to her sermon, but was even less focused, more distracted, than she'd been in the morning. So when her doorbell rang she left her desk with some relief.

It was her brother. 'Thought I'd take a chance on you being in, Sis,' he announced airily. 'I have a gig not far from here, a bit later, and was hoping you might be able to give me a bite to eat.'

'You could have rung,' she said, trying to sound severe. 'What if I hadn't been here?'

Peter was unrepentant. 'I would have gone round the corner and found a caff. But you *are* here, aren't you? So it's okay.'

Callie sighed in mock exasperation and went through to the kitchen, Peter trailing behind.

The contents of her fridge were not promising: she hadn't exactly had a great deal of time to shop for food. There *were* eggs, though, and a packet of cheese. 'Omelette?' she suggested. It was a favourite standby for her, one of her few culinary specialities.

'Perfect.'

Peter straddled a kitchen chair, back to front, and watched her as she broke the eggs into a bowl and whisked them. 'So, Sis. How is your first week going, then?'

This time her sigh was perfectly genuine. 'Well, apart from having to see Adam, and apart from being verbally attacked by a priest who thinks... thought... women clergy are the scum of the earth, and then having him turn up murdered, it's been just fine.'

'Murdered? You're joking!'

She delved in the drawer beneath the hob and found the frying pan. 'I wish I were.'

'Did *you* do it, then?'

'Certainly not.' While the frying pan heated, Callie grated a handful of cheese. 'Though I suppose I had good reason.'

'Hmm,' said Peter thoughtfully. 'Who was he, then? I wonder if he was anyone I knew?'

'Why should you know him? He was a priest, not a musician.'

Peter laughed. 'Oh, come on, Sis. I'm gay, right? And this is London. I probably know more priests than *you* do.'

'Very funny.' She made a wry face at him.

'Seriously. I could tell you such stories about some of the things I've seen in the club where I play... I mean, a few months ago, there was this guy—he wasn't wearing a dog collar, but I could tell he was a priest, it just stuck out a mile. And there was this rent boy, and—'

Callie interrupted his story; any illusions she'd had about the clergy had been pretty much demolished recently, but this was more than she wanted to know. 'Well,' she said, 'his name was Father Jonah. Jonah Adi-something. He was Nigerian. That's about all I know about him.'

'Doesn't sound familiar,' he said, almost regretfully. 'And I think I would have remembered someone like that.'

Callie dropped a knob of butter into the frying pan and swirled it round as it melted and sizzled, then poured in the beaten eggs. At that moment the doorbell rang again.

'I'll get it, shall I?' Peter suggested helpfully.

'Thanks.'

He was back in the kitchen a minute later, just as the eggs were beginning to set. 'Police,' he whispered with a melodramatic raising of his eyebrows. 'They want to talk to you, Sis.'

She should have expected it, but her stomach plummeted in instinctive dread. 'Oh, great.'

'They seem very nice, though,' Peter added reassuringly. 'Not bad looking, either of them. In fact, the younger one is quite cute.' He grinned.

'Has any one ever told you that you're incorrigible?'

'Frequently.'

The police would just have to wait a minute or two, Callie decided. Unrushed, she sprinkled the cheese over the eggs and watched it melt. At just the right moment, with skill and timing born of experience, in one fluid movement she flipped one half over the other and slid the perfectly-cooked omelette onto a plate. She set it on the kitchen table and beckoned her brother. 'Eat.' Only then, her heart fluttering with apprehension, did she go through to the sitting room to face the police.

⟩〰⟨ ⟩〰⟨ ⟩〰⟨

In the absence of any family, Father Vincent Underwood was the one who made the formal identification of Jonah Adimola's body, as well as supplying the police with a photo of the dead man, taken at last year's Patronal Festival. In the afternoon a junior police officer had called at the house and asked him to accompany him to the mortuary. It had been a deeply upsetting experience for him, and he was glad that he didn't have to go back out that evening.

Vincent and Marigold Underwood rarely spent an evening together at home; he often had church business to attend to, in his study or elsewhere, and she not infrequently went out with friends. That night, though, she declared that she was coming down with a cold, and cancelled her plans for a bridge evening at Beatrice's.

Indeed, her eyes were puffy and her voice hoarse, Vincent observed. Her nose appeared to be running as well; she continued to dab at it with a handkerchief, blowing it periodically.

She had also lost her appetite. 'You should eat something,' Vincent urged her, but she pushed the food round on her plate listlessly. Neither one of them seemed much inclined to conversation.

By unspoken agreement, they both descended to the kitchen and sat in front of the television set, Marigold in the old arm chair and Vincent pulling up a kitchen chair a short distance away.

Wordlessly they sat through two tired old sitcoms with loud laugh tracks, repeated for the umpteenth time, followed by a cutting-edge drama in which young people with ugly haircuts and uglier clothes spoke in incomprehensible accents and did things together which the Underwoods had never even contemplated. Then the news came on.

It was a short item near the end of the broadcast, during the section devoted to local news. The footage shown was the same that Vincent had seen earlier: the church, the crime-scene tape, the voice-over about the murder. This time, though, they identified the murdered man as Jonah Adimola, curate of St Mary the Virgin, Marble Arch, and ended with a few words from a police spokesman. 'This was an horrific crime,' he stated. 'No arrests have been made. We are pursuing our enquiries. If anyone has information relating to this case, please contact the Metropolitan Police on the following number…'

Marigold blew her nose and swallowed hard, looking down at her lap. 'Terrible,' she whispered, so quietly that it seemed as if she didn't mean to be overheard.

Vincent was touched. Marigold didn't really know Jonah; her contact with his curate had been so infrequent, so impersonal, that she must surely be experiencing emotion on *his* behalf. For Vincent to lose his curate like this was most unfortunate, and it pleased him that his wife realised the extent of his loss.

'Terrible isn't the word,' he stated portentously. 'I just don't know what I shall do without him. This is a large parish. I can't possibly run it without a curate.'

She raised her eyes. 'What…'

'I'll ring the Bishop in the morning,' Vincent decided. 'And the Archdeacon. I'll tell them that they'll need to sort it out.'

The weather girl was now predicting a beautiful day tomorrow, gesturing at bright orange suns dotted over the outline of the country.

Vincent switched off the television, then looked at his wife. She was definitely coming down with something unpleasant; her colour wasn't at all good. 'Marigold, my dear,' he said, all solicitude. 'Shall I fix you a whisky with lemon and honey? That will help you to sleep.'

She hesitated, then nodded. 'Yes. That would be good,' she said huskily. 'Thank you, Vincent. You're very… kind to me.'

ტოოა ტოოა ტოოა

It was late evening before Frances made contact with Leo. Every time she tried to ring, his line was engaged, until finally she heard his voice, weary and verging on hoarseness.

'Oh, thank God, Leo,' she said.

'Frannie?'

'I've been trying for hours.'

'I've had to ring round all the clergy,' Leo explained. 'And everyone wants the whole story. I'm sick and tired of repeating myself.'

'The police…'

'They've been to see you, then? Did you get my message first?'

'No,' she said. 'They came to the hospital, while my mobile was still switched off.'

Leo swore, an Anglo-Saxon expletive which would have sounded shocking from the mouth of almost any other clergyman. 'What did they ask you? What did they tell you?' he added. 'And what did you tell *them*?'

They compared notes and discovered that they had received pretty much the same information from the police, and had given them corroborating accounts of the evening's events.

'Thank God for that,' Leo said. 'And you didn't say anything about…'

'About Oliver? No, Leo—of course not. He doesn't have anything to do with this. And besides,' she assured him, 'I just wouldn't. You should know that.'

'I do, pet. It's just that… well, they asked me whether I was alone last night. You know—if there was anyone who could vouch for my alibi, after I'd taken you home. And I said that I was. Alone, that is.'

Frances groaned. 'So you lied to the police.'

'I had to,' he stated. 'I'm not proud of myself, but I didn't feel I had a choice.'

'I'm sure it's not important.' She tried to sound confident, reassuring. 'You don't need an alibi, anyway. Why should you? They can't suspect you, surely.' Then her confidence faltered, and she finished on an uncertain note. 'Can they?'

⚬⚬⚬

Surprisingly—perhaps it was the whisky—Marigold fell into a sound sleep almost as soon as her head met the pillow. Her dreams were formless at first, unmemorable, then she seemed to open her eyes to see her father standing beside her bed, so real and solid that she felt she could reach out and touch him. 'It will be all right, Marigold,' he said in a soothing voice. 'I'll sort it. Believe me, sweetheart. No one will ever know.'

Marigold struggled to consciousness, fighting off the mists of sleep, finding herself feverish and tangled in the bedclothes. She switched on the bedside lamp.

No, her father wasn't there. How could he be? He'd been dead for twenty-five years. He couldn't sort it. Not this time. No one could sort it this time.

Breathing hard, almost gasping for breath, she turned off the lamp and lay in the darkness, straightening the damp sheets and trying to make herself comfortable. But sleep eluded her after that, and for hours she thrashed around, enmeshed in her own misery, tears dampening her pillow.

Chapter Eight

Callie was anxious to see Frances, to talk to her face to face, but that would have to wait: on Thursday morning she was scheduled to have what was to be a weekly staff meeting with Brian Stanford, and she couldn't very well cancel that in her very first week.

She went round to the vicarage and was met at the door by Jane, who must have known she was coming but who regarded her with suspicion.

'Brian is expecting me,' Callie stated.

'Yes.' Jane opened the door wider to let her pass. 'He's in his study.'

Callie went through to find Brian reading the morning paper. He shut and folded it as soon as she entered.

'Here. Have a seat.' He gestured to a comfortable leather chair, the twin of the one in which he sat.

Jane, who had followed Callie, hovered at the door. 'Would you like some coffee now?' she addressed her husband.

He looked at his watch. 'Perhaps a bit later, dear.'

She retreated with a fixed smile, leaving the door slightly ajar.

Callie had been out first thing in the morning to buy a newspaper, and though the murder was mentioned on its inner pages, the story contained no more information than had been on the evening news. She nodded toward Brian's paper. 'Not very informative,' she said. 'Have you heard any more? Have the police been to see you?'

He pressed his thin lips together repressively. 'I don't really think we should talk about it, Callie. It's too serious a matter for idle speculation.'

The implied rebuke stung, yet in a way she was relieved. The murder had so dominated her thoughts; a distraction at this point was to be welcomed.

'Fine,' she said meekly. 'What shall we talk about, then?'

'Well.' He tented his fingers. 'I'd like this weekly meeting to be a useful one for us both—a sort of a debriefing, if you like. I hope you'll feel free to ask me any questions you have about the parish, about the people in it, about things that may have happened to you. Tell me about your experiences, your expectations. And there is a practical side to it as well—we can use it as a planning session. For instance, it's none too soon to start talking about Christmas.'

'Christmas?' she echoed. Christmas was so far from her mind that it seemed a complete non sequitur.

'Christmas. We need to plan the services, decide what your role will be—that sort of thing.' He leaned over to his desk and retrieved his diary. 'I hope you've brought your diary. It will be an essential part of these meetings.'

To her relief, she had it in her handbag.

'Now. Christingle,' Brian said, thumbing through the back pages of his diary.

A quarter of an hour later, Jane again appeared at the door. 'I've made your coffee,' she announced, bringing in a tray.

Brian, deep in discourse about the Nine Lessons and Carols, looked annoyed, but he thanked his wife and indicated where she should put the tray.

'I do hope that's all right,' said Jane.

'I'm sure it will be fine, dear.'

She seemed inclined to linger, but Brian waited pointedly for her to go, his finger marking the place in his diary. Eventually she went, with a little flounce and a clearing of her throat.

Why, Callie wondered, was Jane behaving like that? What did she think Callie was going to do in her absence—seduce her unattractive, middle-aged husband?

⁂

Callie was still bemused when she left the vicarage. Jane had managed two more interruptions, to collect the coffee tray and to ask Brian when he might be finished with the meeting. She had even extracted a promise from him that he would take her out to lunch when Callie had gone.

On her way back to her flat, Callie made a detour via the nearest shop. Peter's visit had highlighted the sorry state of her fridge, so she stocked up on a few things—as much as she could easily carry home.

As she climbed the stairs, she could hear the telephone. Sprinting up the last few steps, dropping her carrier bags on the landing, she fumbled for her key and made a lunge for the phone.

The voice on the other end was tentative, not immediately identifiable. 'Is this the curate?'

'Yes, this is Callie Anson.'

'This is Dennis Harrington.'

She had to think for a second before conjuring up a mental image of the old man she had visited with Brian on Monday. That seemed such a long time ago, on the other side of the gulf that was the murder of Father Jonah.

Dennis explained that he had tried to ring the vicar, but there was no reply, and the recorded message on the answerphone said that in a pastoral emergency the caller should contact the curate instead, giving her number.

'Has something happened to Elsie?' Callie asked, jumping to the most logical conclusion.

'No, it's not my Elsie. She's...' He faltered. 'Could you come? Now? We need to talk to someone.'

'Yes, of course. I'll be there as soon as I can.'

She quickly shoved the perishables into the fridge and went back out again, hoping she could remember her way to the

Harringtons' flat, wondering what it could possibly be about. Surely the police hadn't been to see them?

Dennis was waiting for her at the open door of the flat. He was wearing the same green cardigan that he'd worn on Monday and the same wary smile; the only thing that betrayed his agitation was the bright red colour of the tips of his prominent ears. 'Come in,' he said with excessive politeness. 'Kind of you to come so quick, girl.'

'I'm glad you rang me,' she said, meaning it.

He lowered his voice and spoke rapidly as he ushered her through to the lounge. 'Mind you, my Elsie wasn't keen. She wanted to see Father Brian. Him, or nobody. Especially not some woman. Nothing personal, girl. But she just can't get her head round the idea, even though I told her what you said. About the Jesus and the Disciples and such like.'

She'd actually got through to him, then, Callie realised with some satisfaction, even as she wondered anew at what this was all about.

Then she saw Elsie, propped up in the corner of the oversize sofa. She was tiny, birdlike, her eyes bright with tears as she raised them to the newcomer.

Dennis performed the introductions. 'Elsie, this is our new curate.' His voice became tender, proud. 'And this is my Elsie.'

Callie leaned over and took the small, twisted hand in her own for a moment; it felt like an assortment of loose bones in a sac of jelly. 'It's a pleasure to meet you. Your husband has told me so much about you.'

Her words were acknowledged with a nod, but that was enough. She could see that Elsie was by no means a well woman, and she was clearly in distress as well.

'Would you like some tea, girl?' Dennis offered.

The suggestion was tempting, but Callie decided it was better to get on with it. 'No, thanks, I'm fine.'

Dennis sat down next to his wife, and indicated that Callie should sit in the chair opposite them. She complied.

The Harringtons looked at each other; something wordless passed between them, possibly the acknowledgement that he would do the talking. He cleared his throat. 'It's our son,' he said. 'Our Stu. You remember?' His eyes moved to the photo on the mantel shelf above the electric fire.

'Yes, of course. He's in America. Has something happened to him?'

'Well, you could say that.' Dennis cleared his throat again, painfully. 'He rang us this morning.' He looked away from Callie and spoke rapidly, as though this were the only way he could get through what he needed to say. 'He said his partner had just died. I thought he meant a business partner. But he meant... something else. His partner was one of them rock-and-roll blokes. A drummer, I think he said. And he died of that AIDS.'

'Ah,' said Callie neutrally, as the pieces all fell into place.

Still Dennis did not look at her. 'He said they'd been together for nearly twenty years. That they loved each other. As much as if they were a man and woman, properly wed.'

Elsie spoke for the first time, her voice soft and hoarse with pain. 'We never even suspected. He was such a handsome boy. So popular with the girls at school.'

'We never thought our son, our Stu, could be one of them homos.' The words were almost ripped out of Dennis. 'Nancy-boys, we used to call them.'

There was a brief silence, as Callie tried to think what the Harringtons wanted from her. Did they just need to share their shock and grief with someone, or was there more to it? Were they seeking answers to questions they dare not frame, or some sort of reassurance?

'What did we do wrong?' Elsie whispered. 'We tried to bring him up right. We thought we *had*. But we went wrong somewhere.'

Inevitably, Callie thought about her brother.

⁕⁕⁕

Somehow Callie had always known Peter was different from the boys she was at school with, even when he was very young.

He wasn't interested in playing with the shiny toy cars which their parents bought for him; instead he crept into Callie's room to play with her dolls and stuffed animals. And rather than engaging in rough-house games with the little boys next door, he sought out his sister's company, though she was nearly four years his senior.

In those days, of course, Callie didn't have a label for it. All she knew was that her brother was different, and when, years later, it was finally spelt out, she assimilated the knowledge as though she were slipping into an old, comfortable garment. It was not a surprise.

She had no patience with those who claimed that being gay was a choice, or that someone could be made gay, either by family circumstances, early childhood experiences, or some later corrupting influence. Callie had known Peter from his birth, and none of these things had ever altered in the slightest what was already there. Being gay was part of what Peter *was*, the essential him, as much of his makeup as his speckled hazel eyes and his recalcitrant cow-lick, as his self-mocking humour and his musical talent. It had always been there.

She was the first one he told, when he had figured it out for himself. It was shortly after he hit puberty, when the attention of his school-mates was fixed obsessively on girls, and he realised that his lack of interest was all part of the pattern.

At first, he wanted to tell their parents right away. But Callie counselled caution. 'It's not that I think you're going to change your mind or anything. You're young, though, and that's what they'll say—that you're too young to know, that you might change. They might pressurise you to try going out with girls.'

So Callie became his confidant through his teen years. Her time at university was punctuated with endless confessional phone calls as he fell in and out of love with alarming frequency. She listened, she consoled; she never judged.

Just before he left school, not quite eighteen years old, he told their parents, coupling it with the announcement that he would not be going to university as they expected, but planned to make his way in the world as a free-lance musician.

Their father was a bit stunned at first; like Callie, though, he soon came to see that it was something he'd really known all along.

Their mother found the second announcement far more alarming than the first. He would ruin his life if he didn't go to university, she stated in no uncertain terms. Callie had done what was expected of her—university, then following their father into the Civil Service—and Peter must do the same. Anything else was unthinkable. They had sent him to a good public school; how could he contemplate wasting their money and displaying such ingratitude?

The admission that he was gay she simply dismissed. He just hadn't met the right girl yet, she said. Not surprising, when he went to a single-sex school. And everyone knew that public school boys were like that—experimenting with each other in the absence of a female alternative. It was a phase. He would outgrow it. Once he went to university, as he surely must, he would meet lots of lovely girls. One of them, she assured him, he would want to marry, and all this nonsense would be forgotten.

Despite the fact that Peter had not gone to university, had not met any girls, and showed no signs of settling down and getting married to anyone, Laura Anson continued to persist in ignoring what she did not wish to believe about her son. Occasionally she still tried to introduce him to daughters of friends, eligible young women of whom she approved.

Needless to say, Peter didn't take his boyfriends home to meet his mother. Callie was the one to whom he'd always introduced them, one by one.

Often she wished that, like Stu Harrington, Peter could find a long-term partner.

It wasn't, she knew, for lack of trying. Peter was both a romantic and an optimist—perpetually looking for true love, and always certain that *this* time he had found it. Each new relationship was embarked upon with enthusiasm and wholehearted commitment, and the inevitable disappointments, while crushing and painful, were never long-lived. The next time, he continued to believe, it would be different. Mr Right was out there, and any day now he would meet him.

⟨≈⟩ ⟨≈⟩ ⟨≈⟩

The Harringtons were staring at her, waiting for her to say something. With a sinking sensation in the pit of her stomach, Callie suddenly thought what it might be. 'Your son,' she said gently. 'Stu. Is he... does he have... ?'

Elsie gasped. 'No! No, not that.'

Her husband reached over and took her hand in his with infinite tenderness, then addressed Callie. 'We just want you to tell us, if you can, how it could have happened? How could a boy who was brought up in the Church turn out like that? Like Elsie said, what did we do wrong? Or did he get corrupted by Hollywood, by America?'

Callie took a deep breath, aware that her choice of words was important, and aware as well that the Harringtons would probably not like them. 'I don't think he was corrupted,' she said. 'Not by Hollywood or anything else. And I don't think it was anything you did. Some people are just... made that way.'

'You mean he was *born* like that?' Dennis demanded incredulously. 'Born perverted?'

'Perverted is a harsh word,' Callie said. 'These days, most people don't think in those terms. We're more enlightened than we used to be. Being gay isn't any better or any worse than being straight. It's just... different.'

Dennis' mouth worked wordlessly, and he narrowed his eyes at her with such suspicion that Callie was sure she knew what he was thinking: he was wondering, no doubt, whether she was one of *them* as well.

'No,' she said to his unasked question. 'I'm not gay. But I have a brother who is, so I do know what I'm talking about.'

'Aren't you... ashamed of him?' whispered Elsie. 'Ashamed to admit that he's... like that?'

'Not at all. He's my brother, and he's the way God made him. That can't be wrong.'

'But it *is* wrong!' Dennis sat upright, his hand gripping Elsie's. 'It's a sin!'

'Father Jonah said so,' Elsie added. 'When Father Brian was on holiday, he came to preach at All Saints'.'

'And he said as it was a sin,' Dennis continued firmly. 'A horrible, horrible sin. A perversion of nature, and a sin against God.'

Father Jonah, Callie registered in a part of her brain. Did the Harringtons know that Father Jonah was dead? 'Not everyone in the Church feels that way,' she said.

'But it says it in the Bible!' Dennis stated. 'Father Jonah told us so. See if you can explain that, missy!'

Callie sighed to herself. Where to begin? 'Jesus never said anything about it—not that we know about, anyway. He didn't say a great deal about sex at all, as a matter of fact.'

Dennis stirred uncomfortably at the mention of a word his generation didn't much like to be spoken aloud in public.

'The only story I can really think of is the one where the woman is caught in adultery,' Callie went on. 'And Jesus doesn't condemn her. He says that it is not for us to judge each other.'

'But this is worse than adultery,' Dennis insisted. 'It's unnatural. And the Bible says that men who… you know… with other men should be put to death.'

'That's the Old Testament,' she pointed out. 'The Old Testament also says that men who trim their beards or cut the hair on the side of their heads should be put to death. And I don't see that happening very often these days.'

She caught the ghost of a smile on Elsie Harrington's face, and began to think that perhaps—just perhaps—she was beginning to reach them.

⁓⁓⁓ ⁓⁓⁓ ⁓⁓⁓

Callie and Frances managed to catch up with each other in the afternoon, and as it was a beautiful early October day, unseasonably warm, they decided to meet in Hyde Park, where the open spaces afforded them a privacy which would not be possible in the hospital cafe.

The sky was a pale blue, with a few high clouds which cast no shadows; the leaves of the trees were touched with colour, shimmering liquid gold in the sunlight. The two women met at the north end of the park, near Lancaster Gate, where an area of Italianate columns and fountains acted as a sun-trap.

They hugged, then sat for a moment on a bench, hardly knowing where to begin. Then Frances said, 'Let's walk, shall we?'

'Good idea.'

They set off along one of the wide paved walkways, taking the turning signposted toward Kensington Gardens and the Peter Pan statue. Strolling in companionable silence, they found it difficult to broach the subject that was so much on their minds.

Callie opened with a relatively neutral topic. 'Have you had a busy morning, then?'

'Yes.' Frances shook her head ruefully. 'I had to deal with the family of a man who died yesterday. They really needed to talk to someone about it all. You know—those little, simple questions like "Where do people go when they die?" and "What is the meaning of life?" How about you? You've been busy?'

'I had a meeting with Brian this morning.' Callie hesitated. 'And at lunch-time I had to go and talk to some parishioners who have just found out that their son is gay.'

'They didn't take it well, I presume?'

Callie grimaced. 'Not at all. They're quite elderly. It was a great shock to them—they didn't have a clue.'

'Why didn't Brian talk to them, then?'

'He was out when they rang, and they were desperate.'

'Well,' said Frances, 'you probably had more constructive things to say to them than Brian would have done.'

'I'm not sure,' Callie confessed, clenching her hands into fists in her pockets. 'They seemed convinced that being gay is about the biggest sin in the book—the Bible, that is. Father Jonah had told them that it was a perversion of nature, and that AIDS is God's judgement on wicked sodomites. Can you believe it?'

'Father Jonah?' Frances echoed, startled, and Callie realised that she had brought up the subject without meaning to.

'Yes,' she said. 'I'm not even sure they knew about... well, about what happened to him. To Jonah.'

'Have the police been to see you?' Frances asked abruptly.

'Yes. Late yesterday afternoon. I tried to ring you, after.'

'I took the phone off the hook,' Frances admitted. 'I was afraid... well, I was just afraid. They tracked me down at the hospital after lunch,' she added. 'Two policemen. DI Stewart, the older one was called. He gave me his card. And a younger blond one.'

'Those are the same ones who came to see me. They knew all about the... the altercation on Tuesday night. They knew I was involved.'

'Leo told them, I believe.'

Callie made a face. 'I thought Leo was your friend.'

'Do you think they wouldn't have found out?' Frances gave a sharp, bitter laugh. 'Vincent Underwood would have fallen over himself to tell them. At least Leo was able to put in a good word.'

'Why would he need to?' Callie glanced at her friend. 'I answered their questions. I told them the truth about what happened. I'm sure you did, as well. What do we have to be afraid of?'

Frances stopped walking; Callie took another step, then halted and turned to face her. 'Did they tell you how he died?' Frances asked quietly.

'He was murdered. Strangled, apparently.'

'With my stole,' Frances stated.

'Your stole? But... oh, my God.'

'I left it in the vestry after the service. I was going to collect it later.'

Callie had to remember to breathe. The mental image was so vivid, so horrible, so obscene. 'But they can't...' She couldn't finish her sentence.

'They can,' Frances whispered. 'Oh, Callie. I'm sure they think I killed him. They didn't come out and say it, but I know that's what they think.'

On Thursday afternoon, Neville and his sergeant met up for a quick meal of egg and chips at the station's canteen to compare notes. Neville had spent the morning attending the brief, formal inquest—at which an open verdict had been recorded—then holding a press conference. Cowley had been dispatched to St Mary the Virgin's clergy house to oversee a search of the premises.

'Guv, the man was more than a loner—he was a freak,' he stated as they sat down with their trays. 'A religious nutter. He didn't have a life.'

'What do you mean?'

'No telly. No personal letters. Just a load of boring old theology books—shelves and shelves of them.'

Neville looked at him sceptically. 'He can't have spent his whole life reading theology books.'

'Well,' Cowley admitted, 'there were some magazines, as well. On his bedside table. A stack of them. "New Directions", they were called.'

Neville choked on a chip. '"Nude Erections"? Porn? Good God, man.'

Cowley grinned, enjoying his boss' confusion. 'Not quite, Guv.' He spelled it out for him. 'N-E-W, D-I-R-E-C-T-I-O-N-S. Religious stuff—they all had pictures of crucifixes and statues on the cover. Nothing saucy, believe me. Not a tit or a bare bum in sight.'

Both hungry, they applied themselves to their food in silence for a moment.

'Diary?' Neville asked between bites, shoving a bit of egg onto a chip with his knife.

'It was on his desk, Guv. I checked it.'

'And?'

'Just church services and meetings, apparently. It was all in code,' Cowley mumbled through a mouthful of chips, then swallowed. 'I rang his vicar, that Underwood bloke, to ask him about it. Turns out that MP is Morning Prayer, EP is Evening Prayer, and M is Mass. Oh, and FIF is Forward in Faith. Underwood explained that it's a society against women priests. He went to their meetings regularly.'

'No unexplained dates or assignations?'

'Zip.' Cowley tapped the side of his nose. 'Not that he put in his diary, anyway.'

'Computer?' asked Neville hopefully.

'No computer. All his sermons were on file, all in longhand.'

Neville sighed with regret. 'So no Internet porn, then.'

'Like I said, he lived in the stone age. No mod cons. If he used a computer at all, he used someone else's. Maybe at the library or something.'

'That won't help us.'

Sid Cowley gulped down half a cup of strong, hot tea, shoved his tray aside and lit a cigarette. 'What now, Guv?' he asked.

'I just can't believe that the man didn't have any secrets,' Neville mused, almost to himself. 'It's not natural. There must be something we've missed.'

The sergeant bristled, as if he had been criticised. 'Believe me, we turned that place over. There's nothing else to find there.'

Neville drummed his fingers on the table. 'Got any plans for tonight, sunshine?'

'What did you have in mind?' Cowley looked at him suspiciously.

'Clubs. Pubs. Soho, the West End. Take that photo we got from Underwood. I've given it to the press, but take a copy with you. Ask around. See what you can find.'

'What are you going to do, then, Guv?'

'I'm going back to see Frances Cherry. I have a few more questions for her.'

⚬⚬⚬

Callie bought a copy of the evening paper as she made her way home, shaken, from her meeting with Frances.

She put the kettle on and brewed a pot of tea, feeling she would probably need more than one cup to settle her down. Half-afraid of what she would find, she leafed through the newspaper to see if it was any more informative than the morning paper had been.

The evening paper had indeed caught up with the story, having decided that it was a rather juicy one: not just a run-of-the-mill murder, but one involving the Church, with the potential for some rather choice scandal. The upper half of page five was devoted to the story.

Their reporters had evidently scratched around for someone with unsavoury knowledge about the dead priest, but their story revealed that they'd come up empty-handed. 'Father Jonah Adimola was a model priest, admired and beloved by all who knew him,' the article began, beneath a large and rather dramatic photo of him in a chasuble. 'His outspoken beliefs and adamant public opposition to women priests had made him a few enemies on the larger stage, yet his private life was seemingly above reproach.'

Callie scanned the article quickly, looking for Frances' name, or her own. She discovered that the writer was more subtle than that.

'Our reporters spoke to members of Father Jonah's congregation at St Mary the Virgin, Marble Arch, all of whom are stunned by their curate's murder. Everyone told the same story: He lived alone in the clergy house. He did his job, and did it well. As far as anyone knew, he had no secrets, and nothing to hide.

'Father Jonah Adimola, aged 31, came to London from Nigeria as a mature university student. He read theology, then went on to train for ordination in the Church of England. He was unmarried, and seems to have had no ties to the large Nigerian community in London, instead spending all of his time in his parish.

'Yet someone murdered Father Jonah Adimola on Tuesday night, in the vestry of St John's Church, Lancaster Gate, where he had been for an evening meeting. Police confirm that the post-mortem results indicate he was strangled, and that the murder took place at some time between eight PM and midnight. They confess themselves baffled at this seemingly motiveless crime.

'Father Vincent Underwood, the vicar under whom Father Jonah worked, declined to be interviewed, declaring himself too grief-stricken to talk to the press.'

Callie's tea grew cold, forgotten as she read the article over and over again. What, exactly, were they trying to imply?

'Seemingly above reproach.' 'As far as anyone knew, he had nothing to hide.' Did that mean the writer, or the police, suspected that he *did* have something to hide? Were people, in fact, protesting too much?

Father Jonah's death was not an accident, and that left two choices. Either, Callie thought, it was a random crime, with Father Jonah an unfortunate victim who was in the wrong place at the wrong time, or he had been targeted. If he had been targeted, then there must have been a motive. No matter what people said about his blameless life, there must have been something in it which had made someone want to kill him.

Yes, he had hated women priests; she had experienced that for herself, but as difficult and upsetting as she had found his antagonism toward her, there had been nothing personal in it. He hated what she stood for, without making any effort to know *her* as a person.

He had also hated what was, for him, the sin of homosexuality. There had been a glimpse of that as well that night, when he'd jumped to conclusions about her and Frances, and it had been more than confirmed by what the Harringtons had said.

Was that hatred, too, an impersonal one? Or was there something in it which touched him more closely than he would ever have admitted?

As Callie had discovered, especially at theological college, often the men who spoke most loudly against homosexuality were the ones who feared it most, either because of their own experiences or their unacknowledged desires. Was Jonah Adimola one of those men?

Did he, in fact, have something to hide?

Absently she picked up her mug and sipped, grimacing at the shock of the cold tea.

A moment later she went to the telephone and rang her brother's number.

He answered just as she had counted the maximum number of rings before his answer machine would kick in.

'What's up, Sis?' he wanted to know. 'Any more from the police, then? Did that dishy blond one try to chat you up, or do you think I'm in with a chance?'

She was in no mood for his banter. 'Listen to me seriously, Peter.'

'I'm listening.'

'Have you seen the evening paper? About the murder?'

Peter admitted that he had.

'The priest who was killed—the one they were asking me about. You've seen the photo?'

'Yes. Very nice, too. I'd go so far as to say drop-dead gorgeous. Oops—unfortunate choice of words.'

'Stop it,' she said severely. 'I just wanted to know—have you ever seen him before? In a gay club, or... well, you know. Around.'

Peter chuckled. 'If you want to know was he part of the scene, then the answer is no. I've never run across him, anyway. And I certainly would have noticed him, and remembered him.'

Callie felt let down, deflated, as she rang off. Peter's testimony wasn't definitive—after all, Jonah might have been extraordinarily careful and secretive if he were indeed living a double life. But if she'd hoped for instant confirmation of her gut suspicions, then she was disappointed.

Chapter Nine

Leo Jackson's early life, one of many children in the family, growing up dirt-poor in a Jamaican slum, had been a life in which beauty was at a premium. In their home there was no music, no art—just a struggle for existence, for enough food to keep the increasing numbers of mouths fed. That was one reason why, from an early age, the Church had meant so much to Leo. There, if not at home, beauty was to be found: beauty in the structure and language of the liturgy, beauty in the music, and beauty in the colours of the windows. Most beautiful of all, in young Leo's opinion, was the painted reredos behind the altar, with its glorious haloed saints and its radiant golden-haired angels. Those angels, sweet-faced and boasting magnificent multi-hued wings, had sustained him through years of ugly poverty, fuelling his dreams that one day he would escape to a better life.

As a teenager, he had been shipped off to England with an older sister who was emigrating with her new husband, and Leo had put Jamaica behind him once and for all. He found his home—and his vocation—in the Church of England, throwing himself into his work with all the passionate devotion of which he was capable.

He scarcely ever thought about his past—not even about the angels.

Until the day that Oliver Pickett turned up on his doorstep, wanting to talk about faith.

He'd looked at Oliver with a faint shock of recognition. Did he know him? Had he seen him before?

And then the penny dropped, as the memory resurfaced. Oliver had the face, the form, the pure golden beauty of the angels on the reredos. All he lacked was a pair of multi-coloured wings.

At that point, Leo never dreamed of aspiring to Oliver's love. All he wanted was to be able to look at him, to revel in so much beauty in one human form. To have that love bestowed upon him had been nothing less than a miracle: a life-transforming, life-enhancing miracle.

Now, though, Leo stirred restlessly in his oversized bed, half asleep, reaching with longing for someone who wasn't there.

He and Oliver had agreed that with all of the police and reporters swarming about the place, they had better be cautious; Oliver had not been to the rectory since the fatal Tuesday night.

Feeling the cool, smooth cotton of the pillow under his hand rather than a silky fall of golden hair, Leo sighed and dragged himself to consciousness. He stretched his hand out for the alarm clock and squinted at it in the half-light: it was nearly six o'clock, his usual time to get up.

Too early by far to ring Oliver, though. Oliver was a night owl, not a morning bird. He would not appreciate being waked from his slumbers, even by words of love and endearment from Leo.

Leo squeezed his eyes shut and tried to recapture the way it had been, just a few days ago. The way it should have been today: the long, pale limbs sprawled on the bed, the golden hair spread across the pillow.

Well, there was no point wishing for what might have been. Sighing, he got up and went for a shower.

An hour later—showered, shaved and breakfasted—Leo went into his study and reached for the phone. It was still too early to ring Oliver, but there was another phone call he needed to make. He'd been trying to reach Frances without any success, and now was his best chance, before she went off to work. The hospital's rules against mobile phones being switched on within its premises was a damn nuisance, he'd discovered, and made it almost impossible to get in touch with her during the day, since she was never at her desk.

Graham was the one who answered, and when he put Frances on, she sounded groggy.

'I didn't wake you, did I, pet?' Leo asked.

'Not really. I mean, I haven't really slept,' she admitted. 'I tossed and turned for hours. I suppose I finally started dozing a couple of hours ago.'

He was stricken. 'Oh, I'm sorry. I didn't think.'

'It doesn't matter,' she said wearily. 'I needed to get up soon anyway. This is my morning for taking the service in the hospital chapel.'

'Well, I won't keep you long. But I just wanted to see how you're doing.'

'Thanks, Leo.' She sighed. 'The answer is: not very well.'

It wasn't like Frannie to let things get to her, Leo knew. Through all the acrimonious debates about the priesting of women she had kept her cool, even in the face of active hostility and almost insurmountable odds. 'The police. Are they hassling you, love?'

'I'm sure they don't look at it like that,' she said wryly. 'They're just doing their job. But I wish their job didn't involve trying to pin a murder on me. Odious as the man was, I didn't kill him.'

'I know. I know.'

'I had one of them here again last night, going over everything again,' she confided. 'I'm sure they think I did it. In the end, I told him that if I were to murder every male priest who ever gave me grief, I would be a very busy woman indeed, and the Diocese of London—hell, the whole Church of England—would be seriously short of clergy.'

Leo chuckled in spite of himself. 'You tell them, pet.'

'The trouble is,' she analysed, 'they just don't have anyone else in the picture. Did you see the evening paper last night?'

'Yes. Wasn't that a masterpiece? Seemingly motiveless crime, indeed.'

'Graham's going out for this morning's papers. I wonder whether they'll all have picked up the story.'

'Journalists hunt in packs,' Leo said caustically. 'Where one goes, the others are never far behind.'

'Maybe I should stay at home and draw the curtains, then.' She sounded only half joking.

'Not a bad idea, Frannie love. It can only be a matter of time till someone tells them about what happened on Tuesday night. The only reason they haven't sniffed it out already, I reckon, is that Vincent was too grief-stricken to talk to them.' His voice was mocking. 'Balls,' he added succinctly. 'What a drama queen.'

'But what about you?' she asked. 'Have you been... okay?'

'The police haven't been back, and I've sent a few journalists packing,' Leo said. 'I suppose it was inevitable that they should come sniffing round here, since the murder happened in my church.'

'And... Oliver?'

'He's not here, if that's what's worrying you,' he replied a bit more sharply than he'd intended, then relented. 'Sorry, Frannie. I know you have my best interests at heart.'

'I just don't want you to get... hurt.'

Get caught was what she meant, and Leo knew it. He acknowledged it with his next words. 'We're cooling it at the moment. We both thought it was best, under the circumstances.'

'That's good.'

Leo heard the rattle of the letterbox. 'Post,' he said. 'Or perhaps it's the paper. I'd better run, pet.'

'Thanks for ringing.'

'Not at all. Take care of yourself,' he cautioned. 'And keep in touch. You know where to find me.'

The newspaper was on the mat, and so were several pieces of post. Leo carried it all through to his study, intent on checking out the paper. But one of the letters caught his eye: the return address was Downing Street.

'What on earth?' Leo muttered under his breath, reaching for his letter knife.

The letter was written on heavy crested paper. He opened it, staring for a minute before his brain took it in. The gist of the letter was simple: the Prime Minister's Appointments Secretary was happy to inform him that Her Majesty the Queen had approved his nomination as Bishop of Brixton. Downing Street would be making the announcement on Tuesday.

He stopped, and whistled. 'Well, I'll be damned,' he said softly. 'Bishop.'

He remembered now that he'd been chatting with the diocesan Bishop at some clergy gathering or other, and the Bishop had asked him whether he would be interested in a suffragan post, if he were to be approached. Leo had said yes, without taking the question seriously; he'd thought it was just a hypothetical one.

Evidently there had been more to it than that.

It was probably, he realised, a simple case of tokenism, of political correctness: the Church was anxious to be seen to promote minority candidates to high office, and a prominent black diocesan bishop had recently announced his retirement.

But he would take it. He would take it.

A voice at the back of his mind reminded him about Oliver. Oliver…

Leo shook his head to dispel the voice. He wasn't about to give Oliver up, not now that he'd found true love for the first time in his life. He wouldn't think about that now; he would worry about it later.

⚬⚬⚬ ⚬⚬⚬ ⚬⚬⚬

DI Neville Stewart was already at his desk—had indeed been there for some while already—when Sid Cowley arrived. 'About time,' he said sourly, looking up from the pile of morning newspapers he'd been perusing. 'It's fine for some.'

Cowley checked his watch ostentatiously. 'I was out late last night, remember.'

'Sorry,' Neville muttered. 'I didn't mean to take it out on you. But the papers have really got me wound up. Bloody press.'

'What do they say?'

'It's what they *don't* say.' Neville slapped his palm down hard on the papers. 'Just lots of innuendo, implying that we don't know what we're doing.'

'You talked to them yesterday,' Cowley pointed out. 'You dished out the results of the p.m., didn't you?'

'Yeah, yeah. I thought if we let them off the leash a bit, fed them a titbit or two, got them on our side, they might be able to turn something up. Something that would help us, as well. But they haven't come up with anything more than we have. To hear them tell it, the man was a bloody saint. No skeletons in *his* closet. Oh, no.'

'I saw the evening paper.' Cowley pulled up a chair next to Neville's desk. 'The way I read it, they haven't found anything yet. But they're still digging.'

'And what about *you*? Have you found anything?'

'Nothing, Guv,' Cowley admitted. 'I did like you said. I was out half the night, showing that photo round the clubs, the pubs. No one recognises him. He really doesn't seem to have had a life. No women. Nothing at all like that.'

'But someone killed him,' Neville said forcefully. He ran his hands over his face, rubbing at his cheeks. 'It's just not the way these things work. Not in my experience.'

'There are such things as random crimes,' Cowley offered. 'Sometimes people are killed for no good reason.'

Neville glared at him. 'There's no evidence of robbery, or attempted robbery. No evidence that anyone broke into the church. No good explanation of what Jonah Adimola was doing in the vestry, for that matter. Why did he go back, after he left Vincent Underwood? Why, unless he was meeting someone?'

'You think he'd arranged to meet someone?'

'I don't know what to think,' Neville confessed. 'I just know that it's two days on, and we haven't got any further than we were when we started. I'm bloody tired, and I'm fed up.'

'Frances Cherry,' Cowley said. 'What about her?'

Neville smiled grimly. 'At least the press haven't got on to her yet. That's one small satisfaction.'

'Do you still think she could be in the picture, Guv?'

'I think, my lad, that she's absolutely all we've got at the moment. After all, she did have a blazing row with him. And it was her stole round his neck—we mustn't forget that little fact.'

⚭⚭⚭

Lilith Noone had, she always liked to think, grown up with newspaper ink in her veins instead of blood. Her father had owned and operated a small weekly provincial newspaper, as had his father before him. To be a journalist herself was what she had always wanted, but she had long since set her sights higher than the family business.

Just as well, really, as her older brother had been the one anointed to take over. Her brother was the brilliant one in the family, or so everyone thought. And her younger sister was the beautiful one, with a career as a fashion model. Lilith, stuck in the middle between the family's two shining stars, had to make do with ambition and cunning.

She had both in abundance, along with a huge competitive streak, and those qualities had helped her to land a job as a reporter on the staff of the *Daily Globe*.

But she had always considered herself a bit apart from the run-of-the-mill tabloid journalist. To put it in its simplest form, she had class. She was well dressed, well groomed, well spoken. People who would run a mile at the sight of one of Lilith's seedier colleagues would hesitate when Lilith approached them, and in that millisecond was her advantage. All she needed was that moment of initial contact, she often told herself, and they were hers.

She'd been a bit late getting on the bandwagon with the Jonah Adimola murder; her editor had given the story to one of the young male journalists. But when he'd made no progress at all, Lilith was invited to take over.

She read her way through the morning papers, then planned her strategy. The others seemed to be wasting their time trying to ferret out Adimola's background, looking for scandal or the hint of scandal; she would, therefore, do something different. She would, literally, return to the scene of the crime.

Churches were not really Lilith's patch. Yes, she'd once covered a 'naughty vicar' story, insinuating herself into the confidence of a woman who'd been pawed by the vicar in question during a counselling session. But that was about it. Still, she felt that she looked the part—modest black pumps, a knee-length skirt and twin-set—as she sauntered into St John's Church, Lancaster Gate, on Friday morning.

The crime scene tape had gone, and the church seemed deserted. Disappointed, she was about to go, when she heard the sound of a hoover from somewhere at the back.

She followed the noise, stopping at the door of the small room where a woman pushed the hoover back and forth. For a moment the woman was unaware of her presence, giving Lilith a chance to observe her and decide on her approach.

She was young—just a girl, really—and with her spiked orange hair and nose ring, not at all what one might have expected to find in a church. Perhaps she was just the cleaner, then, Lilith concluded with disappointment. Churches probably had to take what they could get these days, like everyone else, even if they sported nose rings and green fingernails.

Changing direction, the girl spotted Lilith and switched off the hoover. 'Sorry,' she said. 'I didn't hear you. Can I help?'

Lilith had read, as had everyone, that Adimola's body had been found by the church's sacristan. She hadn't even been sure what a sacristan was, but had looked it up in the dictionary, and found that it was a 'person in charge of a sacristy'. Scarcely more enlightened, she had looked further to discover that a sacristy was 'the room in a church where sacred vestments and vessels are kept'. The sacristan had not been named; Lilith assumed it to be a man.

'I was looking for the sacristan,' she said.

'That's me.' The woman shoved the hoover into the corner. 'What can I do for you?'

'I'm Lilith Noone, and I was wondering if you'd possibly have a few minutes to join me for a coffee.'

The sacristan wiped her hands on the back of her jeans and shook the hand which Lilith extended. 'Willow Tree,' she introduced herself. 'Please don't laugh.'

'It's a lovely name,' Lilith assured her.

The girl smiled, but warily. 'Thanks. You wanted to see me about…?'

'About the terrible thing that happened here the other night.'

Willow's face clouded. 'I'm not sure that I should. You're not police, are you?'

'Not police, no. Someone who is as concerned as you are that justice should be done.' She smiled her most ingratiating smile, followed by her favourite 'crusader for truth' expression.

'Well…'

'I'm dying for a coffee, actually,' Lilith added. 'Is there a proper coffee shop round here?'

Willow succumbed to her charm. 'Actually,' she said, 'I was just about to make one for myself. I suppose you could join me, if you'd like.'

'That would be lovely.'

'It won't be very up-market,' Willow said, leading her out of the room and locking the door behind her. 'No cappuccino or latte. In fact, it's pretty foul. But it's fair-traded, at least.' They went through to the church hall, which boasted a small kitchen, and Willow set about making the coffee. Lilith leaned against the counter, pondering her next step.

'I was actually here the other night,' Willow confided. 'Serving coffee before the meeting.'

'The meeting?'

'You know. The Deanery Clergy Chapter meeting. The… um, murder… happened after the meeting.'

'And you were here.' Lilith modulated her voice to conceal her excitement.

'Yes, though I left before the row. I didn't hear about that till afterward.'

'The row?'

Willow looked slightly abashed, as if she'd betrayed something. But she continued. 'Father Jonah and Frances Cherry, apparently. She's a hospital chaplain. It must have been quite a barney—she threw a glass of wine over him.'

Lilith's fingers itched for her notebook.

'That's why he was in the vestry,' Willow added. 'He needed to get cleaned up.'

'Any idea what this row was about?' Lilith asked casually.

Willow shrugged. 'The usual, I imagine. Women priests—he just couldn't cope with the idea. I don't get it, myself. What possible reason is there why women shouldn't be priests?'

'I can't think of a one,' said Lilith, who had never given the subject so much as a passing thought.

She accepted a cup of coffee from Willow and sipped it. 'Mmm. That's just what I needed.'

'Things are getting better in this deanery, though,' Willow added conversationally. 'There's a new woman curate at All Saints'. She was here the other night, as well.'

'Was she involved in the row, then?'

Willow shook her head. 'I'm not sure. As I said, I didn't actually see it.'

Feeling a bit bolder, Lilith said, 'That room that you were hoovering just now. Was that…'

'It was where I found him. Yes.' Willow's voice held a slight tremor. 'The police have finished in there now. So I was cleaning it up. They made a frightful mess, with fingerprint powder and all of that. They took my fingerprints,' she added, looking at her green-nailed fingers as if there might be some residue remaining on them. Then her voice changed and she said briskly, 'I don't have to be at work till noon today, so I thought I'd pop in this morning and deal with it.'

'Would you mind terribly if I had a look round there?' Lilith asked.

Willow hesitated. 'Well, you've been in there already,' she said at last. 'I don't suppose it would do any harm for you to see it.'

'I know this must be difficult for you, but if you could just show me where....' She paused delicately.

'All right, then.' Willow checked her watch, finished her coffee, took Lilith's empty mug, and washed up before leading the way back to the vestry.

'Is the room usually locked, then?' Lilith enquired as Willow fished the key out of her pocket.

'Not usually. The sacristy is locked, because that's where the silver is kept. But there's mostly just vestments in the vestry.' She shoved the door open and indicated the large chests along the wall, fitted with shallow drawers. 'The chasubles and other flat bits are in the drawers. The copes are hung on hangers in the wardrobe, along with albs and surplices and cottas. It's part of my job as sacristan to keep everything tidy and in good condition and put away properly.'

Lilith scanned the room. Evidently Willow had just about finished cleaning up after the police; the tops of the chests were dust-free and all of the drawers were neatly shut. The only thing which seemed out of place was a long white garment draped over a chair in the corner. 'What's that?' Lilith asked. 'I'm so ignorant about these things. I don't even know what it's called.'

'Oh, that's a cassock-alb.' She picked it up and held it against her. 'I just left it there because I don't know who it belongs to. It's certainly not Leo's.'

'Leo?'

'Leo's the rector. And he's... well, he's huge. This is tiny.'

Lilith saw that there was a small case on the chair which had been hidden by the garment. She went over to examine it, and discovered that it had a luggage label attached to the handle. 'The Reverend Frances Cherry,' she read aloud. There was also an address, which she didn't vocalise but committed to memory with a facility born of long practice.

'Oh! She must have left it the other night,' Willow said. 'She was doing the service with Leo.' She stopped suddenly and put her hand over her mouth.

She'd gone very pale, Lilith observed; her kohl-rimmed eyes were wide with shock. 'What is it? Is something wrong?'

'It's just… oh, I've just realised.' Willow took a deep breath as she dropped the white garment back on the chair. 'He… Father Jonah. He was strangled with a stole. A blue and white stole. I didn't think about it at the time—I was too… shaken up.'

'Didn't think about what?' Lilith moved closer, put a hand on the girl's arm.

'It was *her* stole. Frances Cherry's. I should have realised. I should have told the police.'

'Never mind,' said Lilith, her soothing voice masking her triumph. She wanted to shout; she wanted to crow. Instead she soothed. 'Never mind, Willow. I'm sure the police have figured it out by now.'

⟨∞⟩ ⟨∞⟩ ⟨∞⟩

Friday was Callie's official day off. Her first week in the job had been so full of experiences that it seemed strange to her to have a whole day ahead of her with nothing in the diary. She spent the first part of the morning perusing the newspapers, then decided that she needed to distract herself by going out.

The shopping she'd done the day before had been a stop-gap measure. Now, she realised, was her chance to do a proper, planned shop. She checked the contents of fridge and cupboards and made a list. Callie liked being organised; a well-stocked kitchen would help her to feel more in charge of her life.

There was a mini supermarket in the neighbourhood which would have most things she needed, so she headed there first. She pushed her trolley up and down the aisles, trying to stick to her list and avoid impulse purchases—all of those things like biscuits and chocolate bars which the supermarket planners seemed determined to tempt her with at every turn.

She was in the bread department, trying to decide between a wholemeal loaf and a granary one when she heard someone call her name.

Callie turned, a loaf in each hand, to face Adam.

'Hi, Cal. Fancy meeting you here,' he said, grinning at her.

'Day off,' she stated, as though she needed to explain why she should be in a supermarket on a week day. How inane she sounded, she berated herself as soon as she'd said it.

'Me, too. How about that?'

'Brian's day off is Saturday,' she heard herself saying. 'So he suggested that I should take Fridays.'

'What a great coincidence to run into you.' Adam turned away from her and beckoned to a girl who was just coming round the end of the aisle, pushing a trolley. 'Come here, sweetheart,' he addressed the girl. 'There's someone here I want you to meet.'

Callie's first thought was that she was very young; she looked scarcely out of her teens, though she must have been a bit older than that. She was also very blond. Her silver-gilt hair was fine and wispy, cut short in a sort of pixie style which added to the impression of extreme youth. And she was thin, with that model-like adolescent scrawniness so much coveted by the young—long legs, narrow hips, and scarcely any chest at all. She wore a pale blue shift dress, the exact colour of her eyes, and a lacy cardigan. Looking at her, Callie felt old, frumpy and overweight. She wished she'd put on make-up; she wished she hadn't worn her oldest and most comfortable pair of jeans.

Adam draped an arm round the girl's shoulders and smiled down into her face. 'Darling, this is Callie Anson. My friend from theological college.' He raised his head, meeting Callie's eyes. 'And this, you've probably guessed, is Pippa. Pippa Fairchild. My fiancée.'

'Pleased to meet you,' said Pippa with a seemingly genuine smile, putting her hand out. 'I've heard so much about you.'

Callie was still holding the bread. Feeling foolish and clumsy, she put it down and took the thin, cool hand which Pippa offered. 'Good to meet you,' she murmured.

'Isn't this nice?' Adam said heartily. 'Listen, Cal. Do you have plans for lunch?'

'No.' The word was out before she'd had time to think.

'Great! You can come to my place, then. You can see my new flat. And the two of you can really get to know each other.'

She collected herself, realising it was probably too late to escape, but needing to try. 'My shopping,' she protested. 'I have to finish. And I have to take it all home and get it put away.'

'That's all right,' Adam assured her, looking at his watch. 'We're not quite finished, either. Shall we say three-quarters of an hour? Half-past one?'

'All right,' Callie capitulated.

'You know where it is? Just across from Christ Church, on the corner. Number 63. The ground-floor flat.' With a wave, he and Pippa disappeared round the end of the aisle.

'Damn, damn, damn,' Callie muttered to herself. How could she have been caught off guard like that? She grabbed a granary loaf and tossed it in the trolley, then went straight to the till.

Fifteen minutes later she was home, shoving her perishables into the fridge. This wasn't how she'd planned to spend her afternoon—not at all. She'd thought she would organise the fridge, rearrange the cupboards, get everything in order. She'd thought she would make herself a sandwich, listen to *The Archers*, go for a walk in the park, maybe even read a novel. Later she would prepare a nice meal for herself, ring Frances and have a long, luxurious soak in that wonderful Victorian claw-foot bath.

But now…

There was just about time to take a quick shower. 'Damn,' she repeated again as a jet of cold water caught her unprepared.

Rummaging in her chest of drawers, she found a colourful jumper, which she pulled on over a clean pair of khaki trousers. Why was she bothering? she asked herself, even as she applied lipstick and blusher. Why was she doing this for Adam, when he had Pippa? And besides, she had begun to stop loving him.

At least she thought she had.

⟳⟳⟳

Lilith Noone went straight from St John's Church to the address she'd memorised, which turned out to be a vicarage in Notting Hill. She took a taxi: after all, it was a business expense. The boss didn't like them to avail themselves of taxis on a regular basis, but Lilith told herself that in this case, time was of the essence. If she didn't get to Frances Cherry soon, someone else was bound to do so.

She rang the bell, waited a moment before ringing it again, and had just about given up when she heard the sound of approaching footsteps.

The man who opened the door blinked at her in the sunlight, as if he were emerging from some dark cave. He wore a clerical collar and had spectacles and a tidy beard. 'Yes?' he said.

Lilith made a guess. 'Are you Reverend Cherry?'

'That's right. Can I help you with something?'

'I was wanting a word with your wife,' Lilith said. 'Frances Cherry.'

Now he was looking at her with sudden suspicion. 'You're not from the police, are you? She's already talked to the police. Twice. And if you're from the press, she has nothing to say to you. And neither do I.'

'Just a moment, Reverend Cherry.' She spoke quickly, before he had a chance to shut the door in her face. 'I'm here because the press has got hold of the story about your wife's altercation with Jonah Adimola.'

He looked stricken, and his exclamation was involuntary. 'Oh, no!'

'It's important that I talk to her. Otherwise... well, it won't be very pleasant for her. But I can help her.'

'She's not here.' He regarded Lilith gravely, sizing her up. Then, reaching a decision, he opened the door more widely. 'She should be back soon. I suppose you'd better come in.'

⌘⌘⌘

Adam's flat was the ground floor of a large and beautifully-proportioned Georgian house. He was waiting at the door for Callie, and greeted her with an unexpected kiss on the cheek. 'I'm so glad you could come on short notice,' he said. 'Running into you like that, Cal—I suppose it must have been God's will.'

She could think of another way of putting it, Callie said to herself as he ushered her into the sitting room.

'Pippa wasn't meant to come down till tomorrow,' Adam went on. 'But since it was my day off today, she decided to call in sick to work, and make it a long weekend.'

'That's nice,' said Callie falsely. 'What sort of work does she do?' She was sure he'd told her, but it was one of the things she'd blocked from her mind after that excruciating conversation in which he told her that he was going to marry someone else.

'She's an infant school teacher.'

That figured, thought Callie.

'It will be so useful when we're married. She'll make a wonderful vicar's wife,' he went on enthusiastically. 'And a wonderful mother.'

Pippa came through and went straight to Adam, winding her arms round his waist. 'Everything is about ready, darling,' she said, with a smile of greeting in Callie's direction. 'If you'll deal with the wine, I'll give Callie a little tour of the flat. I'm sure she'd like to see it.'

'Yes, of course I would,' Callie confirmed.

'Right, sweetheart.' Adam gently extricated himself from her arms and kissed her on the nose, then left the two women alone together.

'This is the drawing room,' Pippa began. 'Obviously.'

It was, Callie saw, a lovely room, with original features intact: an elaborate ceiling rose, plaster mouldings round the high ceiling, a marble fireplace. But a slightly bizarre note was introduced by the room's main wall decorations: Adam's collection of African tribal masks. His parents had been missionaries, and the collection was impressive. Seeing them, though, gave Callie an unexpected pang; the masks had adorned Adam's room at theological college. The grotesque faces were familiar to her, as familiar as old and dear friends—friends who had witnessed some of the most significant events of her life. 'Do you like the masks?' Pippa asked.

'Yes, I do.'

'I think they're a bit creepy. But I'm sure I'll get used to them.'

You'd better, Callie thought. Adam would rather cut off his arm than give up his beloved masks.

'I'll show you the kitchen at the end,' said Pippa, leading the way into the corridor. 'Come this way.' She opened a door into a bathroom. 'The little room,' she said coyly.

Callie gave the response she supposed was expected of her. 'Very nice.'

'And there are two bedrooms. This is Adam's room.' Pippa threw open the door.

Strangely, it did not affect Callie as much as the masks had done. She'd never seen any of the furniture before, and the bed—a double bed, rather than the narrow one he'd had at college—sported a smart new duvet cover in fashionable earth tones. The ratty old Indian throw which had covered his bed for all the time she'd known him was no more. That, she knew instinctively, would be down to Pippa.

Pippa was moving on to the next door. 'And this is Adam's study. It has a sofa bed, so it's also the guest room.' She pointed at a suitcase. 'It's where I stay when I visit. Until our wedding.' She added, lowering her voice confidentially, 'Of course, as Christians, Adam and I don't believe in sex before marriage.'

Callie stared at her in astonishment, then saw that Adam had come up behind them. He shot Callie a nervous look; it was the most discomfited she had seen him since he had suggested this bizarre get-together. She didn't say anything: let him sweat for a few minutes, she thought.

He put his arms round Pippa from behind. 'Everything is ready,' he said quickly. 'Shall we eat?'

'Oh, here you are, darling!' Pippa purred. 'I was just telling Callie why we plan to get married so soon. We just can't wait much longer, can we?'

'That's right.'

'The wedding will be at Christ Church,' Pippa went on in the same confidential tone. 'And Richard—Richard Grant, Adam's vicar—says he won't marry us if we've been living in sin. So the answer is to get married as soon as we can.'

'Seems sensible to me,' Callie said in a neutral voice. 'Better to marry than to burn—isn't that what it says in the Bible?'

Adam relaxed visibly. 'Lunch is getting cold,' he said. 'Let's eat.'

ⓒ∞∾ ⓒ∞∾ ⓒ∞∾

Much later, soaking in her fragrant bubble bath, Callie tried to make sense of it all. What on earth had got into Adam?

He had certainly had no objections to sex before marriage when they'd been together.

It wasn't that they'd jumped into bed five minutes after they'd met. It hadn't been like that at all; after all, they *were* both Christians, and preparing for ordination to the priesthood. Almost a year into their relationship, though, when they'd started talking seriously about marriage, about a future together, things had progressed. They were both relatively inexperienced in such matters, but what Adam lacked in experience he made up for in enthusiasm. It was a mutual decision, a natural outgrowth of their growing love and commitment. Callie had gone on the pill, and they'd begun sleeping together.

Theirs was a fairly liberal theological college, and a blind eye was turned to that sort of thing, especially when it was understood that they were engaged, that they would marry. On most nights, Adam would slip along the corridor to Callie's room, or she to his, and they would squeeze together into a narrow bed, holding each other tight beneath Callie's flowered duvet or Adam's Indian throw.

What had Adam told that innocent child Pippa about their relationship? Had he told her that they were just friends? One thing for sure: he certainly hadn't told her the truth.

And as well as sex, there was another of Adam's appetites which Pippa seemed to have been successful in quelling.

At college, Adam had practically lived on bacon sandwiches. For a special treat, he loved nothing so much as a thick steak, barely cooked and oozing with juices.

Now, it seemed, he was a vegetarian.

'We don't eat meat,' Pippa had announced, in the same proprietary and self-righteous tone in which she'd divulged their sexual abstinence. 'Adam and I believe that eating meat is as bad as murder.'

She had produced a dish of lentils and marinated tofu, which, though it didn't taste as bad as it looked or sounded, made Callie long for a juicy burger.

Adam had tucked into it with evident enjoyment. Was he indeed a reformed character?

In any case, there were things about Adam that she suspected he would not like Pippa to find out.

Callie smiled grimly to herself. Not that she'd ever tell her, but it did make a pleasant fantasy to imagine the look on Adam's face if she did.

Chapter Ten

Saturday was Jane Stanford's favourite day of the week. Throughout his ministry, Brian had taken it as his day off, and they had spent it as a family day. When the boys were young and they'd had a parish in the country, that had meant rambles in the countryside and outings to sites of interest. Latterly in London, they often visited museums. Jane enjoyed planning their Saturdays, something Brian was glad to leave to her.

Now the boys were gone. Over the past few years Charlie and Simon had seemed to have more things of their own to do at weekends, so Saturdays were as often as not spent in the parish, with Brian relaxing at home before the demands of Sunday took over his life. Jane was the fierce watchdog and guardian of their sacrosanct Saturday privacy, leaving the phone unanswered and turning people away at the door. Anyone foolish enough to try to drop by the vicarage on a Saturday would be sent away with a flea in their ear; gradually the word had got round, and few parishioners would dare to chance it, even in extreme emergency.

On this Saturday, therefore, Jane was surprised to hear the doorbell ring. It was still quite early in the morning, and they were getting ready for a rare day out: they planned to drive to Oxford and take the boys to lunch. Jane had been looking forward to it for days, with a longing anticipation which surprised her. It had been less than a fortnight since they'd seen Charlie and Simon, but it seemed a lifetime to their mother.

She went to the door with a mingling of impatience at the interruption and goodwill engendered by her excitement about seeing her sons in just a few hours. If it was a parishioner, though, she would have no hesitation at seeing them off, and quickly.

Jane didn't know the woman on the doorstep; she was not a member of the congregation. But she was nicely dressed and looked most respectable, so Jane was not quite as ferocious as she might have been. 'Can I help you?'

'I'm so sorry to disturb you,' said the woman in a genteely-accented voice. 'But I saw that this was the vicarage, and hoped you could help me to find the curate.'

'Certainly.' Jane pointed toward the church. 'The church hall is behind the church, and her flat is above the hall.'

'Thank you so much.' The woman turned to go, and Jane closed the door, putting the incident out of her mind almost as soon as she had done so. Today she would see her sons; nothing could take away from her joy in that.

For the second morning running, the phone, ringing early beside the bed, woke Frances from sleep.

This time, though, it was not the welcome voice of Leo.

The man identified himself as a journalist with one of the major Sunday papers. 'I was wondering, Reverend Cherry, whether you might want to comment on the story in this morning's *Globe.*'

'No, I would not!' she snapped, slamming down the phone.

That call was the first of several. After the second one, Frances stopped answering them and sent Graham to the nearest newsagent's shop for a copy of the *Globe;* after the tenth one she took the phone off the hook. And before Graham had returned, someone rang the doorbell. Frances ignored it, drawing the curtains at the front of the house. When she'd said it to Leo the day before, it had seemed almost a joke. Now it wasn't funny.

Graham managed to get past the hopeful man at the door and found Frances in the kitchen, drinking strong coffee. He dropped the tabloid on the table in front of her.

'I've had a look,' he said with an apologetic grimace. 'It's not as bad as it might have been.'

Frances was trying not to blame Graham, but it was proving difficult. How had he been so easily taken in, so naïve? She'd come home from work to find him with that journalist woman, talking to her over a cup of tea. Frances had soon sent her packing, in spite of her protestations that she was there to help her, to give her a chance to recount her side of the story.

'I didn't tell her anything that she didn't know,' Graham had insisted afterward. 'She knew about the row with Jonah. And she knew about your stole.'

'About my stole?' Frances echoed in horror. 'Oh, God.' She couldn't believe it. Who would have told her that, if not the police? And she was sure that was one thing they'd been anxious to keep under wraps when it came to the press. 'So what exactly *did* you tell her, then?' she demanded.

'Just that it wasn't like you to lose your temper like that. And that he had provoked you. He'd started the argument. That's what you said to me about it, anyway.'

Now Frances opened the tabloid and stared at a fuzzy, blown-up photo of herself from some years earlier. She recognised it as one that had been taken when she'd stood in Dean's Yard during the General Synod vote on women's ordination. The eleventh of November, 1992—a date she would never forget. The photo, which had appeared on the front page of several newspapers the following day, was cropped to remove those packed around her, showing only Frances with her banner reading 'Women Priests: The Time Has Come'. The headline, running across the top of the page, said '*Globe* Exclusive: The Militant Woman at the Centre of Murdered Priest Mystery.'

Lilith Noone had been given a prominent by-line. 'This reporter has learned,' she wrote, 'that a short while before he died, the murdered Nigerian priest Jonah Adimola had a public and heated row with the Reverend Frances Cherry, a prominent campaigner for the rights of women in the Church of England. Adimola, who was known to have disagreed strongly with the legislation which allowed women to be ordained as priests, is said to have provoked Cherry with taunts, and she reportedly reacted by throwing a glass of wine over him.

'The petite red-head was in the forefront of the Movement for the Ordination of Women,' the story went on. 'She campaigned tirelessly for that cause, and was triumphant when, after years of debate, the General Synod of the Church of England voted by a narrow margin that women could be ordained. Cherry herself was amongst the first women to be ordained, in April of 1994. She now serves as a full-time chaplain at St Mary's Hospital, Paddington. She lives with her husband, the Reverend Graham Cherry, a vicar in Notting Hill. "It's not like Frances to lose her temper like that," Graham Cherry told this reporter in an exclusive interview. "Jonah Adimola started the row. He was incredibly rude to her."

'Adimola, who preferred to be called "Father Jonah" by his parishioners at St Mary the Virgin, Marble Arch, was murdered some time on Tuesday night in the vestry of St John's, Lancaster Gate, a neighbouring church at which he—and Cherry—had attended a meeting that evening. Police are baffled by the murder of a man who, up till now, was not thought to have enemies.

'Frances Cherry has been interviewed twice by the police, her husband has confirmed. No arrests have yet been made.'

Well, Frances reflected ruefully, the woman had done her homework. You had to give her that. She'd obviously been through the archives at the *Globe*, to have come up with that old photo and the background information.

And she was skilful as well, managing to imply far more than she said. Graham had opined that it wasn't as bad as it could have been: what, though, could have been worse than giving the impression that the police were on the brink of arresting her for murder? Perhaps they were, or perhaps this article would itself be a catalyst, goading them into taking action.

Then she realised what Graham meant. There was one thing that Lilith Noone knew, but which she had withheld in her article: that Frances' ordination stole had been the means of Jonah Adimola's death.

Frances supposed she should be grateful for small favours. But she very much feared that she hadn't heard the last from Lilith Noone.

⌘⌘⌘

On Saturday morning, Callie knew that she would have to pay the price for her day off. For one thing, she hadn't yet finished her sermon, and time was running out. She got up early, went to her desk and concentrated on it, blocking distractions from her mind. When she finally got to the final 'Amen' and looked at the clock, she realised with a feeling of panic that there was barely enough time to get dressed, and none to have breakfast, before she had to go to the church to say Morning Prayer. Afterward, she promised herself, she could pop down to the shops for the newspapers, and possibly even stop by the bakery and treat herself to a danish pastry. She could munch on it, in lieu of breakfast, while skimming through the papers. With any luck they would have had enough of the Jonah Adimola murder by now and would have gone on to the next big thing.

She clattered down the stairs of the flat, glancing at her watch. No more than a minute to spare.

A woman was at the foot of the stairs, blocking her way. Callie had never seen her before, and assumed that she was a parishioner she hadn't met yet.

'Excuse me,' Callie said, hoping that the woman was going to the church hall rather than looking for her. She could just about squeeze past her in the narrow stairway.

'Are you the curate?'

Damn, thought Callie. 'Yes,' she admitted.

'Could I possibly have a word?'

'I'm sorry—I can't stop just now. I'm due to say Morning Prayer. Might you be able to come back later, or another time?' She hated to turn anyone away, but what would Brian think of her if she couldn't even be on time for Morning Prayer on his day off, the first day she was on her own?

'Can I come to the service?' the woman asked, stepping aside so Callie could pass.

'Yes, of course. Anyone can come.'

Not that many people ever turned up for it. On two mornings that first week, she and Brian were the only ones there; on Monday there had also been one old lady, and on Thursday two men had showed up.

Saturday drew a rather larger congregation, Callie discovered, with five people including the woman who had come to see her. Breathless, she slipped into her stall and picked up her prayer book.

After the brief service, the woman waited at the door for Callie. 'Could we go somewhere for a coffee?' the woman suggested.

That suited Callie very well. If they went toward the local shops, she could stop at the newsagent's on her way back home. 'There's a Starbucks not far away,' she suggested.

Walking along, they made small-talk about the pleasant weather; Callie surreptitiously glanced at the woman, trying to make some assessment of her. She was probably about Callie's age, or a bit older—it was difficult to tell. Her clothing was classic, discreet, and she wore her long hair in a rather elegant upswept style.

At one point in their progress, they had to step off the pavement to avoid a man jogging along toward them in the direction of Hyde Park. As he drew close, Callie recognised him as Richard Grant, the man who had set himself up as an arbiter of his curate's morals. She'd not actually spoken to him at the Clergy Chapter meeting, and wasn't sure whether he'd recognise her or not.

But she was, of course, wearing her clericals, so she would be difficult for him to miss. He was not: his abbreviated jogging shorts displayed muscular legs, as tanned and sinewy as his arms. He slowed a few feet short of them, smiling at Callie in recognition, then jogged in place as he said hello. Callie stopped and returned the greeting, her companion pausing at her side.

'Beautiful morning,' he added.

'Yes.'

'Are you settling in well?' Richard Grant asked.

'Very well, thank you.'

'Adam seems to be taking to it like a duck to water.' His ascetic face creased into a smile. 'I'm very fortunate to have him.'

'Yes, I'm sure,' was the only response Callie could make to that statement.

'That was quite a business the other night,' he said.

'The meeting, you mean?'

'The row. He really went for you, didn't he?'

'It was a bit upsetting,' she admitted. 'But not nearly as upsetting as the fact that he's been murdered.'

Richard Grant shook his head with a pious expression. 'God metes out judgement in mysterious ways,' he said obliquely.

'What do you mean?'

'It's not for me to judge, of course, but I can't help feeling that Jonah Adimola's sins caught up with him.' With that, he nodded at her and resumed his long, loping strides toward the park.

Callie and her companion stepped back onto the pavement. 'Who was that?' the woman asked.

'Richard Grant. He's the vicar of Christ Church. It's up Westbourne Terrace.'

'And who is Adam?'

For a parishioner, the woman asked a lot of questions, Callie said to herself. 'His curate. Adam Masters.'

'A friend of yours?'

'I know him a bit,' she said cautiously, with an escalating feeling of unease.

'Was he at the meeting the other night?'

Callie stopped and turned to face her. 'Just a second,' she said. 'Why do you want to know? Who are you? You haven't said.'

'Let's just say I'm someone who is interested in the truth. Isn't that what you clergy are supposed to be all about?'

The penny dropped. 'You're a journalist, aren't you?'

She raised her chin and looked Callie in the eye. 'I'd like to help you. I'm in a position to be able to do that. All I ask is a few minutes of your time.'

∞∞∞ ∞∞∞ ∞∞∞

Earlier in the week, Neville had hoped for a Saturday off, but clearly that was not meant to be. Instead, exhausted and dispirited, he dragged himself into the station early, stopping on his way to collect a sheaf of newspapers.

This time, in spite of the fact that he'd once again spent a late night in some of the seedier establishments of Soho—all in the interest of truth and justice, of course—Sid Cowley was already there, sitting at Neville's desk reading a newspaper and smoking a cigarette.

'Morning, Guv,' he said cheerfully.

Neville scowled. 'You're awfully bright this morning. Does that mean you've found something?'

'In a manner of speaking.'

Instantly awake and invigorated, Neville demanded, 'Tell me!'

Cowley made an expansive gesture with his cigarette. 'I met a very nice young lady in one of the clubs.'

'She recognised the photo? She knew Jonah Adimola?' Neville's voice was eager with hope.

'Well, no,' Cowley admitted. 'But she seemed to take a fancy to me, and when this business is all over, we're going to meet up for a drink.'

Neville stared at him, biting back a string of expletives. When he had himself under sufficient control to speak, he said, 'Bloody hell, man! We're in the middle of a murder investigation, and you're out there chatting up girls?'

'Just following instructions, Guv.' Cowley didn't look or sound in the least bit repentant. 'You said to talk to as many people as possible.' His smirk conveyed a clear message: you're just jealous, Guv.

He wasn't going to win this one, Neville could see, and if it put Cowley in a good mood, he supposed he shouldn't knock it. He gave an ostentatious sigh. 'Point taken.'

Cowley took a last long drag on his cigarette, then stubbed it out in an empty coffee mug. 'At any rate, Guv, I've been through the papers. Have you seen them yet?'

'No.'

'I didn't think so.'

It was difficult for Neville to tell whether he was being smug, or something else. He dumped his armload of papers on the desk. 'Why? What's up?'

'Do you want the good news or the bad news first?'

Oh, God, Neville thought. 'Give me the bad news.'

The sergeant waved a copy of the *Globe*. 'That Lilith Noone woman. She's sniffed out Frances Cherry.'

This time Neville made no effort to check the single sturdy Anglo-Saxon expletive which rose to his lips, adding, 'How the hell did she find her?'

'Beats me, Guv. She's talked to her husband, she claims. And she's written all about her background as a campaigner for women priests. "The Militant Woman at the Centre of Murdered Priest Mystery".'

Neville snatched the paper and scanned the story.

'The kicker is at the end,' Cowley pointed out.

'"Frances Cherry has been interviewed twice by the police, her husband has confirmed. No arrests have yet been made." Oh, great,' Neville said bitterly. 'Talk about setting an agenda for us. If we don't arrest the woman, everyone will want to know why. Not least the Chief Superintendent.' He threw the paper down on his desk. 'After that, what could possibly be the good news?'

'She didn't mention the murder weapon. Either she didn't know, or...'

'Or she'll drop the other shoe later. I wouldn't put it past her.' Neville shook his head. 'Well, Sid, I suppose we should be grateful for small favours.'

The door of the Christ Church vicarage was opened by a motherly-looking woman with short grey hair.

'Is the vicar in?' Lilith asked. She hoped that she had allowed enough time for him to complete his run.

'Do you have an appointment, dear?'

'Well, no.' She assumed a beseeching expression. 'But I need to see him. It's important.'

The woman seemed to be sizing her up, then nodded. 'Come in. I believe he's just out of the shower. I'm sure he can spare you a few minutes.' She ushered her into a study a few feet from the front door.

Lilith had only a brief wait before Richard Grant joined her—barely enough time to scan the book shelves and glance at the photos on display. The former contained a prodigious number of Bible commentaries, and the latter were uninteresting, showing several well-scrubbed and interchangeably smiling young people.

In place of his running gear, he was now dressed in an electric blue shirt with a very wide plastic dog collar, emphasising his long neck and prominent Adam's apple. 'My wife said you needed to see me,' he said, smiling at her in an encouraging way; his teeth were even and white.

'Mr Grant?'

'Please. Call me Richard.'

Lilith rejoiced inwardly: clearly he did not recognise her at all, and he was going to be a piece of cake. He hadn't even asked her who she was or why she wanted to talk to him. The women—Frances Cherry, Callie Anson—had given her a bit of trouble, but Graham Cherry, and now Richard Grant, proved that she hadn't lost her touch with the opposite sex. Men, especially clergymen, were so trusting…

He indicated that she should take a seat, and he sat across from her.

'Now,' he said. 'How can I help you?'

'I've been very upset by what happened… to that priest. Father Jonah.'

A small frown appeared between his brows. 'Jesus said that you should call no man "Father", save our Father in Heaven.'

This was going to be even easier than she'd thought. 'You didn't approve of him, then?'

'Well.' He cleared his throat. 'It's not for me to judge. But that "Father" business is just an indication of how far he was from following the true path. The Biblical path.'

'He was a priest, though. In the Church of England.'

'The Church of England? You would never have known it.' Richard Grant tented his fingers together and studied them. 'Jonah Adimola was part of that section of the Church—a small and shrinking segment, I'm happy to say—which happily flouts not just the Bible, but also Canon Law.'

'What do you mean?'

'Romanisers.' He almost spat the word. 'If you went into their churches, you'd never guess you weren't amongst the papists. Candles. Incense. And statues! We're forbidden by God's Word—by the Ten Commandments, no less—to worship idols, yet their churches are full of them. "Their idols are silver and gold, even the work of men's hands." They pray to them, and I find that disgusting. An affront to God.'

'In the Church of England?' Lilith said again. It was certainly not the way she remembered the church of her childhood, which had involved long and tedious sermons and endless singing of the Te Deum. Parish Matins, dry and dusty, with not a statue in sight…

'Oh, certainly. As I say, though, you wouldn't know it. They—some of the Anglo-Catholics—even use the Roman Missal instead of the Prayer Book or Common Worship. And that is expressly forbidden.'

Lilith was beginning to understand why Richard Grant, with his own peculiar slant on things, had spoken of God's judgement on the murdered priest. 'Is that what they do at St Mary the Virgin, then?'

'I'm not sure about that,' he admitted—the first time he had expressed uncertainty to her about anything. 'You wouldn't catch me in that church. Nor any of my congregation, either.'

'You *did* know Fa… umm, Jonah, though?'

He sniffed. 'Yes, I knew him. We were in the same Deanery.'

'But you weren't friends or anything.'

Richard Grant leaned forward and addressed her earnestly. 'We didn't see eye-to-eye about most things. But I wouldn't want you to think that there were no points of agreement. In fact, there were two things on which we most definitely agreed.'

Lilith could scarcely imagine what they might be. She waited.

'Women priests, for one.'

Startled, she blurted, 'You don't approve of women priests, either?'

'Certainly not. It is not right for women to have authority over men. St Paul is very clear on that point.'

Words of protest sprang to her lips, quickly suppressed, and she found herself feeling a sudden and unexpected sisterhood with Frances Cherry. It was that sort of attitude which had kept women in all walks of life in their place for hundreds of years, and had prevented able women from achieving equality with their male colleagues.

Better to change the subject before she lost her temper with him. 'You said there were two things,' she stated. 'What was the other one?'

'The sin of homosexuality,' Richard Grant said immediately. 'Jonah and I were of one mind on that. Holy Scripture condemns it, and all right-thinking people can see how abhorrent it is.'

Welcome, thought Lilith ironically, to the Church in the twenty-first century.

⚬⚬⚬ ⚬⚬⚬ ⚬⚬⚬

Neville was at his desk on Saturday afternoon, sifting through a pile of witness statements and interview notes. Either there was something he'd missed, or the right questions had not been asked, because he felt no closer to finding Jonah Adimola's killer than he had three days ago.

A welcome interruption was provided when Mark Lombardi put his head round the door. 'Sorry to bother you, Nev,' Mark apologised.

'No problem.' He dropped the piece of paper he'd been reading. 'I'm starting to go cross-eyed.'

Mark hesitated. 'Could I ask you something?'

'Ask away.'

'Have you interviewed someone called Callie—or Caroline—Anson?'

The woman who had been with Frances Cherry during the famous row, Neville remembered. Quite an attractive woman, in an understated sort of way. He wondered why Mark wanted to know. 'Yes, we have,' he confirmed. 'A couple of days ago—early on. Why—is she a friend of yours or something?'

'I know her a bit,' Mark confessed, seemingly embarrassed.

'She's not a suspect, if that's what you're wondering,' Neville volunteered. 'At least, not at the moment. I'm not really at a point where I can rule anybody out, quite frankly, but she doesn't seem to be in the picture.'

'Thanks,' said Mark, looking relieved. 'So the investigation isn't going well?'

'You could say that.' Neville sighed and placed his palm on the stack of papers. 'I've never known a case like it.' He put on a thick Irish brogue and added, 'It almost makes me wish I was back in the ould country, digging peat.'

⚭⚭⚭ ⚭⚭⚭ ⚭⚭⚭

In spite of the knowledge that he was to be a bishop, Leo was feeling restless and unhappy. Not only had he not seen Oliver, he had not even spoken to him on the phone for two days, his attempts to reach him thwarted by an ever-present voice-mail message. He hadn't wanted to impart the news of his appointment in such an impersonal way, so had just left messages asking Oliver to get in touch. So far, Oliver had not rung him back.

According to the letter he'd received, the appointment was due to be announced by Downing Street in just three days. He needed to talk to Oliver before that, and preferably face-to-face.

Even if it hadn't been imprudent to contemplate going to Oliver's digs to see him, it wasn't an option: he didn't know where Oliver lived. They'd always made contact on Oliver's mobile, and met up in neutral places or Leo's rectory. So he could only try again on the phone.

This time he was more importunate than ever. 'I love you,' he said to the impersonal voice-mail announcement. 'I miss you like hell. I really need to see you. It's urgent. Please ring me, darling.'

A few minutes later, the phone in his study rang; Leo pounced on it. 'Yes?' he said eagerly.

'Hi.' Oliver's voice was casual, offering no apologies. 'You said you needed to talk to me?'

'I do.' Leo took a deep breath to still the pounding of his heart. 'I know it's not possible for you to come here right now, but can we meet somewhere?'

There was a long pause. 'I don't think that's a good idea. We agreed, remember?'

'I know we agreed not to meet. But something... well, there's something I need to talk to you about.'

'Why can't you talk to me now?'

'I need to see you,' Leo insisted.

'You're not... it's not over, is it?' For a moment Oliver sounded like a forlorn little boy rather than the self-assured young man Leo had known him to be.

Astonished that Oliver could even contemplate such a possibility, Leo was emphatic in his denial, overflowing in a flood of words. 'Good God, no! Is that what you thought? I love you so much, Oliver. You know that. You're everything to me. I adore you. You've made me the happiest man in the world, and I couldn't imagine living without you. Nothing's changed. Not between us.'

'Then what...?'

'Meet me tomorrow,' Leo said. 'Tomorrow afternoon, three o'clock. At the Albert Memorial.'

⌘⌘⌘

Callie's mother rang her on Saturday afternoon. 'It's not that I read the *Globe*, of course,' Laura Anson said. 'But my cleaning lady does. There was an article this morning. Isn't that Frances Cherry a friend of yours?'

'Yes.'

'Well, it sounds to me like she murdered that black man. Did she?'

'Of course not,' Callie said stoutly.

'I knew that no good would come of you getting involved with the Church,' her mother continued. 'Didn't I tell you?'

She had told her, over and over again: Callie was mad to give up a good job in the Civil Service for the poor pay and reduced social status of the Church. It wasn't worth having the argument again. 'Yes, Mum,' she said.

'And why should I have to find out about this from my cleaning lady? You haven't been round in over a week. You haven't even rung me.'

Callie cringed guiltily. It was true: her mother had been just about the last thing on her mind this week. 'Sorry, Mum,' she said. 'I've had a busy week.'

'I thought vicars only worked on Sunday. Surely you could have found time to call round to see your mother.'

'In the first place, I'm not a vicar. And the clergy work hard, all week,' she defended herself, then added, with sudden inspiration, 'Why don't you come here tomorrow? You could see my flat. And I'm preaching my first sermon in the morning. You could come and hear me.'

'Oh, I don't think so,' Laura Anson said. 'I like my lie-in on a Sunday. You know that.'

Callie resisted the urge to slam the phone down. 'Well, I'll try to see you in the week, then.'

'Ring before you come,' her mother instructed. 'I do have quite a few things on.'

'All right.'

'You couldn't come this evening, could you? I'm having a little bridge party, and someone's had to drop out.'

'No,' said Callie. 'No, I can't come this evening.' Her stomach gave a little lurch.

⌘ ⌘ ⌘

With everything that had happened in the week, Callie had managed to put her date with Mark Lombardi almost entirely out of her mind. Now, though, the moment was drawing near.

They were just going for a pizza, she told herself as she surveyed her wardrobe after a lingering bath. Nothing heavy. Nothing formal. She should probably dress quite casually. Certainly not clericals.

Jeans, then, but not the ratty pair she'd worn on her day off when she'd so unfortuitously run into Adam and Pippa.

And with the jeans, perhaps a nice jumper. She pulled out one in which she always felt good—deep cherry red cashmere, with a flattering neckline. Peter, whose taste in clothes was impeccable, had bought it for her last Christmas.

She put it on, and surveyed herself in the mirror. Not bad. And besides, it was just a casual date, she reminded herself. A pizza. Nothing more.

Round her neck she fastened a chain with a delicate handfashioned silver cross, an ordination gift from Frances. She brushed her hair and put on a little make-up.

No matter what she told herself about this evening, Callie felt like she was sixteen again, getting ready for her first formal date. She caught herself smiling into the mirror, her cheeks flushed becomingly and her eyes bright.

'Snap out of it,' she said aloud, scowling at her image. 'It's just a pizza.'

⌘ ⌘ ⌘

They'd made arrangements to meet at the corner of Farringdon Street and Clerkenwell Road. Callie saw, as she approached, that he had got there first; he was looking off in the other direction, watching a boisterous group of youths who surged along the pavement.

He was better looking than she had remembered, Callie realised: when they'd met, she'd viewed him through the filter of her Adam-misery rather than assessing him on his own merits. His black, curly hair was attractively mussed, and he had a beautifully shaped mouth.

He saw her, and his mouth curved in a spontaneous smile which lit his face and reached his brown eyes.

Callie's stomach flip-flopped. Unlikely as it seemed to her, this gorgeous man was unmistakably glad to see her.

Chapter Eleven

Mark led Callie through the streets of Clerkenwell, seeming to know exactly where he was going.

'I hope you don't mind coming this far,' he said. 'It's a bit quieter than the West End. Leicester Square has some good places to eat, but it's no place for law-abiding people on a Saturday night.'

'I've never been to this part of London before,' she admitted.

'Little Italy. I grew up here.'

They passed by Italian restaurant after Italian restaurant; as the enticing smells wafted out toward them, Callie grew hungrier and hungrier, her mouth watering. Lunch seemed a long time ago.

'This looks like a good place,' she said longingly as they walked under a red restaurant awning. A large group of people sat round a table just inside the window, tucking into delicious-looking food: crisp-crusted pizzas, bowls of fat olives, glistening salads, pasta dripping with sauce. It reminded her of Venice, and she saw that it was called La Venezia.

'No,' said Mark, continuing to walk. 'We're not eating there.'

'You know of somewhere better, then?'

He turned and grinned at her. 'No. There's no better restaurant in London. But we're not eating there.'

Perhaps it was too expensive, Callie told herself, disappointed.

'If you must know,' he added, 'it's my family's restaurant. My parents run it. And we're not eating there tonight.'

◦◦◦◦◦ ◦◦◦◦◦ ◦◦◦◦◦

The place he took her to instead was just round the corner. 'They do wonderful pizzas here,' Mark promised her as the waiter led them down a flight of narrow stairs into a sort of cellar. The walls were painted white, and the decor was like something out of a movie, classically Italian: red-and-white checked tablecloths and wax-encrusted Chianti bottles holding candles. It was atmospheric, even romantic.

They looked at the menu and ordered food, discovering that they both loved mushrooms and pepperoni on pizza. The waiter brought fizzy water and a bottle of wine.

'I shouldn't,' said Callie.

'Don't be silly.'

'I have to preach tomorrow morning. My first sermon.' But she allowed him to pour her a glass.

They talked, their conversation as effortless and natural as it had been at their first meeting as aeroplane seatmates. He asked her about her new job; she found herself telling him about her first week, and the difficulties of getting up to speed when there were so many new people she needed to get to know. She told him about the Harringtons, about her various home visits to parishioners and other activities of the week. And she talked at some length about Brian, and her hopes for establishing a good working relationship with him.

The one thing she didn't want to talk about was the murder. Somehow it didn't seem appropriate to introduce it into the conversation when she was having such an enjoyable evening, so she skirted round the subject, and Mark didn't bring it up either.

He did, though, talk to her about his work as a policeman. His job, he told her, was nothing glamorous, and nothing high-profile. He worked as a family liaison officer, which meant that he was on hand to deal with people who had suffered some sort of violent crime within their families. It was a difficult job in many ways, and often open-ended as far as results went, but satisfying for someone who liked working with people as he did.

The pizzas arrived, and Callie found hers as good as Mark had promised. They managed to polish off the whole bottle of wine by the time they'd finished the main course; Callie was feeling distinctly mellow when the tiramisu arrived, then discovered that it was not only delicious, but redolent with alcohol.

'It seems to me that we're both in the people business,' Mark summed up. 'Our jobs are pretty similar, as a matter of fact—dealing with folks who are in pain and need help. We have different employers, that's all. I work for the Metropolitan Police, and you work for God.'

That struck Callie funny, and she laughed with alcohol-induced mirth. Mark joined in, which set her off all the more; soon they were both limp with laughter.

The waiter, smiling indulgently, presented them with tiny glasses of a pale yellow liqueur along with their coffee. 'On the house,' he said.

'Oh, I really shouldn't,' Callie demurred, but nonetheless she downed it in one gulp. It burned all the way down, bringing tears to her eyes. She choked. 'What *is* that?'

'Limoncello.' Mark took a more demure sip of his. 'Italian fire-water.'

'Oh, help.' She reached for her water glass and drained it, then took a gulp of coffee, which she discovered to be scalding hot and strong enough to strip paint. Was she making a fool of herself? she wondered in the part of her brain which was still functioning. It wasn't like her to be so carefree, so talkative, so uninhibited.

'Seriously, Callie.' Mark pulled his coffee toward him and gazed down into the dark murk rather than looking at her. 'I realise we haven't known each other for long. But I do feel that... well, there's something I want to ask you. It's a bit cheeky, and feel free to say no.'

Oh, Lord, she thought: was he about to make an indecent proposition?

'Have you ever thought about having a dog?'

'A *dog*?' She stared at him, wondering if she'd heard aright.

'There's this lovely little dog,' he rushed on. 'She belongs to the family I'm dealing with at the moment. But they can't keep her because of what's happened. They were going to have her put down. I couldn't bear that, and said I'd try to find a home for her.'

'A *dog*?' Callie repeated, still in shock.

'I'd have her myself, of course. But my hours are so long and irregular. It just wouldn't be fair. It seems like you're different, though—you work pretty close to home most of the time, from what you've said, and you're in and out of your flat all day. And you're so close to Hyde Park, for walking.'

'A dog?' This time her tone was speculative.

'She's a lovely dog. And she'd be good company for you,' he added.

That much was true: how nice it would be, Callie thought, to come home to find something waiting for her. As a child she'd always wanted a dog, but her mother had claimed herself to be allergic to them, thus effectively closing off any discussion of the matter.

A dog. 'Why not?' she said it recklessly, knowing that she was tipsy, that she might regret it in the morning.

Then again, she might not.

⁂

On the surface, at any rate, normality had reasserted itself in the Underwood household. Routines were resumed: Vincent was busier than ever with church services, and Marigold was once again lunching and spending evenings out with her friends. The only references to Father Jonah's murder were indirect, as Vincent kept Marigold apprised of his campaign with the Bishop. 'I don't know how he can possibly expect me to carry on without help,' he complained after each fruitless phone call. 'I mean, how am I supposed to have High Mass without a deacon?'

But while Vincent was away at church each morning, Marigold went out to the newsagents. She avoided their usual newsagent, the one who delivered their copy of the *Telegraph* each morning. Instead she went rather farther afield, to an anonymous shop just off Oxford Street. There she would buy a copy of every daily domestic paper, then hail a taxi to take her home with her burden. Back at home, in the privacy of her bedroom, she combed through the papers and clipped out any item having to do with the murder. Already she had quite a collection.

Sunday morning's paper yielded a rich harvest as well. The broadsheets had sober reports of the murder as part of their weekly news overviews, and the tabloids continued with their attempts to find a fresh and sensational angle.

The Globe on Sunday once again featured a story by Lilith Noone, with the usual photo of Father Jonah blown up large under the screaming headline 'Did This Priest Deserve to Die?'

She had, it seemed, spoken to Richard Grant, 'the respected Vicar of Christ Church, Westbourne Terrace'. He had expressed the opinion that Father Jonah's murder demonstrated God's hatred for idolatry and Romish practices.

'Even if, as Richard Grant believes, this murder was God's judgement on faulty theology,' the article concluded, 'it was carried out by human hands. The police have yet to discover whose hands they were.'

Marigold's own hands shook as she wielded the scissors.

⌘ ⌘ ⌘

It was time, thought Lilith, to view those Romish practices for herself. As far as she'd been able to tell, no member of the press had yet been successful in getting Vincent Underwood to speak to them; she was ready to have a go, and Sunday morning at his church seemed the best place to try.

She arrived in plenty of time, to make sure of a seat. She needn't have worried: the church was far from full. Somehow she suspected that the same would not be true of Richard Grant's church, a short distance away geographically but as different as it could possibly be. She'd had a peek into Christ Church after her interview with Grant, and had seen what must once have been an ornate interior, now stripped of decoration. The pews had been ripped out and replaced with folding chairs, and the main feature at the front of the church was not the altar, but a large projection screen and a platform for musicians, equipped with microphones, loudspeakers and a drum kit. Grant had told her that they filled it every Sunday with young and old, people from all walks of life. People who loved the Lord Jesus and were eager to hear His Word proclaimed.

All Saints', where she'd been in unexpected attendance at Morning Prayer, had been very different from Christ Church, of course, and she expected that Vincent Underwood's church would be similar to that one. But nothing she had seen the day before at either church, or indeed at the church where the body had been found, could have prepared her for the sensory splendour of High Mass at St Mary the Virgin, Marble Arch.

The church interior itself was beautiful to look at, a Victorian confection of stone and carved wood and stained glass. Colourful statues, some bedecked with tiny gold crowns, were attended by ranks of flickering candles. The main altar, and the altars in the side chapels, were covered in fabrics rich with embroidery and held elaborate silver crucifixes and towering candlesticks.

Even before the service began, the smell of incense was strong, as if it permeated the very walls of the place, mingling with the candle-wax and the flowers.

The ringing of a silvery bell heralded the start of the service, and the sparse congregation struggled to its feet. A robed choir entered singing, processing in a cloud of fragrant smoke behind a huge silver cross. The priests followed; there were three of them, two of them quite elderly, wearing vestments so heavy with gold that it seemed impossible that the men remained upright within them.

Lilith was vaguely able to follow the service. Mostly, though, she just drank it in: the ethereal voices of the choir, the chinking of silver chains, the chiming of silver bells and the chanting of the priests, the choking haze of incense, the intense pinpoints of light from the candles shining through the smoke. Sounds, sights, smells. For the faithful, the other senses would have been engaged as well, as they tasted the communion wafers on their tongues and felt the wine going down their throats in a warming stream, as they touched their foreheads and breastbones and shoulders in their elaborate crossing rituals.

This was Father Jonah Adimola's world, Lilith told herself. Only last Sunday he would have been a part of all this, wearing those very vestments and chanting those timeless words. At that moment she experienced a revelation: it would be impossible to find out what had happened to him without comprehending that fact.

The police were looking in the wrong place. They should be here.

☙ ☙ ☙

After the service she took her time. First she ascertained from a member of the congregation which of the priests was Father Vincent Underwood. As she'd suspected, he was the youngest of the three, though even at that he must have been pushing sixty, with his florid face and thatch of white hair.

Everyone seemed to be drifting toward an adjoining room, so Lilith followed. She discovered that coffee was on offer, weak and tepid and barely drinkable, but she bravely struggled through a cup as she hovered on the fringes of the crowd, eavesdropping on conversations. Fortunately for Lilith, it wasn't the sort of church where the regulars made any effort to greet visitors, nor did they view them with suspicion. Visitors were a fact of life, to be taken for granted and tolerated, if not necessarily encouraged to return.

She wasn't surprised to find that the main topic of conversation amongst the congregation was their dead curate, and speculation ran riot.

'Who do you think killed him, then?' said an elderly man with copious hair sprouting from his ears to a younger man in a spotted bow tie.

'It must have been that woman. I read about her in the paper. That hospital chaplain. She was a flaming feminist, wasn't she? Just the sort who couldn't stand a man like Father Jonah.'

'Well, no one else could have done it. I mean, you couldn't ask for a better priest than Father Jonah,' opined Ear Hair.

'I'm surprised the police haven't arrested her. D'you think they will? Or will she get away with it because she's a woman?' speculated Bow Tie.

'A woman, and a priest.' Ear Hair shook his head. 'Or at least she *thinks* she's a priest, even if some of us know better.'

Bow Tie sighed. 'When's the funeral to be? Have you heard anything about that?'

'I asked Father Vincent,' Ear Hair stated. 'He says it won't be just yet, as the police haven't released the body. But when it happens, we won't have seen anything like it. A Requiem Mass with all the bells and whistles.'

'I may have to take time off work, if it's not at the weekend. Sounds like it will be worth it, though.'

Lilith tuned in to the conversation on her other side. 'Did you see this morning's *Globe*?' a woman in a bilious green dress demanded indignantly.

Her companion, whose nose was in unfortunate disproportion to the rest of her face, shook her head. 'My husband won't have that rag in the house. What did it say?'

'That horrible Richard Grant. You know, from that happy-clappy church up the road.' Green Dress made a face as if she had a bad smell under her nose. 'He had the nerve to say that Father Jonah deserved to die!'

Big Nose gasped. 'No!'

'Those Evangelicals. They think they know everything.'

'Oooh. I just wish Father Vincent would talk to the *Globe*. He'd set them straight, all right,' Big Nose stated.

Father Vincent himself, having divested himself of his sumptuous vestments, was moving round the room in his black cassock, making soothing noises to his parishioners. Though she was too far away to be able to hear what he was saying, Lilith turned her attention to him, watching his body language and his face.

He was good at it, she soon realised. There was a certain aloofness about him that seemed very reassuring, if a bit condescend-
ing. But judging by the faces of those he spoke to, condescension
seemed to be what they wanted from him. A scornful phrase of
Richard Grant's lingered in her mind: 'Father knows best.' He'd
said it as a condemnation of Anglo-Catholicism, a denunciation
of the need to defer to an all-wise priest rather than establishing
a personal relationship with Jesus.

Presumably Father Jonah had also wielded that sort of authority within the parish.

The congregation seemed inclined to linger, everyone needing
to have a word of comfort or reassurance from their priest. Lilith
waited: she was in no hurry, and the fruits of her eavesdropping
would provide her with material for future stories. After a bit,
though, they began to drift off to their Sunday lunches, and
eventually it seemed as though Father Vincent was about to
follow suit.

Lilith approached him, smiling. He gave her an enquiring
look.

'Father Vincent?' she said in her most obsequious voice.

'Yes?'

'I was wondering whether I might have a word with you.
About Father Jonah.' She hesitated, then added, 'I'm Lilith
Noone, from the *Daily Globe*.'

Father Vincent regarded her for a moment, as if weighing up
his options. Then he nodded his head. 'Yes, Miss Noone. Yes,
I'll talk to you,' he said in measured tones.

He arranged two folding chairs facing each other, while she
took her notebook from her handbag.

His cassock, she observed as they sat down, was made of a
finely woven, expensive-looking cloth, piped round the edges
with satin. The sleeves had turned-back cuffs with little satin-
covered buttons, and the garment had been skilfully cut so that
the buttons did not strain round the contours of his ample
stomach. It almost certainly had not been bought off the peg.
Father Vincent, then, must be rather better off than the average

clergyman. Did he have private means? Lilith jotted a cryptic note, reminding herself to look him up in *Who's Who*.

He pre-empted her first question. 'It's a terrible business,' he said heavily. 'Who would have thought it? Last Sunday he was here. And now…'

'Now he's dead,' Lilith finished for him. 'And the police don't seem to be making any progress in finding out who killed him.'

He frowned. 'It should be obvious, shouldn't it? I've told them so myself. And your story in yesterday's paper—clearly you know as well as I do that it was that woman who did it.'

'Frances Cherry?'

'Of course. Who else? She was the one who hated him, because he had the courage to speak the truth to her, to expose the lie she's living.'

'The lie?' Lilith echoed, her interest quickening. Was Frances Cherry perhaps having an affair?

'Her delusion that she is a priest.' Father Vincent folded his plump white hands over his portly belly. 'Anyone who knows anything about theology will know that it's no more possible to ordain a woman than to ordain my wife's cat.'

In his smugness and self-certainty, Lilith thought suddenly, he was not unlike Richard Grant. She suspected that neither man would welcome the comparison.

⚭ ⚭ ⚭

Callie's sermon had gone very well; she'd been complimented on it by various people after the service, and only a few of them had been patronising. And much as some had muttered about the tediousness and irrelevance of Harvest Festival, Callie had quite enjoyed it. Inappropriate as it may have been to sing 'We plough the fields, and scatter' in the centre of London, she'd found it a refreshing change from the bland hymns of the long weeks after Trinity.

She'd gone home afterward, and found that the flat seemed unaccountably empty to her, the hours stretching out to Evensong and beyond. She tried ringing her brother; receiving no reply, on impulse she rang her mother instead. After all, she needed to see her mother at some point: why not this afternoon?

'I hope you're not expecting to be given lunch,' Laura Anson said. 'You know that I never cook on a Sunday any more.'

'No. I'll eat something before I come.' Callie made herself a sandwich and heated up a tin of soup. As she ate, she allowed herself to dwell on the subject which she'd managed to banish from her mind during the morning service: the events of the previous evening.

What had it all been about? she asked herself. She'd had a wonderful time, and had laughed more than she had in ages. Though she and Mark came from very different worlds, they seemed to have much in common. Conversation had never lagged; there had been no awkwardness between them.

But there seemed to be no hint of romance, either.

He'd been courteous, friendly. Nothing more, surely.

Had she just imagined that spark of pleasure in his eyes when he'd seen her?

Maybe he was gay. Somehow she didn't think so: after years of exposure to her brother's friends, Callie's 'gaydar' was pretty finely honed, and Marco exhibited none of the signs.

Maybe he was married, or in a relationship.

Maybe he was just looking for a friend.

Or maybe, she told herself with a wry smile, it was all about the blooming dog. Would he have gone to so much trouble just to soften her up so she would agree to take the dog?

Why did it matter? Did she fancy him, then?

She did find him very attractive, Callie admitted to herself. And then she realised, with a little shock, that it had been at least 24 hours since she'd thought about Adam. Surely that must be some sort of record. Something to be celebrated, even.

Callie poured herself a modest glass of wine from the bottle in the fridge, partly in celebration and partly to fortify herself for the visit to her mother.

Why had she said she'd go? It had to be done, she told herself philosophically. And at least it would take her mind off Mark.

The sun was dropping toward the horizon, its rays angling sharply, as Leo Jackson, dressed in jeans and an open-necked shirt rather than his clericals, walked through Hyde Park on Sunday afternoon. Indian summer continued unabated, with a lingering warmth in the air, and the park was full of skateboarders, dog-walkers and babies in push-chairs. The leaves of the trees were well advanced in their annual transmutation from green to gold.

Leo, though, scarcely noticed any of it. He was in a state of emotional turmoil.

His steps quickened as he approached the Albert Memorial, which gleamed an almost impossible gold in the slanting sunlight. Leo had always enjoyed the overblown statement of grief—mingled with an aggressive assertion of Empire—which was the Albert Memorial. He particularly loved the enormous sculptures at the corners, depicting the four continents, and had a special fondness for the be-tasseled camel which represented Africa; its rather stupid face betrayed no alarm at the woman in the Egyptian head-dress who straddled its hump so precariously, one arm cradling a crook while the other reached out to rest its hand on the well-muscled naked shoulder of a handsome young man.

Leo walked straight past the camel without a glance, his eyes searching instead for a human figure.

Oliver was there, sitting on the steps with his back to the gigantic representation of the Prince Consort. Leo, his heart pounding, forced himself to approach slowly, while all he wanted to do was run to Oliver and sweep him into his arms. He knew that he couldn't do that; he couldn't even touch him, not out here in public.

'Hi,' said Oliver casually, squinting against the rays of the sun, as Leo stood a few feet in front of him at the bottom of the steps.

Leo opened his mouth, wanting to say so much but managing only 'Hello.' He rocked back on his heels, his eyes feasting on his beloved. It seemed like weeks—months—since he'd seen him, though it had been a mere five days. Often as his thoughts had lingered on Oliver's beautiful face, he had forgotten how very blue the eyes, how very golden the hair—rivalling the gilding on Albert himself, he told himself with besotted wonder.

'You said this was important,' Oliver reminded him after a moment.

'Yes.' Leo sat down on the steps with a careful foot or so of space between them, and turned his face away from Oliver, looking across at the Royal Albert Hall. No point beating round the bush, he told himself. 'I've had a letter,' he said. 'They want to make me a bishop.'

'A bishop?'

The alarm in Oliver's voice drew Leo's eyes back to his face. 'Don't worry,' Leo said quickly. 'It won't make any difference. Not to... us.'

'But it will have to make a difference. I mean... you know. You know what happened before. That other bloke.'

'This isn't the same situation at all.' Leo had been through it all in his own mind, over and over, so the words came out in a practised stream. 'In the first place, no one knows. Not about you, not about *us*.'

'That woman knows,' Oliver pointed out. 'The one who came to tea.'

'Frannie. She's my friend. She won't say anything—I can promise you that.'

'You can't be sure.'

Leo nodded firmly. 'I can be sure. Frannie won't give us away.'

'But what if someone *does* find out?'

Again Leo turned his face toward the Royal Albert Hall, unable to bear the strength of the emotion engendered in him when he looked at Oliver. 'I won't give you up.' He said it with simple force. 'Never. Nothing is worth losing you. It's taken me so long to find you, and I couldn't bear to go on without you.'

'So you're saying...'

'If it came down to a choice, I'd choose you.'

'But you're willing to lie about me, so that you can be a bishop. Why don't you just tell them to stuff it?'

This was something else Leo had had ample time to think through, relentlessly examining his own motivations and aspirations. 'It's not as simple as that,' he said. 'I'm not an ambitious man—not for myself, anyway. I've never gone out of my way to seek preferment. I've never cosied up to people who could advance my career.' He stretched his legs out. 'As a black man, though, and a gay man, I owe it to other people like me to take what's offered. To be their spokesman, their advocate, if you like. I feel I can change the system more effectively from the inside than from the outside. Do you understand what I'm saying?'

'I think so.'

'The system is going to change. The *Church* is going to change. It has to. I want to be a part of that change, and I do think that I have something to offer.' He swallowed. 'The day will come when we, and people like us, can be together without being afraid of being found out, or of what others will think. That's what I long for, and what I hope to help bring about.'

'It's all very well to say that, but it's in the future. Where does that leave us now?'

Leo sighed painfully. 'This is the difficult bit. For now, we'll just have to stay apart. Until everything is signed and sealed. It's the sacrifice I... we... have to make. And it will be as hard as hell. But it won't last forever, and then we can be together again.'

'Yes,' said Oliver. 'Yes, I understand.'

⚬⚬⚬ ⚬⚬⚬ ⚬⚬⚬

Mark had promised to ring in the evening to talk about the dog, so after Evensong Callie went back to her flat as quickly as possible. She could hear the phone ringing as she mounted the stairs and made a mad dash to answer it, her heart thumping.

She reached it in time, but it wasn't Mark: it was Peter.

'Hi, Sis,' he said breezily by way of greeting.

'Oh, hi.' Callie tried to keep the disappointment out of her voice.

'My call-minder said that you rang and didn't leave a message. Hope it wasn't anything important.'

'I just wondered what you were up to this afternoon, whether you were free.' She sighed. 'I went to see Mum instead.'

'Oh, Lord.'

'It had to be done. I hadn't been in more than a week. She was starting to be a martyr about it.' Peter, she knew, would understand all too well.

'I just don't get it,' he said. 'She never seems glad to see us. She does nothing but complain when we're there. But if we don't come, she puts on the martyr act.'

'Well, that's the way she is,' Callie said philosophically. 'She isn't going to change.'

'Enough about Mum,' Peter pronounced, and the tone of his voice altered. 'Sis, I have to tell you. Something wonderful has happened.'

'You've met someone,' Callie guessed.

'Yes! He's fantastic. He came to the club where I was playing last night, and… well, what can I say?'

'Spare me the gory details,' she laughed.

'Well, I'll spare you the *gory* details, at least, but I have to tell you about him. He's a fashion designer. Very high-powered, apparently.'

'Sounds interesting.'

'He's going to Milan this week, flying out tomorrow morning.'

'That's a shame,' Callie sympathised.

'No, not at all.' Peter sounded triumphant. 'He's asked me to go with him, Sis!'

'Can you manage it?' she asked practically. 'What about work?'

'Oh, I don't have that much on this week. Just a couple of gigs. I'll cancel.' She could imagine him waving a hand in airy dismissal. 'I'll be back in time for my regular Saturday night gig.'

'Well, I hope you have a good time.'

'Don't worry—I will,' Peter assured her. 'I'll give you a ring when I get back.'

Love at first sight yet again, Callie thought ironically as she put the phone down; she might have found it easier to believe in if it didn't happen to him with such frequency. She kicked her shoes off and flopped on the sofa, feeling exhausted, wondering whether she ought to summon up the energy to make herself something to eat.

Before she'd decided what to do about food, the phone rang again, and this time it was Mark.

'Are you in for the evening?' he wanted to know.

'Yes. Unless I decide to go out and collect a takeaway,' she thought aloud as her stomach rumbled with hunger.

'Well, I can bring her round right now.'

'Bring her round?'

His voice was patient. 'Bella. The dog.'

'She's called Bella?'

'It's Italian for beautiful. And she is, Callie. Wait till you see her.'

She'd begun to have second thoughts about the dog in the clear light of day. What on earth had she let herself in for, under the influence of alcohol and Mark's persuasiveness? 'I'm just not sure,' she said doubtfully.

He seemingly chose to misunderstand her. 'Oh, she's beautiful all right,' he said. 'And you don't have to worry about her gear—I'll bring it all. Bed, food, lead.'

'All right, then,' she capitulated.

'I'll be round in a bit. Say, three-quarters of an hour. And,' he added, 'if you can hold out that long, I'll pick up a takeaway on the way. Indian, or do you prefer Chinese?'

'Either. I don't mind.'

'Brilliant. See you soon.'

Having been dragged out of her lethargy, Callie looked round the sitting room and tried to decide what she needed to do before he arrived. She retrieved her shoes, fluffed up the sofa cushions, and looked for a duster, which she flicked over the

mantelpiece and coffee table. There was wine in the fridge, so
that was all right, though her lunch dishes were still in the sink.
She washed them up and put them away, then laid the table,
using her favourite mats. That still left time for a quick shower
and change of clothes. She was just giving her face a critical look
in the mirror when the bell went.

Callie threw the door open breathlessly.

'Hi,' said Mark, a dog in his arms. 'This is Bella.'

The dog was a cocker spaniel, black and white. Her head
was mostly black, with a white blaze, and her body was mostly
white, flecked with black spots. Callie, who had had little experience with dogs and was no great judge of such things, could
see that she was indeed beautiful, with her long silky ears and
her enormous dark eyes.

Bella raised those eyes to Callie and wagged her tail; as Mark
delivered her into Callie's arms, she lifted her head and licked
Callie's chin.

Till that moment, Callie had been sceptical about love at first
sight. Now, though, she knew that it was possible. 'Hi, Bella,'
she said softly, cradling her in her arms.

Chapter Twelve

Neville had been dreading Monday morning. He was scheduled to have a meeting with Detective Chief Superintendent Evans, and he knew that it wasn't going to be pleasant.

The meeting was to be in DCS Evans' office, which made things worse. Evans was fiercely territorial; his office was very much an extension of himself.

Neville knocked on the door at the appointed time, which happened to be quite early. 'Come in,' barked Evans.

Edging through the door, Neville was confronted with the sight which greeted all comers: a wall completely covered with photos of Evans' family—wife, children, grandchildren, a veritable tribe of Evanses.

In the centre was a large and rather flattering studio portrait of Mrs Evans. The lovely Denise, Neville said to himself reminiscently.

Once upon a time, Denise had been DCS Evans' secretary. Young and single, she had been the object of many a fantasy at the station.

It wasn't that she was particularly beautiful. Denise was a pretty enough girl, with youth and a good complexion on her side, but her chief attraction was not her face. To put not too fine a point on it, she possessed a magnificent pair of breasts—the envy of all the women, and the focus of lust in all the men.

They'd virtually queued up to go out with her, Neville recalled. He'd even taken her out once. Only once, though:

he'd found her a bit on the dim side, and not at all forthcoming with her favours.

And old Evans was clearly smitten with her, from the very beginning. He couldn't keep his eyes off her, could scarcely keep his hands off her either.

It had been a standing joke at the station. The desk sergeant had even started running a book on the outcome: would Evans be successful—as none of the rest of them had been—in seducing Denise, or would she have him up on sexual harassment charges?

But they had underestimated Denise. She had confounded them all, displaying rather more cunning than anyone expected of her.

It would seem that she'd always had her eye on the higher prize, if prize it could be called. She had played the Anne Boleyn game, refusing to sleep with Evans—giving him enough to keep him interested and coming back for more, but not enough so that he ever became bored or took her for granted.

And in the end it had paid off for her. Five years ago DCS Evans had divorced his comfortable middle-aged wife and married the lovely Denise.

In spite of the fact that he had grown children and an increasing number of grandchildren, Evans and his young wife had promptly started a new family. There were now two children under five, with a third on the way.

It must have been the money and the status which attracted her, Neville concluded dispassionately as he faced Evans across an expanse of desk. She certainly hadn't married him for his looks: DCS Evans was no oil painting.

He had a heavy prognathous jaw, his vast chin jutting out to create an underbite. And his eyebrows, several shades darker than his greying hair, were wild and bushy, overshadowing his rather small eyes. It was an easy face to caricature; many a young policeman with rather more artistic talent than discretion had doodled a cartoon image—caterpillar eyebrows, lantern jaw—during the long briefing sessions of which Evans was fond.

The eyebrows were lowered now, the piggy eyes boring holes in Neville. 'Well?' Evans said, and it was obvious that he wasn't asking after Neville's health.

Neville decided on the cautious approach. 'You wanted to see me, sir.' He said it in a neutral voice, careful not to sound apologetic or defensive.

'Damn right I wanted to see you. What, exactly, have you accomplished this weekend on the Adimola case?'

'Well, sir, we're still making enquiries. There's a full team out—'

Evans' voice cut across his. 'Because it seems to me that Lilith Noone has been a lot busier than your lot.' His palm slapped down on the tabloid spread across his desk. 'The Cherry woman on Saturday. That happy-clappy lunatic on Sunday. And Vincent Underwood this morning. Have you seen it?'

'Not yet, sir.'

'Perhaps we should be hiring Lilith Noone to replace you, Stewart. Do you think that's a good idea?'

Neville gulped. 'No, sir.' But he filed the remark away for future reference: it was a good one, and he might be able to use it on Cowley at some point.

The DCS bent his head to the newspaper, squinting at it; vanity prevented him from using the reading glasses he so badly needed. 'The bloody woman's damn clever. There's no denying that.'

'What does she say, sir?'

'It's more what she *doesn't* say. She's always careful to stay just the other side of libel. But she keeps having a go at us. Implying that we should have made an arrest by now.' This time it was his fist rather than his palm making impact with the paper. 'And damn it, man, she's right.'

'Does she say exactly who we should be arresting?'

'Not in so many words. She's too clever for that. Listen to this.' Evans adjusted the angle of his head and squinted down. '"Father Vincent, who worked with Jonah Adimola on a daily basis and knew him perhaps better than anyone else in London did, emphasised what a gentle man he was. 'Everyone in the parish loved him,' he told me with a catch in his voice and tears in his eyes. 'I can't imagine anyone wanting to murder him. Father Jonah had no enemies—none at all.' He admitted, though, that outside of the parish, Father Jonah may have upset people who held less traditional views about the church. 'He always stood up for what he knew was right, even if it wasn't popular. He didn't hesitate to speak out about abominations like so-called women priests, and I suppose there were those who might have resented that. Taken it personally, even.'"' Evans raised his head to glare at Neville. 'Could that be much clearer? A bit farther on in the story, she mentions—oh so casually—that Underwood had witnessed the row between Adimola and Cherry. "'It upset Father Jonah deeply,' Father Vincent said sorrowfully. 'She went for him, out of the blue. And so soon after that, he was dead. I suppose we must regard him as a martyr for our cause.'" You have to hand it to the woman, don't you?'

'Underwood told us that he was sure Cherry had done it,' Neville pointed out.

'I have no doubt that he told her exactly the same thing. She just knows better than to say it in so many words.' Evans sighed and shook his head, more in sorrow than in anger. His temper tantrum had run its course.

Neville stifled a sigh of relief. He, like everyone else, knew that Evans was prone to these little outbursts, but was essentially a reasonable man. If one could manage to weather the tantrums without responding in kind, there was a good chance of having a civilised and fruitful discussion.

'Sit down,' said Evans. His desk was compulsively neat, empty of messy in-trays and out-trays, holding only a writing pad and pen, and an open file, squared with the edge of his blotter. He picked up a page of notes. 'All right, Stewart,' he said. 'Where, exactly, are we? Let's talk it through. Starting from the beginning.'

Neville reminded him, as concisely as possible, what had been done by his team of detectives. Everyone at the fateful clergy meeting had been interviewed, some more than once; none of them, apart from Frances Cherry, had an evident motive for murder, and she had an alibi, unless you accepted the possibility that Leo Jackson was in it with her or prepared to lie for her. Various members of Jonah Adimola's church had also been interviewed, turning up absolutely nothing. His flat had been searched, with a similar result. Enquiries had been made in clubs and pubs, as they looked for possible clandestine activities and associates; no one admitted to knowing the dead priest, or ever having seen him before.

'What about the crime scene forensics?' Evans prodded.

'Plenty of fingerprints. Mostly Leo Jackson's, and the sacristan woman's. Some of Adimola's, a few of Underwood's—remember, Underwood took Adimola there after the wine incident. And Frances Cherry's, of course. She was there earlier in the evening, before and after the service.'

'So even if there were fibres or other evidence of her having been there, it doesn't pin anything on her.'

'Unfortunately not. The same is true of Jackson, of course.'

Evans looked up from his notes. 'You have reason to suspect Jackson, then?'

'Not really. Not unless he and Cherry are… involved. Having an affair or something like that.'

'And that's possible?'

'Possible, certainly,' Neville confirmed. 'They seem very protective of one another. I have a strong feeling that they're hiding something, and that would explain it.'

'Hmm.' Evans digested the scenario, drawing his brows together. 'I suppose we could lean on them a bit more.'

'I'll see to it, sir.'

'Good.' Evans checked his notes. 'Now, what about the p.m. report? Anything there that helps us?'

'He was strangled. Garrotted, really, with that stole. From behind. So he had no defensive injuries.'

Evans gave him a shrewd look. 'And a woman could have done it?'

'No problem.' Neville had been through this in his own mind, had wondered the same thing: after all, Jonah Adimola was a tall man, and Frances Cherry quite a small woman. 'He was sitting down when it happened. In a chair. You saw the body in situ. The murderer came up behind him. Caught him by surprise, evidently. It was just a matter of whipping the stole round his neck and twisting it. Anyone who was reasonably fit could have done it.'

'But it doesn't sound like a casual sort of murder,' Evans reasoned. 'Not, for instance, a thief breaking into the church, looking for something to steal.'

'No,' Neville said. 'That's unlikely. Highly unlikely. I would say that he was almost certainly killed by someone he knew.'

Evans thumbed through the file and extracted a sheet of hand-written notes. 'I've been checking into the Nigerian angle,' he said. 'I've been in touch with the Nigerian embassy in London, and with the Foreign and Commonwealth Office. Unofficially, of course—any official enquiries could take years, especially dealing with Lagos.' He pulled a wry face.

'Have you found anything, sir?'

'Nothing. He didn't seem to have been involved with the Nigerian community in London. And as far as they can tell me, his life in Nigeria was as blameless as his life in the UK. No criminal record, no evidence that he was anything but an upright citizen. And I checked with the Home Office,' Evans added. 'Lunar House. His immigration status was above-board. Proper papers and documentation. All permissions in order.'

It was up to Neville to voice it. 'So we're no further ahead at all, sir.'

Evans tapped his pen on his writing pad, frowning. 'Well, as Lilith Noone so helpfully points out at every opportunity, *someone* killed him. And even if we don't have much to go on, everything we do have points in just one direction.'

'Frances Cherry,' Neville stated.

'Frances Cherry. Not least, Stewart, because he was killed with her stole. Don't forget that little fact.'

'It's the one thing that Lilith Noone doesn't know,' Neville said, almost to himself.

'And had better not find out.'

'No, sir.'

Evans fixed him with a piercing look. 'Lean on her, Stewart,' he ordered. 'Lean on Cherry. And do it soon. Time is marching on. We need to make an arrest, sooner rather than later.'

☙☙☙

Lilith Noone was feeling depressed. On the one hand, she knew that she had cause to be elated: her continuing stories on the Adimola murder were streets ahead of anything the other papers had been able to come up with, and her exclusive interviews with the people involved were the envy of her colleagues.

But on the other hand, Lilith realised that unless something unexpected were to happen, she was nearing the end of the road.

She had spoken to Graham Cherry, to Richard Grant, to Vincent Underwood—all of the gullible male priests. The women—Frances Cherry and Callie Anson—had refused to talk to her. Perhaps she could get to Leo Jackson, if she were lucky. Maybe.

Where could she go from here? How could she follow up the brilliant story she'd written on the Underwood interview?

She sat at her desk with a tepid cup of coffee at her right hand and tried to think what to do. She could cobble together something from the overheard conversations after the church service, but that wasn't really sensational enough.

On impulse, she picked up the phone and rang the police station, asking in her most honeyed voice to be put through to Detective Inspector Neville Stewart.

'Can I tell him what it's in regard to?' asked the operator.

Restraining herself from correcting the woman's grammar, Lilith said sweetly, 'The Adimola case. I have some information which will interest him.'

He picked up the phone almost immediately; Lilith recognised the soft Irish accent from his television appearances. 'Hello?'

'Good morning, Inspector Stewart.'

'Who's speaking?' He sounded brusque, rushed.

'Let's just say it's someone who is as interested as you are in finding the person who killed Jonah Adimola,' she said.

Now his voice was wary. 'You said you had information.'

'I do.' She paused strategically. 'I know about the murder weapon. About Frances Cherry's stole. And if you don't want me to print it, perhaps you could tell me exactly where you are in your investigation. Whether you're close to making an arrest. The *Globe*'s readers want to know. It's their right to know.'

'Lilith Noone!'

'Correct, Inspector. If you could just—'

Just before he slammed the phone down, he cut her off with an Anglo-Saxon expletive telling her where to go, and leaving her in no doubt that he meant it.

⚬₩₩₯ ⚬₩₩₯ ⚬₩₩₯

Callie woke up feeling happy. For a moment she wasn't sure why, then she remembered: Bella.

Her feet fumbled for her slippers; she pulled her dressing gown round her shoulders and went through to the kitchen, where she'd put the dog basket. That had seemed the best place, just to be on the safe side, though it had been a wrench to leave her there.

Bella was awake, her tail wagging with delight as Callie opened the kitchen door.

'Hi, girl.' Callie flopped on the floor and was rewarded with ecstatic face licks.

But the floor wasn't very warm, and Callie wasn't sure how soon the dog would need to go outside.

'I'll get dressed,' she said to Bella. 'Then we'll go walkies.'

It was a pain to be on the first floor; she couldn't just open the door and let Bella into the garden. Not that there was a garden—just a patch of grass which would have to do for emergencies. Fortunately Hyde Park was only a few minutes away.

She dressed quickly; she could shower later, Callie told herself. With a sense of doing something momentous, she clipped the lead onto Bella's collar. Her dog. She was walking her dog.

The early morning mist hung low, giving a slight air of unreality to the proceedings. She'd never been out in the park this early, Callie realised. But she was not alone. Scores of others were engaged on similar business, and they greeted one another with familiarity and warmth. Several people spoke to her: commenting on the weather, admiring Bella, asking how old Bella was.

She had, Callie recognised, just joined a club—the fraternity of dog-walkers. The thought made her smile.

⚭ ⚭ ⚭

Later, after her shower and before it was time for her to join Brian for the Monday home communion visits, Callie rang Frances. It had been a couple of days since she'd talked to her, she thought guiltily, and Frances must be going through a bad time, after that horrible newspaper article.

Callie knew that Frances usually worked at her desk on Monday mornings, going into the hospital toward lunch time. She tried the home phone, half expecting it to be off the hook, and was surprised when Frances answered right away. 'Hi, Callie.'

'You knew it was me?'

'We've invested in a caller display phone,' Frances explained wryly. 'Needs must. This is a vicarage, after all. We can't very well leave the phone off the hook permanently. This way we can answer when we recognise the caller or the number.'

'Sounds like a good idea.'

'I sent Graham out on Saturday afternoon to buy it.'

'How are you coping?' Callie asked.

Frances gave a shaky laugh. 'All right, I suppose. All things considered.'

'Have the police been bothering you?'

'No. That's one thing to be thankful for.' She sighed. 'It's just that I feel so... so violated. That dreadful article. And the one today, with all of Vincent Underwood's poisonous innuendo.'

'I haven't seen that one yet,' Callie admitted, realising guiltily that she'd been so wrapped up in Bella she hadn't even thought about buying a paper.

'You can imagine what it says.' Frances changed the subject abruptly. 'Enough of that. How did the sermon go yesterday?'

'Oh, fine. I had some compliments.'

'What else is new with you?'

Callie looked across at the sofa, where Bella had settled down and made herself at home. 'You won't believe it,' she said, smiling. 'I have a dog.'

༄༅ ༄༅ ༄༅

On reflection, Lilith decided that Leo Jackson was her best hope for a new angle on the story, and settled on a careful approach, planning to observe him at a distance before trying to talk to him. Her starting point would be his church, where he was bound to show up sooner or later.

While doing her homework on Frances Cherry, she had also done her homework on Leo Jackson: she knew that he was something of a lefty when it came to various social causes, and had made his church into a centre for like-minded people. She knew that he was considered a high flyer, someone with good career prospects in the Church. She knew about his West Indian background; she'd seen a photo of him.

Yes, she knew the facts about Leo Jackson. But nothing in those bare facts had prepared her for the sheer impact of the man.

She was at the back of the church, fingering the leaflets for Amnesty International, Christian Aid and Traidcraft, when he arrived to take the lunchtime service. He strode toward the vestry, his colourful dashiki contrasting with his clerical collar.

Leo Jackson, she saw, was a good-looking, sexy giant of a man. Charismatic, larger than life. The sort of person who was supremely comfortable in his own skin. She felt slightly breathless as he swept past her.

He was, in fact, just the sort of man she could fancy. In spite of the fact that he was a vicar.

Up till now, dealing with the dried-up sticks of clergymen she'd encountered thus far, she'd adopted a conservative look, her twin-set-and-pearls persona. Now, though, she sensed that something else might be called for. Something a little more blatant, more appealing to a red-blooded man. Leo Jackson, she could see, was certainly that.

So she went home, all the way to her Earl's Court flat, and, chameleon-like, changed her clothes—and her whole persona.

A dress with a bit of cleavage, spike-heeled shoes instead of flat pumps. She unpinned her neat French twist and ran her fingers through her hair, mussing it up artfully; she re-did her make-up, applying a glossy lipstick. She even took the time to paint her nails.

If she played her cards right, she might strike it lucky; she might get more than an interview out of Leo Jackson. Not right now, of course—that would be unprofessional. But when the police finally got round to arresting Jonah Adimola's killer, then it would be a different matter.

Her active imagination carried her along in that vein as she returned to Lancaster Gate. She'd got beyond the preliminary stages of seduction, picturing the strong muscles of his shoulders, almost feeling them beneath her fingers, when she reached the rectory and rang the bell.

He opened the door quickly, towering above her, scarcely allowing her enough time to adjust the angle of her cleavage to provide him the best view. 'Yes?' he said.

'Hello, Mr Jackson. I'm Lilith Noone, from the—'

His face changed. 'I know exactly who you are, Ms Noone,' he cut across her in a voice cold with barely disguised anger. 'Did you think I wouldn't be expecting a visit? After what you've already done, I assumed I'd be next on your hit list.'

'Then you'll talk to me?' She licked her lips and looked at him through her eyelashes.

'Like hell I will.' Then, as he shut the door in her face, he told her where to go, uttering exactly the same Anglo-Saxon expletive that Inspector Stewart had used. It was, thought Lilith, extremely unbecoming from a man of the cloth.

And if it was ever in her power, she would make sure that he regretted it.

Neville, realising that time really was running out for them, took a chance that he would find Frances Cherry at home. He debated about ringing her ahead of time to make sure, then decided that the element of surprise would work in his favour. If she wasn't at the vicarage, they could probably track her down at the hospital.

Sid Cowley went with him, and on the way they discussed their strategy. 'We were pretty gentle with her before,' Neville said. 'I think it's time to shake her up a bit.'

Cowley, who had watched too many police shows on television, suggested, 'How about good cop/bad cop?'

'It might work. Which would you like to be?'

The sergeant took a thoughtful drag of his cigarette. 'Bad cop would be fun.'

'Right. And we—you—go for the jugular about Leo Jackson. She won't be expecting that, I reckon.'

As in the past, it was Graham Cherry who answered the door to them. 'Frances is here,' he said, adding protectively, 'Is it really necessary to talk to her again? I'm sure she's told you everything she knows. Everything that happened. I'm afraid you'll upset her if you start pressing her.'

'It's necessary,' Sid Cowley said, already slipping into his bad cop role. 'A man's been killed. We haven't made an arrest yet. And that upsets *us*.'

'Would it be all right if I sat in?' Graham requested. 'I won't say anything, but I'd like to be there for moral support.'

Neville thought quickly. If they were going to press her about a possible affair with Leo Jackson, it wouldn't be good to have her husband there; she might be less forthcoming and less inclined to come clean. 'No, I don't think so,' he said. 'Sorry, but we need to talk to her on her own.'

Graham, too, had seen his share of cop shows. 'What about a solicitor?' he asked. 'Isn't she entitled to have a solicitor present?'

'Certainly she is,' Neville said.

'Why do you think she needs one?' Cowley added belliger-ently. 'We're just going to ask her a few questions. If she doesn't have anything to hide, then why should she need a solicitor?'

Graham Cherry led them through to the kitchen, where Frances was boiling the kettle for coffee. 'The police would like a few words with you, Fran,' he warned her.

Neville looked round the kitchen and decided it was as good a place as any for the interview; there was a table where they could sit. And he was getting tired of the endless interviews conducted in clergy studies, surrounded by dusty tomes. 'We can talk to you right here,' he said. Graham retreated, casting an apologetic glance at his wife.

If she was nervous, she didn't betray it. 'Would you like some coffee?' she asked, smiling. 'It's the good stuff, not that rubbish they serve at the hospital.'

'That would be grand,' Neville said.

They sat at the table while she poured the boiling water into a cafetière and rounded up several mugs.

'Mind if I smoke?' Cowley asked, reaching for his cigarettes.

Frances hesitated for only a second. 'All right. This will have to do for an ash tray, though.' She passed him a clean saucer, then cracked the window open.

Cowley made a ceremony of lighting up and taking his first drag as Frances pushed down the plunger and poured out the coffee. 'Milk? Sugar?' she offered.

They adjusted their coffees to suit themselves; Frances took a mug through to Graham before joining them at the table.

'I've told you everything I know,' she began. 'We've been over it all more than once.'

'We'd like to ask you about Leo Jackson,' Neville said, stir-ring his coffee.

'Leo?' She sounded surprised, and perhaps a bit wary.

'You've known him for a long time?' asked Neville.

'Yes, I've told you. We've been friends for years.'

Neville took a sip of coffee. It was very hot, but it was delicious. 'Good coffee,' he approved, continuing with a question to which he knew the answer. 'Leo Jackson isn't married, is he?'

'No.' It was a monosyllable, and now Neville was sure that she looked wary.

'Does he have a girlfriend, perhaps? Someone special?'

'A girlfriend? No, I don't think so.'

Cowley spoke. 'You don't think so. Does that mean you don't know for sure?'

'His private life is his own business,' she stated after a split second's hesitation.

'You haven't answered the question.' Cowley stared at her insolently, dragging on his cigarette. 'Do you know for sure? You're supposed to be such great mates, after all. You must know.'

Frances was silent, biting her lip.

'I'd like to suggest,' Cowley said before she could reply, 'that you do know. That you know very well. That, in fact, you and Leo Jackson are more than just friends.'

'More than just friends?' She sounded genuinely puzzled.

Cowley leaned forward. 'Are you shagging him?' He blew smoke in her face. 'Are you and Leo Jackson lovers?'

She flushed a deep red. 'No! How dare you suggest such a thing?'

'Don't you think he's attractive, then?'

'He's quite an attractive man. But that has nothing to do with it,' she snapped.

He sneered. 'You want me to believe that you just don't fancy him.'

Frances looked toward Neville in appeal. 'You don't seem to understand. I'm a married woman. *Happily* married. And,' she added, 'a priest. As is Leo.'

'Yes, I understand,' Neville said soothingly. 'You're out of line, Sergeant Cowley.'

Cowley wasn't ready to give up. 'It's in the papers every day,' he stated. 'Supposedly happily married people, having it off with someone else. Vicars, too. They're the worst. Naughty vicars. Don't you read the papers?'

'I don't suppose Reverend Cherry reads that sort of paper,' Neville put in with a reproving look at the sergeant.

'Or maybe you don't fancy him because he's black. I suppose you might be a racist.'

'You have to believe me.' Flushing, Frances ignored Cowley and addressed Neville. 'I am not a racist. Leo and I are friends. Nothing more.' She paused. 'And besides—what does it have to do with you? I thought you were concerned with finding out who killed Father Jonah, not digging into the private lives of everyone who ever knew him.'

⁂

Callie had a busy morning, accompanying Brian on his rounds as he visited the shut-ins and dispensed communion.

Since her emotional visit with Dennis and Elsie Harrington the previous week, she had spoken to Dennis several times on the phone, ringing to see how they were coping. Although he hadn't been very forthcoming, he had seemed to appreciate the calls.

So she was surprised when he opened the door to them little more than a crack. 'My Elsie's very poorly today,' he announced flatly. 'Well under the weather, she is. I think it best if you don't come in just now, Father.'

'I'm sure she'd like to see me,' Brian said. 'She'll be wanting the Sacrament.'

'Not today, Father. Maybe another day.' He closed the door.

'Well!' said Brian. 'That's a first.' He shrugged and they went on to the next visit.

But Callie couldn't help worrying about them. Now, of all times, she would have thought that they would have wanted the comfort of the Sacrament, of Brian's soothing words. She realised, as well, that Dennis had not been in church on Sunday; according to Brian, he never missed a week, so that was additional cause for concern.

She tried to put it out of her mind, and succeeded fairly well by the time Brian suggested they go their separate ways for an early lunch and meet up again in an hour.

If she grabbed a sandwich, there ought to be time for a quick walk, she told herself as she turned eagerly for home. Then she was seduced by a butcher's shop window, displaying an inviting array of prime cuts of meat.

A bone, she thought. She should get a bone for Bella.

'A knuckle bone, my love. That's what you want,' the butcher advised her. 'A nice knuckle bone. They don't splinter like other bones. Won't get stuck in your doggie's throat.'

'Thanks. How much will that be?'

'No charge, my love.' He wrapped the bone in greaseproof paper. 'Anything else, my love? I have some lovely steaks today. Scottish beef. Sirloin, fillet.'

It seemed mean to take his bone without buying anything. On impulse, Callie pointed to the steaks. 'I'll have two of those. The fillet, I think.'

'Oh, very nice, too.' The butcher chose the two best and winked at her. 'I hope he's worth it, my love.'

Was he worth it? Callie pondered the question, handing over the money—a shocking amount for just two pieces of meat. Enough to feed an African village for a week, most likely.

It had been another lovely evening, filled with laughter and warmth. He'd provided the takeaway, a massive amount of Chinese food. They'd eaten, they'd talked, they'd played with Bella. He'd been in no rush to leave. And when he'd finally gone, it had been with the promise of returning on the following night. 'To keep an eye on Bella and see how she's settling in,' he'd said. 'I feel responsible for her.'

She still couldn't quite figure out what he wanted from her.

Did it matter? She enjoyed his company; he made her feel like an interesting person. So what if he didn't reciprocate her growing sense of attraction?

If he just wanted to be friends, then friends they would be, she decided.

Better, thought Callie wryly, a good friend than a bad lover.

She was almost home. Her footsteps quickened and she bounded up the steps, Marco forgotten—almost.

Bella was waiting for her at the door, her feathery tail wagging her whole body with ecstasy. Unconditional love on both sides, totally reciprocated. Callie swooped her up in her arms joyously.

Chapter Thirteen

It was only later, during her lunchtime walk with Bella, that Callie realised she hadn't told Brian about her Thursday visit to the Harringtons. The visit had happened after their staff meeting; Friday had been her day off, Saturday had been Brian's, and Sunday had been so busy with Harvest Festival that the matter had slipped her mind.

As soon as they met after lunch, Callie told him. She didn't expect him to be very happy about it, and she was right.

'Why on earth didn't you tell me?' Brian demanded.

'There just wasn't a chance,' she explained lamely, detailing everything that had happened since then.

'You should have rung me straightaway. I can't believe you didn't tell me something as important as this.' He frowned at her. 'I'm the parish priest, Callie. I have the cure of souls of this parish. That means it all comes down to me. My parishioners are *my* responsibility, not yours.'

'Sorry, Brian.'

'As a matter of fact, you were out of line going to see them without me, let alone without telling me. They were trying to reach *me*, and you went instead.'

Callie bit her lip. 'It was an emergency. They were distressed, and needed to talk to someone…'

'It could have waited until I'd finished lunch.' His eyes were narrowed, and the line of his mouth indicated his displeasure.

'Sorry,' she repeated, feeling miserable. Just over a week on the job, and already she'd badly blotted her copy-book. She had disappointed—even angered—Brian, and had jeopardised their working relationship. Maybe she was in the wrong line of work after all.

⌇⌇⌇

After the police left, Frances sat for a long time at the kitchen table, staring into her now-cold coffee, numb with shock.

She was already late for work, and she knew that she ought to talk to Graham and tell him what DS Cowley had suggested about her relationship with Leo. But ridiculous as the allegation was, she couldn't bear to face Graham just now. Nor could she face Leo.

With a chill feeling in the pit of her stomach, though, she realised that she had to tell Leo. The police would probably ask him about it as well, hoping to catch him out, hoping that he would betray something to confirm their suspicions. She had to warn him.

It wasn't something that should be done over the phone. With sudden resolution, Frances dumped the cold coffee down the sink, grabbed her handbag and went through to the front door, calling out to Graham as she passed his study. 'I'm off to work now.'

'But what about—' he called after her.

She shut her mind to the concern in his voice and hurried toward the nearest bus-stop. Seeing a number 94 disgorging passengers, she broke into a run and caught it just before it pulled away from the stop. She squeezed into an empty seat at the back, breathing heavily, her chest constricted with pain, unnoticed tears on her cheeks.

The other passengers were locked into their own private worlds, staring straight ahead, looking out of the window, or reading a newspaper; no one paid her any attention. Only the conductor, a grizzled and wiry black man with liquid brown eyes that reminded her of Leo's, gave her a kindly look. 'You okay, ma'am?' he asked as she flashed her season ticket at him.

Her response was brusque, mechanical. 'Yes. Fine.' He shook his head and moved on.

When the bus reached Lancaster Gate, she barely waited for it to stop before swinging herself off the back platform and turning toward St John's Rectory.

A smile split Leo's face at the sight of her on the door step. 'Frannie, love!' he boomed. 'You must have read my mind. I was just thinking about ringing you. Come in, pet. Come in.'

He led her upstairs to his private sitting room. It was a comfortable room with a superb view, looking out over Hyde Park. Frances ignored the view and collapsed onto a squishy leather sofa. 'Oh, Leo,' she gulped, tears very close to the surface.

'Frannie, love—what on earth is wrong?' He sat beside her and put his arm round her shoulders. 'Talk to Leo, pet.'

She didn't want to tell him, but knew that she must. It was painful, it was embarrassing. 'I have to warn you,' she said. 'The police—they'll probably be back to talk to you.'

'Oh, them.' He gave a dismissive shrug. 'I can handle the police. You don't have to worry about me.'

'They've just been to see me.' She took a deep breath and plunged on, not looking at him. 'They made some crazy accusations. They thought—they think—we're... having an affair. You and I.'

Leo's laugh rang out, loud and incongruous. 'What did you tell them?'

'I told them it wasn't true. That it was unthinkable.'

'Oh, pet! Don't you fancy me just a little bit, then?'

'Leo!' She turned horrified eyes on him, swimming with tears. 'It's not a joke, Leo.'

'Sorry, pet.' He gave her a contrite squeeze.

'Don't you see? I didn't understand, at first, what they were getting at, or why they thought it was important. But then I figured it out. They think we're in it together.'

'In *what* together?' He frowned, baffled.

'The murder. Jonah. They think we killed him, one or both of us, then gave each other alibis.'

'But why would we do that?'

'I'm not sure what they think. Maybe because he insulted me,' she guessed. 'And he insulted you. I suppose they think that's reason enough.'

∽∾∽∾∽∾

'The way I look at it,' Cowley said as Neville drove back toward the station, 'they did it for one of two reasons.'

Neville was bemused at the way Cowley had got the bit between his teeth on this one. He'd seemed to be going through the motions on this case until now, very much taking a back seat and doing what he was told, but the interview with Frances Cherry had empowered him in some way. 'Tell me,' he invited.

Cowley paused to light a fresh fag, then chucked the match out of the window. 'It could have been the woman priest thing,' he said. 'Like we thought before. The row, and all that. Adimola must have really pissed them off, and they could have come back a little bit later, while he was still in the church, and offed him together.'

'Or?'

He took a long, contemplative drag. 'Or he could have been blackmailing them.'

'Blackmail?' Neville sat up a bit straighter.

'Say Adimola found out that they were having it off. Maybe he saw them together somewhere, and put two and two together. Who knows how he found out. But say he did?'

'It's a thought,' said Neville slowly. 'It's a thought.'

'And there was something Vincent Underwood said,' Cowley went on. 'He said that he and Adimola left the church together, remember? And that Adimola said he'd forgotten something, and went back.'

It was a detail which had puzzled Neville at the time, and had nagged in the back of his mind ever since. Why would Jonah Adimola say that? What was his real motivation for going back into the church? 'So you think he'd arranged to meet them there?' he said with rising excitement.

'It's possible.'

'It would explain a lot,' Neville reasoned.

'Say the row was a total red herring,' Cowley continued. 'Say they'd already set up a meeting.'

Neville took it a step further. 'The row might even have been staged.'

'To give Adimola a reason to be in the vestry. But then Underwood got involved, and he had to get rid of him before the other two came back to meet him.'

'And they came back as arranged,' Neville concluded, 'and killed him. To shut his mouth and protect their guilty secret.'

'That's it,' Sid Cowley declared triumphantly. 'That's it, Guv.'

Neville put on his indicator and turned at the next corner. 'I think we need to talk to Leo Jackson right now, don't you?'

Leo finally managed to calm Frances down. 'We had nothing to do with it,' he reminded her. 'That's our best defence, pet. They can't pin something on us that we didn't do.'

'But they can try,' she warned.

'They can try, but they won't get anywhere. We're innocent.'

Frances twisted her wedding ring and drew a ragged breath. 'Yes, I suppose you're right.'

'Trust me, pet.' He scrutinised her closely. 'Would you like some tea? You look like you could use it.'

'I really ought to go to work. I'm late already.' She sounded half-hearted at best.

'On second thought,' pronounced Leo, 'you need something a bit more bracing than that.' Waving away her unspoken protest, he went to a cupboard and produced a bottle of whisky, then sloshed a healthy portion into a glass. 'Drink this,' he ordered.

Frances didn't argue. She took a tentative sip, shuddered, and downed most of it in one gulp. 'Thanks, Leo. I did need that.'

As he poured a glass for himself, Frances remembered what he'd said when she arrived. 'You said you were just about to ring me,' Frances recalled. 'I don't suppose it was ESP. What was that about, then?'

'Oh, that.' Leo sat down across from her and turned the glass in his massive hands. 'I wanted to tell you something, Frannie love. I didn't want you to read it in the papers first—I wanted to tell you myself.'

The worst-case scenario emerged full-blown in her mind and she gasped in horror. 'Oh, Leo, no! They haven't...'

'No, no, no.' He laughed and put up a reassuring hand. 'Nothing like that, pet. It's *good* news. Or I suppose it's good.' Leo paused and announced, 'They're going to make me a bishop.'

'But that's wonderful news!' Impulsively she went to him and gave him a hug.

'Mind the glass, pet,' he chuckled.

She returned to the sofa. 'Tell me about it. All the details.'

'Bishop of Brixton. It will be announced tomorrow. That's pretty much all I know at this point,' he said. 'I've had a chat with the Appointments Secretary. And I'm due to see the Diocesan Bishop at the end of the week.'

'You deserve it, Leo. No one deserves it more than you.'

'Unless it's you, Frannie love,' he said quietly. 'You're one reason why I'm taking it. I want to be able to make a difference when the battle for women bishops starts in earnest. As a bishop myself, I'll have a voice that will be heard. On that issue, and so many others. A voice for the excluded and the marginalised.'

'Your voice will always be heard.' She smiled at him fondly. 'No matter where you are.' Then a disturbing thought struck her. 'But what about...'

'Oliver?' he finished for her. 'It's okay, pet. I've talked to him about it, and it will be all right. He'll manage. I'll manage.'

'You're giving him up?' Inwardly she sighed in relief. 'I know that must be really difficult, Leo, but it's the only way.'

He straightened and stared at her. 'Give him up? I'll never do that.'

'Then what...'

'He's the love of my life,' Leo stated simply. 'The Church may not be ready to accept that yet, and we both have to be prepared to wait things out a bit.'

Frances felt once again that dread which had possessed her when she'd first met Oliver. 'You *will* be careful, won't you, Leo?' she pled with him. 'Oh, you must be so careful.'

'Yes,' he said. 'I'll be careful.'

The doorbell rang; they looked at each other.

⌒⥣⥢ ⌒⥣⥢ ⌒⥣⥢

Marigold Underwood lunched with two of her friends at a favourite restaurant in Knightsbridge, chattering to them as though nothing in her world had changed. Their children, their lovers, their husbands were—as always—the main topics of conversation. Since she had nothing to add on the first two topics, Marigold contributed a few amusing anecdotes about her cat Jezebel, and facilitated a gossip session about another friend who had been seen in the company of an unknown man.

'I heard he was gorgeous,' sighed Beatrice enviously.

'And young,' added Georgina with equal envy.

Then suddenly, that topic of conversation exhausted, they turned on Marigold.

'My cleaning lady showed me this morning's *Globe*,' Georgina said. 'Did you know? There's an interview with Vincent in it. All about that murder.'

'Oh, really?' Marigold managed to sound surprised.

'I saw it, as well,' Beatrice admitted. 'There's even a photo.'

'Is it any good?' Marigold asked brightly.

'Oh, quite.'

Beatrice had always been a good liar, Marigold reflected. That was why she was so successful in carrying out her affairs.

The photo, as she knew herself, was not at all flattering, though it was quite accurate. It seemed to capture the essence of Vincent in all his pomposity. His round face wore a bland, self-satisfied smile and his plump hands were folded on his stomach in a most characteristic pose. There was something about it that made her want to tear it from the paper and rip it to shreds, to destroy that smug smile.

The article had hinted, discreetly but unmistakably, at the accusation which Vincent had made from the beginning, to her and anyone else who would listen: Frances Cherry had killed Jonah.

Marigold wondered now, as she had from the first, whether Vincent really believed that.

◦꧁◦ ◦꧁◦ ◦꧁◦

Lilith was in a panic. With the wilful lack of co-operation from Leo Jackson and DI Stewart, she really had reached the end of the road. She sat at her desk and went laboriously through her notes. There was nothing there from which she could cobble a story. Nothing.

Her editor had been delighted with the Underwood interview, heaping effusive praise upon her. 'Well done, Lilith,' he'd said. 'Just the sort of work I like to see in the *Globe*. You leave the reader wanting more. And I know you'll give it to them tomorrow.'

But what was there left to give?

Just one thing, and that was her ace in the hole.

Frances Cherry's stole.

She'd threatened DI Stewart with it, in the heat of the moment, not seriously intending to follow through with her threat. Or at least not yet.

Who, though, was she protecting?

The police, who had stonewalled her at every turn? Frances Cherry herself, who had unceremoniously thrown her out of her house and refused to make any comment at all?

They hadn't made her life easy. And all she was trying to do was her job.

The public had a right to know. That was the founding principle of journalism, and one to which she had always subscribed.

The public had a right to know, and her editor had a right to expect a good story.

Why had she even contemplated wimping out now, when she had the best story of all in hand? Surely she, Lilith Noone, was made of sterner stuff than that.

Her fingers hovered over the keyboard and the words began to appear on her screen. 'This reporter can reveal exclusively…'

ᏛᎳᎯᎦ ᏛᎳᎯᎦ ᏛᎳᎯᎦ

'Well, really!' said Jane Stanford indignantly, when Brian told her that his curate had visited the Harringtons without him, and had then failed to tell him. 'That woman's getting above herself, Brian. I did warn you.'

'I'm sure it was an honest mistake,' he back-tracked. 'After all, I scarcely saw her after that, except for Sunday. And it was a busy day.'

She ignored him. 'She's only been here for five minutes,' she fumed. 'Already she's going behind your back.'

'I need a curate,' he said mildly.

'You need a curate, yes. But you don't need *her*.' Jane frowned. 'That woman is going to be more trouble than she's worth. Mark my words.'

ᏛᎳᎯᎦ ᏛᎳᎯᎦ ᏛᎳᎯᎦ

Not sure whether she'd get into even more trouble with Brian, but feeling that she had to do it, Callie rang the Harringtons late in the afternoon. 'I just wanted to make sure you were both okay,' she said to Dennis when he picked up the phone.

'As well as might be expected,' he replied.

'I was worried about you. And so was Father Brian,' she added. 'Why did you send us away?'

There was a long pause on the other end. 'Father Brian,' he said at last. 'We were… well, we were embarrassed. About our Stu, and all. Father might not understand.'

'But you rang him on Thursday. You wanted to talk to him.'

'We were upset. We needed to talk to somebody. Afterward, though, we thought better of it.'

'You talked to *me*,' Callie pointed out.

'Oh, that was different, girl. You're… well, you seemed to understand. And as I said, we needed to talk to somebody. Then we thought you'd probably tell Father, and we were afraid to face him.'

'He's your parish priest,' she said firmly. 'Believe me, he's not going to pass judgement on you and Elsie, or your son, or anyone else.'

'We'll think about it,' Dennis conceded. 'In the mean time, though, girl, if you want to come and see us, we wouldn't turn you away.'

Callie exhaled in a whistling breath as she put the phone down. Going to see the Harringtons without Brian would certainly get her into even hotter water. But they needed her. How could she let them down?

⌘ ⌘ ⌘

Neville rang Detective Chief Superintendent Evans' secretary on the way back to the station, and as luck would have it, Evans was in his office and available to see Neville immediately.

He said hello to the secretary as he went in. When the lovely Denise had married Evans and given up the job, she'd chosen her own replacement: middle-aged, flat-chested, and plain as a boot. But she was a nice woman, and could be relied upon to warn people if her boss was in a particularly foul mood. She also seemed to have a soft spot for Neville. 'He's not too bad at the moment,' she told him. 'Better than he was this morning.'

Thank goodness for small favours, thought Neville.

This time he was invited to sit. 'What progress have you made?' Evans wanted to know.

'Not as much as I'd like,' conceded Neville. 'We've talked to Cherry and Jackson. Separately, of course. Neither one of them would admit anything about an affair. They were both pretty angry at the suggestion, in fact. Jackson practically chucked us out of the door.'

'That doesn't mean anything.'

'No, sir. I know.'

Evans stroked his long chin. 'What was your gut feeling about it? Did you believe them?'

'I'm not sure,' confessed Neville. 'They seemed sincerely shocked at the question. But they could just be good actors. If it were true, though…' He explained DS Cowley's theory about blackmail as a motive for Jonah Adimola's murder.

'Possible,' Evans said thoughtfully. 'It would certainly explain a great deal.'

'What would you like us to do now, sir? Shall we arrest Frances Cherry? Her connection with the murder weapon—'

Evans' phone rang. He picked it up with a frown. 'I thought I told you— Oh. All right, then.' There was a brief pause, then he went on. 'Yes. Yes, I'm glad you rang, darling…. Don't panic. I'm sure… Yes. All right…. As soon as possible.' He put the phone down and turned back to Neville. 'You were saying, Stewart?'

'I wondered whether you wanted us to arrest Frances Cherry. If we brought her in, we might be able to break her down.'

There was a small frown between Evans' heavy brows, and he seemed to look at Neville without really seeing him. 'I don't think that's necessary just yet,' he said. 'Let's give it another day and see what happens.'

'The blackmail scenario is the closest thing to a plausible motive that we have,' Neville pointed out. 'Everything else we've looked at is a non-starter.'

But Evans was no longer listening. 'Not now, Stewart,' he said dismissively. 'Go home and catch up on your sleep, man. We'll talk about it tomorrow.'

～～～ ～～～ ～～～

Neville could certainly have used the sleep, but he was too keyed up to contemplate that. On impulse, he rang Mark Lombardi on his mobile.

'I wondered if you'd like to meet up for a drink,' he suggested. 'Or even a bite to eat, later. A curry, maybe.'

'Sorry,' said Mark. 'I can't do it. I have… plans.'

'Plans? That sounds intriguing.' Neville laughed. 'What's her name, then?'

Mark, though, was evasive. 'Let's do it another time,' he suggested. 'Soon.'

Leo had already had a full afternoon: he'd spent time calming Frances down, and he'd been subjected to a visit from the police. Both of these things had been unscheduled, and had taken valuable time. But there was one more thing which *was* scheduled, and which couldn't be avoided.

Late in the afternoon, a photographer arrived at the rectory. He was to take the official photographs of Leo in advance of the announcement of his new appointment, photos which would be available for the press and media. It was the last thing, really, that Leo needed at that moment.

In spite of that, he switched on a smile and welcomed the man. 'Where would you like to take them?' he asked. 'Here at the rectory, or in the church?'

'Maybe we'd better do it both ways,' the man suggested. 'It's good to have a variety.'

Leo led him into his study and posed at his desk as the man snapped away.

'Now,' said the photographer, 'before we go to the church, I wonder whether we might take one or two with your family? That's what I usually do, if they're willing and you don't have any objections.'

'I don't have a family,' Leo said.

'No? No wife and kiddies?'

'No. I'm a bachelor.'

The man looked round speculatively. 'You live in this big house all by yourself, then?'

'That's right.'

'Seems a shame, somehow.' As they headed toward the church, he continued to chatter companionably. 'Me and the wife, we've got three kiddies. Two boys and a girl. Don't ever believe it if people tell you that boys are more trouble than girls. Our boys have never given us a minute's worry. But the girl, our Kayleigh—that's another story. She's twelve now. Twelve going on twenty-one, the wife says. Wants her belly-button pierced, if you can believe it! Twelve years old, and wants a pierced belly-button. Can you feature it?' He shook his head in wonderment. 'She says all the other girls are doing it. Of course, the wife has put her foot down. Ears, maybe, she says, but no belly-button. Not at twelve.'

Leo let it all wash over him; his thoughts were elsewhere. The photographer's innocent question, and his automatic response, had triggered a flood of emotion which he had to hide—from the man and from his camera.

No family. A bachelor. Just a few short weeks ago he would have said it light-heartedly, with more relief than regret. God had been good to him. He had his friends, he had his church: why would he need anything more than that?

But that was before Oliver had entered his life. Now he knew that he needed more. Now he knew, from experience, in the depths of his soul, that there was profound truth in the Genesis account: 'It is not good that man should be alone.' Man was created for love, for companionship, and once that had been experienced, it was unthinkable that it should be taken away.

How much easier it had been, before.

And how unfair it was. If Oliver had been a woman, had been his wife or his fiancée, he would have been at his side today, sharing his joy in this public recognition of his abilities and accomplishments. Proud of him, and proud to be there with him.

For Leo, for Oliver, that wasn't an option.

Somehow he got through the photo session, managing not to betray his raging feelings. Then he went back to the rectory and poured himself a whisky, settling down in the upstairs sitting room to drink it.

The sun was low in the sky, casting long shadows over Hyde Park. For just a moment there was a magical effect, as the tops of the trees were gilded with liquid light, glowing warmly in the gathering dusk. Unnoticed, they had started to turn colour, and the sun now pointed out their new autumn finery by adding some gold of its own. Then the sun sank a bit further, and the trees were just trees again.

Oliver had come into his life like the sun, illuminating his hidden corners, throwing everything into sharp relief. More than that: Oliver had changed him. And Leo hadn't even noticed. Once—not so long ago—he had been alone, but he had never felt lonely.

Now he was profoundly lonely. Not much more than twenty-four hours since he'd seen Oliver, and he was more lonely than he'd ever been in his life.

Was it worth it?

Sipping his whisky slowly, he asked himself the question: did he really want to be a bishop?

Everything he had achieved in the Church had been done, in his mind, as a representative of his race. To prove that a black man—and one who had grown up barefoot in the slums of Jamaica—could do as well in the Church as anyone else: that was his underlying motivation, always. This appointment was the culmination of all he'd striven for on behalf of his race.

And as he'd told both Oliver and Frances, it gave him the most wonderful platform from which to campaign for change in the institution, an unparalleled opportunity to speak out on behalf on all the causes that mattered to him. That was not to be dismissed lightly.

And yet, and yet…

He was beginning to realise the cost involved. His life would no longer be his own, and it wasn't just because of the enormous time commitment. He would be putting himself in the public eye far more than he'd ever done, subjecting himself to the relentless glare of publicity. His life would have to be seen to be above reproach.

That, even if he could manage it, was so unfair for Oliver.

Oliver's life, as well as his own, would change beyond recognition. He would have to be prepared not only to wait out the initial period of separation, but to skulk around after that, hiding in the shadows. Living a lie.

Leo acknowledged that he hadn't fully thought through what it would mean to Oliver, or what he was asking of him. And that was assuming that they'd pull it off, that the press wouldn't sniff Oliver out and subject them both to the most horrible ordeal imaginable.

Again he asked himself: was it worth it?

Perhaps it wasn't too late to change his mind, Leo told himself suddenly, finishing his whisky. If he were to pick up the phone this minute and ring the Appointments Secretary…

He half rose from the sofa, then sank back again, groaning as the realisation hit him with full force. It *was* too late. Everything had been set into motion. The Diocesan Bishop, the Archbishop, the Prime Minister, the Queen… all had given their stamp of approval. The official photos were even now being printed off, the press releases were written and at the ready. Tomorrow, at noon precisely, it would happen. And there was nothing he could do now to stop it.

⚭⚭⚭

Callie had laid the table, using her favourite mats, and had added a few twinkling tea-lights. The steaks were seasoned and ready for the grill; a big bowl of salad awaited dressing. She'd bought a punnet of late strawberries for pudding, and had chosen a bottle of red wine at the off-licence, wishing that Peter—something of a wine expert—had been around to advise her instead of off cavorting in Milan.

Now she was on the sofa with last Friday's *Church Times*, which she'd been too busy to read until this evening. Bella was beside her, snuggled close, her head on Callie's knee, and Callie fondled her soft ears as she read. It was almost impossible to believe that Bella had been with her for only twenty-four hours. They had bonded; they were a family now.

The doorbell rang about seven. Callie carefully moved Bella aside and went to answer it.

Mark was smiling. 'How's my beautiful girl this evening?' he asked.

A shaft of wild joy, dazzling and unexpected as a rainbow, shot through Callie, but it only lasted for a heartbeat. Mark wasn't looking at her, she realised—he was looking past her, into the room.

He was talking about Bella.

Chapter Fourteen

Neville knew that he should have followed DCS Evans' advice and had an early night, but he'd been far too restless for that. Instead, for lack of a better drinking partner, he'd gone out with Sid Cowley. They'd had a curry, and then had gone on to a pub where he'd had at least one Guinness too many. Cowley's fault, of course: Neville wasn't about to let down the honour of his race by letting some poxy little lager-swilling Englishman out-drink him.

And *why* had he let Cowley talk him into the vindaloo? he wondered in the middle of the night, tossing and turning in an agony of heartburn. He hoped that Cowley, wherever he might be, was suffering as much as he was. If not more.

That proved to be a vain hope when his phone rang at an unconscionably early hour. Neville reached for it, half awake and in pain, knowing only that it was still dark and he hadn't had nearly enough sleep. 'Morning, Guv,' said Cowley's cheerful voice.

Had he not even been to bed, then? 'Good God, man! What time is it? What do you want?'

'*The Daily Globe*,' Cowley said succinctly. 'You need to see it. It's bad, Guv.'

Neville slammed the phone down, cursing Cowley and Lilith Noone in equal measure. Surely the bloody woman hadn't carried through on her threat? Not even Lilith Noone, not even the *Globe*, could be that irresponsible, could jeopardise their investigation like that.

He took the time to shower, letting the hot water sluice over his face and scrubbing himself hard, as if he could get rid of the residue of the vindaloo and the Guinness that way. Then he dressed and went out into the dark.

It was raining. Hard. After the fine weather of the past weeks, that came as a shock. Neville sprinted to the corner newsagents'; the unaccustomed exercise was another shock to his system.

There was a caff on the opposite corner, its lights shining invitingly through steamed-up windows and dingy net curtains. Dodging the earlybird traffic, Neville dashed across and found an empty table, amongst the off-duty taxi drivers and shift-workers who frequented the place at that hour. The smell of bacon frying was overwhelming; ordinarily he found it the most enticing of smells, but not this morning. He ordered black coffee, and spread the damp *Globe* open on the chipped Formica table.

The story wasn't difficult to find; it had not been relegated to the obscurity of the back pages.

A mug of coffee was slapped down beside the paper, and he sipped it absent-mindedly as he began to read. It was boiling hot, and as corrosive as battery acid; his beleaguered stomach, still reeling from the vindaloo, contracted queasily in protest. Neville didn't notice.

oⅢ⅏ oⅢ⅏ oⅢ⅏

Frances, feeling battered, buried her head in her pillow and was only dimly aware that she was alone in bed. Graham had said something about getting up early to work on a funeral sermon, she recalled, reaching for the clock.

It was later than she'd thought. Either she'd slept through Graham's alarm, or he'd waked without its help and switched it off. She'd better get going if she wasn't going to make a habit of being late for work, she realised with a stab of panic.

She was still gathering her strength to throw the duvet off when Graham pushed the door open with his foot, holding a cup of tea in one hand and an envelope in the other.

'Why didn't you wake me?' she demanded.

'You needed your sleep.' His voice was firm.

'But I'll be late!'

Graham put the tea down on her bedside table. 'The world won't come to an end if you *are*, Fran. You always put in extra hours. No one will mind if you're a bit late.'

She closed her eyes in exasperation. Graham meant well, but he was far more laid back than she when it came to time-keeping. He might not be late to his own funeral, as the saying went, but he had certainly been late to several other people's—knowing full well that they wouldn't start without him.

'Drink your tea,' he said. 'I have something to show you.'

There was a note in his voice which quelled her protest before it rose to her lips. Graham was serious, and if she wasn't mistaken, he was upset.

'What is it?' she asked apprehensively. 'Bad news?'

He gave her a wry, reassuring smile. 'Actually, it's *good* news. Or at least *I* think so.'

'What?'

'Heather is coming home for Christmas after all.'

'But that's wonderful!' She sat up quickly, almost knocking her tea over. 'How do you know? Did she phone while I was sleeping?'

Graham waved the envelope in his hand. 'She's written.'

'A *letter*?' Frances couldn't recall the last time they'd had an actual letter from Heather. It had been years—probably not since she was at school. Communication since then had always been in the form of phone calls or e-mails. Frances wasn't even sure she would recognise Heather's handwriting. 'I suppose she's split up with the new American chap and she's coming home to recover,' she guessed.

'Not quite right,' said Graham. 'On either count.'

Frances put out her hand for the letter, but Graham withheld it. Instead he handed her a photo. 'Brace yourself,' he warned. 'The chap isn't... well, he isn't exactly what you might have expected. And they haven't split up.'

Frances was unable to absorb what she was seeing. Heather, in a bedraggled-looking lace dress, clasping an equally bedraggled bunch of flowers. The man who stood next to her, his arm protectively round her shoulders, was tall and skinny and wore a tie-dyed t-shirt. His thinning hair was grey, long and braided into a pair of meagre, greasy plaits which hung halfway down his chest. And his thin forearm, which reached across to clasp Heather's free hand, was adorned with a colourful tattoo of a green-scaled, red-eyed dragon. With his weathered, seamed—one might even say wrinkled—face, and his wispy, drooping grey moustache, he looked to be closer to sixty than fifty. Old enough to be her father; older, certainly, than her parents. 'His name is Zack, it would seem,' Graham said dryly.

'Zack.' Frances' mind was still a blank.

Graham held the letter up and read from it. '"We're coming home for Christmas, so you can meet him. I know you'll love him, Daddy, just like I do."'

'Heather loves an ageing hippie called Zack,' Frances said, trying to take it in. Then she realised something else. 'She said "Daddy". She didn't write to both of us, then?' She knew that Heather had always been closer to her father, but she couldn't help a fleeting twinge of jealousy.

He smiled apologetically. 'She thought you'd be upset. She wanted me to break it to you gently. To show you the photo, then tell you.'

'Tell me what, exactly?' Her first—unwelcome—thought was that Heather was pregnant. But as soon as the words were out of her mouth, Frances knew. This was no ordinary photo: it was a wedding photo. The lace dress. The flowers. 'They've got married, haven't they? Oh God. They're married.'

'Last week, apparently.'

Why didn't Graham seem surprised? Suspicion assailed Frances. 'Did you know anything about this before?'

'Well, not exactly.' Graham didn't look at her. 'But she'd sent me a few e-mails mentioning Zack. She sort of hinted at it.'

'Oh, great. And you didn't tell me.'

'You've had other worries on your mind,' he reminded her.

'That doesn't mean I wouldn't want to know about my daughter—my only daughter—getting married to an old man she's known for five minutes.' Again she put her hand out. 'Can I read the letter?'

Graham sat down on the edge of the bed. 'I'll read you bits of it.'

'All right,' she conceded.

'"We're so happy. I never knew what true happiness was until now. Zack is older than I am, and he's been married before, but he is so wise and so good. Now everything is right. So right—you just can't imagine, Daddy. But I know you'll understand."'

'Why does she think *you'll* understand?' Frances demanded.

He ignored her and went on. '"Yes, I realise that we haven't known each other long, but when the right person comes along, you just *know*. Mum might have a hard time with this. I know she's always had a clear idea of the sort of man she wanted for me, and Zack is nothing like that. There's the age difference, of course, and he's not a Christian—he's a pagan, and our wedding was a druid ceremony. I'm sure she'll be disappointed in me, and upset that you weren't invited to the wedding. I don't want her to disapprove. Please try to help her understand. I want you both to love Zack. He's the best thing that's ever happened to me."'

Frances sighed. 'What else?'

'"He is a vegan, of course, and I have become one as well. So Christmas lunch will be a bit different this year! I'll send Mum a recipe for nut loaf."'

'Oh, great.'

Graham pulled a face, then said, 'And there's one more thing, Fran.'

'Tell me.' Her heart sank at his tone.

'"In case you think we got married because I was pregnant, Daddy, I can assure you that I'm not. In fact, we won't be having children at all. Zack had a vasectomy about thirty years ago, after his first wife had her fourth baby. I hope you don't mind."'

No grandchildren, then. Frances' eyes pricked with tears, for herself and for Graham. 'Does it bother you?' she asked.

Graham turned the letter over in his hands, looking thoughtful. 'I suppose if I'm honest, Fran, I'm a bit disappointed. I would really have liked to have grandchildren one day.'

'Well, I wouldn't rule that out.' Frances gave a bitter laugh; if she didn't laugh, she knew she would cry. 'The one good thing is that, at his age, he won't live forever. When he pops his clogs, she'll still be young enough to have babies with someone else.' Her laughter bubbled over into hysteria, and she collapsed back onto the pillows, unable to stop. Tears ran down her cheeks; still she laughed.

It was infectious, of course, and Graham joined in. The letter fell to the floor and they clung together, both shaking with mirth.

⁂

Neville rang Cowley on his mobile. 'Where are you now, Sid?'

'At the station. In your office. Where are *you*?'

'On my way.' That was a slight exaggeration. He ran back to his flat, changed into dry clothes, and equipped himself with an umbrella.

Cowley was indeed in Neville's office. Sitting at Neville's desk, in fact, and eating a greasy bacon sandwich.

Again Neville's stomach did a flip-flop. 'Ugh, how could you?' he groaned. 'After that vindaloo?'

'That was hours ago.' Cowley grinned cheerfully, seeming none the worse for wear.

Neville threw the newspaper, now thoroughly wet, on the desk. 'Well, what now?' he asked, though he knew the answer as well as Cowley did.

'We'll have to arrest her,' said Cowley, stuffing the last bite of his sandwich into his mouth and reaching for his cigarettes.

Yes, they would have to arrest her. They had no other option at this point. 'But first we have to get the go-ahead from Evans,' Neville pointed out. 'And I'm the one who's going to have to tell him,' he added, almost to himself. 'Unless he's already seen it.' He didn't know which would be worse; on the whole he preferred not to have to break the news himself, though Lilith Noone's words were seared on his memory: 'It is a week today since Jonah Adimola was brutally murdered, and the police seem no closer than ever to making an arrest, this in spite of the fact that he was strangled with a garment which belonged to the radical feminist priest, the Reverend Frances Cherry, with whom Adimola had a public row just a short time before his murder.' A garment, he thought: made it sound like she'd strangled him with her knickers. God, what a genius that wretched Noone woman was! She'd managed to land them deep in the brown stuff, all right, and make it sound even worse than it was.

'Better you than me, Guv.' Cowley struck a match on the scarred wood of Neville's desk and inhaled as the flame caught.

Neville looked at the clock. Evans might be in his office by now, or on the way. At any rate, his efficient and admirable secretary would probably be at her desk. He picked up the phone and rang her extension. 'Neville Stewart,' he identified himself. 'Is he in yet? I need to see him, urgently.'

'The *Globe*,' she guessed. 'I read it on the Tube.' She sighed regretfully and went on. 'I'm sorry, Inspector Stewart, but he's not in. And he's not likely to be in for a few more hours, at least.'

'But it's Tuesday,' Neville said stupidly. Why would Evans not be at his desk on a Tuesday morning?

'It's his wife,' she explained. 'She's gone into labour. Prematurely, apparently. He's with her at the hospital. They've been there since half past two this morning.'

'Oh, Lord.'

She anticipated his next question. 'And he's not reachable. You know how hospitals are when it comes to mobile phones.'

Neville did know. 'So what are we supposed to do? It's urgent,' he repeated.

'If he rings in at some point, I'll tell him to get in touch,' she promised. 'It's the best I can do.'

Cowley had been listening to one side of the conversation with interest. 'So what's up?' he asked when Neville had put the phone down.

Neville told him. 'We can't do it without his say-so,' he finished. 'Not unless we're prepared for him to have our guts for garters. So I suppose that means we cool our heels for a bit, until the lovely Denise gets round to presenting him with the latest Evans sprog.'

'That could be hours,' Cowley pointed out. 'Days, even. My sister, she was in labour for forty-seven hours.'

'Oh, great,' Neville groaned. 'I suppose we'd just better hope that this baby is in a big hurry to be born.'

Cowley dragged on his cigarette and twisted his mouth into a grin. 'Poor little bastard. When he sees his father's ugly mug, he'll probably want to turn round and go back where he came from.'

∽♦∽ ∽♦∽ ∽♦∽

Callie spent the morning with Brian, whose fortnightly turn it was to take assembly at the local primary school. This time, he told her, she would observe and assist. Next time she could do the lion's share of it, while he watched her. And the time after that, she would be on her own. School assemblies, he made it clear, were a curate's province, freeing up the vicar for more important parochial responsibilities. What those responsibilities might be, he didn't say.

At lunch-time she hurried home to Bella. The heavy rain, early on, had prevented more than a token walk first thing in the morning, but the rain had eventually given way to watery sunshine and she was anxious to take her for an extended walk while she had the chance.

They headed for the park, where Callie was glad to see that only a few of the leaves had come down in the storm. Under the new-washed sky the rest seemed, all at once, to have transformed themselves, flaunting shades of ochre, crimson, russet, copper, lemon and lime in numberless combinations, unique as snowflakes.

Even as a child, Callie had looked forward to autumn, the start of the academic year, with its promise of new beginnings. She'd loved all its trappings: crisp new apples tucked in new lunch-boxes, pristine new exercise books, and new pencils, freshly sharpened, in shiny new pencil tins. Though she knew that autumn was the winding-down season of the year, sliding toward winter, to her it had always been an exhilarating time.

After the daytime warmth of the past few weeks, in the wake of the storm it seemed suddenly colder, with a definite autumnal nip in the air. That didn't seem to bother Bella, who trotted along quite happily, sniffing all the interesting scents which the rain had brought out. But Callie found, after a while, that her fingers were getting cold. And when she turned toward home, she saw that a black cloud had bubbled up behind her, looking more ominous by the minute.

She didn't have an umbrella: a mistake, she knew, as the first fat drops pelted down.

They weren't all that far from the council flats where the Harringtons lived, and on impulse Callie started off in that direction at a brisk walk, Bella trotting along eagerly at her side. She was already quite wet when Dennis opened the door. 'Well!' he said. 'You look like a drowned rat, girl. Come on in and dry off. I'll put the kettle on.'

'I've got my dog with me. I hope you don't mind.'

Dennis bent over, creakily, and fondled Bella's ears. 'No, I don't mind. I like dogs. I didn't know you had one.'

'I've only had her for two days.'

'I used to have a dog myself,' he said, straightening up. 'When I was just a lad. A little terrier, he was. Name of Spot. I suppose you can guess why.' Dennis chuckled. 'In them days, dogs had names like that. Spot, Blackie, Rex, Prince, Daisy. *Dog* names. Not like nowadays, when you hear people calling their dogs "Henry" and "Cynthia" and such like.'

'Her name is Bella,' Callie told him with pride. 'It's Italian for "beautiful".'

'She is that,' he acknowledged. He led her through to the lounge, which was empty and chill, and switched on a bar of the electric fire. 'That'll warm you a bit,' he said. 'That, and a good cup of tea.'

'Is Elsie…'

'Not so good today,' Dennis admitted. 'Had one of her bad turns this morning, did my Elsie. The doctor came out and all. Said that bed rest was what she wanted.'

'Oh, then perhaps I'd better go,' Callie said.

'Not at all, girl.' He shook his head vigourously. 'She's doing what the doctor ordered—sleeping. And I'm glad of the company, to tell you the truth.'

He made tea for both of them and brought it through to the lounge. Callie accepted it with gratitude, while Bella sat decorously at her feet.

'I was watching the telly a bit ago,' Dennis said. 'Saw on the news as our Area Dean is going to be Bishop of Brixton.'

'Leo?' Callie exclaimed. 'That's great!'

'You know him, then?'

'Not very well,' she confessed. 'I've met him once or twice.'

Dennis tapped the side of his nose. 'I suppose they put it on the telly because he's… you know. Black. There aren't many black bishops, are there, and I reckon the Church wants everyone to know that we're moving with the times.'

'He's a good man,' Callie said stoutly. 'My friend Frances Cherry thinks the world of him.'

'Ah, now.' Dennis put down his tea cup. 'Would that be the Frances Cherry we've been reading about in the papers?'

Callie sighed; she should have known that Dennis would read the *Globe*. 'On Saturday, yes. But you mustn't believe everything you read in the papers.'

'Oh, I meant today's paper, girl.'

'Today?'

'I think it's in the bedroom.' He got up and tiptoed from the room, returning half a minute later with a tabloid. 'Right here,' he indicated, opening it and pointing. 'Sure sounds to me like she's involved with that murder. Bad business, that. Doesn't do the Church no good for priests to go round killing one other.'

'Frances had nothing to do with it!' Callie said sharply as she reached for the paper.

'How can you be sure?' He shook his head. 'Mind, I'm not saying you're wrong, girl, but in my experience, there's no smoke without fire.'

༺༺༺ ༺༺༺ ༺༺༺

Lilith read the press release about Leo Jackson's appointment with great interest. Religious affairs—other than in the strictly literal sense, as in 'Vicar Bonks Organist's Wife'—were not usually the province of the *Globe*. But what a fantastic story she could write about this—nothing, she was sure, that any of the other papers would do. Already she could visualise the headline: 'New Black Bishop Linked to Priest's Murder.'

Great stuff—and it would show that supercilious bastard what happened when you crossed Lilith Noone. She hadn't imagined that her opportunity for revenge would come quite so soon, and in this form. Almost a gift from God, she decided, smiling to herself.

She sketched something out on her computer, then decided that she'd better run it by her editor. E-mail was the most efficient way to do that, so she sent the first draft off to him and worked on polishing and expanding it until she received his reply.

'I don't think so,' he said tersely. 'Not our kind of story.'

Lilith was stunned and incensed. Not our kind of story? What did he mean? True, the other papers probably wouldn't touch it with a barge pole, but the *Globe* never backed away from stories because they were a bit controversial, or teetering on the brink of libel or good taste. That was their speciality, for God's sake.

She picked up the phone and rang him.

'It's a great story,' he said in a conciliatory voice. 'But I just don't think we want to go there. Not at the moment.'

A nasty suspicion struck her. 'It's because he's black, isn't it? The race card, and all that.'

He didn't deny it. 'It's speculative, that's all. And negative.'

'Everything we do is negative,' she said bluntly.

'I disagree. We've been building up a lot of sympathy in the black community with your articles about the murdered African priest. That's the sort of thing we want, Lilith. A black victim, and the system doesn't care. As long as it's the system—and the police—that we keep pressurising, everyone will be happy.'

'But…'

'Your pieces have been great up till now. Just right. Give me another one like that for tomorrow, and I'll print it gladly.'

It was not what she wanted to hear. She slammed the phone down. What on earth was she going to write about?

⌘⌘⌘

Frances checked the list of new hospital admissions. When anyone put 'C of E' as their religious preference on their admission form, she liked to pay a quick call on them and offer them the opportunity to receive the sacrament, or just to talk.

It was a bit of a nonsense, really. Most people who weren't actively something else—Roman Catholic, Baptist, Muslim—put down 'C of E', and very few of them had any interest or involvement whatever in the Church. Almost all were the 'hatch, match and dispatch' sort of Anglicans, who liked the Church to be there at significant moments in their lives, but didn't want it to impinge otherwise. Still, even amongst the majority of nominal Anglicans there were those who considered their hospitalisation to *be* a significant moment, warranting the presence of a priest. Perhaps they were dying, or perhaps they were frightened, or lonely.

Many sent her away, of course; it was those who didn't who were often her most satisfying and rewarding contacts. After all, she'd first met Callie Anson at the bedside of her dying father.

Her first 'cold call' of the afternoon turned out to be a middle-aged man facing a major operation. He had no family, seemingly no friends, and he was terrified. He wasn't interested in the sacrament, but he did want to talk.

An hour later, with the promise of a visit the next day, Frances moved on. This time it was an elderly woman, also alone. She'd been passing the time with magazines and newspapers, which were strewn about her bed, and received Frances with scepticism.

'I'm not really a church-goer,' she warned. 'Christmas and Easter, if I'm lucky. You won't want to talk to me, I reckon.'

'It doesn't matter,' Frances assured her. 'I just wanted you to know that I'm here, if you do want to talk.'

'I don't hold much with women priests,' the woman said frankly.

Frances' smile didn't waver. It wasn't the first time she'd heard that, and sometimes it was stated far more bluntly and hurtfully. She'd visited people who refused to receive the sacrament from her, who demanded to see one of her male colleagues instead—a 'real' priest, as they usually put it. 'Well,' she said, 'if you'd rather talk to someone else, I can arrange that.'

'Wait a minute.' The woman stared at her, narrowing her eyes. 'You're that Frances Cherry, aren't you?'

'Yes, I'm Frances Cherry.'

The woman's hand scrabbled amongst the pile of reading material on her bed. 'The one in the *Globe*.'

Now her smile felt fixed, artificial. 'I was mentioned, yes. A few days ago.'

'Today!' said the woman as she triumphantly retrieved the tabloid. 'It says, near enough, that you killed that black man. If it's true, why haven't the police arrested you? What are you doing *here*, when you should be in gaol?'

Frances' mouth went dry with shock. She put out her hand for the paper, but the woman withheld it, clutching it to her chest. For a moment they were frozen like that, staring at each other, then Frances turned and fled.

⁂

Marigold came home from an afternoon of shopping, feeling more like herself than she had for some time; retail therapy always did the trick for her, and it was a shame she hadn't tried it days ago. New shoes, new bed-linens, and a fashionable new winter coat had been purchased and would be delivered in a day or two.

She would be going back out later for a bridge evening, so she'd asked the daily to prepare a light supper for her and Vincent.

They ate in the dining room, the table properly laid, though it was only cold: smoked chicken breast, salad, and fruit.

'Have you had a good day?' she asked dutifully.

Vincent, facing her across the table, shook his head. 'The Bishop still hasn't done a thing about getting me some help. I just can't keep up this pace, Marigold. And a church with the importance and prominence of St Mary the Virgin—it's just not right.'

She made soothing noises.

'It's because we're High, you know,' he went on.

Marigold nodded. She'd heard it all before.

'If we were some lower-than-the-floorboards Evangelical lot, or flaming liberals, they'd be falling all over themselves to sort it out.'

She spooned some chutney onto her plate. One of Vincent's adoring churchwomen had made it, and it was really rather good. Better than store-bought—even Fortnum's.

Vincent was working himself up to a rant. 'And speaking of flaming liberals, to add insult to injury, they've gone and made that Leo Jackson a bishop! Bishop of Brixton, if you please!'

'Did I know that?' She frowned, trying to remember.

'It's only just been announced, today. I heard it on the news.'

Marigold said what was expected of her. 'That's appalling.'

'Appalling is the word. And unfair! He's much younger than I am, he hasn't been ordained as long. He wasn't even born in this country!'

'It's because he's black,' she pointed out. 'You wouldn't *want* to be Bishop of Brixton. Bishop of Kensington, maybe, but not Brixton.'

He scowled at her, in one of those moods where he was not prepared to listen to reason. 'That's beside the point! They've had plenty of chances to give me preferment, if they'd wanted to. But again and again, I've been passed over, because of my Churchmanship. It's out-and-out discrimination, I tell you! These days you have to be a wishy-washy liberal to get any-where in the Church. You have to overlook the abomination of women so-called priests, for a starter. They promised, when they passed that lamentable act, that we traditionalists wouldn't be discriminated against. But they lied about that, like they've lied about so many other things. We few who hold to the true faith of the Church are the ones who have been marginalised and ignored.'

'I'm sure you're not being ignored,' she tried to soothe him. It was the wrong thing to say.

'Just name one traditionalist, one member of Forward in Faith, who's been promoted! You can't, can you?'

Marigold sighed to herself, relieved that she was going out.

Before she left, an hour later, she put her head round the door of Vincent's study to let him know she was going. His back was to her; he was on the phone. The Bishop again, she supposed—bothering him at home, most likely. That was certain to endear him to the Bishop and the Church hierarchy.

'Vincent? My taxi's here, so I'm off now. I shouldn't be too late.'

He put the phone down quickly and spun round. 'All right, dear,' he said heartily. 'Have fun.'

⁐⁐⁐

One week. It was almost impossible to believe, thought Callie as she laid the table, that exactly a week ago she'd been working herself up into a stew before the Deanery Clergy Chapter meeting. Looking at herself in the mirror, worrying about facing Adam for the first time.

With everything that had happened since, that had faded into insignificance.

A man was dead, and Frances… It just didn't bear thinking about, the agony her friend was going through at the moment.

And tonight Mark was coming back, yet again. To see Bella, of course, she reminded herself. He'd said that it wasn't fair for her to feed him for a second evening in a row, and had insisted that he would cook for her instead. He would bring the ingredients and the wine; all she had to do was lay the table.

He arrived on time, greeted Callie warmly and Bella effusively, then opened the wine, pouring two generous glasses. 'You can relax in the sitting room and drink it,' he said, 'or you can keep me company in the kitchen.'

She followed him toward the kitchen, Bella at her heels. 'If that won't distract you.'

'Believe it or not, I can cook and talk at the same time. As long as I don't step on Bella.'

Callie leaned against a counter and watched him as he skilfully and rapidly chopped an onion, then scooped it into a saucepan with a glug of olive oil. 'Who taught you to cook like this?' she asked, impressed.

'*La mia mamma, naturalmente,*' he said lightly. 'She's the best cook in the world. *La migliora cuora.* Bar none. I told you my parents have a restaurant. *Un ristorante.*'

'Yes, of course. We saw it. La Venezia.' She added shyly, 'Maybe we could go there some time.'

'Perhaps.' He opened a tin of plum tomatoes and ran the knife through them. 'Unless you can get fresh ones, in season, these tinned ones make the best sauce,' he told her. 'You have to use good Italian ones, of course.'

'Are we having pasta?'

'We are.' Mark went to one of the bags he'd brought and pulled out a flat box. 'I would have made my own, but I didn't have time.'

'You make your own pasta?' She really was impressed.

'It's not difficult. I'll show you some time.'

'Great. I'd like that.'

'My mum made this,' he confessed. 'I begged it off her.' He opened the box to show Callie.

The pasta was, she thought, almost too pretty to eat: little nests of creamy-coloured noodles, still soft, curled in twin rows.

'Oh, yum.' The onion was throwing off a most delectable smell, and her mouth was beginning to water.

Mark took a sip of his wine, then started snipping fresh herbs with her kitchen scissors.

Callie took a rather larger sip of hers, seeking courage. She had something she needed to say to him, and it was going to require all of the bravery she could muster. And the longer she waited, the more difficult it would be.

'Listen, Marco,' she said tentatively. 'Can I ask you about something?'

'Sure.' He turned to grin at her. 'As I said before, I can cook and talk at the same time.' His grin widened, and he winked. 'Unless you're going to ask me for my mum's secret recipe for the best pasta sauce in the world. Then my lips are sealed.'

She gave him a weak smile, then plunged in. 'I know I don't have any business asking you this.'

'Now you have me worried.'

'It's my friend Frances. Frances Cherry.'

She had his attention. For a moment he paused, before deliberately turning back to his snipping. 'Yes?' he said neutrally.

Callie couldn't stop now, and it came out all in a rush. 'I know it's not your department or anything. And you couldn't really tell me if it was. But I just thought you might have heard something. She's terribly upset. I rang her this afternoon, and she was crying. There was a story in the *Globe* today. She's sure that she's going to be arrested. For a murder she had nothing to do with.' She found, to her horror, that she was on the brink of tears herself.

Mark put the scissors down and turned to face her. 'It *isn't* my department,' he said, unsmiling now. 'I don't know anything about that case. Not officially.'

'I'm sorry. I shouldn't have asked. I'm just so worried about Frances, and I didn't know where else to turn.'

'It's good of you to be so worried about your friend.'

'Frances…' Callie searched for the words to explain. 'She's more than a friend to me. She's been my mentor. My inspiration. At times she's been more like a mother to me than my own mother. I'd do anything to help her.'

Mark studied her for a moment, then nodded, as if making his mind up. 'I'll see what I can find out,' he conceded. 'I can't make any promises, obviously, but I know one or two people who might tell me something. Given the proper incentive, that is.'

'Oh, Marco! That's so kind! Thank you so much.' She tried to smile, and started crying instead.

'Now, now.' He took a step forward and folded her in a comforting hug.

Callie assumed he would have done the same for any friend in distress, but that didn't stop her from enjoying it, in spite of the circumstances.

Chapter Fifteen

Wednesday morning's *Globe* was the first issue for several days in which no by-lined piece by Lilith Noone appeared. Leo's appointment was noted in one small and noncommittal paragraph buried deep on an inside page, bearing the alliterative headline 'Black Bishop for Brixton'.

Other newspapers gave more coverage to the appointment, quoting liberally from the press release and running the official photos. In fact, Leo's phone had begun to ring immediately after the announcement, with journalists anxious to set up interviews, in addition to friends and colleagues congratulating him.

Every time the phone rang he'd reached for it, his heart lurching with hope. So many people ringing. But none of them were the only person he really wanted to talk to: Oliver.

On Wednesday, though, he awoke early and with renewed hope. Surely Oliver would ring him today. And in the mean time, he had a very busy day ahead of him. The religious affairs correspondents for the *Times* and the *Telegraph* were coming to interview him first thing in the morning, one after the other, before his weekly meeting with the Archdeacon. The *Church Times* were planning an extensive feature, and were sending someone in the afternoon. Even the *Guardian*, not ordinarily known for their religious coverage, were interested in Leo because of his reputation as an activist for liberal causes, and their reporter was coming at tea-time.

The postman brought the first trickle of congratulatory letters from quick-off-the-mark well-wishers, and more were sure to follow over the next few days. Answering them, if only with no more than a brief acknowledgement, was going to keep him busy, Leo realised, bemused. His life had changed, and there was no going back now.

Still, every phone call engendered that rush of adrenaline, that upsurge of hope. Oliver *would* ring. He *must*.

⌒◌⌒◌⌒◌

In the wake of Tuesday's sensational story, various people went out early to buy the *Globe*, fearing even more unwelcome revelations by Lilith Noone. Frances and Graham, Callie, Neville Stewart and Sid Cowley, and even Marigold Underwood breathed sighs of relief that not a word was said about Jonah Adimola's murder: no more dramatic disclosures, no sly innuendo about anyone's involvement or the police's deficiencies.

Lilith Noone, it would seem, had run out of steam.

Lilith herself was, of course, the one person who was not happy about this development. In fact, she was profoundly depressed by it.

It hardly seemed worth getting out of bed, she felt. Why should she? She was washed up. Finished. She'd staked her reputation on this story, and it had fizzled out. The police hadn't risen to the bait. Nothing had happened; no arrest had been made. There was no where else for her to go.

She wrapped the duvet more closely round her, shivering. The room seemed chillier. Perhaps, Lilith told herself, she was coming down with something. Her head was throbbing, and was her throat sore? She must be developing a nasty cold.

Bed-rest was what she needed. She'd been working so hard lately that she hadn't been taking proper care of herself.

If only there were someone else here to bring her a cup of tea. But she was alone—quite alone.

Feeling thoroughly sorry for herself, Lilith reached for the bedside phone and rang the receptionist at the *Globe*. She wouldn't be coming into the offices today, she said. She was quite poorly, sickening with something. It might be days before she was well enough to come in.

Her efforts to go back to sleep were not successful. Someone in the flat upstairs was taking a shower, and the pipes were making a dreadful racket. And the state of her bedroom was beginning to oppress her. To put it bluntly, it was a tip; in the past few days, when she'd been working flat out on the Jonah Adimola story, it had crossed the line from being merely untidy to being a disaster area. Discarded clothes lay on the floor in piles, where she'd stepped out of them, and drawers were pulled half-open, spilling over with lacy, frilly bits. Every flat surface held dirty tea cups and coffee mugs, plates with crusts and crumbs. On the evidence, she'd been living on caffeine and adrenaline, with just a bit of toast to keep body and soul together. It was no wonder she was ill.

And she was hungry. Feed a cold, she told herself. She struggled out of bed, rooting on the floor for her dressing gown. It was under a layer of clothes from yesterday, and her slippers proved even more elusive. 'Oh, forget it,' she muttered crossly, padding barefoot to the tiny kitchen.

It was definitely colder than yesterday, Lilith realised, and not just because she was ill. She hadn't switched the heating on; there was a real chill in the air, and her feet were freezing on the uncarpeted kitchen floor. She pulled her dressing gown round her and shivered as the kettle took its time to boil. The bread was beginning to go mouldy, she discovered, and the biscuit tin was empty. Desperate, she scraped and picked the green mould from the least-affected slice of bread and popped it in the toaster, holding her hands over it to warm them.

She wasn't surprised to find that the milk had gone off. The old bottle in the fridge had actually coagulated into solid lumps, and the newer one had been left out on the counter—for how long?—and smelt sour. She couldn't cope with milkless tea, so it would have to be black coffee. Not the best thing for a cold, she was sure.

Lilith put the coffee and toast on a tray and took them back to her bed. After consuming them, she wished she hadn't, not least because the coffee gave her heartburn and the toast left crumbs in the bed.

Maybe she should get up and watch some daytime television, like a lady of leisure.

Finding her slippers this time, she went through into the other room—the room with her computer, the television, and other accoutrements for living and working. She was dismayed to find that it was in no better shape than the bedroom. More dirty cups and mugs and plates, and untidy stacks of papers and books rather than piles of clothes. But at least it was warmer, or it would be once she'd switched on the electric fire. Shoving some things aside to make space to sit on the sofa, she deployed the remote control.

Morning television, she soon discovered, was even grimmer than she'd imagined. On BBC 1, loudmouthed designers were taking an ugly house and transforming it into an even uglier one. BBC 2 was given over to children's programming; unidentifiable creatures in primary colours romped round the screen, speaking in high-pitched voices. On ITV, a woman with a shaved head and a bad attitude—almost worse than her grammar—was pouring out her heart to a seemingly sympathetic host and being heckled by the studio audience. Switching to Channel 4, her last hope, she found the home of educational broadcasting. If she'd wanted to know the basics of contract law, she would have been in luck.

Wishing she had cable, Lilith switched back to ITV, and in spite of herself got involved in the woman's story. Yes, she'd slept with her mother's boyfriend, she admitted. And she'd sold one of her mother's rings to finance a dirty weekend with said boyfriend. But they were in love. Didn't that make it all right? Her mother didn't like that ring much and probably wouldn't even miss it. Besides, what her mother didn't know wouldn't hurt her.

She appeared surprised when it was pointed out to her by an astute member of the audience that it was likely her mother would now find out.

In fact, it seemed that the programme makers were a step ahead of her. The mother was backstage, watching on closed-circuit. And the two-timing boyfriend was in a separate room, also watching. Just as the host was about to reveal this fact to the hapless woman, and usher one or both of the other parties onto the stage, Lilith's phone rang.

'Oh, bloody hell,' she said, grabbing it with one hand and turning down the volume with the other.

'Lilith Noone? Sorry to bother you,' said a diffident voice— young, male. 'The receptionist said that you were at home today, not feeling well.'

'That's right.' On the telly, the mother had run out onto the stage, her face contorted with rage. She made as if to grab her daughter's hair, then seemingly realising that she was not possessed of any, she took a swing at her instead—and missed. Burly guards stepped out and pinned her arms but she wriggled away from them just as the boyfriend approached from the other side.

'She didn't want to give me your home number,' he admitted. 'But I told her it was important.'

Wretched woman, Lilith thought—she'd tear a strip off her the next time she saw her. Did 'sick' no longer have any meaning?

The boyfriend had more hair than the daughter. Lots more, flowing down over his biker jacket, blending with his scraggly beard. His wronged lover seized him by the beard and pulled him onto the floor, pummelling him with her fists.

'I'm really not well,' Lilith protested. 'I hope to be back at work tomorrow. Can I take your number and ring you then? Or perhaps you could speak to someone else at the paper.'

The daughter launched herself from her chair and entered the fray. She went for an easy target: her mother's prominent eyebrow ring, which she grabbed and twisted.

'It's important,' the young man repeated. 'And I won't talk to anyone at the *Globe* but you.'

The mother screamed, blood running down into her eye. She elbowed her daughter in her ample stomach, then kneed the recumbent boyfriend in the groin.

Lilith could read their lips clearly, but imagined that if the volume had been audible, she would have heard little but bleeps: it was, after all, nearly twelve hours before the watershed.

He was persistent, you had to give him that. 'What is it in regards to, if you don't mind me asking?'

'I'd rather not say over the phone. I need to see you,' he said politely but firmly. 'Today. In private.'

Lilith sighed. Then a niggle of excitement, some sort of instinct, kicked in and she switched off the television, giving him her whole attention. 'Does this by any chance have to do with Jonah Adimola's murder?' she demanded. 'Is that why you need to talk to *me*?'

'Well, not exactly,' he said. 'But it has to do with someone associated with it.'

Now she was truly engaged. 'Who is that?'

'Leo Jackson,' said the young man softly. 'The new Bishop of Brixton.'

Lilith's eyes narrowed; her heart beat faster. 'Where shall we meet?'

'Can I come to you at home? This afternoon, perhaps? I could come after three.'

She looked round the flat. Well, it couldn't be helped. 'Yes,' she said. 'Come after three. As soon as you can get here.' She gave him the address.

'I'll see you, then.'

When he'd hung up, she sat for a moment with the remote slack in her hand, intrigued and excited. Then she remembered what she'd been doing, and turned the telly back on. The credits were rolling; the injured parties were nowhere to be seen. Now she would never know.

※ ※ ※

Frances rang Callie during her morning break. 'It's been ages since we've seen each other,' she pointed out. 'I know you're very busy, but could we get together one day, even if it's just for a coffee?'

Callie mentally checked her diary, feeling a bit guilty. She'd been thinking about Frances a great deal, and had spoken to her almost daily, but her free time had been absorbed by Bella... and Mark. She *must* make time for Frances. Especially now, when Frances had so much on her mind. So much hanging over her head. 'I have a staff meeting with Brian tomorrow morning,' she said. 'But I'm free at lunch time.'

'Shall we meet up then? You name a place.'

Bella would need to be walked. 'Why don't you come here?' Callie suggested.

'I don't want to put you to any trouble.'

'I won't go to any trouble,' she assured her. 'I'll pick up some sandwiches, and heat some soup.'

'Sounds great,' Frances agreed. 'I'll see you about one tomorrow, if that's all right with you.'

'That will be wonderful. Besides,' Callie added, 'you haven't met Bella yet. You have to meet Bella.'

'I'll look forward to that.'

Callie hesitated for a moment. 'How are you feeling today? About... you know.'

'Nothing in the *Globe* this morning.' Frances gave a shaky laugh. 'Which was a great relief. And no police knocking on the door. So I suppose I would describe myself as cautiously hopeful.'

⌘⌘⌘

Neville was frustrated but resigned. A whole day lost: Evans hadn't even bothered to ring him, and twenty-four hours later there was as yet no word. Denise, it would seem, was still in labour. Eventually, though, there would have to be a resolution to the situation. The baby would come, dead or alive, sooner or later.

In the mean time, Neville applied himself to clearing his desk of accumulated paperwork. He began to read through all the interview notes, hoping that something he'd missed would jump out at him, something that would suddenly make everything crystal clear.

He didn't need Sid Cowley at this point, finding his presence a distraction rather than a help, so he'd sent him off to talk to a hysterical American tourist whose wallet had been lifted from her handbag during the Changing of the Guard outside of Buckingham Palace.

As lunch-time approached Neville began to flag, and welcomed the appearance of Mark Lombardi at his office door with more than usual enthusiasm.

'Are you busy, Nev?' Mark asked cautiously.

'Not at all.' He threw down the papers in his hand. 'How about getting some lunch?'

'Here?'

The station's catering didn't appeal to him at the moment, and he longed for a pint of Guinness. 'Let's go to the pub.'

'Sounds good to me,' Mark agreed.

When they got to the pub, and worked their way up to the bar, Neville's caution and good sense overcame his craving for Guinness. After all, Evans might reappear at any moment, and when that happened he would need all his wits about him. 'I'll have an orange juice,' he said with a grimace of regret.

'On the wagon?' Mark grinned at him, bemused.

'Let's say, on duty.'

Mark ordered a bottle of Peroni and they glanced at the menu. It didn't require more than a glance; the menu was a modest one, and reassuringly unchanging.

'Steak and kidney,' Neville said. 'And chips.'

'Fish and chips,' Mark decided.

'You're not going for the spag bol, then?' Neville teased.

Mark shuddered. 'Not on your life.'

Someone was just vacating a table, so they appropriated it quickly.

'I thought you'd be up to your ears in that murder,' Mark said, pouring his beer.

Neville looked at it enviously, though he'd never even fancied trying that watery Italian lager that Mark liked. What was the point of drinking something you could see through? Something that, not to put too fine a point on it, looked like pee? Probably tasted like it, as well. 'Well, I am, in a manner of speaking. But the lovely Denise has given me an unexpected breather.' He explained about Evans' unavailability.

'So that means you haven't arrested Frances Cherry?' Mark asked carefully.

'Not yet. Not till Evans gives the go-ahead.'

'But you *will* arrest her.' It was a statement rather than a question.

'I don't think we have much choice, to be frank.' Neville shook his head. 'And I'm sure that Evans will agree with me, given the position we've been put in by the *Globe*.'

Mark leaned back in his chair and took a sip of his beer. 'Do you think she did it?'

'I'm not sure,' he admitted. 'Let's put it this way. There isn't anyone else in the picture at the moment. And as Lilith Noone so helpfully pointed out, it *was* her… umm… "garment" round his neck.'

'What sort of garment are we talking about here? Something frilly and unmentionable?'

Neville laughed. 'Good Lord, no. Far from it. The opposite, in fact. Something liturgical—I think that's the proper term. It's been a long time since my days as an altar boy.'

'The mind boggles.'

'Anyway, why are you so interested?'

Mark looked away, studying the label on his beer bottle. 'I suppose I'd better confess, Nev. Someone I know… is rather worried about Frances Cherry.'

If he hadn't just been reading through the files, Neville might not have made the connection. 'Caroline Anson, isn't it? Callie? That curate. You said that you knew her.'

'That's right.' Still Mark studied the beer bottle. 'She's a friend.'

The penny dropped. 'Ah,' said Neville. '*That* kind of friend.'

Mark flushed. 'I don't know what you mean.'

'Oh, I reckon you do, mate,' Neville smirked. 'She's quite attractive, if I recall. A bit prim for my taste, in that black clerical get-up. But I dare say you could set me straight about that. Appearances can be deceiving.'

'I certainly couldn't set you straight,' snapped Mark. 'It isn't like that. We're just *friends*.'

'You don't fancy her, then?'

Mark was silent for more than a few seconds. 'To be honest,' he admitted, 'I do.'

'Well, then.'

'Well, what?'

'Go for it, man!' Neville put his glass down on the table with enough force to splash a few drops of orange juice on his jacket sleeve. 'She's not attached, is she? What's stopping you from taking things a step further?'

Again Mark was silent. 'I wouldn't just want that kind of meaningless fling,' he said at last. 'She'... well, she's special. Different. Not like any other woman I've ever met.'

This was, thought Neville, sounding serious. 'We're not talking the big "L" word here, are we, mate?' he probed.

Mark pressed his lips together and watched the bubbles rise in his beer glass. 'Could be. I haven't known her for very long, it's too soon to say, but... well. It could be. As I said, she's different. Special. And we get on so well together, it's like we've always known each other.'

'All the more reason to go for it, I would have thought,' Neville pointed out. 'You're not... well, you're not unattractive yourself, though it pains me to say it.' He grinned. 'I don't suppose she'd run a mile if you made a move on her.'

'It's just not that simple.' Mark's voice was quiet but firm.

Neville rolled his eyes. 'Tell me. Tell your Uncle Nev what is so damned complicated about it.'

At that moment their food arrived, and for a few minutes after that they applied themselves to it. But Neville wasn't about to let the subject go.

'What's so complicated?' he repeated. 'Okay, you respect her too much to have a meaningless fling. Then why not a relationship? A real, honest-to-God grown-up relationship?'

Mark speared a stray pea before it rolled off his plate. 'She's going to be a priest.'

'So what? I assume that priests are human beings under those dog collars. Though,' Neville added, 'judging from my experiences of Father Flynn and Father O'Malley, I'm not so sure about that after all.'

Mark smiled. 'An *Anglican* priest.'

'That should make it even easier. Anglican priests don't take vows of celibacy. Apparently they're allowed to be human,' said Neville thoughtfully. 'Most of the ones I've met on this case have been, more or less. Human, that is. Maybe that's the difference between them and the Catholics.'

'I *am* a Catholic,' Mark pointed out. 'Or at least, that's the way I was brought up. Like you, Nev. Mass every Sunday, and Holy Days of Obligation.'

'The Holy Father and I parted company a long time ago,' Neville said wryly.

'I still go to Mass when I can,' admitted Mark, as though he were confessing some shameful secret. 'Though it's not as often as my parents would like. My mum goes nearly every day, in fact. She practically runs the Italian church in Clerkenwell. Padre Luigi would be totally lost without her.'

Once again the penny dropped for Neville. 'So this is about your family, isn't it?'

Mark shrugged his shoulders. 'Can you imagine what my mum would say if I brought home a woman in a dog collar? It's bad enough that she's not Italian. But an Anglo, and an Anglican priest, all at once! A woman priest, for God's sake!'

'She might be more upset if you brought home a *male* priest.' Neville grinned provocatively. 'Even an Italian one.'

Mark roared with laughter. 'You're right about that, Nev.'

'Well then, mate.' Neville put his cutlery on his plate and his elbows on the table, looking directly at Mark to emphasise the importance of his words. 'Here's how I see it. What is it that your family want you to do?'

The reply was prompt. 'Marry a nice Italian girl. Have lots and lots of *bambini*. It's what they've always wanted.'

'And have you done it?'

'You know I haven't.'

'Well, then.'

Mark drew his brows together, puzzled. 'I don't see what you're getting at.'

'I'm just saying,' Neville elaborated, 'that for all these years you've known what your family wanted you to do, and you haven't done it. Haven't paid it a blind bit of notice, from what I've seen. So why, my friend, should you start worrying about it now?'

Neville could see that Mark was wavering, that he had no good answer for that one. He put on the broadest of Irish brogues. 'Listen to your Uncle Nev, me boy. Faith and begorrah, would he lead you astray?'

'Regularly,' Mark confirmed, laughing.

❦ ❦ ❦

Lilith was feeling much better, she discovered. She showered and dressed, then went down to the corner shop for fresh milk, fresh bread, a packet of ham, and a few other necessities. For lunch she made herself a ham sandwich, and afterward she set about tidying her flat—or at least the more public rooms—as it hadn't been tidied in weeks, if not months. She threw away a bin full of old newspapers and other rubbish; she washed up a mountain of stained mugs and food-encrusted plates. She even ran the hoover round and fluffed up the cushions on the sofa.

Her antennae were quivering. She didn't know what the young man—who had not given her his name—wanted to talk to her about, but she knew in her bones that it was going to be good. Her instincts for these sort of things were always on target.

Leo Jackson, that arrogant son-of-a-bitch. Did he have his hand in the collection plate, then? Or up the skirt of the young man's girlfriend or sister, perhaps? If so, the world had a right to know. Especially now, since he was going to be a bishop. Bishops had to be whiter than white—even if they were black, she told herself with self-righteous smugness and not a glimmer of irony. If he'd done something wrong, Lilith was glad that she was in a position to be the instrument of justice. Justice—that was it. Revenge had nothing to do with it.

⌒⟋⟍ ⌒⟋⟍ ⌒⟋⟍

Callie had promised Dennis Harrington that she would bring Bella back to see Elsie. When she rang the bell, shortly after lunch time, there was a several minute delay before he came to the door. 'My Elsie's not so good today,' he told her quietly.

'Oh, I'll go then. We can come back another day.'

Dennis shook his head. 'She says she wants to see you. You and the pooch.'

He'd managed to get Elsie from the bedroom into the lounge, and that is where he ushered Callie and Bella.

Callie hoped that her shock didn't show on her face. Elsie looked so frail, so shrunken, like little more than a bundle of blankets on the sofa. But the old lady was smiling with delight. 'Oh, isn't she lovely!' she cried. 'Come here, you dear thing.'

Bella padded up to her, and was rewarded by having her ears scratched.

There was a plate with a half-eaten slice of cake on the little table beside Elsie. Bella raised her head and sniffed in that direction.

'Oh, she wants some cake,' Elsie said. Before Callie could protest, Elsie's shrivelled hand reached out to the plate and broke a piece off, then held it out for Bella, who downed it in an instant.

'She likes my Elsie's fruit cake,' Dennis observed with satisfaction. 'Clever little thing, isn't she?'

'I'm not sure cake is good for her,' Callie said faintly.

'Oh, it won't do her no harm,' he assured her. 'My little Spot, he used to eat anything that was going. There wasn't such a thing as special food for dogs in them days. And you never saw a healthier dog.'

Elsie stroked the soft head. 'I wish I had something for her,' she fretted. 'A little ball, or one of them squeaky toys.'

'Never mind. She really likes being stroked,' said Callie. For a few minutes they chatted about Bella; Callie related the story of how she had come to adopt her.

Dennis was watching Elsie all the while with keen protectiveness. 'I don't want you to get worn out, Elsie love,' he said. 'Don't you think it's time for you to go back to bed?'

'I am a bit weary,' she admitted. 'But we have guests.'

'They'll come back another day.' Dennis shot Callie a look. 'Won't you?'

'Oh, yes. Whenever you like. But we really must go now.'

'Tomorrow,' Elsie said promptly. 'Dennis can go to the market in the morning and get a little toy for her.'

'That isn't necessary.'

Elsie spoke for both of them. 'It's something we'd like to do.'

'It's very sweet of you.' Callie stood to go.

'Come in the afternoon—that will give me time to get Elsie up and dressed,' Dennis said as he escorted her to the door, adding quietly, 'I'm that worried about her, girl. She's just not herself. Not since... well, since last week.'

'Yes, I'll come. Of course I will,' Callie assured him.

Tomorrow morning, she remembered with a sinking feeling, was her weekly staff meeting with Brian. How much of this did she dare to tell him?

꧁ ꧂ ꧁ ꧂ ꧁ ꧂

By three o'clock, Lilith's living room, kitchen and loo were virtually immaculate, though she hoped her visitor would have no reason to enter her bedroom. From his voice on the phone, she reckoned that he was far too young for her. Not that she was all that scrupulous about such distinctions.

She didn't want to think how long it had been since a man of *any* age had been in her bedroom. Such was the fate of a tireless seeker after the truth, she told herself virtuously. It just didn't leave any time for a private life.

Deciding that it was late enough in the afternoon to offer him tea, Lilith was putting some biscuits on a plate when the doorbell went.

He *was* very young, she saw immediately. Probably not much older than twenty, if that. His was a boyish slenderness, long-legged and thin-hipped. Far too waifish for her taste, even if he hadn't been so young: Lilith preferred a man with a bit of meat on his bones.

The boy, as she now thought of him, was well-scrubbed, dressed in clean denim jeans and an Arsenal tee shirt, and shod in expensive-looking trainers. He wasn't wearing a jacket, and shivered in the chill of the October afternoon. 'Miss Noone?' he said, putting his hand out politely. 'Lilith Noone? I'm Oliver Pickett.'

She took his hand; it was freezing. 'Come in, Oliver,' she said. 'Come in and get warm.'

She'd left the electric fire on and he went to it immediately, warming his hands close to the glowing bar. 'I didn't realise it was so cold outside,' he said.

'Would you like a cup of tea?' Lilith suggested.

'That would be just the thing. Very kind.'

She brewed the kettle, made the tea, and brought it through. Oliver had moved away from the fire and was browsing along her book shelves. 'You have some interesting books,' he remarked.

'Do you like to read, then?'

'Oh, yes. Very much.' He had a very engaging smile and a pleasant speaking voice, without a distinct accent of any kind.

Lilith indicated a chair, the one nearest the fire, and took a seat on the sofa, facing him.

'Thank you very much,' he said, and repeated it when she handed him a cup of tea.

He wasn't exactly chatty, she realised. Perfectly polite, but not forthcoming. Perhaps this was going to be harder work than she'd anticipated. Or maybe he was just nervous, and needed to be put at his ease.

'So, Oliver,' she said after a few minutes of meaningless social chat. 'You wanted to see me. You said it was important.'

'Yes.'

'You said,' she prompted him, 'that it was about Leo Jackson.'

'Yes.' He lowered his head; his blond fringe obscured his eyes.

'Well,' she said, 'I'm all ears.'

Oliver Pickett put his tea cup down abruptly; Lilith could see that his hands were shaking. 'I hardly know where to begin,' he said, almost in a whisper.

'Begin at the beginning.'

He took a deep breath and looked away from her, staring at the glowing bar of the electric fire. She had to strain to hear his voice. 'What would you say if I told you that Leo Jackson had… had sexually abused me?'

Chapter Sixteen

At twenty-two minutes past ten on Wednesday night, Denise Evans, exhausted and battered, gave birth to a son. He was nearly a month premature, and had been through the same ordeal as his mother, but he was alive and relatively healthy. 'He's a fighter, all right,' said the doctor, handing the tiny scrap of humanity to his father.

'He's an Evans.' His father spoke proudly, for of that fact there was no doubt: already the Evans jaw was in evidence.

Detective Chief Superintendent Evans had not left his wife's side for more than a few minutes at a time since they'd arrived at the hospital, over 44 hours ago. So he, like Denise, was badly in need of sleep.

But there were things that needed to be done.

Neville was in bed, asleep, when the call came. He squinted at the clock: it was past eleven.

Evans wasted no time on the preliminaries. 'Get yourself and your sergeant down here to the station. Now.'

'Your wife, sir? How is she?' Neville dared to ask, albeit with trepidation.

'She's fine. We have a son.'

Neville could hear the smile in Evans' voice. That was all right, then. At least the old man ought to be in a good mood.

As soon as Evans had put the phone down Neville rang Sid Cowley's mobile. Knowing Sid and his propensity for late nights, he figured the chances were at least fifty-fifty that he wouldn't be at home.

Cowley didn't answer for almost a minute, and when he did he was breathless and brusque. 'Cowley.'

'Evans wants us at the station. Now.'

Cowley swore picturesquely.

'Are you at home?'

'No, Guv. I'm at the....' There was a pause and Neville could hear him consulting someone else. 'At the Regent Palace Hotel. Piccadilly Circus.'

Neville sighed. 'I won't ask. I don't suppose you're fit to drive?'

'No,' admitted Cowley. 'I've had a few.'

'Then I'll collect you on my way. Wait for me at the corner of Regent Street and Piccadilly.'

Cowley was standing at the corner, smoking, when Neville pulled up thirty minutes later. He looked surly and cold, his free hand jammed in the pocket of his leather jacket.

Neville adopted a conciliatory tone. 'Sorry about this, Sid. Not my idea, as you can imagine.'

'Your timing couldn't have been worse, Guv.'

He wasn't going to ask, but Cowley told him anyway. 'That American bird. The one who had her wallet half-inched this morning?'

'Yes?'

'Well, you *did* tell me to settle her down, didn't you, Guv? You said I was to make sure she didn't go home with a bad impression of London.'

Neville had pictured a middle-aged woman with middle-age spread, waddling round London in white trainers and a tan trench coat, a camera round her neck and a baseball-capped hayseed husband at her side. It would seem he'd been wrong. 'Just out of university, or college as she called it,' Cowley told him. 'It's her first trip abroad. Her first day in London. So I took you at your word, Guv. I thought since there wasn't anything else going on, I'd show her a few of the sights.'

Neville groaned. Somehow Sid always managed to twist his words to justify whatever he wanted to do. It was a gift. 'What sights did you show her, then?' he asked dryly.

'Oh, we went on the London Eye. I'd never been. It was really something, Guv. You ought to try it.'

'I'll keep that in mind. Next time I have a day with nothing to do. Some time in the next millennium, that will be.'

Ignoring the sarcastic interruption, Cowley went on. 'Then we went to the Tower of London. And she wanted to see St Paul's Cathedral, so we went there. Then I took her to Madame Tussaud's—thought she'd enjoy that. Later on we had a bite to eat.'

'My, you *are* conscientious in pursuit of your duty,' Neville commented ironically.

'She seemed to appreciate it,' Cowley said, unruffled. 'Would you believe it? She thought that I talked really posh! Just like the people on the telly, she said. "I could listen to you all day and all night." That's what she said.'

'So you took her at her word. And that's how you ended up at the Regent Palace Hotel?' suggested Neville.

Cowley grinned. 'Well, let's just say that we were getting down to some serious cultural exchange.'

'Is that what they call it now?' Neville muttered sourly.

'You're just jealous, Guv.' Cowley sounded smug.

Maybe he *was* jealous, Neville admitted to himself—if not to Cowley. First Mark Lombardi with his curate, and now Sid and his American bird. Was this the first sign that he was reaching middle age, this envy of younger men's love lives? Was he afraid that he would soon be over the hill, past it, unable to pull a girl to save his life?

It didn't bear thinking about.

☙☙☙

Evans was waiting for them in his office.

'It took you long enough.' Fortunately, he was smiling.

'I had to collect Sergeant Cowley, sir.'

'Yes, yes.' Evans waved the two of them into chairs. It was a measure of his frame of mind; usually he would have made them stand. 'Now. Let's talk about Frances Cherry. I understand that the *Globe* has forced our hand a bit.'

'That's right, sir.' Neville leaned forward. 'It's my opinion that we should arrest her. Not that I'm totally confident we'll get anything out of her that she hasn't told us already, but it would give us a fair crack at her.'

Cowley, who was usually silent in Evans' presence, was emboldened to add, 'And it would send a message—to the bloody *Globe*—that we're doing something other than sitting on our bums and twiddling our thumbs.'

'"A woman is helping the police with their enquiries." That sort of thing,' Neville amplified.

'Well, what are you waiting for?' Evans said beneficently. 'Go and arrest her.'

Neville stared at him. 'Now? At midnight?'

Evans stroked his massive chin—heavily stubbled and not a pretty sight. 'It's too late to get it into the morning papers, I suppose. And she probably wouldn't be able to rouse a solicitor very easily at this time of night, so it would just be wasting our time.'

'Our initial six hours would be gone before we could do anything,' Neville pointed out.

'We'll give her a few more hours of beauty sleep,' decided Evans. 'Bring her in at six. Or seven.'

'Yes, sir.'

'And speaking of beauty sleep, I think I could use a bit of that myself.' Evans yawned. 'You chaps, as well. Go home and grab a few hours. I shall do the same.'

Neville and Cowley rose at the same time as Evans.

'But before you go,' Evans said, 'I have something to show you.'

He handed a photo to Neville: a Polaroid snapshot of the newest member of his family. The baby was red, wrinkled, and ugly as sin, his head way out of proportion to his tiny body and the Evans jaw all too clearly evident. 'Isn't he beautiful?' Evans almost cooed.

'Lovely, sir,' Neville confirmed.

Cowley, looking over his shoulder, agreed. 'Nicest looking baby I've ever seen, sir.'

On their way back to the car, Neville repeated Cowley's words mockingly. '"Nicest looking baby I've ever seen, sir." Don't you think that was overdoing it just a shade, Sid?'

Cowley gave a self-righteous smirk. 'It never hurts to keep on the big man's good side.'

'I think the big man's gone soft in the head,' Neville muttered. 'Beauty sleep, indeed. That man could sleep for a hundred years, like bloody Sleeping Beauty, and he'd still look like the back end of a bus.' He sighed. 'Let's go home, Sid. Like Evans said.'

'Can you drop me back at Piccadilly Circus, Guv?' Cowley requested, getting into the car. 'I have some unfinished business to attend to. And sleep doesn't come into it. Not right away.'

'It's past midnight,' Neville reminded him. 'What makes you think she'll be waiting for you?'

'Jet lag,' Cowley said succinctly. 'That, and my legendary charm.'

'Well, you and your legendary charm had better be back here at the station by half-past six in the morning, or…'

'Yeah, yeah.' Cowley shrugged and flipped open a new packet of cigarettes. 'I'll be here.'

☙☙☙

Marigold had not had a proper night's sleep for more than a week. Her father continued to appear to her in dreams, as real as he'd been in life. His message to her was a comforting one. 'No one will ever know, Marigold. I've sorted it. I'll always look after you. You're all I have, my dear. I'll make sure that you're all right.'

As long as he was there, talking to her and soothing her fears, she felt good—warm and cherished, like being wrapped in the softest goosedown duvet.

Then he would vanish, and she would wake. That waking was the worst part of it: the desolation as she realised that she was on her own, that her father may have provided for her financially, but he had died and left her alone. He was now beyond helping her; he could never put things right.

Following that bitter knowledge, the demons would attack her, those demons of memory, and she would be awake for hours. The vivid dreams of her father stirred up things that she thought she'd put behind her long ago. She longed, with a fierce longing, for him to return to her in life and hold her in his arms once again, soothing her as he had done when she was just a fractious child.

She needed to talk to Vincent. She knew that. There were so many things unsaid between them through the years; she had always found it safest that way. When things were verbalised, they could never be taken back, and Marigold had always erred on the side of caution. Besides, if one asked questions, one risked getting answers one didn't want to hear.

But she *would* talk to him. She must.

⌘⌘⌘

Frances and Graham were sleeping when the doorbell went, a bit before seven in the morning.

'The postman,' Graham guessed, peering at the clock. 'Were you expecting a parcel or anything, Fran?'

'No.' Frances was wide awake immediately, reaching for her dressing gown. In her bones she knew what it was; she'd been mentally preparing herself for this moment. Oddly enough, her first thoughts were for Graham. She must be calm for him. If she allowed herself to become upset or agitated, he would be even more distressed.

'Shall I get it?' Graham offered.

'No, that's all right. I'll go.'

They had come for her. So this was what it felt like. As she went down the stairs, Frances thought of all those figures of history whose blood must have run cold at moments like these: Anne Boleyn, waiting to be taken to the Tower; Marie

Antoinette, hearing the approach of the tumbrel; that other Anne—Anne Frank—as the SS burst through the concealed door of the Annexe.

She opened the door. Outside was no bloodthirsty mob, no armed thugs, no terrifying henchmen. Just the two policemen whom she'd come to know: DI Stewart and DS Cowley.

'Good morning,' she said calmly.

It was DI Stewart who spoke first. 'We're sorry to disturb you so early in the morning, Reverend Cherry.'

She could almost believe that he *was* sorry. DI Stewart seemed to her, in the contact she'd had with him, to be a decent man, just doing his job—a job that was occasionally difficult, but which had to be done. She didn't blame him for that.

DS Cowley, on the other hand, appeared to take positive pleasure in what came next. 'Frances Cherry, we are arresting you on suspicion of the murder of Jonah Adimola,' he said, smiling. 'You do not have to say anything. But it may harm your defence if you do not mention, when questioned, something which you may later rely on in court. Anything you do say may be given in evidence.'

Frances had heard the words before, on innumerable television programmes. Now, as she stood in the entrance hall of the vicarage, wrapped in her dressing gown and shivering at the blast of cold which followed the policemen in from the street, the whole scene possessed an air of utter unreality.

'Come in,' she said mechanically, registering that they had already done so. 'I assume it's all right for me to get dressed?'

'We'll wait here,' DI Stewart said. 'Take as much time as you need.'

She went back upstairs; Graham was still in bed.

'Postman?' he asked.

'No, it's the police.' She made an effort to sound as normal as possible.

'Stewart and Cowley again?'

Frances nodded, opening the wardrobe. Should she wear clericals? she wondered. It might help, might give her a useful bit of gravitas.

'Isn't it a bit early for them to come calling? Honestly, I think you should complain to their superior, Fran. This is getting to the point of harassment.'

She pulled out a simple black skirt. 'They're arresting me. Taking me to the station, presumably.'

Graham sat up in bed. 'Arresting you? They can't!'

'Oh, they certainly can.'

'But you had nothing to do with it!'

'Then I don't have anything to worry about, do I?' She'd been through it in her own mind, trying to convince herself. 'The *Globe* has pushed them into this. Lilith Noone, suggesting every chance she gets that they're derelict in their duty. I think the police feel they have to go through the motions—to be seen to be doing something.'

'I'll come with you.' He threw the duvet off and swung his legs out of bed.

'No, you won't. I'm sure they won't allow it.' Frances decided on a black clerical shirt, the closest thing she had to an official-looking uniform. The police ought to respect a uniform.

'A solicitor,' Graham said. 'You'll need a solicitor. A good one. I'll find one for you. Several of my parishioners are solicitors. I'll ring one of them.'

In her anticipation of this moment, Frances had thought about it, and had already decided that she didn't want Graham's parishioners involved. On principle. 'No, Graham. I'll deal with it,' she said gently.

'Isn't there anything I can do?' His voice was anguished.

'You can ring the hospital and tell them not to expect me,' she said. 'And ring Callie Anson. I'm meant to have lunch with her today. Ring her and tell her I can't make it. And,' she added, without a trace of irony, 'you can pray.'

Traffic was already quite heavy, building up to the morning rush hour, and progress toward the police station was slow. Frances was grateful that the police didn't try to make conversation. The last thing she needed was a discussion of the weather or the traffic.

They arrived at last, and the two men escorted Frances into the police station.

Now, she thought, Stewart and Cowley were on their own territory. Up till then, her encounters with them had been conducted within her world: at the hospital, at the vicarage. That had given her a certain advantage, at least psychologically. Now *they* had the advantage, and not just because she was literally their prisoner. This was an alien environment for her, one about which she knew nothing, but one in which they worked daily and were totally comfortable.

'This is the custody sergeant,' DI Stewart was saying. 'Sergeant Pratt. We're going to turn you over to her now. We'll see you again later this morning.'

The uniformed woman was evidently expecting her. She was also smiling, which Frances took as a good sign. 'Come this way,' the woman said, leading her into a small room. 'We need to take care of a few technicalities. I promise you it will be painless. Would you like a coffee?'

On a nervous, empty stomach that could have disastrous consequences, Frances decided. 'No, thanks.'

'All right, then. Have a seat.' As she pulled a form toward her, she eyed Frances' clerical collar and said, 'I have to tell you that this is the first time I've ever booked in a priest.'

'What a funny coincidence.' Frances gave her a tight smile. 'This is the first time I've ever been arrested.'

They both laughed. Frances felt no hostility coming from the woman; rather, there was almost a tenuous sense of rapport. She must have been near Frances' own age, or perhaps a few years younger. Her greying hair was cut very short—almost as short as a man's—and she had a crooked nose which looked as though it had been broken. In spite of that, her face was kindly and her smile pleasant.

'In that case, I'll tell you what we're doing,' Sergeant Pratt said. 'First we need to fill out this form, with your essential details. Then I'll run through what you can expect during your stay with us. And if you have any questions after that, I'll be happy to answer them, if I can.'

'Fine.'

'Name?'

'Frances Cherry. The Reverend. Mrs.'

Sergeant Pratt's pen moved across the paper. 'Do you have a middle name at all?'

'Mary. But I don't use it. Frances Mary Cherry sounds a bit odd.'

The sergeant smiled. 'Parents never know, when they give girls a name, what will eventually come after it. I certainly never expected to have a surname like Pratt. My husband's to blame for that.'

Frances looked at her name badge: it read Sergeant S. Pratt. She was emboldened by the woman's friendliness to ask, 'What is the "S" for, then? Susan? Sarah?'

She made a face. 'Promise you won't laugh?'

'Promise.'

'My friends call me Sally. But I was christened "Salome". If you can believe it.'

Frances couldn't imagine anyone less suited to the name, suggestive as it was of sensuality and wild abandon. And in combination with the down-to-earth surname, it seemed nothing less than ludicrous. 'I can see why you go by Sally.'

'We digress.' Smiling, she bent her head again to the paper. 'Date of birth?'

Frances supplied it.

'Occupation?'

'Clerk in Holy Orders. That's the official title.'

'Height?'

'Five foot two. Do you need it in centimetres, or is that good enough?'

'Old money is fine with me.' And so it went on, until all the pertinent details had been filled in, and the form was passed across for Frances to sign.

'Now,' said Sergeant Pratt, 'I'm going to ask you to hand over all of your possessions, for safe-keeping.'

'All of them? My handbag?'

'That's right. And I'll need your watch as well, and your belt if you're wearing one.'

'My belt? What on earth for?'

For the first time, the sergeant avoided Frances' eyes. 'It's the rules, I'm afraid.'

So she wouldn't hang herself in her cell, Frances realised. It hit her forcibly, then: she was in custody. Not just here of her own free will to answer a few questions, but in police custody.

She removed her belt and handed it over, along with her watch and handbag. Sergeant Pratt put them all in a large plastic bag and sealed it, wrote out a list of the contents, then had Frances sign it.

'Now, Reverend Cherry.'

'Please. Call me Frances.'

The sergeant nodded, with a brief smile. 'All right. Frances. It's time for you to think about ringing a solicitor. If you don't have one, I have a list. After that, we'll give you some breakfast. It will probably be several hours before you are interviewed, so I'd suggest that you do eat something. It's not the Ritz,' she grinned, 'but the food is fairly reasonable.'

'No bread and water?'

'You've seen too many movies.'

'Or cop shows. My husband loves them,' Frances admitted. 'Inspector Morse, especially.'

'Well, then. If you've watched cop shows on the telly, inaccurate as they are about a lot of things, you probably know that you can be held here for an initial period of six hours,' Sergeant

Pratt went on. 'That's from the time I booked you in, not from the time you were actually arrested.'

'And then?'

'Then, in the event that the Inspector wants to keep you here for longer, with my permission—or another custody sergeant's, whoever is on duty—he can extend that by another eighteen hours.'

'That's twenty-four hours! I could be here overnight!' she realised, horrified. Graham would go spare.

'Yes, until this time tomorrow morning. I don't think it's likely, though,' she said reassuringly.

'After that you have to let me go?'

The sergeant hesitated for just a second. 'In cases where it's felt necessary, and a superintendent authorises it, I can allow a further twelve hours. After thirty-six hours, if they want any more time, it has to go before a magistrate.'

Frances shut her mind to that possibility. 'You have a lot of power, then,' she observed.

'I'm responsible for the care and well-being of everyone here in custody,' Sergeant Pratt said. 'Feeding and watering, medical care. Allocating cells and interview rooms. Keeping the solicitors happy. Not to mention all of the paperwork. Believe me, it can be quite a job. I have a detention officer to help with the donkey work, but it keeps me busy.'

'Then I shouldn't delay you.'

The sergeant leaned back in her chair. 'Don't worry. This is my slow time. I've just started my shift, about an hour ago. I've been round and checked up on everyone who came in during the night. That's when we get most of our customers.' She grinned. 'Drunks. Domestics. The odd burglar. You know the sort of thing.'

Frances wasn't sure that she did. Inspector Morse never dealt with drunks or burglars.

'I usually catch up on my paperwork about now, until the solicitors start arriving. They start coming in about half-past eight, and then things get really busy. It's all go after that.'

'When do you get to go home?' Frances asked, partly because she was curious, and also because she felt that as long as Salome Pratt was there, responsible for her welfare, she was in safe hands and nothing too terrible could happen to her.

'My shift ends, theoretically, at three in the afternoon. But there's always a bit of an overlap with the person on the next shift. I have to fill them in on everyone and their state-of-play before I hand over.' She leaned forward. 'Enough about me, though. Do you have any questions you'd like to ask? Things I haven't been clear about?'

'Will I be... in a cell?' Frances asked, afraid of the answer.

'Not just now.' The sergeant gave her a reassuring smile. 'For one thing, there isn't one available. It was a busy night, and they're all full, at least till the solicitors start arriving to bail them out. And I don't really think it's necessary. You're not a danger to yourself, or to society, are you?'

'Not the last time I checked.'

'They're a pretty stroppy lot this morning,' the sergeant said. 'Two of them cussed me up one side and down the other, and used a few words I'd never heard before. And I thought I'd heard them all.'

Frances tried to imagine dealing with people like that on a daily basis, and felt thankful that she'd gone into hospital chaplaincy rather than prison chaplaincy. 'That must be difficult for you.'

Sergeant Pratt's grin was rueful. 'Listen. I have three teen-aged sons. There isn't anything I don't know about dealing with stroppiness. I could write the book on it.' She added, 'You have kids?'

'One daughter.'

'You're lucky,' she said succinctly. 'Girls must be so much less trouble than boys.'

Frances kept her reservations about that to herself.

'Anyway, I have a little room I can put you in, where you'll be more comfortable,' the sergeant went on. 'With any luck, you'll be out of here and back home in a few hours.'

'Thank you.' Frances was as grateful for the words of encouragement as she was for the preferential treatment.

'Now. You need to ring a solicitor.' She produced a photocopied list and a thick directory. 'If you don't know one, you can pick someone from this list. Or if you have your own solicitor but need the phone number, here's the Law Society directory.' She stood. 'Come with me. There's a phone in the room where I'm putting you. Feel free to use it, if you want to ring your husband.'

She led Frances down a short corridor and opened the door of a small room. It appeared to be a disused office, perhaps in between occupants. There was a desk with a phone, a desk chair, and another chair, which looked marginally more comfortable. The pin board was empty, bearing faint ghostly rectangles where sheets of paper must once have been, and the lighting, when the sergeant pushed the switch, was garish and fluorescent. 'The detention officer will bring your breakfast in a few minutes,' she said. 'He's called Jim. If there's anything you need, you can tell him. Or give me a shout—I'll be round and about, and I'll let you know when your solicitor gets here.'

The room was windowless and airless, almost more frightening than a cell. Frances had never thought of herself as being claustrophobic, but already she could feel the walls closing round her. She didn't want Sergeant Pratt to go; she didn't want to be left alone in this room, waiting. Waiting for Stewart and Cowley to begin the third degree.

As if reading her mind, Salome Pratt patted her arm. 'You'll be all right, Frances. Neville—DI Stewart—is a good man, and fair. You don't have anything to be afraid of with him, as long as you tell the truth.'

'What about Cowley?' Frances blurted.

'Ah. Cowley.' Sergeant Pratt's face darkened. 'I know I shouldn't be saying this, but I'm not so fond of Sid Cowley. Fancies himself rather too much than is good for him, if you know what I mean. But DI Stewart will keep him in line. You'll see.'

A solicitor. Frances sat with the list in front of her on the desk, paging through it. She'd thought ahead of time about what she *didn't* want—not one of Graham's parishioners, not one of the the hospital's solicitors. But she hadn't progressed any farther than that.

Then, like an answer to prayer, a name came into her head—a name she hadn't thought about in years. Triona O'Neil.

Frances had met Triona O'Neil back in the heady days of the battle for women's ordination. Well over ten years ago, now.

Triona had been very young. Much younger than Frances. She was newly over from Ireland, reading law at King's College, London. A Roman Catholic, but an ardent feminist. She had come along to one of the meetings of MOW—the Movement for the Ordination of Women—and had enthusiastically thrown herself into the cause. When Anglican women achieved the right to be priested, she reasoned, the Romans would eventually follow. Not that she wanted to be a priest herself: she wanted to be a lawyer, the best there was. So she could fight for the downtrodden and the marginalised.

Frances could picture her now, as she'd been back in those days. Thin as a whip, and full of nervous energy, with curly black hair which seemed almost electrified when Triona was on the move. She had that exquisite 'black Irish' colouring, with alabaster skin and eyes of a blue as dark as the Irish Sea.

Her moods were mercurial and extreme; her enthusiasms were contagious. She was a good person to have on your side, and would make a very dangerous enemy.

She'd been with them through the nail-biting vote, standing with a banner in Dean's Yard on that historic November day. Her banner had read 'Today Canterbury, Tomorrow Rome'.

And she'd come to Frances' ordination the following spring. Then Frances had pretty much lost touch with her. There had been a few Christmas cards, and after that...

Perhaps Triona had gone back to Ireland after she'd qualified. Or maybe she'd married, and had a different name.

'If you ever need a good lawyer,' Triona had said to her once, 'I'll be there for you.' It had been said in the context of some mild form of civil disobedience which a few of them had discussed—something like chaining themselves to the railings of Church House to draw attention to their cause, rather in the manner of the Suffragettes. Although it now seemed incredibly trivial, if they'd done it they might have been arrested. Might have needed a good lawyer.

She certainly needed one now.

Holding her breath, Frances opened the Law Society directory and flipped to the O section.

Yes, she was there. Triona O'Neil, and she was still in London.

Frances exhaled in a silent prayer of thanks.

രുന്ധ രുന്ധ രുന്ധ

She came. 'I never forget a promise,' she said as she was ushered into Frances' little room. 'I told you to call me if you ever needed a good lawyer, and here I am.'

Her voice was just the same as Frances remembered, her lilting Irish accent undiminished. In other ways, though, Triona had changed. Her hair was longer, swept into an elegant twist at the nape of her neck. She'd filled out a bit, as well, from her former skeletal thinness. Both the longer hair and the added pounds became her. Once a striking girl, she was now a beautiful woman. And she was very well dressed: her student scruffiness had given way to a sleek, perfectly cut suit, clearly expensive.

'How are you, Frances?' she asked, then answered herself. 'Silly question. I can see how you are.'

'As well as can be expected. Thanks for coming, Triona.'

Triona lowered herself into the chair by the desk, dropping a pad of paper on the desk's bare surface. 'It's because of the promise,' she said. 'I don't do criminal work, not ordinarily.'

'Then what…'

'I've sold out,' she announced bluntly. 'I've been seduced by Mammon. I work for a big City firm. Corporate conveyancing.'

She pulled a face. 'It's as boring as it sounds. Boring as hell, to tell the truth. But it pays fantastically well.'

'I do appreciate you coming,' Frances said. 'If you'd rather not do it, perhaps you could recommend someone else. I just didn't know where else to turn.'

'Oh, I'll do it.' Triona looked directly at Frances; her eyes were unchanged, still alight with that spark of adventure which Frances remembered so well. 'It will be a challenge.'

She took a pen from her black leather handbag and pulled the pad of paper toward her. 'Start at the beginning and tell me everything,' she ordered.

'Have you read the papers? The *Globe*?' If she had, thought Frances, this might be easier.

Triona waved her hand dismissively. 'I never read the papers. A load of rubbish, in my opinion. I want this in *your* words.'

So Frances told her, beginning with the Deanery Clergy Chapter meeting. Occasionally Triona interrupted her with a question, or a request for clarification, pausing now and again to make notes on her pad. The process lasted the better part of an hour.

'I suppose the police will be wanting to interview me soon,' Frances said. 'Detective Inspector Stewart said it would be this morning.'

Triona paused in the act of writing, her pen poised in mid-air. 'Detective Inspector Stewart, did you say?'

'That's right. And Detective Sergeant Cowley.'

'Neville Stewart?'

Frances nodded. 'That's right. Why? Do you know him?'

'Oh, yes,' Triona said softly, almost to herself. 'I know Neville Stewart. Or at least I used to know him.'

'In Ireland?'

'No. In London.'

Frances waited for more, but Triona remained silent, looking pensive. 'Well, well,' she said at last, with a half-smile. 'It will be... interesting... to see Neville Stewart again.'

Chapter Seventeen

Leo had no intimation that his world was about to fall apart when, early on Thursday morning, he was awakened by an insistent ringing of the doorbell.

His clock told him that it was nearly seven, but there wasn't a hint of sun round the edges of the curtains. He got out of bed and went to the window, pulling the curtain aside.

It was overcast, misty—threatening rain. The golden autumn seemed to have vanished under a cloud.

The bell went again. Sighing, Leo padded downstairs, not bothering to look for his dressing gown. If the postman—or whoever it happened to be—didn't want to see him in his boxer shorts, then he shouldn't be ringing the bell at this unsociable hour.

He opened the door a crack and was blinded by a dozen flashes. He blinked, stepped back, and instinctively slammed the door shut, as much from the shock of the cold temperature as anything else. 'What on earth?' he said aloud.

Now there were voices calling out; he could hear them through the door. 'Mr Jackson!' 'Do you have any comment?' 'Could we have a word?'

Leo stood for a moment, shivering, blinking as the blobs on his retina faded away, trying to fathom what was going on. There were people out there. More than a handful, judging by the noise and the number of flashes. Journalists? Surely a black bishop wasn't *that* newsworthy? He'd spent yesterday talking to journalists; why were they back?

He went to the coat-rack in the hall and found an anorak. Perhaps not the most appropriate garment for the occasion, but at least it would keep him warm—and decent. Shoving his cold feet into a pair of wellie boots, he returned to the door and pulled it open. This time he was ready for the flashes; he shaded his eyes and addressed the person who had been ringing the bell, a weedy man with gingery hair and unfortunate teeth. 'What do you want?' he said fiercely in his most booming voice, drawing himself up to his full, impressive height.

'Would you care to comment on this morning's *Globe*?' the man asked, over the shouted questions of the gathered mob. He was clutching a tabloid, on which Leo could get a glimpse of the screaming headline: 'Randy Reverend' was all he could see.

Oh, Lord, thought Leo. One of the clergy in the deanery must have done something naughty. As Area Dean, and a bishop-elect to boot, he would naturally be the journalists' first port of call for a comment.

But who? he asked himself. Brian Stanford? Jane kept him on a short leash, so he would scarcely have the opportunity to stray. And Brian was so idle that he wouldn't have the energy for it, even if he had the opportunity. Vincent Underwood was too bloodless, too pleased with himself, to lose himself in passion. Surely not the ever-so-upright Richard Grant? Maybe so: those self-righteous Evangelicals, when they fell from their pedestals, usually fell the hardest.

These speculations went through his mind in less than a heartbeat, then he shouted 'No comment!' and slammed the door shut again.

How could he find out? He was, Leo recognised, under siege: he certainly wasn't going to get out of the rectory this morning, to buy a newspaper or for anything else.

Oliver! he thought. He could ring Oliver, and ask him to go out and find a copy of the *Globe*. It would be a legitimate excuse to ring him, to talk to him, however briefly.

He went into his study and rang Oliver's mobile. 'This number is not in service,' announced a metallic voice.

'Oh, hell,' he muttered. He supposed he could ring Frannie, but he didn't want to drag her into this, whatever it was.

And then his eye fell on his iMac computer, its screen-saver beckoning him to the delights of tropical isles, obscuring his half-written sermon for Sunday.

He sat down at the keyboard, went on line, and typed 'Globe newspaper' into Google. The first result listed, half a second later, took him straight to the *Globe*'s home page.

And there it was: the full alliterative headline, emblazoned across his screen. 'Randy Reverend in Raunchy Rectory Romps'.

There was a photo as well. Leo stared in dawning horror at his own face.

❦ ❦ ❦

When Marigold saw how unpleasant the weather was—cold, misty and threatening rain—she almost changed her mind about going out to get the papers. After all, most of the press had gone quiet about the murder several days ago, and even the *Globe* seemed to have dropped the subject. But this had become a habit, a ritual for her. As soon as Vincent was out of sight, on his way to say morning prayer, she slipped out of the house and turned her steps toward Oxford Street.

She never saw it coming. A shadowy figure stepped out of the mist as she went by, and with one swift movement grabbed her handbag and shoved her to the ground, then ran off. It had all happened within a matter of seconds.

Marigold wasn't badly hurt, but she was stunned and shaken up. She lay on the pavement for a few moments, catching her breath, assessing her injuries. Trying to decide whether she could stand without assistance.

An approaching jogger proved to be her own Good Samaritan. He paused when he saw the obstruction on the pavement, and went to her aid immediately. 'Are you all right?' he asked with concern.

'I think so.'

He helped her to her to feet. 'What happened? Can you remember?'

'Well, I'm not sure,' she admitted unsteadily. 'I didn't see anything. One minute I was walking along, and then… something hit me. Someone, I suppose. And my handbag. It's gone.'

'Oh, dear. I don't suppose there's any hope of catching him now,' the man said, shaking his head. 'Never mind. The important thing is looking after *you*, and getting you home.'

'I don't want to hold you up,' she protested, without much conviction. There was something comforting, trustworthy, about the jogger. Something familiar, even. She had no doubt that she was in safe hands with him.

'Don't be silly.' He scrutinised her, then pronounced, "I think you need a cup of tea. There's a little caff just round the corner. Nothing grand, but they do a decent cuppa. Do you think you can walk that far? Or shall I try to find a taxi and get you home?'

She took a few tentative steps. 'Yes, I can walk,' she discovered. 'I must not have broken anything.'

He held on to her arm and led her slowly to an unprepossessing cafe with an inviting smell of freshly-brewed coffee. 'A pot of tea for two,' he ordered, even before they sat down at a table covered with a flower-bedecked plasticised cloth.

The tea came quickly, in a brown earthenware pot, accompanied by two thick white cups and saucers. Nothing delicate about it, but it was what she needed. The man poured, adding two spoons of sugar to her cup.

'I don't take sugar,' she objected.

'It's the best thing for shock. Sweet, strong tea. Drink it.'

Obediently she sipped it, under his watchful gaze. It was almost like she was a child again, her father coaxing her to eat something she didn't fancy.

With a jolt she looked across at the man. Did he remind her of her father? Was that why he seemed so familiar to her?

His face was thinner than her father's, with deep vertical furrows bracketing his nose and mouth, though the eyes—under strong brows—were not unlike. Perhaps it was the hair: salt and pepper, straight, with short back and sides. That, and the thin but muscular forearms, exposed by his jogging gear. Arms very like those which had held her as a child, had picked her up when she'd fallen off her swing.

Suddenly she had an overwhelming desire to confide in this man. He was a stranger to her; he was safe. He didn't know who *she* was, she didn't know who *he* was. She could say anything to him, and it would go no further. She opened her mouth, about to pour her heart out to him.

'It was a good thing I came along when I did,' he said, smiling at her, revealing a set of straight, white teeth. 'But I don't think for a moment it was a coincidence.'

'It wasn't?'

'No. The Lord led me to you, in your moment of need. I don't usually run down that road. But this morning I found myself going that way. Not knowing why. Obviously the Lord had a purpose for it.'

'The Lord?' she echoed.

'Our Saviour, Jesus Christ.'

Marigold stared at him, as if he'd suddenly started addressing her in Swahili.

'Do you know Him as your personal saviour?' he asked, fixing her intently with his deep-set eyes.

The man was religious nutter. She'd been on the brink of confiding in him, and he was a religious nutter.

Now all she wanted was to get away from him. To escape, and try to forget that this had ever happened.

'Thanks so much for the tea,' she babbled, rising to her feet. 'I have to go now.'

He stood as well. 'I'll see you home, then. I'm not allowing you to go off on your own, after what you've been through.'

'No, it's all right. Really.' The last thing she wanted was for him to know where she lived. He'd probably start pushing tracts through the door, ringing the bell and quoting the Bible at her. 'But thank you for everything, Mr…'

'Grant,' he said. 'Richard Grant.'

Richard Grant! No wonder he looked so familiar: she'd seen his photo in the *Globe*, next to the interview in which he expounded his opinion that Jonah had deserved to die.

What a narrow escape she'd had! She'd come within a hair's breadth of spilling her innermost secrets to Richard Grant.

Maybe, she thought gratefully as she hurried away from him, there *was* a God.

⁕⁕⁕

Lilith was feeling very much better on Thursday morning. In fact, she was feeling so well that she was all set to go into the office early and get to work on her next story. This one, she thought smugly, was going to play and play. Oliver Pickett had given her enough material to spin out for days, each story putting a further nail in the coffin of Leo Jackson. She already had her headline for tomorrow's story: as if 'Randy Reverend' weren't bad enough, she was going to skip over 'Pervy Priest' and go straight for 'Bishop of Buggery'. Before someone else thought of it. She had no doubt that her press colleagues would already be onto the story, camping out on Leo Jackson's doorstep. Well, good luck to them. Jackson was unlikely to say anything, and she had Oliver Pickett to herself: he'd promised her an exclusive.

After checking with her editor, she had offered Oliver Pickett money for his story, on the basis that he wouldn't talk to anyone else. But he had refused. His eyes filling with tears, he'd said that he wasn't going public about his harrowing experiences for monetary gain, but to warn people about a relentless sexual predator. So that the terrible things that had happened to him wouldn't happen to anyone else.

They had reached an expedient compromise: Lilith had gone out and bought him a brand new mobile phone, top of the range—a phone for which no one but she had the number. His old phone she kept, and as a precaution she rang the service provider and had it disconnected.

In the end she restrained herself from going in too early. It was better, she decided, to wait until everyone else was at their desks. Then she could make a grand entrance, gather her colleagues' congratulations with gracious aplomb, and smile inwardly at their envy.

∽∽∽ ∽∽∽ ∽∽∽

Neville looked at his watch. The morning was getting on. He and Sid Cowley had shared a leisurely breakfast at the station canteen; they'd discussed their strategy for interviewing Frances Cherry. 'Good cop/bad cop' seemed to be working well, they decided, and they may as well continue with that.

'Well,' said Neville, finishing up his coffee, 'there's no time like the present. Let's go and see whether she's got herself sorted out with a solicitor.'

Cowley took a last drag on his cigarette and stubbed it out in the ashtray. 'Right you are, Guv.'

Sergeant Pratt confirmed that Mrs Cherry's solicitor had arrived, and they'd been in conference. 'I'll get you set up in an interview room,' she promised. 'Give me five minutes.'

While Cowley lit another fag, Neville went looking for Mark Lombardi and found him at his desk. 'I just thought I should tell you,' he said, 'that we arrested Frances Cherry this morning. In case you want to let your girlfriend know.'

Mark raised his eyebrows with a long-suffering look. 'She's not my girlfriend. And she already knows,' he added.

'News travels fast, I see.' Neville was obscurely disappointed.

'She rang me an hour ago. Apparently Frances Cherry's husband had been on the phone.'

'Oh, well, then.'

Mark smiled belatedly. 'Thanks, Nev. I do appreciate it. I don't suppose there's anything else I can tell Callie?'

'We're just about to start our interview. You can tell her that, if you like.'

'Keep me informed,' Mark called after him as Neville headed downstairs to the interview room.

Cowley was standing outside of the door, finishing his cigarette with a long drag; there would be no smoking while the interview took place. 'They've gone in,' the sergeant informed him. 'Cherry and her solicitor. The solicitor's a pretty hot-look-ing bird.'

'Anyone you know?'

'Never seen her before,' Cowley said. He threw the fag end on the floor and ground it out with his heel.

Sergeant Pratt had been as efficient as usual; the taping equip-ment was all set up, and water glasses had been provided. Frances Cherry and her solicitor were sitting at the table, on the side facing the door, as Neville and Cowley came through.

Frances Cherry's hands were clasped together on the table, her knuckles white with tension. She was trying to look calm and not succeeding terribly well.

Then Neville's glance shifted to the solicitor. She was smil-ing at him: a knowing, intimate smile. 'Hello, Neville,' she said softly. 'Fancy meeting you here.'

⁂

Triona O'Neil. He couldn't believe it. After all these years.

'You know each other?' Cowley asked, visibly curious.

Neville sensed rather than saw Cowley's curiosity, nor did he reply; he seemed to have been struck dumb, and his eyes hadn't left Triona O'Neil's face.

'I know what you're thinking,' she said. '"Of all the gin joints in all the towns in all the world, she walks into mine."'

Neville found his tongue. 'Something like that.'

For a long moment her eyes locked with his, then she looked down at her papers. 'Let's get on with it.' Her voice was brisk, businesslike.

'Yes.' Neville spoke into the tape recorder with the necessary preliminaries to the interview: the time, the place, the names of the people present, and a reminder to Frances Cherry that she was not obliged to answer their questions. He looked away from Triona O'Neil for only a split second, as he confirmed the time from the clock on the wall.

The interview began with a few standard questions, most of which they had asked Frances Cherry before. Neville handled those with half of his brain engaged, then he nodded at Cowley to take over and sat back, quite unable to continue.

Memories crowded in on him—vivid, immediate, insistent— too strong to be submerged by an act of will. All of his senses were engaged, not just his eyes: he remembered the musical sound of her laughter, the clean scent of her, the feel of her springy curls between his fingers, the taste of her lips. And other memories on which he dared not allow himself to dwell…

It had been nine years, but it seemed like yesterday.

Neville hated the 'L' word. In his observation, even in these enlightened and hedonistic times, it all too often led to the even more dreaded 'M' word. Commitment with a capital C. Life over.

As far back as he could remember, he had never said the 'L' word to anyone—not even his mother. He had always avoided even thinking about it.

But if Neville Stewart had ever loved anyone, he had loved Triona O'Neil.

ᏯᎳᎴᎧ ᏯᎳᎴᎧ ᏯᎳᎴᎧ

They had met the first time in similar circumstances: Neville was a Detective Sergeant, having recently achieved that rank, and Triona was a newly-qualified solicitor. The attraction had been immediate and mutual.

On that occasion, her client had been clearly guilty; in fact, he had confessed to his crime within twenty minutes. That left Triona free—and ethically able—to accept Neville's invitation to dinner that same night.

It was the middle of a long, hot summer. He took her to a romantic restaurant where they dined in a courtyard, sitting there and talking as others came and went, as the scorching day faded into warm twilight and the stars came out.

Within a week she had moved into his flat.

It had lasted just over three months.

During that brief time, though, Neville had felt more alive, had experienced more intense highs and lows, than ever before or since.

Triona was a creature of passions: exciting, invigorating, and often infuriating. There was nothing lukewarm about her; living with her with was like being on a non-stop roller coaster ride.

The good times were fantastic. They shared a wild, ironic sense of humour and of fun; she made him laugh. She made him happy.

But they also shared a deep streak of celtic melancholy, and they were both quite capable of wounding each other deliberately. Their rows were incendiary. Triona had a very short fuse; while it took Neville longer to get wound up, when he did his temper was equal to hers.

Yet it had ended with a whimper rather than a bang. On a day just like this, Neville remembered, glancing out of the window at the dripping trees. On a miserable, wet October day.

෧෨෧෨෧

Even before the numbness set in, before he'd really taken in what he had read, Leo knew that there was one thing he had to do.

Still sitting at his computer, staring at the screen, he opened his e-mail programme and clicked on the pencil icon to compose a new message.

Leo had never stood on ceremony, and he did not do so now.

'Effective immediately, and with deep regret, I withdraw my acceptance of my appointment as Bishop of Brixton.' That was enough. He signed it 'Leo Jackson, Area Dean of Bayswater.'

At the top he filled in the e-mail address of the Bishop of Southwark, with copies to the Bishop of London, the Archbishop of Canterbury, and the Prime Minister's Appointments Secretary.

Then he clicked the 'send' icon.

It was done.

Leo sighed and closed his eyes.

෧෨෧෨෧

Callie was getting ready to go to the vicarage for her staff meeting with Brian when the phone rang. She'd postponed her departure till the very last minute, hoping to hear something from Mark or Graham.

It was Mark. 'Listen, I don't really have that much to tell you,' he said. 'She's being interviewed right now. They'll break at lunch time. I'll see what I can find out then, and I'll give you a ring.'

She experienced a surge of gratitude, if not relief. 'I really do appreciate it, Marco,' she said. 'I hope you're not getting yourself into any trouble over this.'

'Don't worry.'

Callie wasn't sure, when she'd said goodbye, whether he meant she shouldn't worry about him, or about Frances.

Making certain she had her mobile phone and that it was switched on, she ran down the stairs to the street.

Only then did she discover that the rains had started in earnest. She wasn't about to make herself even later by going back upstairs in search of an umbrella, so she pulled her coat over her head and sprinted to the vicarage.

Jane Stanford met her at the door, viewing her dripping figure with disfavour. She made no move to step aside and let Callie in.

'I'm sorry,' said Jane, 'but Brian isn't here. He's had an emergency call-out. He said to tell you he's sorry to have brought you out unnecessarily, and he'll be in touch later.'

Callie's heart was pounding, both from the run and from the alarming message. 'An emergency? What about?'

'I'm sure if he wants you to know, he'll tell you himself.' A small, mean-spirited smile curved the ends of her mouth. Then she shut the door in Callie's face.

Callie made the return dash to her flat. What, she wondered, was going on? And what had she ever done to Jane Stanford in their brief acquaintance, to make Jane dislike her so?

━━━ ━━━ ━━━

As Mark had predicted, Sergeant Pratt stopped the interview at lunch time, taking Frances away to have something to eat.

Neville and Sid Cowley went back to the station canteen.

'What's got into you, Guv?' Cowley asked bluntly as soon as they had their food. During the two hours of the interview, Neville had said scarcely a word. Cowley had had ample opportunity to exercise his 'bad cop' persona, but there was no counterbalancing 'good cop'. The Inspector had virtually opted out of the interview, and the things he'd said had not contributed substantially to the questioning.

Neville contemplated his lunch: sausages and mash. He found that he had no recollection of having chosen it, and no appetite for eating it. 'I don't know what you mean,' he prevaricated.

'You left me on my own in there! You hardly said a thing!'

'I thought you'd like that. It gave you a chance to flex your muscles.'

'Bollocks.' Cowley peered at him closely across the table. 'It was that woman, wasn't it? The solicitor? You couldn't keep your eyes off her.'

Looking down at his plate, Neville prodded the potatoes with his fork. 'I knew her once, a long time ago. End of story.'

'The hell it is.'

'Anyway,' said Neville, 'I think we're on to a loser. We haven't got any further with Frances Cherry. We keep asking the same questions, and she keeps giving the same answers. It's a waste of everyone's time.'

'What do you suggest, Guv?' Cowley's voice was heavy with sarcasm. 'A bit of input from you would make a welcome change.'

Neville spoke quietly, not rising to the bait. 'I think we should let her go.'

'Oh, give me strength!' Cowley threw his fork down on his tray.

'Then you could get back to your American,' Neville pointed out. 'Frances Cherry could get back to writing her sermon, or whatever it is she does with her time. We could all get on with our lives.'

'Except that we still don't know who killed Jonah Adimola. If it wasn't Frances Cherry, who the hell was it?'

Her experiences—both with the bag-snatcher and with Richard Grant—had shaken Marigold Underwood deeply. She'd been grateful that Vincent wasn't yet home when she arrived back at the house, and had gone to the phone to set about doing what she needed to do: cancelling her credit cards and notifying the police about the crime. She didn't expect that she would ever hear another word from the police; it was unlikely that they would put a high priority on catching a mere opportunistic mugger, or that they would find him even if they did. Still, if by chance her handbag turned up in a bin somewhere, it was good to have the theft on record. It had been an expensive leather bag; she would like to have it back, even empty.

At least she hadn't been badly hurt, though there were a few aches which might be felt later on, might even keep her awake at night. Close examination of her clothing revealed that her stockings were torn, and her new coat had a rip on the side, as well as mud stains.

She was supposed to be meeting Beatrice for lunch; suddenly she just didn't feel up to it. All she wanted was a long soak in the bath and a quiet afternoon by the fire in the drawing room with a pot of herbal tea.

'But how utterly frightful!' Beatrice exclaimed gratifyingly when she rang her to cancel. 'If you're not safe on the streets of Mayfair, then where *are* you safe?'

'That's what I thought.'

'It wasn't your Gucci bag, was it? Tell me it wasn't your Gucci bag.'

'No. It was the Mulberry one.'

Beatrice groaned. 'That's bad enough.'

'I'm quite done in,' Marigold confessed.

'I should think so, too. Take care of yourself, darling. And get that husband of yours to pamper you a bit.'

That, thought Marigold, would be the day.

Then she began to wonder where Vincent was. He was usually home fairly promptly after morning prayer, and spent the rest of the morning at his desk.

It wasn't until she was having a solitary lunch—solitary, that is, apart from her cat Jezebel, who waited with ill-concealed impatience for titbits—that she heard his key in the front door.

'Vincent?' she called.

He came through to the dining room, beaming. 'I wasn't expecting you to be at home,' he said. 'Though I don't blame you for not going out. It's a foul day.'

Marigold opened her mouth to tell him what had happened to her, but changed her mind before the words were formed. How could she explain what she'd been doing out on the streets at that hour of the morning? 'I didn't fancy braving the rain,' she concurred. 'I cancelled my lunch with Beatrice.'

Vincent had left his umbrella in the hall stand, but was still wearing his coat. He reached inside it and pulled out a tabloid—the *Globe*, Marigold saw with a sick lurch of her stomach—and waved it at her with a jubilant grin. 'Look at this!' he boomed, slapping it down on the table in front of her. 'Just look!'

She could hardly imagine what might be in the *Globe* to arouse such glee in Vincent; he hadn't even shown her the issue in which he had been interviewed.

The headline screamed at her: 'Randy Reverend in Raunchy Rectory Romps'.

'Oh, dear God,' she said faintly, her hand to her mouth to hold back the nausea. Then she saw Leo Jackson's photo. 'Oh, the poor man.'

Vincent had clearly expected a different reaction from his wife. 'Don't you see?' he demanded, impatient and disappointed with her. 'His sins have caught up with him. Now he'll have to resign. He can't be a bishop now. Not after this.'

'But why should you care?'

'You know why. Because Leo Jackson is everything that's wrong with the Church of England today,' Vincent declared venomously. 'A liberal.' The word was uttered as a curse. 'Women priests and sodomites at the altar. It's disgraceful. He and his kind have taken this Church down the road to ruin. And now he has to face the music for that. He might even have to resign his orders.' At that he gave a satisfied smile.

Marigold stared at him. It occurred to her that in some ways he was no different than Richard Grant—so sure of himself, so sure that he knew what God wanted. So very, very smug.

She lowered her eyes again to the photo of Leo Jackson. The poor man: this time she said it silently. At least, she thought, he didn't have a wife who would have to bear this disgrace.

∞ ∞ ∞

By lunch-time Callie had heard no more from Mark, neither had Brian rung her. Unsettled and upset, she put on her rain gear, found her umbrella, and took Bella out to the park for a quick walk. Then she turned toward the Harringtons' flat; in spite of everything, she had not forgotten her promise to them to bring Bella back this afternoon. Not that they would want a wet and muddy cocker spaniel in their spotless lounge, but at least she could stop by and say hello.

To her surprise, though, there was no answer to the bell. She waited a few minutes and tried again. Then she got out her mobile and rang their number. She could hear it ringing inside the flat, again and again, until she pushed the button to end the call.

Well, there was nothing for it. She'd have to go home and try to ring them later.

The first thing she would need to do when she got home, Callie realised, was to get Bella into the bath and clean her paws. She'd been spoiled up till now by the good weather; now the more demanding aspects of dog ownership were becoming evident. She looked down at Bella, happily slopping along through the puddles on the pavement, and as she raised her head she caught the headline of a newspaper on a corner news-stand. 'Raunchy Reverend...'

'Oh, no,' Callie breathed, and fumbled in her handbag for some change.

After their acrimonious lunch, Neville and Cowley went back to Neville's office. Neville was in favour of going to see Evans and asking him to authorise releasing Frances Cherry; Cowley was strenuously opposed. 'We need one more crack at her,' he insisted. 'She's bound to cave in and admit that she's been shagging Leo Jackson.'

'The more you badger her about it, the more she denies it,' Neville pointed out.

'Oh, you noticed?'

Neville did not appreciate the sarcasm: *he* was meant to be the sarcastic one. Cowley was getting altogether too big for his boots, he reflected. Next thing you knew, he'd be taking on Evans and telling him what to do.

Someone had been into Neville's office, had left a tabloid on his desk. 'What's this?' he said, picking it up.

Cowley was still in sarcastic mode. 'Looks like a newspaper to me. But maybe you know better.'

Neville didn't even hear him; he was reading the headline, looking at the photo. 'Oh, God,' he said as he scanned the first lines of the story. 'Bloody hell.'

Chapter Eighteen

'Bloody hell.' Neville repeated it for emphasis. He quickly read through the teaser on the front page, then turned to the interior pages, where the story merited a double-page spread. Complete with a large photo of the wronged man, looking very vulnerable and extremely young.

'What?' Cowley, his pique forgotten, tried to read over his shoulder.

'Listen to this. '"He invited me to the rectory to talk about faith, about joining the church,' said anguished Oliver Pickett. 'But he couldn't leave me alone. He kept touching me. He was all over me, like an animal.'

'"I was afraid of him. I didn't know what he'd do to me—how he'd hurt me—if I said no. So I played along with him. I knew it was wrong, but I didn't have a choice.'" Bloody hell,' Neville added again. 'Then it says, "Oliver Pickett's eyes filled with tears as he told me, 'It was horrible, the things he made me do. Things against nature. People like that shouldn't be allowed to be priests. They shouldn't even be allowed on the streets. It's disgusting.'"'

Cowley rocked back on his heels, trying to process the information. 'Leo Jackson's a bloody poofter!'

'So it would seem.' Neville laughed mirthlessly. 'And if that's true, Sid, then we've been barking up the wrong tree.'

With a long, low whistle, Cowley sat down and reached in his pocket for his cigarettes. 'I need a fag, Guv. To help me think.'

Neville read the story through to the end. 'Well,' he said, shaking his head in bemusement. 'Unless Lilith Noone has made this one up out of whole cloth, I'd say that our case against Frances Cherry has just gone straight out of the window.'

Cowley took a long drag and exhaled slowly, watching the smoke through narrowed eyes. 'Not necessarily, Guv,' he said at last.

'What do you mean? If Jackson is… that way inclined, then he and Frances Cherry aren't having an affair. There goes our reason for blackmail. No affair, no blackmail.'

'Not necessarily,' Cowley repeated.

'Okay. Tell me what you're thinking.'

Using his cigarette for emphasis, Cowley outlined his new theory. 'We both thought that Cherry and Jackson weren't telling the truth about what happened that night—that they were hiding something.'

'Yes…?'

'So let's say we've been looking at it the wrong way round. Say they *were* hiding something, but it wasn't that they were shagging each other. They were hiding the fact that Jackson's queer.'

Neville took a deep breath of Cowley's second-hand smoke. 'You're saying that Frances Cherry knew that?'

'She must have, if they were such good chums—like she keeps telling us. She might have even known about this Oliver Pickett, and what Jackson did to him. Jackson was probably with Pickett later that night, and that's what the two of them—Cherry and Jackson—have been keeping from us.'

'Then where does Jonah Adimola come into it?'

Cowley grinned. 'This is the good part, Guv. Say Adimola found out about Jackson shagging Pickett.'

'We're back to blackmail.' Neville nodded; it all made sense. At least as much sense as the previous theory, if not more.

'It could have been blackmail. Or Adimola might have just threatened him that he'd blab, because it was wrong. Everyone says he was a self-righteous bastard, and he was known to be against gays. I suppose the powers-that-be in the Church would have taken a pretty dim view of that sort of carry-on, if he'd made it public.'

'Even those who are in favour of committed gay relationships couldn't condone this,' Neville thought aloud. 'It's practically child abuse.'

'I could imagine Jackson—or Jackson and Cherry—killing him just to keep his mouth shut.'

'And what if,' Neville added, 'Jackson already knew that he was going to be appointed a bishop? That would be a pretty strong motive for shutting Jonah Adimola up. Permanently.'

Cowley inhaled luxuriantly. 'I think we're on to something, Guv.' He exhaled, then added, 'Are you going to ask Evans to let us bring Jackson in?'

'Not yet,' Neville decided. That would take too much time, with the clock running on Frances Cherry's detention. 'Let's have another good go at Frances Cherry, now that we have some new questions to ask her. We can always go after Jackson a bit later.'

Cowley stood. 'Okay, Guv. Let's do it.'

'I never thought I'd say this.' Neville's mouth twisted in a sheepish smile and he waved the tabloid in the air. 'But thank you, Lilith Noone.'

⁂

Lilith herself, unaware of how much joy she had brought to Neville, was still working on her story for the next day's paper when her editor rang.

'Good work,' he said, first thing. 'Everyone's talking about it. That's exactly what the *Globe* should be all about.'

'There's more,' she assured him. 'I've saved some of the best bits out.'

There was a short silence on the other end. 'The thing is, Lilith, we have a couple of new developments that you might be interested in.'

'Yes?'

'First of all, Frances Cherry has been arrested. The police have issued a statement saying that a forty-eight-year-old woman is helping them with their enquiries into the Adimola murder.'

A few short days ago, that would have delighted Lilith. Now it seemed like small potatoes. 'Oh,' she said.

'You can take a great deal of the credit for that, I believe,' he went on. 'So I'd like you to see what you can do with it. You know the sort of thing I mean—the sort of thing you've been doing up till now. Don't name her, but imply as much as you want to. As much as you can get away with, under the law.'

'Yes, all right.'

'And the other thing is, the Church of England has just released a statement. Leo Jackson has withdrawn as Bishop of Brixton.'

Now that was a bit more interesting. And she certainly felt that she could take full credit for it. It was what she'd wanted, what she'd been trying to achieve. Still, Lilith felt a tiny twinge of disappointment in the ease of her victory: she'd been sure that Leo Jackson would have put up a bit more fight than that.

She would have to re-write her story for tomorrow to reflect his capitulation. Well, she reflected, all was not lost. She could still use 'Bishop of Buggery'. As in 'Bishop of Buggery Backs Out in Sordid Sex Scandal'.

⚭ ⚭ ⚭

Leo sat at the upstairs window with its magnificent view of Hyde Park and watched the rain come down. It fell steadily from a bruised-looking sky, dripping from the trees even as, with the help of the north wind, it stripped them of their multicoloured leaves. The leaves dropped in showers, until it seemed there could be no more remaining, but still they tumbled, coating the ground with a beautiful but treacherous carpet of glistening colours. People scurried through the park, almost blown along by gusts of wind, their umbrellas occasionally turning inside out and leaving them defenceless. Some of them slipped on the wet leaves and fell, getting up quickly and resuming their ant-like progress toward a drier place—shelter, sanctuary.

For hours he had not moved. The hurting had not yet started. He was like a man whose legs had been blown off in battle, knowing what had happened—seeing the incontrovertible evidence with his own eyes—yet strangely numb.

Leo was a hollow man, reamed out, an empty receptacle waiting to be filled with pain. He knew that it would come. Teetering on the edge of the abyss, he sensed it was only a matter of time before he tumbled in.

For now, though, his world had shrunk to one sodden landscape, one word, and one name. 'Why, Oliver? Why? Why?'

ᖰᖳᖰᖳᖰᖳ

Frances ate her lunch mechanically, scarcely knowing what she was putting in her mouth.

It had been bad, but not as bad as it might have been. Sergeant Cowley had been foul—offensive in his suggestions about her and Leo. She'd heard it all before, though, and had been prepared. Same questions, same answers. 'No, we aren't.' 'No, I didn't.' 'No.' 'No.'

Triona had assured her that if they didn't come up with anything better than that, they would have to let her go. There were no grounds for holding her any longer. She could be home by tea-time. Home with Graham, revelling in the ordinariness and familiarity of the vicarage.

Then Sergeant Pratt came into her little room and sat down, looking grave. 'I have some bad news for you, Frances,' she said.

Frances bit her lip. 'What?'

'I'm afraid that I've had to authorise custody for a further nine hours.'

'But why?' She had been so sure that Salome Pratt would be her champion, would make sure she was home this afternoon. Now she felt betrayed.

'I had no choice,' the sergeant explained unhappily. 'They have new evidence, or at least a new line of enquiry.'

'They're just saying that!'

'I'm afraid not.' Sergeant Pratt didn't go into details. 'Your detention will be reviewed again tonight, by Sergeant Thorp. I'm sure he'll make certain you're treated fairly.'

Tonight. The word sank in painfully. Was she going to be here overnight? She gulped. 'Are you going to put me in a cell?'

Sergeant Pratt avoided her eyes. 'I think it would be best at this point, Frances. This room isn't very comfortable, and the cells have pretty well emptied out of last night's rowdy crowd.'

'But what about… my things? Am I just supposed to wear the same clothes until you decide to let me go home?' She tried to keep her voice reasonable, but heard a note of hysteria creeping in at the end.

'You'll have an opportunity to shower. And if you'd like to ring your husband and ask him to bring a change of clothes…' The sergeant indicated the telephone.

Oh, brilliant, Frances thought. Graham would be in enough of a state without adding that to it.

She would ring Callie instead. Callie could go over and break it to Graham gently, then help him with putting together the things she would need for an overnight stay.

<hr/>

'Yes, of course I'll help,' Callie said without hesitation. The phone call had been a surprise; she certainly wasn't expecting to hear from Frances directly.

Now she was glad that the Harringtons hadn't been at home, that she was free to do as Frances requested, and do it immediately. She didn't relish going back out into the rain, but needs must, and there was nothing she wouldn't do for Frances.

It was only after she'd hung up that she realised she hadn't mentioned anything to Frances about Leo and the *Globe*. Perhaps it was just as well. Frances had enough on her plate without that. She was better off not knowing.

<hr/>

It was time to return to the interview room. Now that she no longer felt that Sergeant Pratt was on her side, Frances relied even more on the reassuring competence of Triona to get her through what was to come.

Triona gave her arm a squeeze as they went into the room. 'It will be fine,' she whispered. 'Just keep your cool.'

Everyone took the same seats, and once again DI Stewart fiddled with the tape recording equipment, identifying the people present and noting the time.

This time, though, Frances sensed a change in the atmosphere. DI Stewart was visibly more engaged; he exchanged significant looks with DS Cowley. There was something going on, and it made her nervous.

'Reverend Cherry,' DI Stewart began, 'we've been asking you questions about your relationship with the Reverend Leo Jackson. You maintain that you have never had a physical relationship with him, but that you are friends.'

'That's right,' Frances confirmed yet again. 'I've known him for years. We're good friends. Nothing more than that.'

DI Stewart glanced at DS Cowley and gave a tiny nod. Cowley leaned forward and spoke smoothly. 'Mrs Cherry, if you and Leo Jackson are such good friends, then you must be aware that he is gay. Homosexual.'

Frances gasped. How on earth…?

She thought quickly. What should she say? How could she continue to protect Leo, without getting herself in any deeper than she already was?

There was a long pause before she replied. 'Yes,' she said cautiously. 'Yes, I am aware that he has that… orientation.' She wasn't making any admissions about his behaviour; surely Leo couldn't be held to blame for his inclinations, if that was as far as it went.

'So you've been trying to protect a friend,' DI Stewart said in a warm, soothing voice. 'You didn't want to tell us the real reason why it was impossible that you and Leo Jackson should be lovers.'

He understood! Frances turned to him in relief. 'That's right. I couldn't say. It wouldn't have been fair to Leo to have betrayed his friendship by telling you that. If he wanted you to know, it was up to him to tell you.'

DI Stewart nodded, and Frances felt affirmed.

But Cowley wasn't finished with her. 'Since you were such good friends, you must also have known about Leo Jackson's… association… with a man called Oliver Pickett.'

Frances hoped her expression hadn't betrayed her surprise. Had they been talking to Leo, then? Had he told them about Oliver in the hopes that it would let her off the hook? Was Leo being incredibly noble, sacrificing himself and his career for her?

Or were they just setting a clever trap for her?

Cowley asked a direct question. 'Did you know about Leo Jackson and Oliver Pickett?'

She turned to Triona. 'Do I have to answer that?'

Triona shook her head. 'You don't have to answer anything you don't want to.'

'Then I would prefer not to answer.'

Cowley lunged forward, almost snarling. 'Are you aware that withholding information which has a vital bearing on our investigation is a very serious matter?'

'I'm not withholding information. I just don't feel it's my place to discuss my friend's private life. If you want to know about that, you'll have to ask *him*.'

'But you *have* withheld information,' Cowley went on. 'Already. You have deliberately misled us about your relationship with Jackson.'

She shook her head. 'I told you the truth. Leo and I are friends, not lovers. What does his private life have to do with your investigation, anyway?'

'We're the ones asking the questions,' Neville Stewart reminded her.

'To your knowledge, was Leo Jackson with Oliver Pickett on the night of Jonah Adimola's murder?' Cowley demanded.

'I would prefer not to answer.'

Cowley didn't pause. 'Had Jonah Adimola found out about Leo Jackson's little... proclivities?'

'I don't know what you mean.'

'Is that why you and Jackson went back to the church that night to meet Adimola?'

'But we didn't! I've said all along that I went home. Leo walked me home.'

'I know what you've said, Mrs Cherry,' the sergeant sneered. 'But now it's time to tell the truth. Did you and Leo Jackson return to the church? Did Jonah Adimola demand money to keep Jackson's secret, or threaten to make it public?'

'That's absurd,' Frances protested, unable to believe what she'd just heard.

'Did you, in fact, kill Jonah Adimola?'

There was a moment of horrified silence as the question hung in the air. 'No,' said Frances quietly.

'Did Leo Jackson kill Jonah Adimola?'

'No.' Her voice rose. 'No.'

Triona stepped in. 'You are distressing my client, Sergeant. I would like to ask for a pause in the proceedings.'

Cowley scowled and looked at Neville. 'I don't think that's necessary.'

Unexpectedly, DI Stewart failed to back him up. 'Miss O'Neil is right.' He made a statement into the tape recorder to the effect that the interview was being terminated, and switched it off.

⌘⌘⌘

'What was that all about, Guv?' Cowley demanded when they were alone. 'Why did you stop it? I had her. She was about to admit it—I just know it.'

'I disagree, Sid.' Neville shook his head. 'She was genuinely shocked. She had no idea what our questions were leading up to.'

'Oh, I think she did. I think she knew exactly what we were getting at. She was just shocked that we'd figured it all out.'

'It's time,' said Neville, 'to talk to Evans again.'

'Evans?'

'Yes. I think we've been interviewing the wrong person. It's time for us to pull Leo Jackson in.'

Neville knew, without being told, why Evans hadn't insisted on arresting Leo Jackson at the same time that they arrested Frances Cherry. With all the charges of institutional racism floating about these days, one had to be extra careful. And it was, thought Neville, quite right that it was so: he'd been in the force long enough to have seen some pretty obnoxious attitudes—often quite overtly expressed—amongst the people with whom he worked, and those attitudes had resulted in a lot of arrests that should never have been made.

He didn't envy Evans the sort of decisions he had to take, constantly walking a tight-rope of political correctness without a safety net. Evans would be the one whose head would be on the block if they made the wrong move.

Not unnaturally, Evans might take some convincing.

∽∽∽ ∽∽∽ ∽∽∽

'He's just come back in from the hospital,' Evans' secretary told them. 'He's been there for most of the day.'

'We can see him, then?'

'Not straightaway. He's in a meeting. But if you're lucky, he'll see you before he goes back. I'll do my best.'

'You're a star,' Neville told her.

'It's important,' Cowley added.

She shook her head. 'I've never seen anyone more besotted with a baby than he is. It's really quite sweet. He's just brought in a whole stack of new photos.'

They cooled their heels for what seemed like hours, eventually going back down to the canteen for tea. At last, though, Evans' secretary rang on Neville's mobile to say that he would give them five minutes, if they could get upstairs immediately.

Evans was obviously in a hurry to get back to the baby; he already had his coat on when they arrived, and didn't offer them a seat. 'What is it, then?' he said impatiently. 'How are you getting on with Frances Cherry?'

Neville told him as quickly as he could about the latest developments: the *Globe* story, Frances Cherry's reluctance to answer their questions arising from it. 'I'd like your permission, sir, to arrest Leo Jackson,' he concluded. 'In my opinion, he holds the key to this.'

'Hmmm.' Evans stroked his monumental chin, and it was obvious to Neville what he was thinking. 'You're sure it's necessary to arrest him? Couldn't you just question him again?'

'I think it's necessary,' confirmed Neville. 'Besides, if the *Globe* story is even anywhere close to being true, there might be criminal charges arising from that. It's pretty nasty stuff, sir—coercive sex, practically rape. Once we get this other business sorted out, we'll have to look into it.'

Evans didn't look very happy at the prospect. 'Well. All right. But... be careful. You know what I mean.'

'Yes, sir.'

'And what about Frances Cherry? Do we need to keep her any longer, or has she told us everything that she's going to tell us?'

Cowley jumped in, forestalling Neville. 'She's being very uncooperative, sir. And worse than that. She's obstructed our enquiries. Wasted our time. Withheld vital information. And I think—I'm sure—that she knows more than she's telling.'

Evans' piggy eyes swivelled to Cowley. 'You think we should keep her here?'

'As long as we can. Until she tells us what she knows about Jackson.'

'Hmm. I don't suppose it will hurt her.'

'After a night in the cells, she might be a bit more inclined to co-operate,' Cowley asserted. 'We might even be able to charge her with perverting the course of justice, if not aiding and abetting.'

'All right.' Evans was already halfway to the door. 'I really must go. Keep me informed.'

༺༺༺ ༺༺༺ ༺༺༺

Arresting Leo Jackson was, they discovered, much easier said than done. When they arrived at the rectory, just as it was beginning to get dark, they found the door surrounded by wet and peevish journalists.

'He hasn't been out all day,' one of them told the policemen. 'Won't come to the door. Doesn't answer his phone.'

'How long have you been here, then?' Neville asked.

The man consulted his watch. 'Since about half six this morning.'

'And you haven't given up?' Cowley shook his head in disbelief.

'He's got to come out some time, doesn't he?' the man said reasonably. 'He can't stay in there forever.'

'You're certain he's there?' Surely, thought Neville, the journalists must have taken loo breaks, or gone off to get something to eat at some point.

'He's there, all right. We've been watching in shifts. He can't have got out without someone seeing him.'

Cowley didn't bother with the bell; he rapped smartly on the door and called out, 'Leo Jackson, it's the police. Please come to the door.'

The journalists perked up and trained their cameras on the door.

There was no reply, no sound of approaching footsteps. Nothing but silence. Neville stood back and looked up: the house was in darkness, curtains undrawn and lights unlit.

'You're sure he can't have got out?' Neville asked again.

'Sure as sure,' confirmed the patient journalist. 'He's in there.'

Cowley repeated his shouted command, this time ringing the bell as well.

Still no sign of life.

The two policemen withdrew a short distance to confer. Cowley was in favour of breaking the door down.

'You must be joking,' Neville said. 'In full view of those cameras? After what Evans said about being careful?' He could see the newspaper headlines already.

'Yeah, Guv. I guess you're right.' Disconsolately he chucked the remains of his latest cigarette into a puddle; it went out with a satisfying sizzle.

ᴄᴍᴍᴏ ᴄᴍᴍᴏ ᴄᴍᴍᴏ

Tears of frustration and empathy for Frances stung Callie's eyes as she scooped food into Bella's bowl. She still hadn't heard anything from Mark. When he did ring, she decided, she would give him a piece of her mind. What kind of friend was he, to leave her in the dark like this?

When the phone went, she snatched it up, indignation boiling over, ready to accuse him of heartless neglect. But the caller was Graham, ringing to report on his visit with Frances. 'They let me see her,' he said. 'For a few minutes.'

'How was she? How did she seem?'

His sigh was audible down the phone line. 'She was very pale. Very quiet. She wouldn't tell me anything about the questions they've been asking her, but she did say that she was being well treated. That's something, I suppose.'

'When are they going to let her come home?' Callie demanded, concern for her friend sharpening her voice.

'I wish I could tell you. She doesn't have any idea.'

'Let me know when you hear anything.'

'Yes, of course.' He added, 'Thanks for your help with the clothes, Callie. I really appreciated it. So did Fran.'

Then the doorbell rang. It was Mark, there in person.

Callie's anger evaporated at the sight of him, his umbrella streaming with water and his shoes soggy. 'I've been waiting for you to ring,' she said feebly. 'Why didn't you ring?'

'I wanted to come instead. To explain what's going on.' He propped his wet umbrella in the corner and stooped to unlace his shoes, then stepped out of them with a grimace.

'Tell me.'

'It's taken me all day to catch up with Neville Stewart. I kept missing him.'

'Tell me,' Callie repeated.

He looked at her levelly, as if assessing her readiness to hear it. 'It's not very good news, I'm afraid.'

Biting her lip, she steeled herself for the worst.

'She won't be going home tonight. It seems that she isn't willing to answer their questions. So everything has ground to a halt.'

'But they can't keep here there indefinitely, can they?' Callie asked. 'Even *I* know that. If she's not charged with anything, they have to let her go.'

'Thirty-six hours,' he said. 'That's as long as they can hold her, without going before a magistrate.'

'But that's tomorrow evening!' she realised. 'Another twenty-four hours! Surely they won't keep her locked up for another whole day!'

Mark shook his head. 'They might not. But they can if they want to. And just between us, Callie, I think they want to.'

⊙⁓⊙ ⊙⁓⊙ ⊙⁓⊙

Returning to the station empty-handed, without Leo Jackson, Neville decided that they'd have one more session with Frances Cherry that evening. It was as unproductive as he had expected: she now refused to say anything, and after a short while, at Triona O'Neil's request, he called it off.

Triona, he thought, must know as well as he did the game that was being played. If Frances Cherry wouldn't talk, they would hold her as long as they could, until the very last minute of their thirty-six hours had run out. He wondered whether Triona had explained that to her client. Perhaps Frances Cherry just didn't care.

It had been a horribly long day, emotionally and mentally draining; Neville was knackered. As Frances and Triona left the interview room, he hurried out of the station and got into his car. Instead of heading toward home, though, he pulled the car up close to the station entrance and waited.

A few minutes later she came out, alone. Under an umbrella, looking round for a taxi.

Neville leaned across and opened the passenger door. 'Get in,' he said. 'I'll take you home.'

'Are you mad?' she hissed at him. 'I shouldn't even be speaking to you. You know that. We could both land in deep trouble.'

'Get in,' Neville repeated. 'Five minutes, then. That's all I ask. Just talk to me for five minutes. I promise I won't even mention your client.'

She closed her umbrella and climbed in, glaring. 'You have a lot of nerve,' she snapped, as he navigated the car onto a quiet side street and parked it. 'After what you did to me, you bastard.'

'Today?'

'Nine years ago.'

'What *I* did to *you*?' He stared at her in the faint yellow light of the street lamp. 'You're the one who left *me*, Triona. You walked out of my life. I came home one day and you'd packed up and gone. No note or anything. Just gone. End of story.'

'Yes, I left you.' The seconds ticked by before she added, almost inaudibly, 'But you didn't come after me.'

'I didn't even know where you'd gone!'

'You could have found me. If you'd wanted to.'

Neville swallowed a lump in his throat. 'Just as a matter of interest, where did you go? Was there someone else?'

'Not then. Not really.'

'Then why did you leave me?'

She picked at a loose thread on the sleeve of her raincoat. 'I think you know the answer to that. We didn't… want the same things.'

Even now she couldn't say it, and he wouldn't either. She hadn't said it then, but he'd known.

'Did you find what you were looking for? With someone else?' His voice sounded surprisingly detached.

'Didn't you know? I married a colleague, another solicitor, a few months after that.' She was equally clinical, as though she were talking about someone else, about a distant acquaintance. 'It didn't work out. It lasted for six years. But it didn't work. It was a mistake from the beginning.'

He *hadn't* known. In fact, he'd never heard another word from or about her since that grim October day. For months he'd expected to run into her somewhere, in court or at a party, but it had never happened.

'And now?' he said, knowing he had no right to ask but unable to stop himself.

'I'm happily single,' she said firmly.

'No one special?'

'God, no. I'm through with all that. My work keeps me busy enough.'

'After this… after all this is over,' Neville heard himself saying. 'Could we get together for a drink? Dinner, maybe?'

There was another long pause. 'No promises.' Then she looked at her watch. 'Your five minutes are up, Inspector Stewart,' she said briskly, opening the car door and raising her umbrella in one swift movement.

Triona disappeared into the night. Neville sat for a moment before pulling out and turning the car toward home. It was a foul night; visibility was poor. He wasn't entirely sure that it was all down to the heaviness of the rain and the inefficiency of his windscreen wipers. It might have had something to do with the mist of tears in his eyes.

⁂

In spite of his exhaustion, sleep eluded Neville that night. After an hour or two of tossing and turning, he got up and poured himself a stiff whiskey.

Why, he asked himself, had he let her go? At the time he had convinced himself that it was out of indifference. There were plenty of other fish in the sea, he'd told himself defiantly. If she wanted to leave, let her—he'd soon find someone else.

As time went on, though, he'd come to realise that it was more complex than that. He'd been terrified of the feelings she aroused in him; he hadn't been able to handle them, or envision where they would lead him. It was easier—far easier—to let her walk away.

It wasn't that he didn't miss her, or feel pain at her going. But eventually the pain had faded, the wound healed over. He'd managed to forget her. Almost. Only occasionally, in the middle of the night, he would think of her, the scar tissue throbbing to remind him of what he'd lost.

Tonight the scar tissue felt as though it were a fresh wound, still lacerated and bleeding.

After nine years, Triona O'Neil was still the most beautiful woman he'd ever known. The most beautiful, and the most desirable.

Chapter Nineteen

The Stanfords' phone rang in the early hours of Friday morning. It wasn't the first time that such a thing had happened; it was, thought Jane as she struggled to consciousness, something that came with the territory. Part of a vicar's lot. And a vicar's wife's as well.

They kept a phone at the bedside, just like a doctor. She allowed Brian to answer it, but listened to his side of the conversation and tried to guess at the other half. 'Oh, I'm sorry.' 'Yes, of course I'll come.' 'No, I don't know.' 'It's her day off today, so I can't speak for her.' 'Yes, I'll see you soon.'

Brian put the phone down and relaxed back against the pillows for a moment, sighing.

'Dennis Harrington?' Jane surmised. Brian had always told her everything when it came to his parishioners, or *their* parishioners as she liked to think of them.

'Yes. Elsie seems to have taken a turn for the worse. They don't think she has long, apparently.'

'You're going.' It was a statement rather than a question.

'He wants her to have the Sacrament.'

Jane nodded. The usual thing.

'He said,' Brian added, 'that he hadn't heard anything from Callie. That she hadn't come to the hospital.' He turned and blinked short-sightedly at his wife as he reached for his spectacles.

'You *did* tell her, didn't you, Janey? That Elsie was in hospital and wanted to see her?'

She thought quickly, not wishing to incriminate herself or to make any claims which could be disproved. 'It might have slipped my mind,' she admitted.

'Well, perhaps you could give her a ring a bit later,' Brian suggested, getting out of bed. 'I know it's her day off, but she might be willing to make an exception in this case.'

'All right,' Jane agreed, knowing in advance that she just might forget again.

⟨◦⟩ ⟨◦⟩ ⟨◦⟩

The gusty storms of Thursday had given way to grey skies and steady rain. It couldn't be said that the sun rose, but the sky lightened enough to signal that a new day had arrived. Still Leo sat at the window.

Then, suddenly, he rose from his chair. He went through to the bathroom, showered, and got dressed, putting on clean black trousers and one of his uniquely colourful clerical shirts. From his wardrobe he retrieved a small duffel bag, in which he put an extra shirt and a change of underwear. Then he went downstairs, took an umbrella from the hall stand, and threw open the front door.

The crowd had gone. They'd finally given up, he supposed. Only the faithful remnant remained: the weedy ginger-haired man, curled up asleep on the top step, kept relatively dry by a propped-up golfing umbrella.

He scrambled to his feet as Leo opened the door. 'Oh!' he said. 'Oh!' Like some strange little wild creature in a children's book, Leo thought.

Leo stated the obvious. 'The others have gone?'

'The police were here. Didn't you hear them? Everyone else was tired of waiting. After the police left, they all went.'

So they'd had their story after all. 'What about you, my friend?' he asked kindly. 'Why are you still here?'

'I didn't want to give up.'

'Come with me, then. You shall have your reward.' Leo raised his umbrella and walked out into the rain.

The man followed. 'Where are we going?'

'Never mind, my friend. You'll soon find out.'

'Could I ask you some questions?'

Leo shook his head. 'Not now.'

They went through quiet residential streets in silence, over pavements blanketed with slippery leaves, the little man scurrying to keep up with Leo's long strides. Then they turned a corner and were in the Edgeware Road, in the midst of the rush hour. No one gave them a second glance.

Leo was mounting the steps of the police station before his companion realised where they were headed. Lowering his umbrella, he went to the desk. 'I'm Leo Jackson,' he said pleasantly. 'I believe that you want to arrest me.'

ᏩᎳᎷᏜ ᏩᎳᎷᏜ ᏩᎳᎷᏜ

All week, Callie had been looking forward to having a lie-in on her day off. She hadn't set the alarm, and there was no sun to peep round the edges of the curtains to rouse her. So she drowsed a bit, halfway between sleep and waking, until she became aware that she was not alone in the bed.

Bella.

Callie had shut her in the kitchen as usual, but she must not have closed the kitchen door firmly; Bella had left her basket and sought her mistress out some time in the night.

She cuddled the furry little body, stroking her silky ears, taking comfort from her warmth. Bella accepted the caresses blissfully, paying her back with the occasional lick; if she'd been a cat, she would have purred.

For the first time in days Callie thought about Adam, and the old times. If things had been different…

But, she realised with a dawning feeling of liberation, she had no regrets. Not even a pang of pain, thinking of him. At this moment in her life, she would rather have Bella in her bed than Adam. Pippa was welcome to him. In—or out of—her bed.

It was also Vincent Underwood's custom to observe Friday as his day off. His pleas to the Bishop for more help in the parish had still failed to bear fruit, but he'd managed to arrange for Benedict Burton, the retired priest, to cover for him that day and take the services at St Mary the Virgin. So the day was his to enjoy.

His mood, at breakfast, was ebullient. Marigold, still feeling shaky from her ordeal at the hands of the bag-snatcher, joined him at the table to find him reading the newspaper and chuckling to himself.

It was not the *Globe* he was reading, but the eminently respectable and high-toned broadsheet which had been delivered to this house every day as long as Marigold could remember, even back to her childhood. This broadsheet had not found it seemly to enter into the speculations surrounding Jonah Adimola's murder, except in the loftiest manner; today it deigned to inform its readers, in a brief paragraph, that a woman had been arrested in connection with that murder and was helping police with their enquiries.

Vincent read the paragraph out to Marigold as she spooned marmalade onto her plate. 'So the police have listened to me at last,' he said smugly. 'I told them from the beginning that Frances Cherry was the only one who could have done it. After all, it was her stole he was strangled with. I can't understand why it's taken them so long to arrest her.'

Marigold was only half listening. 'I suppose they have to be sure about these things,' she said. 'They can't just go round arresting people without being sure.'

He ignored her, turning back a page and smoothing the paper out on the table. 'Here's something else which will amuse you. "The Reverend Leo Jackson, Area Dean of Bayswater, has withdrawn his acceptance two days after his appointment as the next Bishop of Brixton. The withdrawal was announced by Church House, following unsubstantiated tabloid allegations of sexual misconduct on the part of Mr Jackson. Mr Jackson was unavailable for comment." I'm sure he was,' chortled Vincent.

'It says "unsubstantiated",' Marigold pointed out. 'It might not be true.'

'Of course it's true.' Vincent slathered marmalade on a triangle of toast and bit into it with a satisfying crunch. 'You know what I always say, my dear. No smoke without fire.'

Marigold averted her face from him. Oh, how could he gloat like that, after what he'd once put her through? If it hadn't been for her father…

～～～ ～～～ ～～～

Over a leisurely breakfast of cereal and toast, Callie thought about how to spend her precious day off. The weather was far too unpleasant to contemplate spending any more time than necessary outdoors. She would have to give Bella a couple of walks, and she needed to do a bit of shopping so she'd have food for the weekend.

Apart from that, all she really wanted to do was take a long hot bubble bath, then just slob around the flat, enjoying some quality time with Bella. And if there was anything she could do for Frances…

Or, she thought suddenly, with a sinking feeling, she could go and see her mother.

She hadn't even spoken to her all week. With everything else that had been happening, her mother had been relegated to a nagging twinge of guilt at the back of her mind.

Guilt, and duty. A strong combination, when it came to her mother.

She washed up the breakfast dishes, poured herself another mug of tea, then picked up the phone with a sigh and rang Laura Anson.

'Well, I must say. I'd been wondering what on earth had happened to you,' her mother started off. 'I know you're busy, but at least you could have rung.'

It was all so predictable. Evidently it never occurred to Laura Anson that the telephone worked both ways; she preferred to play the martyr, waiting for calls which never came. Or at least not as often as she thought they should.

'And have you heard anything from Peter?' Laura went on.

'He's gone to Italy. Milan.'

'I *know* he's gone to Italy. With one of his chums, I believe. He rang me before he left. But he hasn't even sent me a card. I thought he might have sent one to *you*.'

'The post can be quite slow,' Callie said.

'That's true,' her mother admitted grudgingly. 'Your card from Venice took ten days.'

Venice. Callie wished, with a sudden and intense longing, that she were back there. Far away from sodden London, basking in the golden Venetian sunshine, in a gondola with…

No, she said sternly to herself. Don't go there.

⌘ ⌘ ⌘

Frances' breakfast—an omelette—had come from the freezer, via the microwave. Neither process had improved it, and it had a tough, rubbery consistency which defied the plastic cutlery supplied to those in custody. Just like airline passengers, thought Frances with grim humour. Neither could be trusted with implements which could be used to harm themselves or anyone else.

Not that she had much of an appetite, though she hadn't eaten much at all in the last twenty-four hours.

Twenty-four hours. It was time to review the custody arrangements again.

Triona arrived a few minutes before eight, and was allowed some time with her client. 'How did you sleep?' she asked.

Triona, thought Frances, didn't look as if she'd slept particularly well herself: her unruffled expression of the day before showed distinct signs of strain. She hoped she wasn't responsible for that. 'Not too well,' she admitted. 'I did manage to doze off toward morning. But it was pretty noisy in the cells for most of the night. And the bed wasn't the world's most comfortable. Not,' she added, smiling ruefully, 'that I'd expect it to be.'

'Well, I'm going to do my best to get you out of here in a few minutes,' Triona assured her. 'They don't have anything to charge you with. It's disgraceful that they haven't let you go yet.'

Sergeant Salome Pratt was back on duty, and that gave Frances some cause for hope.

But Neville Stewart had already talked to Sergeant Pratt. He'd conveyed to her the information that Detective Superintendent Evans was in agreement that Frances Cherry should be held for another twelve hours. It was especially important, he'd said, now that they had Leo Jackson in custody. If the two of them had in any way worked together to commit the murder or cover it up, they would need both of them there.

So when she visited Frances, it was as the reluctant bearer of bad tidings. In spite of Triona's protestations, it had already been agreed. It had been decided, as well, that Frances was not to be told of Leo's arrest. Not for now.

'I don't have anything else to say,' Frances stated. 'They can keep me here as long as they like, but I'm not saying another word.'

Then Sergeant Pratt, perhaps feeling guilty, offered a concession. 'If you'd like to have any visitors today,' she said, 'I could make arrangements for that. Would you like to have your husband come again? Or a friend, perhaps?'

She didn't want to see Graham in here again, Frances realised. He had put on a show of bravado for her benefit, but it had been painful and stressful for both of them. And although she'd like to see Leo, it was out of the question to consider dragging him into this.

Callie, she thought. She would love to have a visit from Callie. Wonderful, normal Callie.

❦ ❦ ❦

Leo Jackson, Neville and Cowley soon discovered, was no more co-operative than Frances Cherry. It wasn't that he was belligerent or contentious: he was acquiescent to the point of passivity.

He refused counsel, in spite of the warnings of the custody sergeant that he ought to have legal representation. 'I haven't done anything wrong,' he said. 'I've answered all of your questions honestly, every time I've talked to you. And now I have nothing more to say.'

Sergeant Pratt had set them up in an interview room, giving them priority over the petty criminals who had come in overnight. Leo Jackson sat on his own at the table, across from the two policemen.

'We'd like to ask you some questions about Oliver Pickett,' said Neville.

'I have nothing to say.' His mouth was curved into a semblance of a smile, but his eyes were shuttered, blank. No matter what the question, he offered the same response.

After half an hour, they gave up.

⚭⚭⚭

Lilith rang Oliver that morning, on the new mobile phone number which only she possessed.

There was loud music playing when he answered; she had to strain to hear him. 'I just wanted to see how you were doing,' she said.

'Yeah. Fine.'

'The story in yesterday's paper—I hope you were happy with it. That you felt I'd got across what you wanted to say.'

'Yeah, it was good.'

He sounded different, somehow, she thought. His accent a bit more pronounced, perhaps; his voice a little slurred. Was it possible that he was drunk? At this hour of the morning?

The poor lad. She supposed he was drowning his sorrows. The abuse he'd suffered at the hands of Leo Jackson had probably scarred him for life. Thank goodness, Lilith told herself virtuously, there were people like her in the world who were willing to take a stand for what was right. To stick their necks out in the pursuit of truth and justice.

'Well,' she said, 'I was glad to be able to help. As you said, people need to be warned about perverts like him. I'd hate to think about anyone else being put through what you were, just because you were afraid to speak out. You should be proud of yourself, Oliver. You've done a great public service.' Just as she had.

'Yeah, the thing is…' There was a long pause, during which the music was turned down to a more civilised volume. 'The thing is, now I feel kind of bad.'

'I'm sure you do. It was a dreadful ordeal you went through. But now it's over,' she assured him bracingly.

'No. I mean… I feel kind of bad. You know? He was… he was nice to me. You know? I think… I think he loved me. You know?'

He really was quite drunk, she now realised. He'd probably been drinking all night.

'*Loved* you?' she said. 'Love? I'm sure that love had nothing to do with it, Oliver. He might have said he loved you, just to get you to do what he wanted. That doesn't mean anything.'

It was as if he hadn't heard her; he went on, 'I wonder if I should ring him. You know? Just to tell him… no hard feelings. I mean, he's a priest. You know? I suppose he'll forgive me.'

'It's him who should be begging *you* for forgiveness. Not that he deserves it, after the disgusting way he's used you! You've done the right thing, Oliver,' Lilith reminded him. 'Now it's time to let it go.'

'You don't think I should ring him, then?' His appeal sounded almost tearful.

'Certainly not!' she snapped back. 'Don't even think about it.'

'All right, then,' he said meekly, terminating the call.

ᚱᚢᚾᛟ ᚱᚢᚾᛟ ᚱᚢᚾᛟ

It was late morning when Marigold had a call from her bank manager. Mr Firth was a man she'd known for years; his firm had always handled her father's financial affairs, and he had personally been in charge of hers since before her marriage to Vincent. He must, she thought, be approaching retirement age. She would hate to lose him, with his quiet competence—and the link, however tenuous, to her father.

'I wondered,' he said, 'whether you might be at all free to call in this afternoon.'

She mentally reviewed her diary: she was supposed to be going to the ballet tonight, and had made an appointment for a manicure and a facial in the afternoon in anticipation.

'Could we make it Monday morning?' she suggested.

Mr Firth cleared his throat. 'Well. It's rather important, Mrs Underwood.'

She sighed. 'All right, then. What time shall I come?'

'Three o'clock, perhaps?'

It would be possible to cancel the facial and still salvage the manicure, if they made it half three. She suggested that minor alteration; he agreed.

'I'll see you then,' he said. 'Thank you for agreeing on such short notice, but I'm sure you'll understand why I thought it was necessary, after we've spoken.'

'Can't you tell me what it's in reference to, Mr Firth?'

He was firm. 'Not over the phone, Mrs Underwood.'

It was only after she'd hung up that she realised: in all the excitement and stress of yesterday morning, she had not notified the bank about the theft of her handbag. She'd cancelled her credit cards; she'd told the police. But she had forgotten about the bank, and her chequebook was in the stolen handbag. Someone had probably been writing cheques left, right and centre on her account.

What a nuisance! How careless of her!

Well, she thought philosophically, it sounded as though Mr Firth had the matter in hand. He would give her a little lecture, she would apologise, and then it would be up to him to sort out the consequences. It couldn't be helped.

Marigold promptly put the matter out of her mind, concerned only that she might find it difficult to pay for the manicure, without either a credit card or a chequebook. Then she remembered that she had a small stash of notes in the drawer of her bureau, kept for emergencies. This would certainly qualify as an emergency.

Callie's duty visit with her mother was just as unrewarding as she had expected. Laura Anson quizzed her relentlessly about the details of Frances' arrest—her information gleaned, she was careful to say, from her cleaning lady, who read the *Globe*. 'And what about this very unsavoury business with this black bishop?' she went on, wrinkling her nose in distaste. 'Honestly, Callie. If I'd known what a sink-hole the Church was, I would never have allowed you to get involved.'

Callie, who had successfully fended off the questions about Frances by feigning ignorance, forbore to say that her involvement in the Church had never been a matter which required her mother's approval; she had been well into her adulthood when the decision had been made. They had had this discussion before; nothing she said would change her mother's mind about it. Or hers.

Why, she thought as she headed back home to take Bella for a quick walk before her appointment to see Frances at the police station, had she not sought a curacy as far away as possible from London and her mother? Yorkshire? Cornwall? Surely they needed curates there as well.

Adam, that was why. Adam was the reason she was in London.

And besides, she told herself, it wouldn't have made any real difference. Her mother would have expected a weekly visit even if she was living at the other end of the country. Or the other end of the world. Barnes, Barnsley, Bodmin or Boston—it was all the same to Laura Anson.

Frances was waiting for Callie's visit, looking forward to it as the high point of her day. Callie, she reflected, was so normal. So sensible, so sane. So untouched by any of this unreal situation in which she found herself: she, Frances Cherry, a priest in the Church of England, incarcerated and implicated in murder. It was hard to believe that outside of the walls of this police station, life went on much the same as ever for most people. Callie was a concrete reminder of that other reality—the world of which she herself had been a part just a few days ago.

When Callie came in, Frances rose and hugged her, metaphorically embracing all that she stood for. And immediately she began talking about everyday, mundane subjects—anything she could think of that was unconnected with this place and this ordeal. 'How is your dog?' she asked.

Callie smiled. 'Oh, she's lovely. Absolutely gorgeous, in fact. I love her to bits.'

'No problems with her? She doesn't chew things up, or mess on the floor?'

'She's not a puppy,' Callie said. 'She's two years old. I don't think I could cope with a puppy. Especially without a back garden. I think that's the worst thing—having to take her out to the park to do her business, even when the weather is foul.'

Frances remembered all too well what it meant to have a puppy. They'd had one, once; Heather had had her heart set on it, had nagged and begged till they'd given in and got her one.

It had chewed everything in sight, including Graham's best black shoes. It had ruined the drawing room carpet, and before it was full grown, at which time they might have expected to reap the benefits of pet ownership, it had run away. Heather had been playing with the puppy in the back garden; with her customary intensity she had got involved in something else—some solitary game—and while she was absorbed, the puppy had wandered off through the gate Heather had left open. They had never found it, never seen it again.

Heather was heartbroken, of course. Inconsolable. She had wanted another puppy, immediately.

But they had learned their lesson. 'When you're grown up you can have one,' Frances had said. Heather, though, had never stayed in one place long enough to have a pet. Maybe now, now that she was settled down with Zack...

'Did I tell you,' Frances said, 'that Heather is coming home for Christmas?'

'Oh, that's great!'

'Well, that's the good news.' Frances gave a bemused grimace. 'The bad news is that she's now a vegan, so turkey is off the menu. To welcome our prodigal home, we'll have to go out and kill the fatted nut-roast.'

They both laughed.

'And she's bringing her new husband with her,' Frances added. 'Husband—can you believe it? She's gone and married some ancient hippie with plaits and a tattoo. And a vasectomy.' Now even that seemed funny, Frances realised, laughing till the tears ran down her cheeks.

⌒⥤ ⌒⥤ ⌒⥤

Marigold's nails looked lovely. She didn't like anything too extreme; on her instruction they had been done in an opalescent pink, as tender as the inside of a sea shell. She examined them in the taxi on the way to the bank, thankful that she had enough left over from the manicure to pay for the taxi. Surely Mr Firth would advance her some cash from her account until such time as a new chequebook and credit cards could be arranged.

Mr Firth's domain was not one of the vulgar high street banks, advertising on television with singing bank managers or animated logos. It was an old-fashioned establishment, proud of its reputation for exclusivity and stuffiness. The interior was as it had always been in living memory: wood panelling, leather chairs, dim lights, thick carpets; there was not a bit of plastic or high-tech computer wizardry in sight.

As befitted a client—never a customer in their parlance—of her longstanding and importance, Marigold was not kept waiting, but was ushered immediately into Mr Firth's sanctum.

'Thank you for coming, Mrs Underwood,' he said with grave courtesy, then asked his secretary—surely she was the same one he'd had thirty years ago, grown old along with him—to bring in a tray of tea.

Marigold had decided to forestall him by confessing; perhaps that would ameliorate the chastisement. 'I know what this is about,' she said as she sat down. 'And I'm so sorry.'

His surprise was apparent. 'You do?'

'The chequebook. I should have rung you, but it slipped my mind.'

Now he looked totally baffled. 'Chequebook?'

'The one that was stolen. I suppose he's written all sorts of cheques on the account. Aren't I insured for that?'

The secretary must have had the tea tray ready; already she was bringing it in, putting it on Mr Firth's desk. The teapot was Georgian silver, and the china was Crown Derby. She slipped silently out again and he poured, using a chased silver tea strainer. 'Do you take sugar, Mrs Underwood? I thought not.' He brought a cup round the desk and handed it to her, then offered her a plate of delicate biscuits. She waved them away.

Mr Firth resumed his seat behind his desk. 'Now, Mrs Underwood. Let's start over. What is the reason you imagine I wanted to see you?'

'I had my handbag stolen yesterday morning,' she said patiently. 'My chequebook was in it. I reported it to the police, but I forgot to notify you.'

He made a noise, clucking his tongue against his teeth. 'You should have told us straightaway.'

'Yes, I know. I'm sorry.' She sipped her tea.

'But that isn't why I wanted to see you.'

'Oh! It isn't?'

'No.' He now took a sip, then put his cup down on the desk. Clearing his throat, he folded his hands in front of him. 'You must understand that this is very difficult for me, Mrs Underwood.'

Now she was beginning to be frightened. Was the bank going under? Had she lost all her money? Had someone been swindling her?

'We've known each other for a good many years,' he said. 'There have been no secrets between us.'

'What's happened?' She could hear the panic rising in her voice.

'My mother celebrated her birthday yesterday,' said Mr Firth, 'and I felt it was important that I take her out for the day.'

Mr Firth had a mother? Heavens, thought Marigold—she must be ancient. But what did any of this have to do with his mother?

'As a result,' he went on, 'I was not here. That is most unfortunate. When I came in this morning I checked through the books, the transactions. That is when I discovered it.'

'Discovered what?' Marigold was almost holding her breath, as much with impatience as with worry. Why all this song-and-dance? Why didn't he just get on with it?

'A substantial sum of money was withdrawn from your account yesterday. Had I been here, of course I would not have sanctioned it. Not without your express permission.'

She exhaled. 'Well, I told you. My chequebook was stolen. The man who took it—he must have done it.'

'No, Mrs Underwood.' He looked at her, his brows drawn together in an expression of sorrow. 'I'm very sorry to have to tell you this. But it was no stranger.'

'Then who...'

'The manager on duty confirmed it. It was your husband, Mrs Underwood. Your husband Vincent.'

Seeing Frances had upset Callie far more than she'd expected. While Frances had made every effort to seem relaxed, even good-humoured, it had come across as febrile, false. Callie knew her well enough to see the tension, the tears, just below the surface, and she was not reassured.

Her day off was not turning out to be a relaxing one. The phone was ringing as she came in the door. Shedding umbrella and coat, she ran for it.

'Oh, you're there, then. Father Brian seemed to think you might be away.'

She recognised the voice of Dennis Harrington. 'How are you, Dennis?' she asked. 'How's Elsie? I've been a bit concerned.

You weren't at home yesterday when I called round. And you didn't answer your phone.'

There was a long, shuddering indrawn breath on the other end. 'You don't know, then? My Elsie—she's gone.'

'Gone?' For a moment Callie didn't understand. Gone into a nursing home? Gone on holiday?

Gone. Oh, God… 'Dennis! She's not—'

'This morning,' he confirmed. 'Gone to be with Our Lord. Called home. She's better off there, mind. Her suffering is over. She's at rest now. And she went peaceful.'

Callie felt as though she'd been socked in the stomach. She collapsed onto the nearest chair. 'Oh, Dennis!'

'I know she's better off,' he repeated, convincing himself. 'But I'm going to miss her so. Oh, girl. I don't know what I'm going to do without her.' He drew another deep breath, then started to sob.

'But why… why didn't you tell me? Why didn't you leave a message?'

He spoke through gulping sobs. 'I asked Father Brian to tell you. Yesterday, when she was took to hospital. She asked for you, Elsie did.'

'He didn't tell me.'

'And again this morning. When they said… when we knew she didn't have long. Father Brian told his wife to let you know.'

Callie didn't understand. It made no sense. 'I would have come,' she said. 'You know I would have come. I didn't know.'

'Father Brian said as it was your day off. He said you might not want to come on your day off.'

'Where are you now? I'll come now.'

'It's too late for my Elsie.'

Tears stung Callie's eyes. 'I'd like to see you, though, Dennis. Where are you?'

'The doctor's just given me one of them sedatives. To make me sleep, he says. So now's not a good time.'

'I'll come in the morning,' she promised. 'First thing, or whenever you like. Ring me when you want me to come.'

The old man wheezed out another gusty sob. 'I just wanted to let you know something else, girl. My Elsie—before she went, she said it was her wish that you should do her funeral.'

'Me?'

'Father Brian tried to talk her out of it. Said you were only new, you'd never done a funeral before. But she had her heart set on it.' He gained some control of his voice and went on, 'You told us as a deacon, that you couldn't do the Mass, but you could do weddings and funerals. And my Elsie remembered that. She wanted you to do it, and that's that. Father Brian had to agree in the end.'

Callie gulped, and her voice came out as a croak. 'I would be very honoured.'

Bella was at her side, sensing that her mistress was unhappy. Whimpering, she tried to climb into her lap as Callie put the phone down.

Callie scooped her up and buried her face in the soft fur. 'Oh, Bella,' she wailed, the tears spilling over. 'Oh, my Bella, it's just too much to bear!'

Chapter Twenty

Marigold made an effort to keep her face composed, for the benefit of the taxi driver. If he had been looking at her in the mirror, he would have seen an attractive woman, no longer young but retaining more than a vestige of good looks, dressed in understated yet elegant clothes. Her hands would not have been visible to him, so he could not have seen that they plucked at each other nervously, picking at the edges of her nail polish. She was not at all conscious of it, either; her mind was too occupied.

What, she wondered, was Vincent up to?

The sum of money involved was not small.

One of the many ways her father had looked after her interests had been to make sure that everything was in Marigold's name. His solicitors had drawn up the papers with great care; when he died, everything of her father's had passed over to her absolutely—the house and contents, the investments, the money. Even before his death, the marriage settlement had been on her, tied up so that Vincent couldn't touch it. Thanks to her father and his solicitors, they'd had an ironclad prenuptial agreement long before it became the vogue in Hollywood.

Vincent, for all of the years of their marriage, had been a kept man. If he needed money, Marigold reasoned, he had his clerical stipend. He could spend that as he liked. Apart from that, she provided the roof over his head and the food on his table. When they took a holiday, it was her money—her father's money—that paid for it.

Her father had clearly known what he was doing. It wasn't that he didn't like Vincent, though he'd never felt that a mere clergyman, even one who was tipped to be a bishop one day, was a worthy husband for his only child—a beautiful child, who might have married a prince. But he had been the first to spot Vincent's weakness. When that unpleasantness had cropped up, Marigold had been shocked to the core; her father, though, had not been unprepared. A tower of strength he'd proved to be; he'd moved swiftly to minimise the damage. He had promised Marigold that no one would know, and he'd kept his promise. Thanks to his intervention, it had never made it to court, never reached the newspapers.

As far as Marigold was aware, Vincent had held to his word that it would never happen again. Maybe it was because she had told him that if it did, she would not hesitate to divorce him without a penny.

What if he had once again strayed from the path? It didn't bear thinking about.

But she could no longer bury her head in the sand; she had to think about it. Because if it were true, this time her father was not there to pick up the pieces. And people would surely find out.

Tonight she would confront him about it. She would ask him about the money.

The rain was beginning to slack off at last. By the time the taxi had reached the house, it was barely misting; Marigold didn't even need to put up her umbrella. She paid the driver and climbed the steps to the front door.

The daily was in the hall, donning her plastic mac in preparation for leaving. 'I've just started a fire for you in the drawing room,' she said. 'I've drawn all the curtains. And I've made a fresh pot of tea.'

'Is Father Vincent in?' Marigold asked.

The daily shook her head. 'He went out after lunch. He didn't say where he was going. But he did say that he would be in this evening.'

'Thank you.' Marigold went through into the drawing room. The fire had barely caught hold, so she gave the coals a stir with the poker, then poured herself a cup of tea.

Marigold sat in her favourite chair by the fire, the tea going cold as she retreated into her thoughts, waiting for her husband.

Jezebel, the heartless cat, sauntered into the room, jumped on her mistress' lap, and not finding it congenial enough, promptly jumped down again and went off to pursue other interests.

Marigold looked down at her empty lap, at her hands, at the ruin of the expensive manicure. 'Oh, no,' she whispered. Silent tears slid down her cheeks.

⁂

'I can't bear it,' Callie repeated into Bella's furry neck.

The doorbell rang. 'Now what?' she moaned; she wasn't expecting Mark until later.

'I finished a bit early and thought I'd come straight here,' he said as she opened the door. 'I tried to get you on the phone but it was engaged. It's stopped raining,' he added, then caught sight of her face. 'Callie! What's wrong?'

'Nothing. Everything.' She put her hands over her face. 'It's all just too much, Marco.'

'What? Tell me,' he ordered.

'My mother is impossible. Frances is locked up in a cell. And now... one of my parishioners has died. Someone I'd come to care about. I didn't even know.' It all came spilling out: how Elsie had gone into hospital and died, and Jane Stanford hadn't passed on the messages. 'It must have been deliberate,' Callie said. 'But I just don't understand it. Why would she do that? Why should she hate me?'

'Has it occurred to you that she might be jealous?' Mark said perceptively.

'Jealous? Of me?' Callie's eyes widened. 'But why?'

'Because you're working with her husband. You're seeing more of him than she is, probably.'

'That's ridiculous! She doesn't need to worry about that!' she protested. 'I don't exactly fancy Brian Stanford.'

'And because,' Mark went on, 'you're younger than she is. And you're so…'

'Anyway, I don't need it.' Her voice caught on a half-sob. 'Not on top of everything else. It's just too much.'

Mark took a step forward and hugged her. She relaxed against him, finding comfort in his sympathy.

He stroked her hair. Callie's heart thumped and her stomach gave a peculiar but not unpleasant lurch. Then his thumb caressed her cheek, and she stopped breathing for an instant. 'Callie…' he murmured.

The doorbell rang. They jumped apart guiltily, as though the person on the other side of the door possessed x-ray vision.

'Are you expecting someone?' Mark's voice sounded strange.

'No.'

She opened the door. Peter tumbled in, dropping carrier bags and embracing his sister, trilling '*Buona sera!*'

The next thirty seconds were chaos. Bella proved herself utterly useless as a watch-dog, throwing herself on the visitor with enthusiastic licks and tail-wags. Callie tried to perform introductions, even as Peter explained why he had arrived unannounced. 'Food!' he said, reclaiming the carrier bags from the floor and holding them up in triumph. 'Italian food! I hope you don't have other plans for dinner tonight.'

'You're cooking?' she asked in amazement.

'Well, no. You are,' he admitted sheepishly. 'But I've brought all the ingredients.'

'Let's see what we have here.' Mark took the bags from Peter and began delving into them. 'Olive oil.'

'Extra virgin,' Peter pointed out.

'*Bellissimo*,' pronounced Mark. 'And good balsamic vinegar.'

Peter rattled off a list, beaming happily. 'Marinated artichoke hearts, olives, Parma ham, Milano salami. That's all for the antipasto. Then there's pecorino cheese, and some Parmesan. And lovely mushrooms. Funghi.'

'Pasta,' said Mark. 'And some good passata. And ciabatta bread.'

'Not to forget the wine,' added Peter.

'I take it,' Callie put in, 'that you've had a good time in Italy?'

'Ah, *la bella Italia*,' Peter sighed. 'In a word, it was bliss.'

'You speak Italian?' asked Mark eagerly.

Peter gave a modest grin. 'I picked up a bit. It's the most beautiful language. And the most beautiful country. I just can't believe it's taken me so long to get there. Why would anyone go to France, when they could go to Italy?'

'Peter's always been good at languages,' Callie said.

Mark examined the outside of the carrier bags. 'You've been to Milano?'

'That's right.'

'Next time you must go to Venice. Milano is all right, but *Venezia è ottima.*'

'You're Italian!' Peter realised belatedly.

'Sono nato a Londra, ma i miei genitori sono veneziani.'

Callie, feeling a bit dazed, carried the food through to the kitchen while the men chatted. When she returned to the sitting room, Mark was putting his coat on.

'You're not going, are you?' She could hear the dismay in her own voice.

'Don't go on my account,' Peter added. 'I'm the gatecrasher here. And there's plenty of food for all of us.'

'I just thought I'd take Bella out for a few minutes.' Indeed, Bella was already at the door, wagging her tail vigourously. 'It will give you two a bit of time to catch up.'

As soon as he'd gone, Peter turned to Callie with a wide-eyed, mischievous look. 'Well, Sis. I must say. You haven't exactly let the grass grow under your feet.'

'It's not...' she tried to protest.

'Oh, I approve. He's a great improvement on what's-his-name.' He added, 'I never did think he was right for you. No sense of humour whatsoever. You're well shot of him.'

She didn't feel equal to replying.

'And,' Peter went on, grinning, 'he's really cute. I don't suppose there's any chance he's gay?'

Callie turned her head away so he wouldn't see her involuntary smile. 'I'm pretty sure he's not.'

'Ah, well.' He sighed philosophically. 'My loss is your gain.'

'But you have this new chap,' she reminded him. 'The fashion designer.'

'Oh, him.' Peter gave a dismissive shrug. 'He's history.'

'Don't tell me it's over already! I thought he was meant to be the great love of your life!'

'Well,' said Peter. 'You know me. I live in hope. But he was dreadful, Sis. A workaholic, and a control freak. A very bad combination, believe me.'

'What happened?'

'He was working the whole week, the whole time we were in Milan.'

'It was a business trip,' she reminded him.

'Yes, but all work and no play… The worst thing was, though, that he didn't want me to play, either. He just wanted me to sit in the hotel room all day and wait for him.'

'Obviously you didn't agree.'

'Blow that for a game of soldiers!' Peter said with feeling. 'I wanted to make the most of it. So I went out all day, every day, and crammed in as much as I could. Galleries, shopping, talking to people and picking up the local colour. Food,' he added, sighing. 'Oh, the food was just to die for!' He gave a meaningful look toward the kitchen. 'Which reminds me, Sis…'

'Yes, I can take a hint.'

⁂

'Are you prepared,' asked Detective Chief Superintendent Evans, 'to take it to the magistrate? I'm sure we could get an extension, if you really want to hold on to her.'

Neville shook his head, defeated. 'There's no point, sir. She's not going to talk. She's refused to say anything for the last twenty-four hours.'

'So you've agreed that it's best to let her go.' Evans' eyes moved between Neville and Cowley.

Cowley, his arms folded, looked disgusted but said nothing.

'It's not as if she'll do a runner,' Neville pointed out. 'If we need to bring her in again, we know where to find her.'

'Very well, then,' said Evans. 'What about Leo Jackson?'

'We have another twenty-four hours.'

'And we're going to hold on to that black poofter till the very last minute,' Cowley put in grimly.

Evans drew his brows together in a thunderous expression of displeasure. 'We won't have any talk like that, Sergeant. Not on this force. One more remark like that and you'll be back in uniform. If you're lucky.'

'Yes, sir. Sorry, sir.' Cowley didn't sound very repentant.

◌❀◌ ◌❀◌ ◌❀◌

When Mark returned with Bella, he took over in the kitchen, promising Peter a pasta con funghi the likes of which he'd never tasted before.

'Oh, what a treasure,' sighed Peter, appropriating the most comfortable chair in the sitting room. 'Cute, funny, and he cooks. What did you say he does for a living?'

Callie smiled from the sofa. 'I didn't say. He's a policeman.'

'Well, I suppose no one's perfect,' he grinned. 'But he's definitely a keeper. I hope you're not going to let this one get away, Sis.' Then he caught sight of her face. 'I'm really sorry,' he said contritely. 'That was a dreadfully insensitive thing to say.'

'Apology accepted.'

'You're not still pining for what's-his-name, are you?'

'No,' said Callie, and as she said it she knew it was true. 'No, I'm not.'

Peter hastily changed the subject. 'So, Sis. I'm totally out of touch with the news. What's been going on while I've been away? Have they solved that murder yet?'

She had almost managed to put her worries about Frances out of her mind; now they flooded back. 'It's been dreadful,' she said with feeling. 'They've arrested Frances. She hasn't been charged, or at least she hadn't when I saw her this afternoon, but they have her locked up in a cell. It's horrible. And that awful Lilith Noone has been writing such rubbish,' she added. 'Stirring things up. Our Area Dean—she's practically accused him of rape and paedophilia.'

'Well, at least things haven't been dull.'

Callie indicated a stack of newspapers beside his chair. 'I've saved all the papers for you. I'm ashamed to admit that I've even been buying the *Globe*, to find out what that terrible woman is writing about my friends.'

'She hasn't written anything about you, has she?'

'No. She did try to talk to me once, but as soon as I realised who she was, I sent her packing. I suppose I had a lucky escape.'

Peter picked up the top tabloid from the pile: that morning's *Globe*, with its 'Bishop of Buggery' headline. 'Good Lord. What's this all about, then?'

'Leo. The Area Dean. He was going to be a bishop, and now he's withdrawn because he supposedly molested a young man. I just can't believe it's true. But he did withdraw, so perhaps there's something in it.'

'Good Lord.' Peter read the story, then found the previous issue to get the background. 'I've never seen this bloke before,' he said, examining Leo's photo on the front page. 'And I'd remember him if I had—he's quite striking, isn't he? He's certainly not part of the regular gay scene.' He scanned Lilith Noone's story, turning to the inside continuation pages. He read for a bit, then stopped short. 'Wait a minute.'

'What is it?'

'This bloke here. The one who says that Leo Jackson jumped his bones.'

'Oliver Pickett,' Callie supplied.

'If his name is Oliver Pickett, then I'm the Prince of Wales.'

'What? What are you saying?'

Peter shook his head. 'I've known him for years.' He tapped his finger on Oliver's photo. 'A well-known fixture on the scene. A rent boy, to put not too fine a point on it. Though he's not a boy any longer. He's one of those lucky ones who's managed to keep his boyish looks—the punters like them to look young. But he's twenty-five if he's a day.'

Callie stared at him. 'And he's not Oliver Pickett?'

'I don't know what his name really is,' Peter admitted. 'But I've always known him as Baz Smith.'

'There must be some mistake.' Callie couldn't take it in, couldn't understand it. 'Did Lilith Noone just make it up, then? Why would Leo molest a rent boy?'

'It sounds to me as if friend Leo has been scammed,' Peter guessed. 'Taken in by a young and pretty face. I've seen it before. And there's got to be money involved somewhere.'

'Money? What do you mean?'

'Well,' said Peter, thinking aloud, 'Baz goes with men for money. That much I know for sure. Say he meets this Leo chap somewhere and does the usual. Then Leo won't pay up, so he gets his revenge by cooking up this story for Lilith Noone.'

'I suppose...'

'Or,' Peter went on, 'what if, after they do the deed, he happens to find out that Leo is high up in the Church? What if he tries to blackmail him, and when Leo won't play ball, he goes to the *Globe*?'

'It's all so... sordid,' Callie blurted. She hated to think about her brother inhabiting a world where such transactions were commonplace.

As if reading her mind, Peter grinned. 'Don't worry, Sis. I've never slept with Baz Smith. I wouldn't touch him with a barge pole.'

'Oh, it's not funny,' she protested.

'The point is, whatever went on between Leo Jackson and Baz, it didn't happen the way Lilith Noone says. Baz is no innocent, no religious truth seeker who was led astray by a predatory older man. He must have known exactly what he was doing when he went with Leo. So why doesn't Leo just come forward and set the record straight? He may have been stupid—or desperate—to go with a rent boy, but it's a far cry from molesting an innocent young man.'

'As far as the Church is concerned,' Callie pointed out, 'it isn't any better. Leo must know that his career is finished, no matter how it happened.'

'Dinner will be ready in five minutes,' Mark called from the kitchen. 'I could use a bit of help.'

'I'll go,' Callie said quickly. She didn't want to think about Leo any more, and she welcomed the excuse to escape.

The table was set, the wine was open—Mark had already poured himself a glass—and the sauce was bubbling away on the hob. 'What can I do?' she asked.

Mark put down his wine. 'I didn't really need any help. Everything is under control. But I seem to recall we have a bit of unfinished business.' He opened his arms, and she went into them.

'Sis!' Peter called from the other room. 'Come here for a minute!'

'Oh, great,' she muttered, leaning against Mark for just a few seconds, inhaling the spicy sweet scent of aftershave mingled with tomato sauce, then pulling away. 'I'd better go.'

'Look at this, Sis.' Peter was pointing to something in a tabloid, and his voice was excited.

'Oh, that's that horrible priest,' she said distractedly, her heart still pounding. 'Father Vincent. He was Father Jonah's boss. He doesn't believe in women priests. It even says so in that article. And he implies that Frances killed Father Jonah. He's not a nice man. And he's homophobic, as well.' She could tell she was babbling, and hoped she wasn't blushing as well.

'Sis, listen to me.' Peter looked toward her, almost through her, as if his thoughts had gone far beyond. 'I know this man. Or at least I've seen him.'

'But he's not part of "the scene", as you call it. He's a priest. He's married.'

'Sis, I've told you before. I probably know more priests than you do.'

༺ ༻ ༺ ༻ ༺ ༻

Marigold was still sitting by the fire when Vincent came in. Her tea had gone stone cold; the fire was little warmer.

'Marigold, my dear!' he said. 'I thought you were going out this evening. The ballet, wasn't it?'

She raised her eyes but said nothing.

'My dear, you must be freezing. It's like the grave in here—the fire's gone out, nearly. Your tea is cold. Shall I make you another pot?' He bustled about, shaking more coal from the scuttle onto the fire and giving it a vigourous stir. 'Can I fetch you a cardigan?'

Such solicitousness was not characteristic of him, thought Marigold dispassionately. It must be his guilty conscience.

Her determination, which had been steadily sliding back toward embracing her usual comfortable course of least resistance, experienced a new injection of resolve. She would not allow him to get away with it.

'Vincent,' she said, and there was something in her voice which caused him to stop his bustling and look at her.

'Yes, my dear?'

She took a deep breath. 'Vincent, we need to talk.'

༺ ༻ ༺ ༻ ༺ ༻

'There was something that happened a few months ago,' Peter said slowly. 'I think I started to tell you about it once. You know that club where I usually play on a Saturday night?'

'I've never been there, but I've heard you talk about it,' Callie confirmed.

'Well, you wouldn't have been there.' He smiled. 'It's men only. Not even fag hags venture in there.'

'Well, what about it?'

'I was playing there one Saturday night. I remember it was dreadfully hot and stuffy—more so than usual—so it must have been some time in the summer. July, probably.' He closed his eyes; it was as if he were reliving the experience. 'And this bloke came in. He wasn't wearing a dog collar, like in this photo, but it was him, all right.'

'Father Vincent? In a gay club?' Callie was sure that his memory was was playing tricks on him.

He ignored the interruption. 'And wait till I tell you the rest, Sis. He sat down at a table, and before too long someone came and joined him.' Peter paused for effect. 'It was Baz Smith.'

'But...' No, thought Callie. It couldn't be true.

'This bloke—this Father Vincent—gave Baz a packet of money. I saw the money change hands.'

'Why would he do that? Apart from... but he wouldn't.'

Peter shook his head. 'Sis, don't be so naïve. Of course he would. And that's what I thought it was, at the time. A simple transaction. I give you money, you... Well, let's not go into details.'

She was thankful to be spared that, but she still didn't understand.

'Don't you see?' Peter's finger punched the photo of smug, sanctimonious Father Vincent. 'I said it was about money, and here's the money. Right in front of my eyes. Literally.'

⁓⁓⁓

'Talk, my dear?' said Vincent. 'Can't it wait till morning? You look all done in. Let me make you up a hot water bottle, and you can have an early night.'

He was treating her like an invalid—an elderly invalid at that—and it made Marigold furious. 'My money,' she said, the words cutting through the atmosphere like a knife. 'What have you done with my money?'

⁓⁓⁓

'Callie, you were at that meeting, where Frances had the row with Father Jonah. Leo was involved, too, wasn't he, and Father Vincent? Try to remember. Did you get the feeling that Father Vincent disliked Leo Jackson, as well as hating women priests?'

Peter's question seemed irrelevant, but now Callie was on familiar ground. 'Yes, he despises him. Because Leo is so supportive of Frances, and women priests in general, and all the sort of liberal causes that Father Vincent hates. Frances told me that Father Vincent is jealous of Leo, and thinks Leo's had preferment in the Church just because he's black and liberal.'

'Well, there you are, then.' Peter leaned back, looking almost as smug as Father Vincent himself. 'Father Vincent was paying Baz Smith to lie about Leo Jackson. Probably to seduce poor old Leo, then go to the press with his outlandish tale of being molested.'

As soon as Peter said it, Callie had no doubt that it was true.

⚬⚬⚬

'Your money?' Vincent said vaguely.

'Did you think that Mr Firth wouldn't tell me? Or that I wouldn't dare to confront you, even if he did?'

'Well, my dear…' Vincent sat down across from her and bared his teeth in a semblance a smile. 'I'm sure there's just been a misunderstanding.'

'If you needed money for anything, all you had to do was ask,' Marigold said. 'You didn't have to go behind my back.' She made herself ask the question, not really wanting to know the answer. 'What was it for, Vincent?'

'I had… debts. I didn't want to worry you.' He didn't meet her eyes.

'Was it the same thing… as before?'

They had never talked about it. Not then, and not in all the years since. She wasn't about to begin now, to rake up the sordid things she'd never even wanted to think about, let alone discuss. Public lavatories, anonymous encounters… Evidently it had being going on for quite some time before he'd been caught. All those supposed late night meetings and visits to parishioners… It might have gone on longer if it hadn't been for that undercover policeman.

Now, she supposed, it would be different. Vincent was no longer the smoulderingly attractive young clergyman he'd been in those days. Now he would probably have to pay for what he needed. Possibly a lot of money. Her money.

'I don't know what you mean,' he said.

She flung the words at him. 'Men. Boys. Whatever.' That was as near as she would ever get to saying it.

Vincent laughed. 'Is that what you think?'

'Because if it is,' she went on relentlessly, ignoring his laughter, 'you are on your own. My father isn't here to save your skin like he did the last time. And I'm not prepared to do it.'

'Your father!' He laughed again, without mirth. 'Your precious father! It always comes down to him, doesn't it?'

⚭ ⚭ ⚭

Callie put her hand over her mouth. It all made horrible sense. 'What are we going to do?'

'Tell the police, I suppose.'

'The antipasto is ready,' said Mark, coming out of the kitchen. 'Did someone mention the police?'

'Marco, listen. We've discovered something. It could be important.' Callie didn't feel up to recapping; she allowed Peter to do it.

Mark didn't need convincing. Antipasto forgotten, he pulled out his mobile and rang the station. 'This is DS Lombardi. Could you put me through to Neville Stewart?' he requested.

'DI Stewart is tied up at the moment,' he was told after an interminable minute of waiting. 'I'll get him to ring you back, as soon as he's free.'

'Could you tell me,' Mark asked, 'whether Leo Jackson is still in custody? And Frances Cherry?'

'Mr Jackson is still with us. DI Stewart is in the process of releasing Mrs Cherry.'

'Thanks,' said Mark. 'Have him ring me as soon as he can. I have some information that could be relevant to his enquiries.'

'Leo's in custody?' Callie echoed.

'Didn't I tell you? Apparently he turned himself in this morning.'

She felt utterly confused. 'But what does Leo have to do with the murder?'

Mark tucked his mobile back in his pocket. 'We don't know that yet. But all this fits together, somehow. It's altogether too convenient, too neat. Whoever killed Jonah Adimola, I think we'll find out that it had something to do with Leo Jackson.'

'Leave my father out of it,' warned Marigold.

'You're the one who brought him up. Like you always do. Your precious father, who loved you so much.'

'How dare you? Where would you be without him?' She demanded. 'In prison, most likely. Disgraced, maybe even defrocked. I mean, look what's happened to that poor Leo Jackson. That could have happened to you, Vincent, if my father hadn't made sure that the papers never got hold of it.'

She paused, astonished to see that he was smiling—and smugly, at that. 'Do you really find it amusing, what's happened to Leo Jackson? That's just sick, Vincent. I know you don't like the man, but...'

It was then that a horrible suspicion dawned on her. 'Vincent! You didn't have anything to do with that, did you? With that young man going to the press?'

He continued to smile. 'It was very clever, if I say it myself. And clever of you to guess,' he acknowledged.

'That's what you did with my money!' Marigold realised. 'You paid Oliver Pickett to go to Lilith Noone!'

He didn't deny it. 'And the Church will be spared a liberal bishop with an agenda which goes against everything that right-minded Christians believe,' he said sanctimoniously. 'You must see that I was right. I did it for the Church.'

It was the most breathtaking piece of self-delusion she'd ever heard. 'You said it was a debt!' she reminded him.

'Yes. A debt to Mother Church.' Vincent folded his hands together complacently. 'I planned it months ago,' he couldn't resist adding. 'I gave him a lot of money and told him what to do—I'd saved the money for the first instalment out of my stipend. But it all came to a head before I could save the rest. That's why I had to go into your bank account.'

'But how could you have planned it ahead of time? You didn't know he was going to be a bishop. No one did. It was only announced this week!'

He smiled. 'You told me yourself.'

'I told you? That's insane!'

'Don't you remember? One day you came home from lunch with your friends—a wee bit tiddly on champagne, if I remember rightly. You said that one of your friends—Beatrice, was it?—was having an affair with a man who worked at Number Ten. He'd told her about the black bishop who was going to be appointed. He told her, she told you, you told me. Simple as that, my dear.'

Dear God, she thought. He was right. That was why it had sounded familiar to her when the announcement was made.

⚬⚬⚬ ⚬⚬⚬ ⚬⚬⚬

They sat down and started to eat the antipasto. Five minutes later, Mark's phone rang.

'What's up?' asked Neville. 'They said it was important.'

'Listen, Nev. Did you ever run Vincent Underwood's name through the computer? Does he have form?'

'Of course we did. It was routine—we ran through everyone connected with the enquiry. Cowley did it, early on in the investigation. I'm sure if anything at all had turned up, he would have mentioned it. To be honest, we didn't expect to find anything, apart from maybe a parking ticket or two. He's a priest, for God's sake.'

'So is everyone else in this mess,' Mark pointed out. 'Frances Cherry, Leo Jackson, all those others. And one of them probably killed Jonah Adimola. Another priest, if I may state the obvious.'

'Yeah, yeah.'

'Well, the thing is, Nev, I've turned something up that just might interest you.' Mark told him, succinctly.

'Bloody hell.' Neville whistled. 'I'm going to go right now and check that computer myself. I'll get back to you.'

Marigold was still for a moment, trying to make sense of Vincent's revelation and her feelings about it. Her feelings about him... Had she really ever loved this man—this loathsome, pompous, cruel man? She supposed she must have done, once; she remembered it intellectually, but not with her heart. She had no recollection at all of how it had felt to love him. Most probably the love, if love it was, had died a death that day she'd found out about his proclivities. The day she learned that he wasn't the man she thought he was, and never had been.

Now she wanted to wound him. 'How did you find Oliver Pickett?' she challenged, adding nastily, 'Did you pick him up in a public lavatory, then?'

Vincent winced. 'Don't be crude, Marigold dear. It doesn't become you.'

'Well, then?'

'I have... contacts.'

'Yes, I'm sure you do. Did you plan it all by yourself, then?' she asked. 'Did anyone else know about it?'

'I didn't need any help.'

She wasn't sure what prompted her next words. 'You didn't tell Jonah, then?'

'Jonah?' Vincent sneered. 'Jonah was a self-righteous little prig. Yes, I told him. And he didn't approve.'

If the first intuitive realisation, about Oliver Pickett and the money, had struck Marigold like a bombshell, the next one shook her to the foundations of her being. She saw the scene her her mind's eye so vividly it was as if it were a film. Jonah—her beautiful Jonah, in the vestry at St John's Church, a stole wrapped tightly round his throat. A stole. Not a garment—a stole. Lilith Noone's coy story in the *Globe* had mentioned Frances Cherry's 'garment', nothing more than that—as though it had been a pair of knickers, or a filmy silk scarf. But just that morning, Vincent had remarked that Jonah had been murdered with Frances Cherry's stole.

'You… killed… Jonah,' she gasped, her chest so tight that she could scarcely breathe.

ᗧᗣᗧ ᗧᗣᗧ ᗧᗣᗧ

Mark had just dished up the pasta when Neville rang again. 'I'm going to kill Cowley with my bare hands,' he said.

'Why? What?'

Peter and Callie were looking at him questioningly.

'I suppose he didn't think it was worth mentioning. It was a long time ago, and it never made it to court.'

'What?' Mark repeated.

'Vincent Underwood was picked up by an undercover cop. Importuning in a public loo. Nearly twenty-five years ago. Somehow it was quashed before anything could come of it—how that happened, I'm not clear. Friends in high places, perhaps. But it's still in the records.'

'I think maybe you need to talk to Vincent Underwood again,' Mark said.

'Damn right I do. I'm leaving right now.'

ᗧᗣᗧ ᗧᗣᗧ ᗧᗣᗧ

'Why?' asked Marigold. She wanted to scream; somehow she managed to control her voice. 'Why did you kill him?'

Vincent shrugged. 'It was so unnecessary, really. My fault, I suppose. I misjudged him.'

'Misjudged him?'

'I thought it would cheer him up, after that unpleasant business with Frances Cherry and Leo Jackson. The wine, the insults. I told him that he needn't worry about Leo Jackson much longer, that I'd seen to it that he would get what he deserved. Jonah got on his high horse—said that it was a sinful thing to do. That God would take care of Leo Jackson in His own time and His own way. He said if I didn't call it off, he was morally obliged to tell the Bishop.'

'So you killed him,' she whispered.

'I had to do it. It was just a bonus that Frances Cherry had left her stole in the vestry.' Vincent smiled. 'Her stole! It was as though it were meant to be—I knew as soon as I saw it lying there what I had to do. I kept Jonah from talking, and got even with that dreadful Cherry woman at the same time.'

'Oh, God.' Marigold covered her face with her hands.

༄ঌ ༄ঌ ༄ঌ

The pasta was delicious, the sauce redolent of juicy tomatoes and succulent mushrooms. But none of them were able to enjoy it properly. Mark had put his phone on the table beside his plate; they all jumped when it rang again.

'I'm stuck in traffic,' Neville groaned. 'It's Friday night, isn't it? Every bloody person in the world trying to get out of town, or into town. It's bloody gridlock. Where are you, mate?'

'Bayswater.'

'Then you're nearer than I am. He lives in Mayfair.'

'Would you like me to go and have a word with him?'

Neville gave a relieved sigh. 'Would you? I have such a bad feeling about this. I don't think we can afford to wait.'

'Give me the address.' He wrote it down on his serviette.

'Don't try to drive,' Neville warned him. 'Believe me, you'll be able to make better time on foot. And thanks,' he added. 'I'll owe you one.'

༄ঌ ༄ঌ ༄ঌ

'You're not going to tell anyone, are you?' Vincent's voice was soft, but Marigold's eyes flew open in alarm at the note of warning in it.

'I shall certainly tell the police,' she said icily.

Vincent stirred the renascent fire, but didn't replace the poker. 'I don't think you will,' he said.

She hated him. It was no longer an absence of love; she now felt a much stronger and more powerful emotion. 'My father should have let you go to prison,' she shrieked at him, heedless of the fact that he had taken a step nearer to her.

'Your father. Your father.' Again that unpleasant laugh. 'You're so deluded about your precious father, Marigold. When are you going to allow yourself to see the truth about him?'

'The truth? The truth is that my father loved me. He took care of me.'

'That's what you want to believe.'

'After my mother died,' she said desperately, 'we only had each other. He was everything to me. And I was his whole world. He loved me.'

'But your father scarcely had time for you,' Vincent said. 'You were raised by a nanny. You never saw him, from one week to the next. That's the truth.'

She had begun to weep, wracking sobs that started in her chest and tore at her throat. 'No! You're wrong! You're lying!'

'He told me so himself, before our wedding. He said he knew he'd always neglected you. He felt rather sorry about it, but said it couldn't be helped. He was a busy man, and he didn't know anything about raising children.'

'He left me all his money! The house, everything! He made sure that I would have a secure future!'

Vincent shrugged. 'Who else was he going to leave it to? A home for elderly cats? As you said, you were all he had. Of course he left his money to you. That doesn't mean he loved you.'

Marigold howled with an agony such as she had never before experienced. And while Vincent stood there smirking at her, enjoying her pain, she made a lunge at him and seized the other end of the poker.

⌘ ⌘ ⌘

'I don't know Mayfair very well,' Mark admitted. 'Do you have an A-to-Z?'

'Somewhere,' Callie said. 'I'm not sure where it's ended up since the move.'

Peter looked at the scrawled address. 'I know where that is,' he said. 'I'll go with you and show you.'

That didn't seem a very good idea to Mark, but he realised it would be the quickest way. He could waste a great deal of time getting lost, or trying to find a map. 'All right, then. Let's go. Callie, we'll be back as soon as we can.'

'I'm coming, too.'

'No,' said Mark. 'Absolutely not.'

'You're not going without me,' she said, with a stubborn look on her face that he hadn't seen before.

'No.' He could, he thought, be equally firm.

'If you don't take me with you, don't bother coming back.'

Mark didn't want to risk finding out whether she meant it. 'All right. But the two of you are staying outside. Understand?'

Callie nodded.

'We're wasting time,' Peter reminded him.

ᖷᖬᖰᐧ ᖷᖬᖰᐧ ᖷᖬᖰᐧ

It seemed to take forever. The back streets were dark, misty, lit only by street lamps and the occasional crack of light shining out between drawn curtains. At least, thought Mark, it was no longer raining. But the wet leaves underfoot were treacherous, impeding their progress if they tried to go too fast.

Then they were in Oxford Street, at Marble Arch. The pavements were as full of pedestrians as the street was of traffic; they fought their way to the nearest crossing, then waited an interminable period while a flock of red buses inched along, blocking the road and giving no quarter to those impatient to get to the other side.

Mayfair, south of Oxford Street, was even quieter than Bayswater. 'Hurry,' Mark prompted, driven by the contagious sense of urgency he'd caught from Neville.

'We're almost there,' said Peter, checking the numbers of the houses they passed. 'It's just down here, I reckon, across from the square.'

Then Callie slipped on a blanket of sodden leaves and tumbled headlong onto the pavement.

'Callie!' Mark stopped abruptly and crouched down beside her. 'Are you all right?'

She grimaced. 'I think I've turned my ankle.'

'She's always been clumsy,' Peter said. 'We should have left her behind to do the washing up.'

Mark realised he was teasing, but at this moment he didn't find it very funny.

'I'm really sorry,' Callie groaned. 'Just leave me here. I'll be all right. Peter can stay with me. You'll be able to find your way now, Marco.'

'No. I'm not leaving you.'

She smiled at him, a rather bewitching smudge of leaf slime on her cheek, and held out her hand. 'Then help me up. I can hobble a few more yards.'

'Don't be silly.'

As they argued, a car came round the corner into the road and pulled up at the kerb beside them. Neville rolled down the window. 'What the hell is going on?'

Mark knew there was no point trying to explain; he merely shrugged.

'I didn't realise you were bringing the entire French Foreign Legion with you!'

Peter wrenched open the door of the back seat, and between them he and Mark got Callie inside.

Two minutes later, Neville and Mark rang the old-fashioned bell of the Underwoods' home, and knocked on the door for good measure.

No one answered. The two policemen looked at each other.

Then the door was flung open, by a woman Neville had seen once before, the day when it all began. She looked terrible: her make-up ruined by tears, her dress spattered with blood, her face distorted into an expression of wild misery. In her hand was clutched a poker, and the matter on the other end of it was in no way related to coal. 'He really loved me,' she said to them in a pleading voice. 'No matter what anyone says, he loved me.' She turned and went back into the house.

As they followed her into her drawing room, and even after they saw what was there, Mark and Neville both thought that she was talking about her husband.

Author's Note

My American readers might wonder why an African priest like Father Jonah would be working in a church in London. A few words of explanation are in order.

First of all, the Anglican Communion is a worldwide umbrella group of national churches with historical roots in the Church of England. The Archbishop of Canterbury is the head of the Anglican Communion, though not in the way that the Pope is the head of the Roman Catholic Church: it is far more amorphous and less centralised than that. Each province has its own rules, its own governing bodies, and selects its own bishops in whatever way it chooses. Naturally enough, the Anglican Church is strongest in countries which are or were once part of the Commonwealth or the British Empire, and this includes a number of African nations. It would not be unusual for a priest from one of these countries to serve in England, the original source of their own religious traditions.

Many of the events in this novel have been reflected in recent happenings in the Church of England and the Anglican Communion, though I was in the process of writing it before these things hit the headlines. The appointment of an openly gay bishop in the Episcopal Church in the USA (the American incarnation of the Anglican Communion) has brought to the fore a number of issues which have long been simmering under the surface of the Anglican Church. Conservative Anglicans worldwide have threatened schism over this issue, and none have been more vocal—or more hard-line—than the African churches (South Africa is an honourable exception). The Anglican Church of Nigeria, extremely conservative on the issue of homosexuality (nor do they ordain women), is in the forefront of the crusade to rid the Church of liberal Western scourges like gay priests. To an extent, their position is understandable: in their own countries, most of the African churches are under threat from a Muslim majority, with Islam's emphasis on personal purity and sexual morality, and this puts pressure on the Christian Church to take an equally conservative moral stand, based on obscure Biblical texts which seemingly forbid homosexual acts.

My problem with this is that they are attempting—with considerable success, it must be said—to force their own agenda onto the worldwide Anglican Communion. Sheer numbers are on their side: there are more Anglicans in Nigeria (over 17 million!) than there are in England. And the Archbishop of Canterbury, a holy and prayerful man, is bending over backward to prevent the dissolution of the Anglican Communion, even to the extent of suspending the U.S. Episcopal Church from full participation in the Communion.

In other words, Father Jonah may be fictional, but the sentiments he expresses are all too real—and all too influential, in my opinion.

Next on the agenda? Women bishops in the Church of England. America, and other provinces of the Anglican Communion such as Canada and New Zealand, have had women bishops for decades. But the legislation which made it possible for women to be priests in the Church of England, passed in 1993 through the efforts of courageous and determined women like my fictional Frances Cherry, specifically excluded women from being bishops. This will be the next battle ground; legislation is already being prepared to allow women bishops by the end of this decade. More hard-line threats of schism will inevitably follow, as happened when women were priested.

I firmly believe, though—and have been saying for years— that it is the issue of homosexuality which will define the Church of England and the Anglican Communion in the forseeable future.

[For further information about the Anglican Communion, visit their web site: http://www.anglicancommunion.org/]

To receive a free catalog of Poisoned Pen Press titles, please contact us in one of the following ways:

Phone: 1-800-421-3976
Facsimile: 1-480-949-1707
E-mail: info@poisonedpenpress.com
Website: www.poisonedpenpress.com

Poisoned Pen Press
6962 E. First Ave. Ste. 103
Scottsdale, AZ 85251